Also by Virna DePaul

Paranormal Romantic Suspense

Chosen By Blood (A Para-Ops Novel, Book 1)

Chosen By Fate (A Para-Ops Novel, Book 2)

Contemporary Romantic Suspense

Dangerous To Her (Harlequin Romantic Suspense)

It Started That Night (HRS – 5/2012)

Shades Of Desire (HQN, SIG Series, Book 1 – 6/2012)

Shades Of Temptation (HQN, SIG Series, Book 2 – 9/2012)

Contemporary Romance

This Magic Moment (A Dalton Brothers Novel, Book 1)

Novellas

A Vampire's Salvation (A Beyond Human Novella)
Wild For Him

CHOSEN BY SIN

(A PARA-OPS NOVEL, Book 3)

Virna DePaul

Sale of this book without a front cover may be unauthorized. If this book is coverless, it may have been reported to the publisher as "unsold or destroyed" and neither the author nor the publisher may have received payment for it.

Chosen By Sin is a work of fiction. Names, characters, places, and incidents are the products of the author's imagination and are used fictitiously. Any resemblance to actual events, locales, or persons, living or dead, is entirely coincidental.

2011 Virna De Paul

Copyright © 2011 by Virna De Paul

All rights reserved.

Published in the United States

Cover design: Elaina Lee
Author photograph: Andrea Bucheli

Printed in the United States of America

ACKNOWLEDGEMENTS

Much gratitude to the people who helped this story take shape, including: Holly Root, Tina Folsom, Nina Bruhns, Amy King, Cathy Perkins, Cyndi Faria, Vanessa Kier, Karin Tabke, Grace Chow, Susan Hatler and Julie Barnard. To Marianne S., who I had so much fun with at RT, thank you for being my scientific guru.

Special thanks to an amazing editor, Rochelle French, and series fans/bloggers/beta readers Tanya, Belinda, Danielle, and Nessa.

To Leis Pederson for giving this series life, and to all the readers who have been waiting for Dex's book—you make my job so much fun. Thank you for your support.

Thank you to my friends and family for supporting me, including Damian B., Bushra E., Suzanne P., Marlene/Trace L., Joe and Char C., and their families.

As always, much love to my boys, CJEZ.

"As when a prowling wolf,
Whom hunger drives to seek new haunt for prey,
Watching where shepherds pen their flocks at eve,
In hurdled cotes amid the field secure,
Leaps o'er the fence with ease into the fold;
Or as a thief, bent to unhoard the cash
Of some rich burgher, whose substantial doors,
Cross-barred and bolted fast, fear no assault,
In at the window climbs, or o'er the tiles;
So clomb this first grand Thief into God's fold:
So since into his Church lewd hirelings climb.
Thence up he flew, and on the Tree of Life,
The middle tree and highest there that grew,
Sat like a cormorant; yet not true life
Thereby regained, but say devising death
To them who lived; nor on the virtue thought
Of that life-giving plant, but only used
For prospect what, well used, had been the pledge
Of immortality."
   —John Milton, Paradise Lost Book IV

"The wolf also shall dwell with the lamb."
  —Isaiah verse 11:16 (Old Testament)
Snort.
  —Dex Hunt, Werebeast

"One strong wolf cannot defeat a pack of dogs; one strong arm cannot defeat many fists."
  —Anonymous
"Bullshit."
  —Dex Hunt, Werebeast

"God makes them, then he mates them."
  —An Italian Idiom
Snort.
  —Jesmina Martin, Vampire

"She who mates with a wolf will learn to howl."
  —A bastardized Spanish idiom
"I'll believe it when I hear it."
  —Jesmina Martin, Vampire

PROLOGUE

LONE PINE, CALIFORNIA
JUST OUTSIDE DEATH VALLEY

Through the open window of his home, Bodin of Hammersham watched the child of his blood even as his own blood ran cold. Outside, the air was dry and humid, but the early evening wind carried a slight promise of rain. Yards away, Bodin's wife, Nicole, stood protectively close to The Boy, deliberately keeping the gathering crowd from getting too close. Nicole's shadowed eyes were filled with regret and indecision. Bodin felt the first, but he couldn't afford to feel the latter.

Oblivious to the intense emotions of those around him, The Boy attacked the trunk of a towering tree with the small wooden sword Nicole had given him. His dirt-stained face, cheeks still clinging to baby fat, twisted into a scowl. Though his lips were peeled back to show off imaginary fangs—the real ones wouldn't emerge for years—their absence couldn't disguise the fact that The Boy, *this boy*, was going to be a formidable warrior. To anyone who took the time to look, his power was as plain as his half-breed status. As obvious as his tawny hair, hazel eyes, and bowed legs, each knee scabbed and bruised from his ceaseless play.

Carelessly, The Boy tossed his sword aside and ran up a small, rocky hill. He'd been at the compound for less than twenty-four hours, yet he navigated the rough, multi-leveled terrain easily, inviting the pack's young ones to play with him without hesitation or shame. If those children and their parents eyed him with disdain or suspicion, he didn't seem to notice or care. But he should.

Because they were right to be disdainful. As a half-breed, The Boy represented everything Bodin and his pack stood against—dilution of pure werewolf blood. The weakening of a powerful bloodline.

Unfortunately, the pack was right to be suspicious. More worrisome was the fact they were becoming envious. Covetous. Wondering if this half-breed was the *kind* of half-breed detailed in the Legend of Wolves. The rare kind that by their inherent power could grant one immortality.

Even Bodin had felt it. That moment of hesitation. The temptation to ask the question: What if? What if he had the power to defeat death? What if he could live forever, rule forever, ensuring his clan's peaceful, productive survival?

But with that thought came another. Rather than just survive, the pack could prosper. Live an eternity with those they loved. Never grow old. Never grow weak.

Defeat. Conquer. Dominate death just as they did their inferiors in life.

And that was the devil's plan right there.

The seed of temptation that grew into something more. Something personal. Something desperate. Something that would eat at a person's soul until everything else became disposable.

Then it would spread.

Because temptation was a greedy bitch. It didn't stay the course, but rather stretched out its vile grip like a spider's web, catching all in its path, until the disposer inevitably became the disposed.

A gift like immortality could produce no other result.

Yes, Bodin knew well about temptation. Just as he knew what had to be.

It was a blessing, really—The Boy's ignorance. Far worse to suffer for even one second the agonizing knowledge of your destiny. That in order to help what you loved survive, you had to destroy it.

Turning away from the window, Bodin schooled his expression into one of resolve. With the return of his daughter, Camille, and her son, The Boy, Bodin had to protect what was his, what had always been his, and what would continue to be his even after he died. Rule and power. Balance. Family. Pride. Endurance.

Survival.

Not one of them was discretionary.

Bodin unlocked the hidden drawer in his desk and withdrew a piece of paper worn thin by centuries of handling. It was the only known record of the Legend of Wolves. Handed down by Bodin's forefathers. Tattered and incomplete. But there was enough writing visible for Bodin to know he was doing the right thing.

Protect the wolf whose ancestry none can see.
Protect the one who can gift immortality.
Cast him out before you let him be found.
He'll drive hell's demons back underground.

His...will give eternal life to a... ther
But only if he's gifted his...

Obserwować Demonie Krawcy.

Two of the lines had faded in parts and were indecipherable. Nonetheless, Bodin read the last line of print out loud. "*Obserwować Demonie Krawcy.*"

Watch The Demon Tailors.

It was his pack's destiny.

Someday—if he was right—it would eventually be *his*.

He strode back to the window and looked once more at The Boy.

"We must find the vampires who took Camille in. Make certain they won't talk. But first …" To his trusted advisor, Franco, Bodin ordered, "Bring The Boy to me."

***

MONTHS LATER
AUVERGNE REGION
FRANCE

Damn dragons had a morbid sense of the dramatic, Bodin thought, even as he led the young vampire forward, her petite shadow dwarfed by his own. His charge huddled closer to him as they walked, the flickering torches on the weathered stone walls of the inner castle doing little to reassure her—or him, for that matter.

The Girl looked like a fairy, with her pale skin and silver hair emphasizing the frailty of her small build. She held Bodin's hand, her grip tightening with each step they took. Her eyes were huge, skipping around her, trying to make sense of the dark, strange place he'd brought her to. When shadows at the front of the huge hall shifted and morphed into individual figures illuminated by the nearby fire blazing in the hearth, pain shot through his chest. Ruthless, the pain reminded him of all he'd lost during almost four centuries of life.

Today, once again, he would be compelled to abandon something he could have loved. In the short time he'd known her, The Girl had come to mean so much to him. He knew it was because in some ways, despite the fact they looked as different as night and day, she reminded him of The Boy.

He'd done what he'd had to in order to save The Boy. And although he hadn't been able to save The Girl's parents, he'd saved her; if not from the sun, then from the crazed weres who'd thought they were doing what Bodin wanted. She would always be his responsibility, but with her had come an inescapable realization—if Bodin continued to hold the werewolf race above all others, his pack would not survive. The time for Otherborn unity had arrived. That was what The Girl had taught him. That was why they were here.

Metal clanked from the armor of the Draci guards as they marched beside them. Among them, a cloaked figure, features indecipherable, kept pace gracefully, its strides so smooth it almost appeared to be floating. Bodin narrowed his eyes, automatically sniffing in an attempt to detect the creature's race, but the smell of the Draci was too overwhelming.

The Girl shivered and he tugged her cloak closer around her. Mentally, he cursed the Draci for adhering to the old ways and using this cold, damp castle for the tribe's important ceremonies. He knew, even from the brief time they'd spent together, that although The Girl was nocturnal, she preferred to leave her lights on and was still prone to nightmares. After Bodin left, she'd likely cry herself to sleep. But leave her he would.

A handful of dragon-shifters stood to the sides of the room, watching him with clear distrust. The alliance between their tribe and his European packs had only recently been forged. If he was going to win these dragons over—if he was finally going to facilitate a modicum of peace between his and theirs—he had to go through with giving them The Girl.

The Draci were a powerful, ancient race that populated Europe in small numbers, but those numbers were dwindling fast due to the difficulty their females had giving birth. Their queen was almost twenty, with two-thirds of her life gone, and yearned for a child of her own before she died.

Bodin sensed The Girl's gaze on him and looked down. The smile she shot him reminded him not of The Boy this time, but of Camille. His darling girl. She used to smile constantly, but he couldn't remember the last time she had. He'd taken her smile away when he'd cast out his own blood. His grandson.

He stopped their forward movement, then crouched in front of The Girl and stared into her eyes. Without saying anything, he nodded. Her smile trembled, but she raised her chin and slipped her hand from his.

She was like Camille in that way, too. Brave.

She knew what needed to be done.

Without hesitation, she stepped closer to the Draci.

Their leader, Lacrosse, ignored her and focused his attention on Bodin. Like werewolves, dragon-shifters looked completely human until they shifted. Then they were the ultimate example of inhuman. Fire-breathing versions of the demons Bodin and his pack were sworn to keep in Hell. His duty was one of the reasons for keeping peace with the dragons now. Keep your friends close, but your enemies closer, particularly if you might need them to defeat a greater, stronger enemy one day.

"You're looking well," Lacrosse boomed out in a voice designed to carry. "Well, but old. We've heard rumors that you found the one to prove your legend true, but if that's the case, your patience is far greater than mine."

At Lacrosse's words, The Girl's gaze once more found Bodin and he silently cursed. He never discussed the legend with outsiders, but some in his pack had. He felt The Girl's curiosity and something else… If she weren't so young, he'd think she was trying to read his mind, but that was impossible. As he now knew, vampires couldn't access their powers until after puberty. But he admired her for trying.

In the face of Bodin's silence, Lacrosse finally looked down at The Girl. He studied her for several seconds, his expression grim, before reaching out to pat her head. Though she automatically flinched back and kept her gaze on Bodin, she didn't retreat.

A Draci female standing next to Lacrosse stepped forward and held out her hand, which The Girl ignored. Eventually, when Bodin refused to acknowledge The Girl's gaze, she took the female's hand and let herself be led away.

And although Bodin waited…

Although he hoped to see her turn and smile at him once more…

She didn't.

In fact, she never looked back.

When she was out of sight, he shifted his gaze back to Lacrosse, who offered him a goblet of wine. Bodin raised the goblet. "To the peaceful coexistence of our people from here forth."

Bodin hesitated only a second before drinking the wine. Lacrosse wouldn't have poisoned it. If he'd wanted him dead, he'd have done the more dramatic thing and burned the flesh from Bodin's bones while The Girl watched.

Still, the spicy wine tumbled down his throat like jagged rocks. Swiping his hand across his mouth, Bodin nodded at Lacrosse much the same way he had The Girl. He turned to leave, but Lacrosse's voice stopped him.

"As I was saying, you're looking old, Bodin. If you've proved the legend true, I'd think you'd have instituted the change by now."

Bodin had trained himself well against such prodding, but the Draci were the last individuals he'd expected to have suspicions. They were such an isolated group. Thousands of miles from the States. How could they…

Bodin turned around to stare directly into Lacrosse's gaze. "I have no idea what you're talking about."

"He's talking about your grandson," a voice whispered from the small crowd. Bodin searched for the speaker. His eyes automatically fell on the cloaked figure, but he couldn't be certain this had been the one who'd spoken.

"The only grandson I have is a bastard werebeast whom I disavowed. I have no idea where he is and I certainly don't care. You can bet if he were part of the legend, neither of those would be the case."

Without bothering to nod again, he left, storming away even as his mind warred with images of The Boy and The Girl. Both vulnerable. Both trusting. Both his, in some way. And both gone from him.

They'd be better off for it.

Hopefully, so would the world.

CHAPTER ONE

SEVENTY-FIVE YEARS LATER
LOS ANGELES, CALIFORNIA

Werebeast Dex Hunt watched as Jesmina Martin, the vampire female who'd first approached him in a Los Angeles sex club less than two nights ago, walked down the dark and deserted street and paused across from her hotel. She looked poised and sophisticated in her tailored black clothes, seemingly unconcerned that she'd pissed him off by snatching his half-feline, half-mage teammate, Lucy Talbot, out from under his nose, then hightailed it out of Dodge before he could get to them. It hadn't mattered that her intentions had been good; he'd been chomping at the bit to find her.

By the way his body was reacting to her, however, maybe he should have hesitated. This was supposed to be about making her sorry she'd messed with him, not satisfying his own desire to be buried inside her lithe, fragrant little body.

"So," he said loud enough for her to hear him. "You still want to fuck?"

Jesmina instantly froze, but he had to give her credit—she didn't jerk in surprise or whirl around at his crude question. Instead, she slowly turned toward him, her fine features illuminated by a nearby streetlight.

Her right eyebrow arched mockingly as she swept her gaze over him, stopping just below his waist where his aching flesh was definitely most happy to see her.

Her lips formed a moue. "It doesn't look like Lucy's doing it for you, were. I suspected as much. She's a sweetie, but clearly too innocent to give you what you need."

Dex glowered at her. She knew he and Lucy were having sex. How? When she'd teleported into their hotel room to grab Lucy, he'd been asleep on the sofa rather than next to the mage in their roomy king-sized bed. He couldn't see Lucy telling her. Had she read Lucy's mind? Because she shouldn't have been able to read *his*. Once he'd discovered that premium gold was one way to stop a vampire from reading one's mind or exercising persuasion, Dex had taken to carrying a charm in his pocket.

He only trusted one vampire, and that was the Para-Ops team leader, dharmire Knox Devereaux, and he only trusted him halfway. Still, when he'd met Jesmina, he'd been tempted to let down his guard, which had made her betrayal sting all the more. Once again, the memory of how she'd played him reignited the rage he'd spent the last forty-eight hours trying to get under control.

Two nights before, he'd been at a bar with Lucy, Wraith, and Caleb O'Flare, his Para-Ops team members. They'd been working, using Lucy as bait for a sting operation. Alone at their table, Dex had spotted Jes the second she'd entered the bar.

Like the other females there, Jes's calculating gaze had swept the room, evaluating the males one by one, trying to find the likeliest source of pleasure. When she'd swept her gaze right past the slick good looks of O'Flare to land and stay on Dex, his heart had thundered and his dick had swelled, pushing against his jeans to get to her. With a knowing smile, she'd strolled up to him, surrounding him in the sultry scent of perfume underlined with something wild and tropical...something that called to his beast.

"A night of passion," she'd offered. And he'd been tempted. So tempted. But he'd been working and then shit had started happening, including Wraith getting shot and Lucy being drugged. He and Lucy ended up back in his hotel room after the entire showdown. He'd been exhausted, and had almost forgotten about the sexy vamp. Almost.

Hours later, he'd awoken in his hotel room to find Lucy missing. Someone had blipped in and whisked Lucy away, and every clue had pointed to that someone being Jesmina.

Dex had been pissed. All he could think about was retaliation. But when he'd realized Lucy was not only safe but had gone with the vamp of her own free will, Dex's anger morphed into its true form—lust.

That lust was still crawling through his veins, even after the two days he'd spent tracking down the vamp. Yeah, Jesmina had done what she thought would help Lucy, and Lucy had been all for it as he'd found out later, but he still wanted answers. And maybe to scratch that itch. But it was a lust he couldn't afford to give free rein, not without revealing its intensity or letting it distract him from what was most important—his job and ultimately, his revenge against his bastard of a grandfather.

"Lucy's exactly what I look for in a bedmate," he gritted out, even though it was complete bullshit. "Beautiful and compliant." Those two words accurately described Lucy. But equally true was that Lucy was more like a sister to him than a lover. Still, she needed someone to help her with the feline heat and since she wasn't willing to let anyone else touch her, that left Dex. Sex was the only way to alleviate the writhing agony feline heat put the werecats in. But although the idea of Friends With Benefits might attract some, he knew the truth. He hated that Lucy had to have sex with someone she wasn't in love with. Their bodies might get into the act, but their minds were elsewhere, making for a vacant experience.

"Sounds quite boring, if you ask me. And given your initial question, you think the same thing or you wouldn't be here."

He smiled tightly. "My question wasn't a statement of intention. You approached me in a crowded bar and asked me if I wanted to fuck. I declined. I haven't changed my mind. I'm just wondering if you ever really wanted to fuck or if the reason you came on to me in the first place was to get to Lucy."

Her eyes narrowed into angry slits before her expression smoothed. She laughed. "Well, there's gratitude for you. So typical of a were. Although I didn't use that turn of phrase, it's as accurate as any. And as you're no doubt aware of by now, I helped Lucy get the information you and your teammates were in dire need of."

It pissed him off that she was right. Thanks to Jes, the Para-Ops team had solved their last case. "The question is why'd you help us?" He stalked toward Jes, crowding her with his body until she was forced to look up at him. He traced her cheek, his blunt-tipped finger rough against her skin. He was far too aware of her skin's silky texture, which made him want to press his lips against every part of her. "Somehow I don't think it was out of the kindness of your heart."

She shivered and stepped back. He clenched his fists to stop himself from reaching for her. Contrary to what he'd implied, resisting her invitation hadn't been easy. He'd wanted to fuck her since the moment he'd seen her. He still did.

But it was more than that.

There was something about this female.

Something about the way she'd watched over Lucy while the rest of them had been dealing with Wraith's assaulter and tending to Wraith's wound.

Something about the way she'd talked about her own friendship with a wraith that she hadn't been able to save.

Something about the way she looked at him as if she could see inside his very soul.

Whatever it was, Dex wanted to know her on a personal level that had nothing to do with sex. But damn if he was going to let her see that.

"You're the one who asked me to hold Lucy for you when the wraith got shot," she pointed out. "I tried to tell you I had information relevant to the felines, but Lucy was the only one who listened. So I gave her the information she asked for. *C'est tout.* That's all."

Abruptly, she turned away from him and walked across the street. She pushed through the glass doors of her luxury hotel and strode toward the lobby elevators.

Dex easily kept up with her.

The night they'd met, she'd told him she lived in France, but despite her faint accent, she'd never spoken French before. It was sexy as hell. More importantly, it revealed she was off balance. Clearly on the retreat. Why?

Because she didn't trust herself to keep her hands off him? Or because she was attracted to him in more than the physical sense, as well? Why else would she be reneging on the offer of pleasure she'd made?

As she waited for the elevator to arrive, he crossed his arms and leaned casually against the wall, ignoring the uneasy way the reception staff was staring at them. "That's all, huh? And it had nothing to do with trying to get your claws into me? *Tres* shame," he mocked.

She was looking increasingly annoyed now. "You're attractive, were, but not that attractive. In fact, to answer your question, no I don't want to fuck. Not anymore. The fact that you and your teammates were so clueless has left me cold."

Despite her words, he didn't buy it. Perhaps his instincts were wrong, then. Perhaps she wasn't actually running from him, but rather resisting him because she knew it was the surest way to get to him. Her tact was working and he suddenly found himself quite willing to play along. "Is that a fact?" Now it was his gaze that traced the contours of her body.

Who cared what her motives were? She wanted him and he sure as shit wanted her. "I have an exceptionally good sense of smell, and what I smell isn't just bullshit, but a female who still wants to be fucked really bad."

"Oh I never said I didn't want to get fucked," she taunted. The elevator arrived with a soft ping. As the door slid open, she stepped inside and turned to stare challengingly at him. "I just don't want to fuck you. So why don't you—"

Her goading finally got to him. With a hand against her shoulder, he lightly shoved her further into the elevator, relishing the way her eyes widened with shock. He was just about to step into the elevator with her when someone called his name.

"Dex!"

He immediately recognized the voice and cursed.

Jes was now flushed and breathing hard, lips pressed together and jaw clenched. But for a second, just one second, he thought he saw disappointment flash in her coal-black eyes. "Looks like your girlfriend's here," she said.

"Damn it, she's not my girl—"

"It was kind of you to come to my defense, Lucy, but unnecessary, I assure you," Jes called over his shoulder.

"Don't be so sure of that," he said darkly.

The elevator doors closed, but not before Jes waggled her fingers in a mocking gesture of goodbye. "*Au revoir*, Mr. Hunt." When she was gone, Dex fought the conflicting needs to punch the wall and grin.

Jes was right. Compliance was boring, especially in bed. The vampire had a mouth on her and a spirit to go with it. Despite his misgivings, he'd love to experience what that mouth and spirit could do when they were horizontal. But obviously, his chance to experience it tonight had passed.

With a growl, he turned toward Lucy, the pretty little feline mage he'd come to care far too much about.

She momentarily paused as he glared at her, but she tilted up her chin and strode toward them. "Dex, I told you she was just trying to help me. Help us! You shouldn't have come after her."

Dex closed his eyes in disbelief. "Goddess help me," he muttered.

Lucy punched him in the arm. His eyes popped open just as she muttered, "Oh stop it."

Things certainly had changed. A few weeks ago, no one, let alone a small feline mage, would have had the nerve to punch him so casually. He'd obviously given Lucy the wrong impression about him. Still, as he stared at her, several uncomfortable feelings washed over him. He actually had to catch himself from shuffling his feet like a kid.

He suddenly felt like a guy whose ex-girlfriend had just caught him with his current girlfriend. No, worse than that. Like a guy whose wife had just caught him in the sack with the mistress he was about to leave said wife for. In other words, he felt crappy. Nervous. Guilty and unsure.

And that was bullshit.

Forget the fact that he didn't do nervous or guilty, let alone uncertainty.

Lucy was his part-feline teammate and temporary lover until she found someone else to help ease her sexual heat. She wasn't his ex, his current girlfriend, or his wife. Their arrangement was for practical purposes only and no feelings or promises had been exchanged—well, except for his promise "to be there" for her sexually when she needed him, which wasn't a vow of fidelity or love.

And the vampire? He barely knew her. Yes, he'd been instantly attracted to her, but he'd been attracted to a lot of vamps, and by the way she'd so easily manipulated Lucy, this one obviously equaled trouble.

So why did the idea of the two of them seeing each other just now have him so freaked? Why did the fact they'd previously double-teamed him, and not in a good way, make him want to alternately shake Lucy and fuck Jesmina senseless?

Rather than dwell on questions he didn't want to answer or feelings he didn't want to feel, he bent down, getting right in Lucy's face, and gritted out, "What the hell are you doing here? I told you to stay at the hotel."

"Since when do you order me around, Dex?" she asked quietly. If their teammate Wraith, the once blue-skinned, hazy-eyed ghost, had asked the question, it would have sounded bitchy. From Lucy, however, the question seemed merely...quizzical. But despite the modulation of her tone, Dex saw her tremble. Some small part of her was having to force herself to keep eye contact with him.

Something perilously close to betrayal squeezed his heart. Was she simply feeling guilty because she'd sneaked out of their hotel room to meet the vamp, or did she actually believe he could hurt her? Both, he realized. Immediately, he straightened and took several steps back. It was as if the newfound distance between them alerted Lucy to his thoughts, for she followed him and laid a hand on his arm.

Dex moved away again, forcing Lucy's hand to drop. Normally, he hated the idea of Lucy suffering, but right now he didn't care.

The others were right. He needed to stop treating Lucy like a child. Only, in so many ways, that's what she reminded him of. She was so small and kind and innocent. Hell, she'd been a virgin the first time they'd done it. But she wasn't as helpless as he'd thought.

She was just like everyone else. She'd played him for a fool. And not just within the team, like O'Flare had once fooled Wraith, but with a vamp she'd just met. "This doesn't concern you, Lucy. This is between me and Jesmina Martin. Jes," he emphasized. "The stranger you decided to trust. The vampire you went off with alone, despite what happened to Wraith at that bar. Remember?"

With each word he spoke, his tone got harsher and harsher. He knew he had to get control of himself. Despite his better judgment, he'd ended up caring about Lucy, but she wasn't his to protect. And of course he didn't care about Jesmina, so why give anyone the impression that he did?

Yet his body was itching to get into the elevator and go after her.

Get the hell out of here, his mind urged.

No fucking way, the rest of him shouted.

One part of him was being especially vocal.

Lucy stepped right in front of him and placed her hand on his arm, her gaze comfortably steady now. "You like Jesmina, don't you?"

Well, shit. Lucy really did have some balls on her. "I want to fuck her, Lucy. I don't have to like her to do that."

Her mouth quirked. "But you're fucking me, and something tells me that's going to get in the way of you fucking her. I thought you just wanted to yell at her, but it's more than that, isn't it? If you want her, Dex, talk to her. I can take care of the heat myself—"

Dex shook his head. "I made you a promise, Lucy. I'll be here for you as long as you need me. No matter how pissed off you've made me, that hasn't changed."

"It doesn't matter what you promised, Dex. If there's something between you and Jes… If she's someone you can care about, even love…"

Yes, he'd definitely given her the wrong idea about him.

He covered the hand she still had on his shoulder with one of his, then gently lowered it to her side. "You don't get it, Lucy," he said, his voice serious. "I like you enough to help you. To sleep with you. It's certainly no hardship for me. But I don't do love. I don't love anyone. I never have and I never will. As long as you understand that—as long as you don't interfere with me and Jes again—we'll be okay."

CHAPTER TWO

FBI Director Kyle Mahone stared at Special Agent Leonard Walker, the new head of the Bureau's Los Angeles office. He wasn't sure why the President had promoted Walker over Mahone's objection, but he'd tried to look at the bright side of things. At least the belligerent agent wouldn't be knocking on Mahone's office door anymore—not from across the nation. It was the first time in years Mahone had left Washington, D.C. for Los Angeles, but he'd had to take his newly formed concerns to this man. Granted, he still outranked Walker, but given the President's faith in him, Mahone had to give

Walker considerable leeway when it came to running his own office—no matter how much it pissed him off.

"Let me get this straight," he said. "You don't see anything remotely disturbing about the fact that three shape-shifters have been killed in the last month, each murdered by other shape-shifters who've immediately confessed with clearly prefabricated accounts of self-defense?"

"A rash of murders isn't evidence of whole scale fratricide, Mahone, which is what you're implying."

"Except for felines, shape-shifters are the most unified Otherborn. Shape-shifters killing other shape-shifters have been virtually unheard of, yet the national incidence of such murders has tripled in the past month. According to my sources overseas, it's nearly quadrupled in France, with London coming in a close second. Plus, in at least half of the killings, there's been evidence of dark magic and satanic rituals involved."

"Shape-shifters have always been the hardest Otherborn for us to track, especially when it comes to mortality rates and criminality. As they integrate themselves more and more into society, it's reasonable we're discovering more about them, not all of it pretty. In any case, confessions, even ones claiming justification, mean less backlog for us. As for the other, maybe they're just getting sloppy about hiding their true religious leanings."

And maybe you're just being lazy, an idiot, or a bigot, Mahone thought, none of which were anything new. But he refrained from saying so. He had more important things to do than try to talk sense into Walker. The first thing on his list was to make sure the debacle that had been the Para-Ops team's last mission was wrapped up as neatly as possible. Then he'd be able to deal with the situation with the shape-shifters and, oh yeah, the Goddess still threatening to bring forth Armageddon.

"Have all the requisite reports been filed with the various local agencies?"

"Not yet, but soon. Damn shame about how that last op ended up," Walker said slyly. "The Para-Ops team wasted time in L.A. when they could have been doing real good somewhere else."

"Real good" meaning something that benefited humans, not vamps or felines. "Somewhere else" meaning anywhere away from Walker's jurisdiction. Mahone recognized the subtle taunts and smiled tightly. "Don't worry about my team, Walker. The President is pleased with the work they've already accomplished. When the time is right, each and every one of the Para-Ops team members is going to get the recognition he or she deserves."

"Of that, I have no doubt." Walker's tone was so smug it made Mahone bristle.

"What the hell does that mean?"

"With all due respect, Director Mahone, it means your so-called team is getting smaller and smaller as we speak. Knox Devereaux and Felicia Locke are too busy protecting themselves. From what I hear, the wraith and her human boyfriend are also on hiatus. Your team is proving what I've always known to be true—ultimately, everyone looks out for the people who matter most—themselves. It's why the War started in the first place, and it's why peace can never last. I know it. You will, too, eventually."

Mahone stiffened. Fed up with Walker's threats, he leaned in close to him. "My team is committed to keeping peace, with each other and within this nation. If you interfere, I don't care how well you've fooled the President—I'll take you out of the equation myself." Before Walker could do more than bluster, Mahone whirled and stalked into the office he was using as his temporary headquarters. He slammed the door shut, then raked his hands through his hair.

Damn, he was getting soft. That someone like Walker could get to him so quickly proved it. He knew it was because Walker's taunts had hit home—it didn't look good for him or the team that they'd wasted so many days chasing after Natia's phantom suspects. The falsification of feline rapes also hadn't helped their cause to promote peace between humans and Otherborn—already there were a growing number of humans ready to believe the worst about Otherborn again. Pockets of protestors were organizing, and Mahone knew they'd soon be sought out by the Quorum.

Despite the progress he and his team had made, the fragile peace that had ended the Second Civil War and given the nation hope was beginning to splinter.

It was bad enough that each Otherborn race fought against each other and with humans. What more if shape-shifters—creatures that could disguise themselves to look like any individual, human or Otherborn—were fighting among themselves and methodically killing each other off? Even worse, Mahone knew shape-shifters didn't worship Satan as a general rule, yet the murders seemed linked to rituals designed to channel spirits from the Otherworld back to earth. When he'd first got wind of the rituals, Mahone had actually tried getting in touch with Essenia. For once, however, the Goddess had remained stubbornly quiet. He was trying to take that as a good sign.

One thing was certain. If Walker wasn't going to look into the matter, Mahone would. He needed to get the Para-Ops team assembled. He also needed to get Knox and Felicia back on board. That meant somehow alleviating Knox's very real and understandable concerns about the threat the Quorum posed to Felicia. As impossible as this latter task seemed, he needed to accomplish it fast.

His phone rang. Automatically, he thought about the Goddess, which was ridiculous. Essenia liked to throw down her threats in person so she could see and not just hear how freaked out he got.

Bitch, he thought as he sat in his desk chair and answered the phone. But even he recognized he felt more exasperated than hostile. "This is Kyle Mahone."

"I was told you're in charge of the Para-Ops team. Is that true?"

The feminine voice on the other line was low and smooth. Cultured. He could tell the speaker wasn't American. She sounded vaguely European. French?

"Who am I talking to?" he asked.

"I'll take that as a yes. I've met your team and I have the highest respect for them. However, based on our interaction, it's apparent you could use some help with Otherborn intel. That happens to be a specialty of mine."

Mahone leaned back in his chair and closed his eyes. The female's voice sounded slightly like Bianca, Knox Devereaux's royal vampire mother, the vampire queen Mahone had once loved and lost. *C'est la vie*, right? "And what makes you think we need your help?" he asked.

"I gave your team several leads. Information about wraiths, as well as the felines."

Ah, Mahone, thought, sitting back in his chair. This must be the mysterious vampire O'Flare had told him about. Knox had never heard of her, and Mahone's people were at this very moment trying to find out everything they could about her but having little luck. Obviously, she was right. He did need better intel about Otherborn if he couldn't even get a handle on one vampire. "Too bad you didn't get in touch with us before I flew my team to L.A. You could have saved us a lot of trouble," he said lightly.

"I'm happy to save you trouble in the future," she replied. "In fact, I'm hoping we can help each other."

Of course you are. "So you're willing to barter information for—" Recalling his recent conversation with Walker, he sat up straight. "Tell me," he said, "Do you know much about the shape-shifter race? Those in Europe, perhaps?" Technically, the FBI didn't have jurisdiction overseas. His special agents had absolutely no authority to work over there. But that didn't mean certain independent contractors—like those on the Para-Ops team, for example—couldn't decide to do a little work on their own. He suspected none of his team members would balk at the concept of plausible deniability. It was one reason he'd chosen them.

"I'm willing to share my information with you, Mahone. About the shape-shifters and other races. The weres. The mages. The question is how much you're willing to pay for it."

His mouth tightened and an odd sense of disappointment washed through him. For some reason, he'd expected better of the vamp. "So this is about money then?"

He heard the female sigh with what almost sounded like regret. "*Oui*, it's about money. A whole lot of money, in fact. But only because the money is necessary to achieve something important. Something that if I can accomplish, you'll be very, very interested in. Whether I share it with you will depend on what happens next."

"Tell me more."

"I will. But first, tell me everything you know about Dex Hunt."

CHAPTER THREE

Jes spotted the diner she was looking for a couple of blocks ahead of her and deliberately slowed her pace. She also placed her hands in her coat pockets, not because of the slight evening breeze but because it would make her look even more laid back.

She didn't actually *feel* that way, of course.

After her close call with Dex outside her hotel last night, her blood still zipped with excitement. Unfortunately, she was also feeling anxious and uncertain when she needed every drop of confidence she could muster to do what was necessary. She couldn't deny, however, that when it came to deceiving Dex, her resolve was splintering.

Oh she'd talked to Mahone anyway. Set things in motion. She'd even arranged to meet Rurik Pitts, one of Dex's former pack brothers, at a nearby diner to learn more about Dex.

Yet she was torn between duty, and her desire and respect for Dex. Bottom line, she liked him. And she wanted him.

She wanted to explore the sexual sparks that flared to life whenever he was near, even if that's all it ever was.

She wanted, for once in her life, to do something simply because it made her feel good. Because it made her feel *alive* for the first time in almost one hundred years of living.

But she couldn't.

As a child, she'd watched as her parents were murdered, and later had witnessed over and over again as members of her adoptive Draci family died. It was just her luck Bodin of Hammersham had saved her only to put her in the care of dragon-shifters whose life span lasted thirty years.

Did that mean she had to spend the rest of eternity standing by and doing nothing while those she loved continued to die?

Non. Absolument non. Absolutely not.

She was a scientist, for Goddesses's sake, one who'd spent years acquiring the skills and the information that might, someday, somehow, be able to keep someone she loved from leaving her again. Maybe she'd even discover something soon enough that she could save Bodin, who was coming to the end of his own life cycle. Each day, Bodin was weakening. So was the peace between the Draci and their natural enemies, the European were-packs.

There was only one problem: Dex could be the answer to all her prayers, but he had every reason to hate Bodin and no incentive to help the Draci or her.

Maybe he'd turn out to be her white knight anyway.

Mentally playing back her thoughts, she shook her head.

Might.

Someday.

Somehow.

Maybe.

When had equivocation become a mainstay of her mental thoughts?

Maybe since the day she'd first heard about the Legend of Wolves. Maybe equivocation had grown as over the years she'd put together the bits and pieces of information that had finally led her to Dex. Bodin's grandson. The one rumored to fulfill the legend. The one who could gift immortality, although no one knew quite how.

It was up to Jes to find out if it was true. And if it was true, how it was possible.

If it was possible.

Was she simply fooling herself? Was she so desperate to save Bodin and her Draci family that she actually believed she could prolong life through manipulating DNA and duplicating the effects of vampire regeneration? After all, she'd fooled herself about someday being able to have a baby—her body just wouldn't carry a fetus to term—so why not this, too?

These were questions she asked herself daily, right along with whether she should even be trying to further her current goal—not to have a baby, of course, since that was now impossible, but to prevent anyone else she loved from dying. Prolonging life through healing illness was one thing, but prolonging individual life spans through science was unnatural, wasn't it?

With Herculean effort, Jes pushed aside her troublesome thoughts. Rita, the old Draci seer who'd lived decades longer than she was supposed to, had often told her that knowledge in and of itself was never a bad thing—what she chose to do with that knowledge was something she could decide if it ever became an issue.

Although Kyle Mahone had been willing to exchange money for the information she could provide him, he'd claimed ignorance of Dex Hunt's medical history. Jes hadn't believed him, but it hadn't mattered. As she'd told Mahone, she was an expert when it came to ferreting out information.

Having reached the diner, Jes pulled open the door and stepped inside. Immediately, she spotted a big, mangy werebeast sitting in a back booth. She made her way toward him, jerking to a halt when a young boy darted in front of her. To her shock, he raced behind her and grabbed hold of her leg.

A couple was hot on his trail. The human male looked completely pissed. There was a female beside him, a pretty feline with a soft and gentle face who nibbled her lip and blinked rapidly to stem her tears.

Instinctively, Jes reached behind her and laid a reassuring hand on the boy's head. Then she peeked into the mind of the angry-looking male.

This was his son. He loved him. But he loved the feline, too, and desperately wanted them to get along.

The human glanced apologetically at her then addressed the boy through gritted teeth. "Give your new stepmom a hug, Eric. *Now.*"

"It's fine, Greg—" the feline began.

"No. It's not. You've been trying so hard and it's your birthday. It's the least Eric can do."

"But—"

"*Now*, Eric," Greg insisted.

Jes twisted and looked back and down.

Eric glared, then shrunk back and dug his fingers deeper into Jes's leg. He met her gaze. "She's not my mother," he warbled, clearly fighting back his own tears. "She'll never be my mother."

No, Jes thought, tugging information from his mind. No one could ever replace the mother who'd died of cancer several years earlier. Just like no one had been able to replace Jes's mother or father, no matter how hard they'd tried.

For a horrible moment, the memories barreled down on her. Fear. Pain. Loss. An illogical feeling of abandonment.

Her parents had left her. It hadn't been their choice, but they'd still left. *Everyone* left her.

The walls of the restaurant blurred and a haze darkened the room. Jes's breath seized somewhere impossibly deep in her throat. A roar built in her ears, and the walls and booths of the diner fell away until all she saw was the boy and his fear.

She'd felt that fear. So had Dex, she realized. Never mind that Bodin had been trying to protect Dex by sending him away to the were orphanage. Dex had felt the loss of love. Of family.

They'd both lost love early, but at least Jes had been loved by others. Had Dex? Had he ever had the chance? Had he ever let someone truly love him?

It struck her then, how desperately she wanted him to be loved. How desperately *she* wanted to be the one to love him.

What a strange thought. She barely knew him. To her scientific mind, love at first sight was impossible.

A foolish dream.

Jes dealt with reality not dreams. So she focused on the facts.

She and Dex had lost family, but they'd both survived.

So would this boy.

Deliberately, she pushed back her sorrow until the world slowly came back into focus. She patted his head and pretended to check out his stepmom, raking her gaze up and down the feline's body. She pasted a playful grin on her face and knelt down. "Do you know what I am?" she asked, letting the tip of a fang show and deliberately flicking her silver hair.

"You're a vampire," the boy said.

"Right. So I can sense things others can't. And I always tell the truth. Your stepmom? She looks okay to me. And I can sense how much she loves you," she whispered. "Give her a chance."

The boy stared at her with a furrowed brow, glanced at his stepmother, then glanced back at Jes. Slowly, the sharp peaks of his shoulder blades relaxed. Hesitantly, he released Jes's leg and stepped around her.

His parents stared at her.

"Thank you," the feline said. "My name is Lisa." She turned to Eric and knelt down to his level the way Jes had. "It's okay. You don't have to give me a hug, Eric. But would you mind—would you mind if I gave you one?"

Eric glanced at all of them in succession. His father. Jes. Then Lisa.

He nodded.

As Lisa enfolded him in her arms, Jes couldn't help noticing Eric's small arms hugging her back. Taking a lurching breath, she made her way to a smirking Rurik Pitts.

Twenty minutes later, she cocked a brow at the big werebeast. "So Dex Hunt is what? Some kind of medical miracle?" she asked, lacing her tone with disbelief despite the fact she believed every word she said.

Pitts frowned. "I'm telling you, Dex was healthier than anyone I've ever met. He never got sick. *Never.* There's something unnatural about him."

"But you were only around him for what? Five years? For all you know, he was sick before and afterwards," she drawled, choosing her words very carefully to play devil's advocate and still speak the truth. Because of her vampire blood, Jesmina couldn't lie. Of course, over the years, she'd discovered there were ways around that, but nothing she was willing to undergo, not when it was just as easy to manipulate people by what one said or didn't say.

Inside, however, it was more difficult for her to remain composed. Excitement thrummed through her. Pitts was on to something. Everything he'd told her merely confirmed what she suspected about Dex.

Protect the one who can gift immortality.
Cast him out before you let him be found.

The Draci believed Bodin had cast out his grandson in order to protect him. Before she'd died, Rita had pounded that belief into Jes, telling her time and again of her duty to discover the truth.

If the legend *was* true, Dex wasn't natural. More like supernatural.

Comprised of the stuff of legends.

But the werebeast leaning back in his booth seat didn't know that. He stared at her as if she was an idiot. Jes took advantage of the extra few inches of space and breathed in shallowly. Not only was he arrogant and condescending, but he was extremely unkempt. Thankfully, she knew from experience that not all werebeasts smelled so bad. In fact, Dex Hunt had smelled *très…délicieux*.

 Even in the packed nightclub that reeked of sweat, alcohol, sex, and drugs, his scent had called to her just as powerfully as if someone had held a glass of pure immaculate blood to her nose. The same thing had happened last night when he'd confronted her outside her hotel. And it had happened again when he'd lost control and pushed her back into the elevator, ready to take what she'd previously offered him.

When Lucy had shown up, it had taken even more self-control than she'd ever thought she'd need to keep herself from taking a bite out of him. *She*—who'd never once drank from a male during sex and who drank blood like clockwork, thus rarely experiencing blood lust—still felt it that night. Her skin had been rippling with desire ever since, and this unkempt were's words only further fueled her determination to see Dex again.

"Listen, sweet cheeks, Dex and I rode together for six years, five of those during the War. We weren't exactly staying in luxury accommodations during that time, either. The Ferals are tough, we keep tough company, and we're a hearty race, but no matter what shit holes we stayed in or what disease-infested company we kept, Dex was the only one of us who didn't end up puking his guts out or oozing puss at one time or another." He smirked, as if he really thought talk of oozing puss would intimidate or sicken her. "What do you care about Dex's health anyway?"

"It's not just his health I care about," she said. "I told you, I have a business proposition for him, and a smart negotiator never goes into a deal unarmed."

Again, all true. She just didn't know if she'd actually make Dex the business offer she had in mind. She couldn't know until she got him alone and had a chance to read his mind again—this time when he wasn't blocking her powers with the gold charm Mahone said he carried.

"He works for the FBI now," she reminded the werebeast. "He's got a pretty good thing going with them. Luring him away won't be easy."

"But you'll do what you need to in order to do it, right?" Rising, Pitts planted his palms on the table and leaned toward her until his ghastly smell made her eyes water. The way he said "it" made it apparent he thought she'd willingly use her body to sway Dex's mind.

She didn't take offense, since he was right.

"So who told you he has a thing for vamps?" he asked.

She raised a brow, which made him bust up laughing. Her heart fluttered, then clenched. *That* was information she *didn't* have before. Dex was attracted to her, but was it only because she was the right race? One of a handful—and who knew how large those handfuls had been—of vampires he'd wanted?

"Oh come on. You didn't know?" He sat down again, still chuckling. "Well, looks like you've got an edge then, sweet cheeks. Dex never could resist your breed's silver hair—kind of ironic, given silver is our weakness, don't you think?"

But only when in wolf form, she recalled.

He glanced insultingly at her chest. "I like my females with bigger tits, of course, but there's no accounting for taste." He threw back the last of his beer before standing. "We done here?"

"Quite done," she said, barely refraining from slugging the asshole. She slid an envelope toward him.

He grabbed it, peeked inside, and grinned. He was almost to the restaurant's outer door before he turned back. "You remember what I told you about my brother, don't you?"

Pitts had told her Dex had killed his "brother," another Feral member. Slowly. Tortuously. And that he'd left the gang immediately afterward. "Murder isn't something I'm likely to forget." Even as she said the words, terrible images of two specific murders flashed through her mind. Two vampires bound just feet from her. Her parents. Left to burn in the sun.

Mama, Papa. Je n'oublierai jamais. I will never forget.

The were continued talking. "Thanks for the money. Easiest cash I ever earned. But I won't even bother to wish you luck. I don't know what you're hoping to do with the info on Dex. Bribe him? Play hardball? Dex plays harder than anyone I've ever met. Remember that."

With that warning, he was gone. He'd wasted his breath.

She knew Dex played hardball. She'd watched him playing as he'd restrained the misguided shape-shifter who'd messed with Lucy Talbot in that Los Angeles sex club. But although Jesmina might look lithe and harmless next to a bulked-up, badass, motorcycle-riding werebeast, she could play hardball with the best of them.

Only in Dex's case, she'd be playing hardball with tools she never liked to use—deceit and trickery, all unspoken but still quite effective. Of course, that was the very nature of playing hardball: you did what you had to do, no matter what.

She picked up her cell phone and dialed Kyle Mahone's number. She'd taken a huge risk telling him about Dex and her intentions, but she stood by it. Dex worked for Mahone. That meant he had to trust him on some level. Plus, Mahone had the authority to give Jes the money she needed to keep her research going. And although he hadn't given her information about Dex's medical history, he'd known Dex carried a gold charm, which explained why she hadn't been able to read his mind either time she'd attempted to.

Apparently dharmire Knox Devereaux didn't mind sharing intel about his species with the Para-Ops team, which actually reassured Jes. Although she'd never met him, the vamp leader was rumored to have the highest regard for honesty and integrity. If he'd shared information with his team members about vampire weakness, Jes was right to have put her trust in them, too. That included Mahone.

When Mahone answered the line, she said, "I just talked to an old friend of Dex's from the Ferals. Everything he said tells me what I believe is true. In order to be sure, I need to run those tests. Once I read his mind and exercise persuasion over him, I'll draw his blood. Since we were interrupted the last time, I'm hoping he'll come to me. If he doesn't show up, I need you to push him in that direction. If I approach him again, he might become suspicious."

She half-listened to Mahone's response, her thoughts already on whether Dex would come to her. On whether he'd still be pissed at her for taking Lucy away from him. Whether she'd actually do what she planned—tempt him, then take his blood before he even knew what hit him—or let him do what she'd been fantasizing about…

Merde. Why was she even thinking in terms of options?

What she was about to do was bad enough. She wasn't going to add whoring to her litany of sins. No matter how attracted she was to Dex Hunt, she wasn't going to sleep with him to get what she needed.

But she wanted to.

And she had no delusions. She was always unfailingly honest with herself even if she couldn't be honest with those around her. Yes, she suffered from survivor's guilt. She also suffered from an unexpected case of lust and respect for Dex Hunt, a male she barely knew, and the one had nothing to do with the other. It would be easier if it did. Easier for her to see him as a means to an end. But it didn't. And she didn't.

She'd seen Dex working with his team, protecting Lucy and Wraith, putting himself at risk for felines he didn't even know. She knew what he was.

A sexy male who'd done what he needed to do to survive.

An honorable male who pretended not to care because he cared too much.

A male who would despise her if he knew the truth.

CHAPTER FOUR

Until recently, the term fuck buddy had never meant anything to Dex. He'd always fucked for sheer pleasure—to receive it and to give it—but lately other needs drove him. With Lucy, his drive was friendship disguised with practicality. With Jes, his desire was driven by something alarmingly primal. Not just seeking pleasure for pleasure's sake, but more like seeking to appease an intense, gnawing need. With each hour that passed, he had to fight the urge to go to her. To take what he'd actually been prepared to take when he'd pushed her into that damn elevator. To give part of himself he'd never been tempted to give anyone else.

Physically and emotionally.

Hell, he hadn't known what he wanted to do most—mark Jes with his scent and his seed, or beg her to hold him while telling him everything about her.

How was that for bat-shit crazy?

Since he couldn't afford even a temporary case of insanity, he'd managed to refrain from doing any of that.

Which meant for now, a fuck buddy was all he was going to be.

Still, while it wasn't exactly torturous stuff, it wasn't turning out to be as easy as it should be, either—not for him and not for Lucy.

"Let go, Lucy. Let me give you this." As Dex spoke, he pressed himself deeper into the mage's body, then pulled out slowly, stroking the tight inner muscles that fluttered around him. Gritting his teeth, he forced his mind to remain distant from the physical pleasure that was racking his body. From his memories of Jesmina.

This was for Lucy. All for Lucy, damn it.

He'd promised to help ease her sexual heat, the heat that lasted seven days and came every seven days simply because she was part feline. She'd agreed, but the fact that she was fighting the pleasure he was giving her, that she always fought the pleasure he gave her, only tortured them both. He fought release because it would only complicate matters between them, but Lucy fought release because she was ashamed of her body's needs, ashamed she needed sexual release so badly that he'd offer to help her in the first place.

Of course, he never let her get away with it. In order to function during the day, her body needed the release that only male penetration and climax could provide her. If he spent his seed inside her, her relief would be even greater and last even longer. But Dex, unwilling to risk exposing another child to the cruelties of the world, always wore protection. Always.

That wouldn't change, even if he ended up fucking Jesmina.

Especially then.

Of course, he reminded himself, that wasn't going to happen. Yet, once the thought formed, so did other thoughts. Other images.

Suddenly, it was no longer Lucy beneath him, but Jesmina.

It was Jesmina's body he covered, her thighs spread and flanking his hips, her heat surrounding him and fluttering with dual pleasure and resistance.

It was Jesmina who fought the pleasure he offered her at the same time that she strained for it.

It was Jesmina who suddenly made him want to lose control, to shoot himself into her creamy depths again and again, to take her several times, in several different ways…

"Dex!"

Lucy's gasp brought him back to the present and he opened his eyes to stare down at her. Shit. He was pounding into her, stroking her breasts, giving her not just sex but taking her. Because he wanted—needed—to take Jesmina.

Cursing softly, he slowed his thrusts so they were once more controlled.

"Sorry," he murmured. "Now come, Lucy. Please," he choked out.

Lucy's dark eyes were dazed, but he saw the guilt that flashed through them. It made him curse again. He hated the fact that she suffered. He felt compelled to help her but—

"Okay, Dex. Thank you."

She closed her eyes. Took several hitching breaths and forced her body to relax. Within seconds, her climax took her. It was a mild one, as most of hers were, but he knew it would give her temporary peace before she needed him again.

He stayed inside her until the last of her tremors passed. Then he withdrew, grimacing at the friction that made his cock jerk from sheer biology.

"I'll be right back," he said. He excused himself to go to the bathroom and took himself in hand. It took mere seconds for him to get off. It took him only thinking of Jesmina.

When he returned to the bedroom, Lucy was covered with the sheet and laying on her side. He sat beside her and touched her hip over the sheet. "You okay?"

She nodded. "Yes. That was—that was wonderful. Thank you."

Dex snorted and shook his head. "It wasn't wonderful, but it can be better, Lucy. Far better. If you let yourself go, if not with me then with someone else, sex can be damn pleasurable. Your orgasm can be amazing."

She smiled thinly. "It can't be that great since you're able to resist it."

"That has nothing to do with you."

"No? Does it have something to do with you not wanting to have a child? So much so that even using a condom isn't enough assurance for you?"

Her question caught him unawares, mostly because it was so spot on. With Lucy's steady gaze on his, Dex thought about lying, then simply shrugged. "I can't have children. I won't. Not even with you, babe." Especially with her. He'd been ridiculed for his half-breed status. Even Knox had been ostracized by most of his clan. How much more would the child of a half-breed were and feline mage suffer?

"Listen, Mahone wants to talk to me about something. I'll come back as soon as I'm done. I know you're heading home tonight. We can—"

Lucy shook her head. "No, Dex. I should never have let this happen again. It's time to stop."

Agreement was on the tip of his tongue, instinctive and swift. But he knew that couldn't be right. "You need it, Lucy."

"I'll always appreciate what you've done for me, Dex, but it's not fair to you. You're not into me, but you're clearly into someone else. You should go see her—"

"Will you stop trying to push me and the vampire together?" he snapped.

"No, I won't. If you're too stubborn to see what's so obvious, then I need to—"

He growled and did the only thing he could think of to shut her up. He dipped his head and placed a gentle kiss on her lips.

Lucy was so surprised she jerked back. He'd never kissed her, not on the lips. The intimate contact merely confirmed how platonic their feelings really were for each other. No thrill ran through him. No response besides shock was triggered in Lucy. It would be so much easier if he wanted her the same way he wanted Jesmina. It would be so much safer.

"You don't get it, little one. I'm a werebeast, shunned by my own people. I couldn't even fit in with the Ferals, a biker gang of werebeast criminals. My destiny is to be alone. I want only one thing, and that's the reason I joined the Para-Ops team in the first place. Mahone promised each of us what we most wanted. You want a cure to your heat. I'm going to get my revenge on my grandfather. Soon. For now, you're actually doing me a favor. I get sex with you. Get to hold a damn good-looking female without having to worry about someone getting clingy and demanding on me."

She crossed her arms over her chest and tilted that adorably stubborn chin of hers. "You can't fool me, Dex. Jacking off in the bathroom after servicing me is not 'sex with me' or something you should enjoy. It ends now."

The little one was pushing her luck. "Never challenge a were, Lucy. Remember what I told you before all this started. I lead. You follow. It ends when I say it does."

"You're not my older brother. You can't protect me forever."

He got up. Dressed. "Look, I've got to go. We'll talk about this later. I don't want you worrying. If—if me taking you without achieving my own release is what's got you hung up, then we'll switch things up." In fact, maybe it was time to do what he'd always known he should and get that vasectomy. Lucy's heat cycles wouldn't end anytime soon and if he was going to come inside her...

"I don't know. This whole thing, it just doesn't seem right, Dex."

"Let me worry about that. I'm going to talk to Mahone." He headed for the door, pausing with his hand on the doorknob when Lucy spoke.

"Children aren't a curse, you know..."

He turned back to her. He thought of the child he'd been. The horrors he'd seen and experienced in the dilapidated were orphanage his grandfather had sent him to. He'd certainly felt cursed back then and sometimes, when his guard was down and the memories sprang upon him, he still did. "Don't, Lucy. I'm not going there."

"You need to talk about it."

She was wrong. Talking about his past, his family, himself, was the last thing he needed. "We'll talk more when I get back. Just not about that."

***

Lucy watched Dex shut the door behind him before screaming with frustration and flinging herself back on the bed. What a mess.

She adored Dex, but someone needed to knock some sense into the were.

Someone needed to knock some sense into *her*.

What had she been thinking, accepting his offer of sex?

Okay, she knew what she'd been thinking. That she was sick of suffering from the heat and that Dex was hot and she respected him and that she knew he cared about her so why not let him help her out?

Well, the "why not" had just walked out the door.

Sighing, she curled onto her side and stared out her small hotel window. Through the sheer curtains, she could just make out the cloudless California sky.

Bottom line, she'd let her own needs overshadow those of her friend's. At least, she'd done so after Dex had met Jesmina. She'd seen for herself how attracted he was to Jes and the fact that Dex hadn't been able to hide that attraction was telling.

Lucy stood, used the bathroom, then studied herself in the mirror. She looked the way she should. Like a female who'd just had sex. Dex's soul patch had even left red marks near her neck and shoulders. She lightly traced the lines with the pads of her fingers.

Yes, she looked like someone's lover even when she'd never really been one.

And maybe that was how it was supposed to be.

Things were changing.

The team was fracturing.

And that made her feel more panicked than she'd felt since peace had been declared.

What was she going to do?

When she was with her teammates, she was more than she'd ever been. More than a mage denying her feline blood. More than a youthful looking female who no one took seriously. Sure, she was the quietest one, the peacekeeper of the group, but that just emphasized the fact that she had a place among them.

Here, now, she was adrift without the others.

But that was something that was going to have to change.

Felicia had Knox, and Wraith had Caleb. Dex deserved his own chance at happiness. To give him that chance, she was going to have to break the fragile connection that he'd initiated between them. For his own good. And for hers.

She had to find her place, as well as the ability to stand in it on her own.

***

Mahone was an excellent FBI agent, Dex thought. He was an even better leader. Political enough to rise in the ranks, manipulative enough to recognize and move pawns where they needed to go, and unassuming enough to fly under the radar when he needed to, which was most of the time. But today something was different.

Dex stared at the human who was pacing his temporary space at the Bureau's office in Los Angeles.

Today, Mahone seemed edgier. Tougher. In attitude and in appearance. It wasn't like the guy really looked different exactly, at least not in an obvious way. Yet he seemed fitter when he'd always been fit. Sharper when he'd always been sharp. And younger...

Dex frowned. For some reason, Dex always thought of Mahone as fatherly, but why? He was mid-forties. No gray hair. Probably quite attractive to most females. Hell, even Knox's mother had fallen for him.

Would Jesmina find him attractive?

Dex jolted at the random thought. Jesus, what was wrong with him? As much as he hated his preoccupation with the vampire, he understood it. The fact he was now thinking of *her* in terms of *Mahone's* attractiveness told him he needed to get his shit together. Now.

He returned his attention to Mahone.

Oblivious to Dex's thoughts, Mahone kept right on talking. "...so I'd like you to go to France to check out the growing division among shape-shifters. Paris has the hottest pocket of infighting, with a rapidly escalating murder rate among the race, but we need to assess the situation before we go diving in."

"What about the Quorum? Do you think they're involved?"

"No reason to think so. Not yet. After what happened with Felicia and the felines, they seem to be lying low. Do you have contacts in Paris?"

He hadn't. Not until recently, Dex thought. Not until he'd met Jesmina. She lived there and had told Dex on the night they'd met that she'd be returning at the end of the week.

That meant he had another excuse to see her again before she left.

He tried to temper any pleasure he felt with thoughts of Lucy, who was right in the middle of her heat. If he went to Paris alone, he'd be gone several days, which meant she'd suffer needlessly during that time. "I think I know someone who might be able to help once I get there, but why not let Lucy go with me? If I go alone, getting the info you want will be twice as difficult given the French bias toward weres."

A bias was putting it mildly. The French were extremely hostile toward werewolves, creatures they deemed to have been cursed by the Gods and in league with the devil. Historically, more people had been tried and put to death for lycanthropy in France than in any other country in the world. Even Jesmina had used the word "were" with a hint of automatic disdain, and she'd been undeniably attracted to him.

"I'm glad you brought up Lucy," Mahone said, looking displeased. "I've been meaning to discuss the amount of time you've been spending with her."

Why? Because Lucy was a member of Mahone's team and he didn't like team members fraternizing? Maybe Mahone just felt protective of Lucy, as Dex did. She seemed to inspire that feeling in males.

Mahone blew out a breath. "Look, I know Lucy has certain *needs*, but I can't afford to have both of you out of the country. O'Flare's going to help Wraith adjust to her new situation. Knox is still determined to keep Felicia safe, which means not letting her set foot out of the Vampire Dome. That leaves only you and Lucy. With everything that's happened with the felines lately, it makes sense for me to keep Lucy nearby. Besides, you'll only be gone a few days."

"When do you want me to leave?"

"This week. Can you get in touch with your contact by then?"

"Yeah," Dex said. "I can." He wasn't sure if Jes would be able to tell him anything about French shape-shifters, but it didn't really matter. Not anymore.

Forces were conspiring to bring them together, and he was tired of fighting them.

He was giving in gracefully.

He'd talk to Jes, fly to France, get the information Mahone wanted, and then things would get back to normal. He'd tell Mahone he was ready to move on his grandfather, and then he'd decide whether he even wanted to be part of the Para-Ops team anymore.

But first, he'd get in touch with Jesmina.

In fact, as he left Mahone, touching Jes was all Dex could think about.

CHAPTER FIVE

Of all the disastrous mistakes he could possibly make, Dex knew he was about to make a big one. Yet, there was no stopping himself. It was late afternoon, the L.A. sun still blazing, so chances were that Jes was inside her room. Sleeping. Warm and drowsy. Vulnerable.

As he stood in front of her hotel room door, his skin rippled with the need of his beast to break through. He tried to keep his thoughts on his mission, on his need to question her about the shape-shifters, but as soon as she opened the door, his ability to reason shorted out.

Her telltale moonlight hair was a disheveled cloud around her face. Her legs were bare, her nipples dark and reaching out to him from beneath a thin long-sleeved tee, her expression devoid of any hint of surprise. Behind her, the shades were drawn and the room cast in shadows.

Without thinking, he stepped into the room, kicked the door shut with his foot, then reached for her and didn't even bother with the niceties.

As if he had every right in the world, he slipped his hand under the fall of her hair and palmed the back of her neck. The way she bit her lip and the way her lids shuttered sent his pulse spiking and his body hardening.

He paused. Waited for her to protest.

But she didn't. His blood raged through him when her little white teeth released the plump flesh of her bottom lip. He followed the movement with his gaze, imagining her teeth lengthening into fangs, penetrating his throat. He nearly grimaced from the quivers of desire that rattled through him with a complimentary need to bury himself in her body. Her lips parted.

"What took you so long?" she demanded.

Eyes widening then narrowing, Dex stepped forward and took her mouth with his. He'd never felt so much a wolf as he did at that moment, swooping down on her like a predator overpowering its prey. Plunging his hands into her hair, he held her still for his kiss, groaning at the warm slick suction that surrounded his tongue and shivered its way down to other parts of his body. His hands followed suit, slipping down to her shoulders, pausing at the graceful swell of her breasts, then separating so that one played with her nipples while the other snaked its way to the juncture of her thighs.

She jolted when he pressed his fingers against her mound, her gasp almost drowned out by his groan of approval. She was warm and wet here, too, her body extending the same invitation she'd uttered when she'd first approached him in that bar.

Firmly, he pressed his thumb against the bud that swelled for his touch. Her thighs trembled, something he barely noticed because of his own shaky limbs. Against his fingers, a gush of moisture soaked the fabric of her panties, making him dizzy with need. His nostrils flared as he absorbed her scent, the spice of her arousal almost drowning out the perfume. He licked his lips, wanting to go down on her, knowing she'd taste like heaven on earth. Instinctively, he pressed his groin against her thigh, her warmth penetrating his clothes and giving him the smallest hint of what he'd feel when he was inside her.

But something was off. Even as she opened her mouth wider, welcoming the aggressive thrust of his tongue, she seemed startled by his passion. Innocence didn't jive with what he knew of her, which admittedly was very little, but she seemed almost frightened. By him or the passion between them? He hesitated and started to pull back.

She'd have none of it. Wrapping her arms around his neck, she deliberately arched her lower body into his hand. Then she dropped her own hand and cupped him through his pants, finding and rubbing the head of his cock with a firm, circular motion.

His eyes rolled back in his head and he struggled for control. There was a reason he needed to pull away. Something important...

Quietly, she murmured, "Take me. Now. I can't—I can't have children. We don't need protection."

Protection. Not needed.

Vampires couldn't lie.

But he wasn't taking any chances. Not with her. Not with anyone.

Using his free hand, he retrieved several condoms from his pocket and held them out to her. "Suit me up," he said.

She looked shocked at his request, which gave him pause. She'd never helped a guy put on a rubber before? But before he could give it more thought, she took one of the packs he held out and did the one thing guaranteed to bring him to his knees.

She lowered herself to hers.

***

With her head bent and her gaze focused on her fingers, which were fumbling with Dex Hunt's zipper, Jesmina bit her lip to stop herself from moaning in confusion and delight. *Now's the time to do it, Jes*, she told herself. *Strip him naked and rid him of the gold he carries, then read his mind and use persuasion on him. You're not actually going to have sex with him, remember? You're a scientist who needs to test his blood; you're not a whore.*

But even at her mental gymnastics, her fingers freed him from his pants and her breath escaped.

Like hell I'm not going to have sex with him.

And it had nothing to do with needing to test his blood.

She wanted him. Inside of her. On top of her.

And he wanted her, too.

His shaft was big and thick, the plum-shaped tip flushing a dark red and reaching almost to his belly button. She wrapped her fingers gently around him, gasping when Dex hissed and jerked as if she'd burned him. Yet she was the one who felt burned. His erection was smooth and hot, and that heat traveled directly from her fingertips to her breasts and in between her thighs. Wanting to heighten that delicious heat, she stroked him, relishing his growl and the way his hands flew to her hair and tugged the strands until she looked up at him.

He was staring down at her, eyes glistening, flags of red on both his cheekbones. He looked inflamed and angry, and she knew he hadn't forgiven her for taking Lucy from him that night to hunt down Alton Maddox. Still, she felt a moment of glee. Dex might be sleeping with Lucy, might even desire her, but right now his body wanted hers. The knowledge made her heady with power. Deliberately, she moved forward, pulling against his grasp, not stopping even when she felt a bite of pain because he hadn't released her hair. Her mouth stopped a mere inch from him and though she strained, he wouldn't grant her any more leeway.

She extended her tongue and laved the underside of his shaft.

His fingers tightened even more and he locked his knees together.

"Feeling a little unsteady, were?" she taunted, then swirled her tongue around him, taking her time before teasingly flicking the tip of him. He moaned and suddenly, instead of holding her back, he was guiding her where he wanted her. Or rather, where she wanted him—in her mouth, where she enveloped him with a warm, moist suction that caused both of them to tremble with pleasure.

He tasted wonderful. Hot and sweet with a slight tinge of bitterness that only made him more nuanced and complex. Kind of like fresh, pure blood. And he slid down her throat just as easily, invigorating and energizing her without any of the guilt that came with needing to survive by taking from another. In this, she took but she also gave. She sucked and sucked until her mouth ached, and then she released him only to rake her fangs teasingly against him.

When he cursed and pulled away, not because he didn't like it but maybe because he liked it too much, she cried out and tried to pull him close again, immediately missing the feel of him in her mouth. He shook his head. "Put on the condom," he gritted out, hands still buried in her hair. "Now."

She obeyed with unsteady hands. When she was done, he helped her to her feet, and with his gaze locked on hers, reached down and ripped her panties off. His hands gripped her hips and with amazing ease, he lifted her up and poised her over his straining flesh, butting against her opening like a stallion ready to bolt out the gates.

After that first time, he hadn't kissed her again. He made no move to do so now, but she couldn't stop her gaze from lowering to his mouth. She wanted that mouth on her. All over her. She wanted his tongue in her again. In other places.

"Look at me," he ordered.

Her eyes jerked back to his. He lowered her onto his shaft, feeding her one inch at a time, jerking one hitching gasp out of her after another. The feel of him stretching her delicate, clasping flesh caused pleasure as sharp as diamonds to rip through her. When he was fully inside her, stretching her almost to the point of pain, she could no longer bear the intensity of his gaze.

She buried her face in his neck and breathed in deep, dizzy from his fresh, clean scent. Without forethought, she nipped him and imagined sinking her fangs into his beautiful skin. Her little bite spurred him into motion and suddenly he was pounding himself into her, alternately lifting her and pulling her, working her over his flesh at the depth he wanted, the angle he wanted, the speed he wanted.

And what he wanted just happened to be exactly what she wanted, too.

The pulses started deep inside her, small, tight little flutters that expanded into rolling, thundering explosions that shook her like a rag doll caught in a hurricane.

"Yes," Dex hissed. "That feels amazing. Keep going."

She didn't know what he meant but then realized that as he kept moving in short, hard thrusts, he was somehow prolonging the pleasure, keeping her on the edge of sensation even as his pace quickened and he reached for his own.

"Holy fuck," he breathed just before he exploded. As he came, he latched onto her breast, sucking her nipple through the fabric of her tee. His grip tightened on her hips to the point she knew she'd have bruises but she didn't care. She felt him pulsing inside her, felt the sucks on her nipple and farther down, deep inside her, and she flew straight into another intense orgasm. Another first for her.

She pulled back, breathing hard, and stared into his pleasure-contorted face. She felt a trickle of liquid on her thigh. Realized the condom had broken. Since she couldn't get pregnant or give him any kind of disease, however, she didn't bother telling him.

When his release ended and his face relaxed, he growled, "We're not done yet."

"No," she breathed in agreement.

Little to no foreplay and Dex had given her multiples right out the gate. She couldn't wait for what came next.

CHAPTER SIX

Jesmina pulled herself out of the tangle of his arms and looked down at Dex. For the first time since meeting him, his expression was completely vulnerable, relaxed in sleep so he could no longer hide himself behind a fierce glower or disdainful sneer. Slightly parted lips revealed just the tips of his fangs. His chest rose and fell with his breaths, the muscles rippling beneath burnished skin. She noticed a soft patch of hair that had tickled her cheek when she'd rested against him, relishing the strong beat of his heart. The flesh between her thighs ached, further evidence of his vitality and health.

Dex Hunt had given her the best sex she'd ever had.

Problem was, sleeping with him hadn't been part of the plan.

Making him think it would happen, yes. Getting him alone so she could use persuasion against him, sure.

But not sex.

Only, resisting the were's touch had proven outside her capabilities. Her response had had nothing to do with her plan and everything to do with the simple fact she'd wanted him. Wanted something for herself when for so long she'd thought only of others. She'd been so far gone she'd even let him strip off her shirt, giving him a good long look at the hideous scars on her arm, which, though ugly, hadn't slowed him down. He'd run his fingers and mouth over the damaged skin just like he did every other part of her body and soon she was too caught up in pleasure to be embarrassed.

Now that the sex had happened, however—now that he was naked, with the gold charm he normally used to block vampire power likely somewhere still in his clothes that she'd kicked into the closet—she still had one thing left to do.

Reading his mind should have been easy given everything she'd taken from him already. But it wasn't. Not for her.

This would be the final violation, the most intimate penetration she could commit, yet she let neither that knowledge nor her unease stop her.

She couldn't. What she found would cement her next move. Either she'd be able to wake Dex and tell him the truth—make her offer—or she'd have to take what she needed and leave. She wanted so badly to be able to wake him...

She slipped inside his mind so gently he'd never sense she'd been there. She prodded carefully but thoroughly, and within seconds had her disappointing answer.

Bodin of Hammersham would get no help here. Not willingly. Dex Hunt hated him—his own grandfather. He wanted to kill him.

Nonetheless, Bodin's plan had worked. By ostracizing Dex, he'd kept him alive.

Dex had no idea what he was.

He had no idea of the immortality he could give.

And hopefully, neither did anyone else.

Soundlessly, she retrieved the supplies from her bag and used persuasion to keep Dex asleep while she drew his blood. It was a particularly hard task since he was sleeping and few vampires could actually accomplish persuasion on a sleeping individual; she, however, had tricks of the trade that other vampires didn't. It was just one benefit of a life dedicated to researching Otherborn, including her own race. She knew how to use persuasion on someone who was sleeping. Knew how to train a vampire mind so the vampire could lie. Knew all kinds of little known facts about vampires and weres and felines...

She smirked.

Oh my.

Yes, she was a virtual treasure trove of information, yet she didn't know the things she'd always agonize over.

Why had she been saved when her parents hadn't?

Why would she live forever when those she loved wouldn't?

Why had she finally met a male who could move her and make her think beyond her guilt and duty, only to have to use him and leave him shortly thereafter?

She would never have those answers, but she might be able to have others.

With Dex's help, with his blood, she could find the key to prolonging the lives of those who weren't born immortal. At least, she prayed to the Goddess Essenia that would be the case.

To accomplish what she wanted and to run all the necessary tests, however, she'd need a lot of Dex's blood. Almost too much blood, since she'd likely never see Dex again and this was her one shot at getting enough samples. She had to be careful, otherwise he wouldn't just be feeling woozy tomorrow—he might not recover. So she used care, taking what she needed and not a drop more.

As she took vial after vial, his scent whirled around her, seeping into her skin and causing her fangs to lengthen despite her efforts to keep them sheathed. As a doctor, she'd always had to exercise iron control over her appetite in order to treat her patients. In truth, it hadn't been all that difficult for her, which simply made it easier to forget sometimes that she actually was a vampire.

Things were different with Dex.

She'd been desperate to bite him as they'd made love, had thought for sure she wouldn't be able to stop herself, but the pleasure he'd given her had combined with her own curiosity, giving her the strength she'd needed to resist. Instead, she'd focused on imprinting him into her memory. The feel of him, his touch, the taste of sucking and licking his flesh were all details she cherished and knew she would continue to cherish for an eternity. Sadness threatened to swamp her, making her fingers tremble, and she mentally cursed.

Focus, Jes. The guy got what he wanted from you. Now you need to do the same.

When she was done and the vials of blood safely stored, she dressed and sat beside him again.

Guilt weighed heavily on her but she told herself she'd had no choice. Dex's blood could save the one person he wanted dead. He never would have given it to her freely and she couldn't let his anger, though understandable, jeopardize Bodin's life. Not when she might have the power to save it. Professionally, she'd sworn an oath to heal all, human and Otherborn. Practically, Bodin's death would cause enormous problems within several Otherborn communities, including the Draci, the community most important to her. And personally, she owed Bodin a debt, one she could repay with Dex's help, whether it was freely given or not.

Yet she still regretted having to deceive Dex.

No matter how this turned out—whether or not Dex carried the gift Bodin thought he did—Dex was special.

She'd seen that for herself when she'd seen him with his team mates. Even the seedy bar they'd been staking out hadn't been able to detract from the bond they all seemed to share.

They were a family.

That knowledge had simply enhanced the attraction and intense pull she'd felt for Dex. They were both castaways. Both orphans. Despite his unfortunate childhood, he'd found his place. And in his arms, he'd given her something far more precious than pleasure. Something she'd never quite felt before.

The certainty that she belonged, too.

But that, of course, was just another cruel lie.

Jes didn't belong. She'd found a purpose but she wasn't indispensable. There would always be another to take her place. Someone willing to save the lives of others rather than live her own.

Except she'd finally lived—for a few brief hours in Dex's arms.

And now she'd have to live without.

Jes rose, then hesitated. She could make him forget their time together, but for some reason she didn't want to. She told herself there was no need. If he'd suspected her duplicity, she had no doubt she'd already be dead

Before she left, she kissed Dex's lips and whispered goodbye.

CHAPTER SEVEN

Dex jerked awake to the shrill sound of his cell phone. He groaned as he tried to move, his limbs as heavy as bags of cement. His muscles, his skin—hell, even his hair—ached. Blinking the haze from his eyes, he took in his surroundings—a swank hotel room designed in minimalist chic. Despite his slowness to wake, he knew exactly where he was and who was supposed to be next to him, yet he was the sole occupant of the bed.

He scanned every corner of the room and strained his ears—maybe she was in the bathroom—but his instincts told him he was alone.

The vamp had wrung him dry then left.

He tried to sort out how he felt about that, but his blasted cell phone continued to ring, making his temples throb.

Growling, he rose, staggering slightly before his feet were steady beneath him. Shit, he felt hung over. Woozy. The same way he always felt whenever he let a vamp drink his blood during a night of frenzied sex. Granted, it hadn't happened in several years, but it was a feeling he never forgot, just like he never forgot the euphoric spike of pleasure that threw him into full-out orgasm the moment a vamp's fangs penetrated his skin. Even so, he didn't remember Jes biting him last night. He checked, but felt no tenderness or puncture marks on his throat.

Apparently, it didn't matter. Sex with her had been more intense than any he'd ever experienced. Even now, just thinking about it, his growing hard-on was threatening to throw off his recently found equilibrium.

With her, inside her, time itself had changed. It had raced on, filling him with a desperate fear that he'd never be able to get his fill of her. Simultaneously, the clock had stopped ticking, allowing him to savor each sensation and every caress until his body had vibrated with something he'd never felt before. He'd emptied himself into the condoms he'd worn, yet when he'd let slumber take him, he'd felt filled with what had always eluded him.

Peace.

Contentment.

Happiness?

But those feelings were distant memories now, taunting him with the proof of her absence. Mocking him for his weakness.

Pull yourself together, Hunt. She was a fantastic lay. That's all. Anything else you felt was just your imagination.

He dug his ringing cell phone out of his jeans pocket and checked the time: 2 a.m.

Still naked, he stepped into the bathroom. "Yeah. This is Hunt."

"Hunt," FBI Director Kyle Mahone snapped. "Where the fuck are you?"

"Where the hell do you think I am?" He saw the note taped to the bathroom mirror and ripped it off.

You were even better than you looked. Jes.

He frowned at the flippant words of praise. What had he been expecting? Her phone number and an invitation to call? He filled a glass with water, then took a long swallow. Mahone's voice crackled out from the phone he still held in his other hand, reminding him that he hadn't even questioned her about the shape-shifters the way he was supposed to.

"Damn it, Dex. Did you hear what I—"

He lowered the glass with a thud. "I'm still in Los Angeles with the team."

"You sure as shit aren't with the rest of the team. If you were, you'd know there's been an attempted murder on a shape-shifter. The culprit, another shape-shifter, got away. Lucy's going to the hospital to talk to the victim."

"Which hospital?"

"Los Angeles Memorial."

"I'll be there as soon as I—"

But Mahone had already hung up. "Shit." Once again, Dex reached out to turn on the faucet, this time to splash some cold water on his face, but a sound drifted toward him from the bedroom.

He froze. Whoever it was hadn't come in through the hotel room door because that was next to the bathroom and Dex would have seen him.

Of course, Jesmina was a vampire with the ability to teleport. Maybe she'd forgotten something. Maybe she'd decided she hadn't had enough of him. But he knew that wasn't the case. She was long gone and now someone was out there while Dex was in the bathroom, buck-ass naked without a weapon.

"Dex, my boy, aren't you going to come out and say hello? Or are you shy now that the lady vampire's gone?"

Despite the months since he'd seen him, Dex immediately recognized the male voice as one belonging to a Feral gang member. At one time, the man's brother had been Dex's best friend. That had been before Dex had killed the man for crimes he'd committed at the were orphanage. "Rurik," he called as he scanned the bathroom for a potential weapon. "What brings you to L.A.?"

"Just seeing the sights with some of the other Ferals." Rurik's voice got louder as he approached the bathroom. "Imagine my surprise when what I spotted was you. And the vampire who met you at the door? Nice."

He didn't bother asking how the were had gotten inside. A third floor balcony would be child's play for Rurik. Dex's gaze landed on a toothbrush, still wrapped in plastic, next to the sink. He snatched it up. "Sorry, but if you were hoping to join in, she's already gone."

"Too bad. Could've been fun. But vamps were always your thing, not mine. Guess I'll just have to settle for killing you."

He was right outside the door. Dex drawled, "Your brother was a pedophile who liked abusing little boys. He deserved exactly what he got."

Dex heard Rurik's roar a split second before he barreled through the bathroom door. Dex grabbed the shower curtain, ripped it off the rod, and flung it toward the large werebeast lunging toward him. Rurik's gun rattled to the floor but he kept coming, barreling into Dex and sending him stumbling back. The back of Dex's knees hit the commode just as he pushed Rurik back into the bathtub. Instantly, he flipped the faucet nozzle so water streamed out of the showerhead, the water preventing Rurik from shifting into his wolf—and immortal—form.

Rurik flailed at the clingy fabric. Just as he swiped a portion away from his face, Dex punched the hard plastic handle of the toothbrush into one of the were's eye sockets. Rurik howled but Dex didn't pause. He slammed Rurik's head against the tub several times until he was unconscious.

Swiftly, Dex patted Rurik down, but the were had nothing on him. Dex grabbed Rurik's gun off the floor. It was loaded with tranquilizers, not bullets. So Rurik's mission hadn't been to kill Dex but kidnap him. Why? So he could torture him first?

"Wake up," Dex growled. He shook the were, then slapped his face several times. Rurik didn't stir.

Damn it, he wanted to question Rurik, make sure he hadn't done anything to Jes, but he needed to get to the hospital, too. He scanned the room as if searching for an answer.

From his position low to the ground, he saw the hairdryer under the sink that he'd failed to spot earlier. He grabbed the hairdryer and ripped the cord out of the appliance. He turned, intending to tie Rurik's hands and ankles, but heavy fingers wrapped around his wrists and wrestled him for the cord. Caught off guard, he sprawled backwards, giving Rurik the chance to twist the cord around his neck. Dex barely managed to keep his fingers between the noose and his flesh.

Abandoning the cord, Rurik wrapped his fingers around Dex's throat, squeezing the air out of Dex's lungs far too quickly.

He grabbed Rurik's thick wrists and tried to pull them away, but the pressure didn't lessen. From the corner of his eye, Dex saw the hairdryer he'd tossed aside. Gasping, he stretched out the fingers of one hand. The appliance was just out of his reach. Dots appeared in front of him and his vision began to dim.

With a frantic lunge, he grabbed hold of the hairdryer's handle and slammed it against Rurik's temple. At the same time, he grabbed the dangling end of the cord, the one that still had the socket prongs attached, and punched the metal into Rurik's other temple. With a vicious twist, he snapped the were's neck.

Rurik collapsed. When Dex rolled him off him, Rurik's eyes were open and unseeing. Dex stared impassively at the gruesome sight. "When you get to hell, tell your brother I send my regards. I'll see you both soon." He turned to retrieve his phone just as it rang. . .

***

Dex jerked awake to the shrill sound of his cell phone. He groaned as he tried to move. His muscles, his skin—hell, even his hair—ached. Blinking the haze from his eyes, he took in his surroundings and...

Shit. He bolted up and the soft sheet covering him fell to his waist.

He was in bed. Alone.

The call from Mahone. Rurik's assault. Even his night with Jesmina.

It had all been a dream. Hadn't it?

But as he scanned the empty hotel room, the scent of her lingered in the air. On the sheets. On him. No, this was her room. He'd had her last night. But now she was gone and his phone was ringing. . .

Ignoring his trembling legs, he lunged out of bed and grabbed his cell phone out of his jeans. "Mahone?"

"Hunt," Mahone snapped. "Where the fuck are you?"

Dex's mind spun, trying to process what was happening. He knew what Mahone was going to say next but how was that possible?

"Where the hell do you think I am?" he asked slowly. He glanced toward the bathroom, but it was dark inside and he couldn't see whether Jesmina's note was taped on the mirror or not.

"Damn it, Dex. Did you hear what I—"

"A shape-shifter's been attacked? And taken to Los Angeles Memorial?"

Mahone's stunned silence told him all he needed to know.

"I'm on my way," Dex snapped before pressing the disconnect button. Slowly, he stepped up to the bathroom doorway, reached in, and flipped on the light. The toothbrush was still there. So was the hairdryer. But there was no note taped to the mirror.

And fuck if that wasn't what pissed him off the most.

***

When Rurik Pitts jerked awake, he was sweating, his chest heaving as he struggled to suck in air. His gaze frantically took in his surroundings and what appeared to be a spotless hotel room. Where was he?

Memory returned. His meeting with the female vampire. His pocket full of cash. Meeting up with a fellow Feral, Antonio. Or at least, someone who'd looked like Antonio.

But it hadn't been Antonio. It had been a shape-shifter. A shape-shifter who'd brought him to a hotel room across from the one where Dex was staying and then introduced him to—

Oh God. His lungs seized and his muscles strained with the effort to move. He tried to grip the sheets beneath him, but his fingers remained stubbornly stiff. He tried to shift his legs, to swing them off the bed so he could stand, to kick out—anything—but they refused to cooperate.

A whimper broke the silence; to his horror, it had come from him.

A faint chant, whispers on the air, drifted toward him. His eyes, the only part of him that seemed capable of moving, whipped his gaze around the room. Finally, he caught a glimpse of bright white skin, but that wasn't what made him whimper again.

He felt it. Something inside him. Something slithering not just through his mind but through his body. His heart constricted as if he was having a heart attack, but Rurik knew what it really was—the thing inside him was squeezing his heart. Letting him know it was there. And that it was pissed.

I'll help you, he thought frantically. I'll try again. Just give me another chance.

Another chance, a nasty voice echoed inside him.

But before Rurik could feel even a moment of relief, the voice continued.

One last chance to get me Dex Hunt.

CHAPTER EIGHT

A few hours later, Dex paced L.A. Memorial's surgery floor. The hospital corridor was dark and deserted, with only faint sounds drifting from the nurse's station down the hall. The wounded shape-shifter hadn't been able to tell Lucy anything before he'd been wheeled into surgery and Dex had offered to wait at the hospital so Lucy could get some sleep.

He wished he hadn't.

Being in the hospital reminded him of how helpless he'd felt just days earlier when Wraith had been admitted. They'd all thought she was dying, but she was fine, now, and driving O'Flare, the pretty-boy psychic human who'd stubbornly chased down a goddess in order to save the female he loved, absolutely insane. O'Flare had even left the Para-Ops team because he wanted to spend time with Wraith. Because he actually thought they were going to live happily ever after together.

Poor SOB. He was trapped now, just like Knox. Tied to females that, despite the joy they might bring them now, would eventually leave them. Of course, O'Flare might not outlive Wraith, but as an immortal vampire, Knox would almost certainly outlive Felicia. The Goddess help Knox when that happened because Dex knew Knox would surely go insane.

As it was, Knox had almost lost it after the Quorum put out a hit on Felicia, all because she'd married a vamp. To stop them from going after her again, he'd even started a rumor that he'd turned Felicia into a vampire. What surprised Dex the most was that Knox hadn't rectified matters by turning Felicia into a vampire a long time ago. But Knox was controlled by his sense of honor; he wouldn't turn Felicia against her will. And because turning a human meant risking a vampire's own life, Felicia refused to give her consent.

If it were Dex, he wouldn't give Felicia the choice. But that was Knox's weakness. His devotion to duty and honor. He hadn't yet learned, despite almost three centuries on earth, that the only duty one carried was to oneself.

Despite pitying his teammates, however, Dex could understand what was controlling both Knox and Caleb. Even those short moments in Jesmina's arms had made him question what he'd believed his whole life—that survival hinged on detachment. Then reality had intruded. When his eyes had opened and he'd realized she was gone, he'd felt the sting of her absence—both times.

Forget about Jes. It was one night, damn it. Forget about feeling sorry for Knox and O'Flare. What you should really be concerned about is that weird-ass dream you had.

After all these years, why had he suddenly inserted Rurik Pitts into his head?

Lingering guilt over having killed Rurik's brother? No, Dex felt no guilt for that. He'd been involved with the abuse at the were orphanage. The only thing Dex regretted was killing him too quickly when he could have made the pain drag out.

Had his conflicted emotions about Jes sought release through a good ol' violence dream? A challenge to defeat Rurik in battle since he couldn't seem to defeat his desire for Jes? But why had the dream echoed some of the reality that had come after it, like Mahone's call, while other parts of the dream hadn't? Why hadn't Jes left him a damn note—

"What's going on in that head of yours, Hunt?"

Dex jerked slightly at the unexpected male voice. Knox Devereaux, royal vamp and Para-Ops team leader, stepped into his line of vision.

"What the hell are you doing here?" But despite his harsh words, Dex couldn't stop himself from smiling. He hadn't seen Knox for some time and while he hadn't exactly missed the dude—

"You're troubled. Why? Something the shape-shifter told you?"

"He hasn't told me anything. He's still in surgery. Did Mahone fill you in on what's happening?"

"Yes. I know you'll be leaving for France soon."

Marriage didn't seem to be doing much for Knox's well being. In fact, he looked like shit, nothing like the happy vamp he'd been on his wedding day. He looked desperate, worried sick that the Quorum would make another attempt on Felicia's life. "So why are you here?"

"Because I need something from you."

"What's that?"

"A promise."

There were all kinds of smart-ass things Dex could have said, but Knox looked serious and Dex suddenly knew what promise Knox wanted. The question was, what would Dex's answer be?

"A promise," Knox continued, "that if anything happens to me, you'll watch out for Felicia. You'll make sure she's safe and taken care of. My parents and children, they'll be fine, but Felicia . . ."

"You blipped yourself all the way down here for that? Are you planning something I don't know about?"

"No, but things will have to come to a head. The Quorum has slowly been getting bolder. Hell, they hired my own brother to kill Felicia."

Not only that, but the league of powerful humans bent on Otherborn destruction had infiltrated the White House to see Felicia killed. "They think she's a vamp now."

"But she's not. She's human and very vulnerable and she still refuses to let me turn her."

"Because she knows you'd be risking your own life to change her," Dex pointed out. "She'll never let that happen."

Knox raked his hands through his hair and cursed. "I'm not going to let anything endanger her. You've proven you're committed to protecting Lucy. And I know how much you like Felicia. So just promise me, okay?"

Dex rubbed the back of his neck, torn between Knox's faith in him and practicality. "You're placing a lot of stock in me, Knox. More than you should. You know I have my own agenda. Mahone has promised to look the other way when I go after the werewolf leader, but who knows how it'll go down."

"You're still bound and determined to kill your grandfather?"

"Of course."

"Of course?" Knox laughed and shook his head. "It's that much of a no-brainer for you? Hell, Dex, you've got a good life now. Don't you think you should forget about the past? Move on?"

"That's easy for you to say, now that you've discovered your traitor father wasn't a traitor after all. But that's not gonna happen with me. My grandfather is a son of a bitch who deserves everything he's got coming."

"Fine. Just think about what I said. And I still want your promise."

"You'd trust my promise?"

"Yes."

Dex hesitated for a few seconds, thinking of Lucy. Of the promise he'd already made her. Since when had protecting women become a pastime for him? Next thing he knew, O'Flare would be extracting a promise from him to care for Wraith. And there was no doubt in his mind that despite his reluctance to label his team friends, he would agree. Why waste any more time, Knox's or his, by denying what Knox already knew Dex would agree to? "I promise."

They stared at each other with mutual understanding and—again, it couldn't be denied—respect. They'd come a long way since trying to kill each other at the Para-Ops team's first meeting. As Knox turned away, Dex stopped him.

"Wait. I have a question for you. Can vampires manipulate dreams?"

Knox frowned. "I've heard it's possible, though I'm not sure how."

"Have you heard of a female vampire with scars on one arm? Like she'd put her arm through a sheet of glass when she was young?"

"Is this about the vamp you met at the club?"

Of course Knox would have heard about Dex's encounter with Jesmina from the others, but Dex still didn't like Knox knowing his business. He supposed it was the price he paid for working on a team, but even when he'd been with the Ferals he hadn't let anyone that close. Not like this.

"I can put feelers out for you," Knox offered.

"She might have something to do with a recent visit from an old friend. One I wasn't particularly keen on seeing."

"I'll take that as a yes. You want a favor from me?"

Leave it to the vamp to push the matter. "Yes," Dex gritted out. What he really wanted was to question Jes himself. Ask her why she'd left so suddenly. Why she hadn't bitten him. But anything Knox found out would be better than what Dex knew now—zilch.

Knox chuckled. "See you soon, Dex."

After Knox left, Dex returned to his pacing. Within minutes, however, the surgery doors opened and a tired-looking human in scrubs walked up to him.

"Mr. Hunt?"

"Yes?"

"I was told you were waiting to question my patient. The shape-shifter that was brought in? I'm sorry to tell you he didn't make it. His wounds were too serious. We tried, but…"

With a sigh and a shrug, the doctor turned away.

Dex cursed. Mahone had the police reports from the responding officers, but Dex had been banking on getting information from the victim himself. Obviously that wasn't going to happen now.

He left to report to Mahone. On his way, he thought about his conversation with Knox. Not the conversation about Felicia, but about Dex's plan for revenge against his grandfather.

What was it Knox had said? *Hell, Dex, you've got a good life now. Don't you think you should forget about the past? Move on?*

But Knox didn't get it. Knox's brother Zeph might have kept secrets from him, but that was hardly the same thing as sending your grandson off to be abused or causing your own daughter to kill herself. Avenging himself and his mother was the only way Dex was ever going to be able to move on. The real problem was that he'd gotten sidetracked.

By the team. The missions. Jes.

That had to stop.

No matter what Knox found out for him, Rurik's appearance in his dream had been a sign that Dex needed to concentrate on his own future.

He was going to kill Bodin of Hammersham. Soon.

But first he had to keep his word to Mahone and figure out why shape-shifters were killing each other.

Since he hadn't been able to question the shape-shifter who'd just died in the operating room, maybe he could question another one. Why not the shape-shifter who'd drugged Lucy at the same bar in which he'd met Jesmina? He'd clued them in to Maddox and his sterilizations, even as Lucy was rifling through the guy's safe. If Dex was lucky, the shape-shifter was still being held in L.A. And if Dex was really lucky, the shape-shifter would know something about these recent murders.

Failing that, Dex would go to France. Hell, maybe he'd track down Jes while he was there. But after the time they'd spent together—after how much she'd affected him—he knew it was the last thing he should do.

CHAPTER NINE

To one who felt and feared, the approach of the end of a world might be experienced as a significant event. To Essenia, it was merely something to stop. A task to complete based on a niggling sense of injustice. If she succeeded, great. If she failed, so be it. Either way, the event would have minimal, if any, effect on her. She'd simply move on to the next task, the next compulsion, with a slightly better understanding of her place in things but no real emotion for the creatures that had come and gone.

Emotion was a tricky concept for her. From what she knew, emotion came with a personal stake as well as fluctuation. Degrees of sensation. For her creatures, both human and Otherborn, anger and passion burned, joy expanded, grief constricted. What she felt, on the other hand, was an appropriate response to certain stimuli—responses that humans might describe as anger, amusement, or pleasure depending on her behavior—but each was felt equally and each was equally forgettable. Other than their ability to effectuate action in others, the feelings were nothing personal to her.

Her beginning and her end were timeless, what happened in between meaningless. There was only her service to drive her.

Until now.

Now she felt something she'd never felt before. Something she hadn't been able to anticipate with familiar detachment. Something quite unexpected.

Hesitation.

It had first hit her during her last visit with the human Kyle Mahone. At the end of his team's last mission, instead of showing satisfaction at the outcome or sneering at her as he was sometimes inclined to do, Mahone had closed his eyes and uttered, "I'm tired." With those words, just for one brief moment, Essenia had longed to close her eyes and whisper that she was tired, too.

What she hadn't known was why.

As such, she'd played the role Mahone had come to expect.

Goddess. Tyrant. Bitch.

Yet, he knew. Knew she was trying to stop something far more powerful than herself from eradicating his world. That knowledge connected them. Made him the one creature that knew her better than any other.

And now it was almost too late.

Just months ago, she'd given him a task. Form a team of humans and Otherborn, and within one year prove her creatures were capable of changing their world for the better or face annihilation. He'd done the first and the team had made strides toward the latter. But things had changed.

Through no fault of hers, he might not get the year she'd promised.

The change of the seasons was upon them.

The gates would soon widen, allowing that flash of simultaneous creation and destruction that had only occurred once before.

Yes, Mahone had good instincts.

He'd focused on the hotbed of activity among the shape-shifters in France. Had put his team on the task. But that didn't mean they had any idea what they'd face. This time, their task wasn't about recovering an antidote from hostile lands or even finding out who was drugging and raping members of the feline community. The danger, Mahone would discover, was one of unimaginable proportions.

It would be, in human vernacular, an unfair fight.

Perhaps giving up would be in everyone's best interest. Accept the turn of the tides in lieu of fighting a losing battle. Once the danger was released, if Mahone and his team failed, then starting over might not be easy.

Starting over couldn't even be guaranteed.

But there it was again. A beat of hesitation, like a blip in a hummingbird's flight. The urge to turn away from what should have been an easy decision.

The urge to mean something personal to someone, if only for a moment.

***

Mahone knew he had to be dreaming, not because he was masturbating, but because he was actually feeling aroused while doing the deed.

He hadn't felt true desire in years, not since the War had started. Not since Bianca...

Release had become about physical relief or relieving stress, but nothing more.

He hadn't been overly concerned. He didn't have the time or energy to devote to any kind of sexual relationship let alone a romantic one, and he'd long ago given up any fantasies of finding love.

All that mattered was his job. Helping his team. And appeasing the Goddess.

If he could do that—

He hissed as fingers—his own, yes, but also another's—wrapped themselves around him.

Pleasure pooled in the bottom of his spine then shot outward. Down his legs. Up his back and through his arms. Everywhere.

Then the pleasure intensified. Thickened. Until his body could barely contain it.

It was too much, even for a dream, he thought.

This is no dream, Human, a feminine voice whispered in his ear, and Mahone suddenly jerked to full awareness.

He was lying in bed, his fingers wrapped around his shaft, his seed erupting from him in euphoric bursts in time with his jagged, almost sobbing breaths. Sweat covered his entire body, soaking the sheets beneath him and dripping in his eyes, nearly blinding him.

What the fuck—

He shouted as another spasm of pleasure shot through him. It was like getting stunned by a Taser, yet like nothing he'd ever experienced.

The edges of his dream flickered in his awareness then disappeared until he didn't even know the source of the mind-boggling wet dream. That wasn't such a surprise. Ever since he'd been approached by the Goddess Essenia, any memories of his dreams vanished instantly upon waking.

That had been fine with him. He'd been glad not to dream of Bianca Devereaux anymore. Glad that the image of her being reunited with her husband could no longer haunt him when his defenses were down. Tonight, as the painfully exquisite shudders still coursed through him, he was even happier not to know their source. Part of him couldn't help wondering, however, if his subconscious had been fighting to let Bianca through.

Only, he'd never felt anything like this, not in dreams about Bianca and not even when he'd been having sex with her.

For a moment, he craved another dreamlike release, the skillful touch of his imaginary woman's hands—

"Human…" Essenia's whisper in his head.

What the fuck?

He shook his head, then threw off his bed covers. Staggering a little, he headed to the bathroom where he splashed water on his face and cleaned up the proof of his release. He waited until the tremors faded and his breathing regulated. Then he carefully made his way back to bed. Hands clasped behind his head, he stared at the ceiling, waiting. Wondering.

Why had he imagined Essenia lavishing pleasure on him, when all he'd known from her was pain?

Yet he'd heard tenderness in her voice. Once.

Just before she'd taunted him again.

After Wraith had turned back into a human, the Goddess had finally visited him only to imply that one of his team was pregnant. So far Mahone hadn't confirmed whether it was true. He figured the news would come to him when it was meant to. One thing was for sure—the pregnancy would mean something. For her to have mentioned it, it had to.

His eyelids grew heavy. He'd been up later than usual, waiting for news on the wounded shape-shifter. By the time Dex had called, telling him the shape-shifter had died on the operating table, it had been nearing six a.m. Now it was almost noon and Mahone had slept the requisite four hours he needed to be in top form. But the dream had drained him in more ways than one, and waiting with bated breath for Essenia to make her next appearance had him on edge. He could use some extra rest.

He let his lids fall completely. Tried, for the first time in a long time, to conjure memories of Bianca. To remember her as she'd been, before the War, before the vaccine had endangered her health, before her husband had risen from the dead. He tried to remember the way her eyes flashed when he was inside her and the way her body clasped his as if she'd never let him go. He tried to recall the feelings of power and pride and sheer joy she'd pulled from him.

But he couldn't.

Instead, when he slipped into sleep, his arms held a woman he'd never seen before. A woman with long flowing hair and a kind, angelic face. A woman who sighed and called him "Human."

CHAPTER TEN

PALADINE ABBEY
AUVERGNE REGION, FRANCE

"Dex was in good health then?"

At Amanda Hammersham's question, Jes's fingers hovered above her keyboard. She was back in France, in the huge, cavernous abbey that she'd inherited from her second Draci family. After renovating and adding much-needed modern touches, the abbey now served as her home, laboratory, and medical clinic. The sprawling building and grounds ensured she and her patients had their privacy while also enabling her plenty of notice if an unwanted intruder approached.

A few days had passed since she'd been in a position to evaluate Dex Hunt's health. Of course, her position had been flat on her back, and despite her plan, the last thing she'd been doing was evaluating him—more like trying to cling to a fraction of her sanity even as he blew her mind.

Memories of the were's vigor and stamina flashed through her. Heat flared across her body, leaving pockets of searing warmth. The intensity of her response surprised her now just as much as it had last night. Deliberately, she kept her gaze on her computer monitor, not trusting her ability to control her expression.

"He appeared to be in stellar health," she said quietly. Thankfully, her voice was as cool and modulated as ever. "I still need to test the samples I took. If he has the gift, he certainly has no knowledge of it."

She still felt guilty for invading his mind. In doing so, she'd violated vampiric notions of honor and morality. Although she hadn't been part of that society for decades, her parents had taught her the importance of honesty and ethics.

In many ways, her actions shamed their memory.

Even so, she should be long past caring now. Long past the need to explain, even to herself, that she read minds not for titillation or personal gain, but for a much greater purpose. Yet it didn't matter. Each time she entered someone's mind without his consent, her sense of identity became more and more lost to her.

"But you really believe he carries the gift of immortality, don't you? Based on a rumor about a werewolf legend? Based on the ravings of a werewolf who's on the verge of senility and death?"

The disdain in Amanda's voice made Jes frown. Bodin of Hammersham deserved respect. He was the ruler of the werewolves, a descendant of the first werewolf to walk the earth. He'd also been Jes's savior and benefactor. He was coming to the end of his life, his muscles withering with age just as much as his brain, but he had led his people for almost five centuries and still received their love and respect. For him to be so easily dismissed, especially by Amanda—his own granddaughter and Dex's half sister—bothered Jes immensely.

Amanda had been given love and support, and most of all, a place in Bodin's life. Those were all things that Jes had craved from the werewolf leader ever since he'd saved her so long ago. Instead, to Jes he'd been a distant guardian. One who time was determined to take away from her. But not if she had anything to do about it. "Bodin must have been confident Dex had the gift. It's the only reason he would have gone to such extreme lengths to keep him away from the pack. To disown him," Jes said.

"He *says* he disowned him because he was a half-breed bastard," Amanda pointed out. "An embarrassment."

Jes immediately bristled at the unsavory description of Dex. Even Bodin, despite his dedication to Otherborn unity, still occasionally expressed disdain for half-breed werebeasts; his lingering bigotry had obviously influenced Amanda. Jes wanted to leap to Dex's defense, tell Amanda she didn't know what the hell she was talking about, but she didn't. Instead of reacting with emotion, she tried logic instead. "A werewolf who'd save a vampire child, a stranger who meant nothing to him, isn't a werewolf who would abandon his own grandson without a better reason than bigotry."

Amanda's eyes narrowed at Jes's subtle jab. "Fine. Even assuming you're right, that means Bodin sent Dex away to protect him. To protect his destiny. Yet you're willing to jeopardize Dex's life for your own purposes."

Jes hesitated. It was a fair accusation, one she'd agonized over. It was why she'd done things the way she had. If she'd had any other choice, she wouldn't have told even Mahone about her research, but she'd needed the money to purchase the high-tech equipment that now awaited her. Plus, there was always the chance something would prevent Jes from continuing her experiments before she could learn the truth. If that happened, she wanted someone else to carry on her research. Amanda had too much at stake, so Jes had chosen Mahone. It had been a calculated risk, but a good one, she'd reasoned. Dex worked for Mahone so on some level Jesmina had felt she could trust Mahone, too. Talking to him on the phone had merely confirmed that she could trust him.

"Of course I don't want to jeopardize your brother's life," Jes said. "What I meant was, I understand what Bodin was thinking. I understand the danger Dex would be in if others knew. Those who don't understand the legend might even begin to hunt all werebeasts and werewolves in general, on the off chance they were similarly blessed, able to give others immortality. But I have no plans of exposing what I know. If it turns out the legend is true and that Dex is part of it, I have his blood. That's all I wanted. It's all I need. I won't tell anyone about Dex." She stared challengingly at Amanda. "Will you?"

"I love my grandfather. If you can do anything to help him live, I want to help, not hinder you."

The werewolf looked at her without guile, but unease flickered through Jes. She was tempted to read Amanda's mind, just to be sure... But she had no reason to believe Amanda was a threat to Bodin, Dex, or anyone else. If she went around reading minds anytime she felt like it, she really would shame her parents' memory. It was why she hadn't invaded Bodin's mind. Why she'd pieced together her suspicions about Dex on her own before ever approaching Amanda. She owed Bodin way too much to disrespect him that way.

Still, because it wasn't just Jes's welfare at stake, Jes reached into Amanda's mind, probing for deceit. Nothing. Either Amanda was telling the truth or she knew how to block Jes's mind-reading powers. Jes prayed it was the first.

Jes turned back to her monitor and her fingers trembled slightly before descending to tap at the keyboard.

Words formed on the computer screen in front of her, the sum of which was the information about various Otherborn during her visit to L.A. She typed the information she'd gathered about the felines, including their own reports of sexual assault and how the reports had turned out to be false, motivated by the need to rid themselves of their sexual heat via sterilization. She added her observations of the one named Wraith and her discussion about wraiths in general with the Para-Ops team. And then...

To be fair, she had to include her observations about Dex, too. As a researcher, gathering information—even information that didn't seem relevant—was critical to help explain, avoid, and duplicate certain results. If something were ever to happen to her, she wanted her notes to be thorough enough that another could take her place and carry on her research.

She typed in Dex's physical condition. The way he'd interacted with his team members in the bar in Los Angeles. The fact that he'd commenced a sexual relationship with one of those team members, a feline mage.

Amanda sidled up to her, hovering over her shoulder, reading the computer screen. Jes's fingers faltered slightly as she typed Lucy Talbot's name, but she forced herself to keep going, only pausing when Amanda spoke.

"I don't like the fact he's sleeping with the mage, even if it is just to alleviate her feline heat. If what you believe is true, how do we know her physical chemistry won't affect him somehow? Or that she hasn't siphoned information from him? The aftereffects of such a mating has never been studied before—"

"—that we know of." Jes forced her voice to remain calm. "Besides, Lucy can't read minds, and even if she could, she can't siphon information that isn't there. Dex Hunt doesn't know what he is. Lucy certainly doesn't. And as for whether or not her body chemistry would somehow affect his gift, there's no reason to think that. It's not like we know how many females he's slept with anyway, or what races they were." Though according to Rurik Pitts, Dex had probably been with more than his fair share of vampires. Again, Jes couldn't help wondering—had he simply been attracted to her vampire exterior? Or had it been *her* he'd truly needed?

"I suppose you're right. So, tell me. Did you find Dex attractive?"

Amanda's tone was teasing, so Jes tried to respond in kind. "You've seen the photos I took. He's an attractive male. Why wouldn't I think so?"

"But did you—"

Afraid of what Amanda was going to ask next, Jesmina said, "I haven't had a chance to see Bodin yet. Have you?"

Amanda frowned. "I saw him earlier. He was fine. The same. Coming in and out of lucidity. It wasn't like he was going to die while you were away. You mean too much to him."

As she occasionally did, Amanda sounded bitter. The werewolf's seeming jealousy perplexed Jes. Over the years, Jes had barely seen Bodin. The only reason he was here now was because he thought Jes might be able to treat him. By natural means or through science. Yet, he had no idea that she knew about the Legend of Wolves or that she'd sought out Dex. The only reason Amanda knew was because Jesmina had finally broken down and asked her to confirm that the rumors the Draci had heard about the legend were true. Amanda had been reluctant to answer at first, but once she'd realized Jes was serious about finding a way to extend Bodin's life, Amanda had verified the rumors.

Amanda had trusted her with that information, and Jes needed to trust her, as well.

She put her hand on Amanda's arm. "Would you go tell him I'm here? And that I'll check on him in a little while. Please?"

Amanda hesitated, then nodded. "Yes. I will. You'll keep me informed about the test results?"

"I will, Amanda. Thank you."

As Amanda left, Jes breathed a sigh of relief before continuing to type up her report, including the details she'd rather keep secret. She noted the fact that Dex had come to her hotel. How many times he'd taken her. How many times he'd come.

How many times he'd made her come.

Once again, her fingers stiffened and fumbled for a moment, and this time she couldn't get them moving again no matter how much she mentally commanded it. Blankly, she stared at the screen.

It wasn't the memory of the orgasms he'd given her that was the cause of her frozen state, though they'd indeed been surprising. Instead, it was the memory of what had happened afterward. How Dex had fallen into an exhausted slumber, but not before he'd wrapped his arms around her and held her as if she was something precious to him.

She typed for another minute, then read over the report.

Then ...

Although she knew it was wrong ...

Although she knew it was a dereliction of her duties, that she should make note of everything she knew about Dex Hunt ...

She hit the delete key over and over again until she'd wiped out all details about their intimate encounter.

She licked her lips. Closed her eyes and breathed in his smell. Felt his touch. Savored his voice and warmth.

She'd never be able to experience the feel of him against her skin again. Not anywhere but here, in her mind. She'd been given one night with him. The fact that he'd taken her...The fact that he'd held her—that he'd cherished her, whispered her name, nuzzled at her hair, and held her through the night—that, at least, she told herself, would be hers alone.

With a sigh, she rose from the computer station. Fantasies could wait. She had work to do.

Hours later, Jes stared at the results of Dex Hunt's blood sample as disbelief rattled through her. She'd known Dex was special, but she'd had no idea how Bodin had identified Dex as one who could fulfill the legend.

It wasn't possible, was it?

But yet it made sense.

Not just werewolf. But vampire, too.

She recalled the words of the legend as told to her by her Draci family.

Protect the wolf whose ancestry none can see.
Protect the one who can gift immortality.
Cast him out before you let him be found.
He'll drive hell's demons back underground.

Protect the wolf whose ancestry none can see, Jes mentally repeated.

Of course. This was how Bodin had known about Dex's gift.

Mixing were and vampire blood, though not exactly common, wasn't unheard of. In all cases, however, the offspring of such a union was a dharmire, one who carried the outward manifestations and sometimes even the powers of vamps. Like Knox Devereaux, Dex's teammate, who was human and vampire, but who presented as a vampire.

Not Dex Hunt.

He was an anomaly, one whose werewolf genes dominated his vamp ancestry.

And an anomaly was consistent with a rare creature, one that might fulfill a legend. His blood might be able to save not only Bodin, but countless others.

A flutter in her stomach told her she was excited. Too excited. If Dex knew, he'd have to accept his destiny, wouldn't he? She'd never force him, but wouldn't he want to help her? Wouldn't he—

No!

She brought that thought to a screeching halt.

Shame on you, she thought. This was exactly what Bodin had feared.

She couldn't think of Dex Hunt as a trophy or a means to an end. His life would be in danger if she ever revealed just how special he was. Every mortal on the planet would be after him. Not only that, he carried enough baggage already from being abandoned by his grandfather. From never knowing the love of his mother.

Had Bodin's daughter fought Bodin's plan to send Dex away or had she simply gone along with it? If so, had she regretted it? Had she longed for the child that had been taken from her, even after she'd had Amanda?

Jes couldn't imagine giving up her child under any circumstances. Once she'd dreamed of having children, but over and over again her body would reject the life as it began to form in her womb, until the doctors had finally told her she'd been damaged beyond repair. She would never be a mother. She'd be alone for an eternity.

That's when she'd dedicated herself to a higher purpose. To healing others. To saving lives by trying to prolong them. But in doing so, she'd cemented herself as an outsider, treating patients whose lives she'd never truly be a part of. Helping families, but never having one of her own.

Nausea made her stomach heave and she bolted to the private bathroom on the other side of her lab. She dry heaved over the toilet, shudders racking her body. When she finally straightened, her reflection in the mirror was ghostly pale. The lack of color, combined with her silver hair that she hadn't had a chance to dye since returning from America, made her look older. Old.

She dampened a towel and pressed it against her face, closing her eyes when another wave of nausea swept over her. Shakily, she clung to the edge of the sink and locked her knees.

What was going on?

She was never sick. The only times she'd ever been sick was when she'd been pregnant.

Pregnant.

With Dex's child?

Instantly, she remembered the trickle of moisture on her thigh, proof the condom he'd used had broken.

Her shocked gaze stared back at her from the mirror, her silver pupils expanding.

Impossible. Not because it was so soon for her to know she'd conceived—fertilization occurred almost instantly. Moreover, vampires were extremely connected to their bodies and could almost always sense the moment a sperm fertilized an egg.

But she hadn't. And she wasn't supposed to be able to conceive at all. That's what the doctors had told her.

Impossible.

It was the same thing she'd thought as she'd stared at Dex's blood results. And as those proved, nature loved a good laugh.

CHAPTER ELEVEN

FBI BUILDING
LOS ANGELES, CALIFORNIA

"Remember, Dex," Mahone said during their final briefing on Dex's assignment. "Flying to Paris is about gathering intel only. The shape-shifters aren't exactly a group the Bureau is prepared to trust. Still, reliable sources overseas tell us there's more infighting than ever."

"You've reminded me of this every hour on the hour. I've made several good connections over the past few days. I'm not stupid, Mahone."

"But you do have a problem blending in, even when you're in the States. You'll stand out even more in France, where Otherborn aren't even publicly acknowledged."

It didn't matter where they were—none of the Para-Ops team blended in. But Dex just shrugged.

He got what Mahone was saying loud and clear.

Forget that the team's leader, Knox Devereaux, had a vampire's silver hair and pupils, that Wraith had once had blue skin and hazed-over eyes, or that O'Flare was an "11" on a scale of one to ten for sexual appeal. Dex was the team's problem child. That's what Mahone meant, and that suited Dex just fine.

"Usually," Dex pointed out, "I have no reason to blend in. Besides, I told you I have another motive for going to Paris now. Once I get you the information you want, I'm going to take some time off. Establishing my presence overseas will allow the agency to deny my involvement in the imminent murder of a certain U.S. were leader. As such, blending in isn't what I'm looking to do."

Mahone narrowed his eyes in warning, causing Dex to blow out an impatient breath. Yeah, okay fine. To get him to join the Para-Ops team, Mahone had agreed to look the other way when Dex exacted revenge against his grandfather, but such things were normally kept on the hush hush. It was yet another example of Dex's inability to blend, he supposed, but whatever. He'd get the job done. Both jobs. He always did.

"Your international travels will provide you some kind of alibi," Mahone confirmed. "At least one the Bureau can use publicly. But that's a secondary goal. We still need you to exercise restraint with the shape-shifters. And that's even assuming they'll talk to you."

"Don't worry. They'll talk to me. I've already made contact with a shape-shifter in France and he's assured me he has influence with the locals there."

"I'm sure you'll wield your considerable powers of persuasion. Then you can tackle your sudden need to deal with personal business."

Dex's mouth tightened. "Wanting to avenge my mother's death isn't sudden. I've put it off for far too long." He might have momentarily put the task aside, but after the close call Wraith had suffered, Dex had been reminded that even an immortal, let alone a half-breed were, had limited time on Earth. Rurik's appearance in his dream had merely reinforced the thought. Vengeance had to be swift or it grew cold, especially when the killer's blood coursed through his own veins. As it was, Dex had already waited decades to get his revenge.

"Just remember, this might not be a quick and easy assignment. Despite your confidence, I have no doubt you'll meet resistance from these foreign shape-shifters. If you're going to be distracted because of this revenge, or even your arrangement with Lucy—"

"I'll get you the information you need, Mahone."

Mahone nodded. "Good. Because frankly, I'll be a little too busy dealing with other matters."

"Like?"

"Like filling the holes in the Para-Ops team that Caleb and Wraith have made. Like trying to track Knox's brother and see what he's managed to find out about the Quorum. Like trying to convince Knox that Felicia is better protected in our hands than solely in his."

Dex didn't even bother snorting at that one. So long as there was a remote chance that the Quorum was still after Felicia, Knox wouldn't let her out of his sight.

It did pose a problem, however, given that the Para-Ops team was now down four of its six members. Strangely, as hostile as their initial team meeting had been, Dex wasn't keen on bringing strangers into the fold. "You're not replacing any of them permanently are you?"

Mahone ran a hand through his hair. "No. At least, I don't think so. Wraith says she's done, but I bet with time she'll change her mind. Still, it's a good sign that the President's willing to up the team members. We're making a good impression on him."

"So why the troubled expression? You worrying about something I need to know about?"

Mahone looked tempted, as if he wanted to unload a huge burden from his shoulders. But then he, like Dex had moments ago, affected indifference with a shrug. "Worrying? That's part of the job, worrying what kind of surprises you guys are going to be throwing at me next."

"There's no surprise where I'm concerned. I just want what you've promised, Mahone. You owe me."

"You never let me forget, Hunt. None of you do. I have a feeling the same will be true of my new recruits." Mahone said it with an edge of amusement that rubbed Dex the wrong way.

Gritting his teeth and trying to play nice, mainly because he was curious, Dex asked, "Who are these new recruits you're targeting?"

Mahone's smile was self-satisfied. "Classified information for the moment."

"Right." Annoyance warred with his own sense of humor. He supposed Mahone had to get his jollies somewhere. Lord knows the band of misfits he'd assembled gave him enough grief without any of them trying. Dex wouldn't want Mahone's job for all the money and fame in the world. "You'll keep an eye on Lucy?"

"Lucy's perfectly able to keep an eye on herself. She'll be fine. Or do you have some reason to worry that she won't be? Has she been—I don't know—*ill* that you're aware of?"

What did Mahone mean about Lucy having been ill? Dex didn't know why, but he suddenly felt like he was playing a game he didn't know the rules to. "She's pretty shaken up by all that stuff that went down with the felines. But as far as I know, her health is normal."

Mahone nodded, but he still looked slightly troubled. Even so, he reassured Dex, saying, "She'll be doing some intel, same as you, only here in the States. Talk to the shape-shifters. Find out what's got them turning against one another. Get back here as soon as you can with the information we need and we'll be able to set our course of action."

"Right." But just as Dex turned, Mahone called out.

"And Hunt?"

Dex cocked a brow at the human.

"Watch yourself. I've got a bad feeling about this. Something's coming. Something none of us are prepared for. At least not yet."

Dex frowned. Again, that feeling of being manipulated. Or at the very least, kept in the dark. But what else was new with Mahone. If the guy had secrets he was keeping, nothing Dex could say or do would drag them out of him. He just hoped Mahone's secrets didn't end up complicating Dex's life even more. "Between each of us, we've danced with the devil more times than I can count. Whatever's got the shape-shifters out of sorts, we'll contain it."

"I hope you're right."

Dex left, but as he did, he heard Mahone mutter under his breath, "Problem is, I don't think you are."

***

Mahone's chest ached with a burning sensation as he watched Dex leave.

If he didn't know better, he'd say the sensation was guilt. Even if it was, so be it. After all, any guilt he felt was well deserved.

When Jesmina Martin had called him, proposing an exchange of money for information, there was no way Mahone could have guessed just how bountiful the information she possessed really was. Or that it would have concerned one of his own team members.

According to Jesmina, Bodin of Hammersham had abandoned his grandson in order to protect him because he believed Dex possessed the gift of immortality. A gift Jesmina hoped to replicate with her test tubes and microscopes. All of her theories were based on the whispered accounts of an old legend, the same legend that predicted a werewolf with an identity crisis would save the world by shepherding a bunch of dark demons back to hell.

What she hadn't known, at least as far as Mahone could decipher, was that shape-shifters were killing each other and that dark magic and incantation spells were somehow involved. But Mahone had certainly made the connection fast enough.

Even if it was only speculation at this point, it was speculation accompanied by a gut feeling that he was right. And Mahone paid attention to his gut feelings. If what he suspected was true, shape-shifters were killing other shape-shifters based on what they truly believed was self-defense. They were killing their own in order to stop those in their midst from bringing dark spirits back to earth.

When he thought about it, it made sense. As Walker had recognized days ago, shape-shifters were mostly a mystery to the rest of the world. That's how everyone preferred it. Shape-shifters were scary not only because of their alien-like exteriors, but because they could travel undetected anywhere and anytime they wanted. They could disguise themselves as someone's brother, mother, or lover, and most people would never know it. Because they were the most feared and least understood Otherborn, they were also the most persecuted.

Since they'd seemed relatively peaceful, everyone had pretty much ignored the threat they posed up to now. That had been a huge mistake.

If the shape-shifters couldn't find a place among the living, why not with the dead? And why not use the dead to avenge themselves against all the living creatures who'd fucked you over in the first place?

A legend. Dex. Dark demons. Shape-shifters performing rituals to raise dark demons.

It had to be more than coincidence.

He'd wait to see if Dex made the same connection—without any help from Mahone. And who knew? Maybe Jesmina would play a role in things, which would validate Mahone's decision to keep their little arrangement a secret from Dex.

Of course, Dex hadn't mentioned a single word about Jesmina to Mahone, but Mahone was no fool. He knew Dex wouldn't be able to resist seeing the vampire again. Mahone had followed Dex the night he'd gone to see Jes at her hotel, and Dex had been inside her hotel room far longer than it would have taken Jesmina to take the samples of blood she'd been after.

However he got the information, Mahone was counting on Dex bringing him back something useful. And if the "good" shape-shifters wouldn't open up to him? Well, Mahone had prepared for that contingency, too.

By strategically leaking Jesmina's suspicions about Dex to several shape-shifters, Mahone was gambling that word would get around and that the "bad" shape-shifters would go after Dex themselves. After all, what better way to get those shape-shifters' attention than to dangle the promise of immortality in front of them. Immortality not just for them, but for the dark spirits they raised.

Of course, that meant others might hear the gossip and go after Dex, too. In effect, Mahone had probably unleashed a whole hella-lotta nasty on the werebeast. Mahone couldn't afford to feel regret or to hesitate because of it.

Mahone would send Dex backup if Dex needed it, but Mahone already had a Goddess threatening him with world-annihilation. Now he had to deal with the possibility that shape-shifters were plotting an apocalyptic revolution of their own. He had nothing to rely on but his own instincts and machinations. It might make him untrustworthy and it might result in his team members dying or hating him, most of all Dex Hunt, but at this point Mahone had no choice.

The pitcher was on the mound and he was stepping up to the plate.

He just hoped when the time came, Essenia would have his back. The only other alternative was her bashing him in the head with the bat then spitting on his body before she wiped out every single living thing on earth.

Game. On.

CHAPTER TWELVE

VAMPIRE DOME
PORTLAND, OREGON

Dharmire Knox Devereaux stared at his wife, Felicia Locke Devereaux, with an expression that could only be described as horror.

She sighed and murmured, "I guess the honeymoon really is over."

"If you honestly think I'm letting you leave here, then yes."

Here, being their home. The Vampire Dome. A place Felicia loved, but not one she was willing to become her prison. She understood Knox wasn't trying to imprison her. He loved her. He was trying to protect her. And she loved him even more because of that. She just couldn't allow it to continue. "I'm a federal agent, Knox—"

"I don't care if you're the President of the United States. Nothing is as important as your life. The Quorum tried to have you killed."

"I haven't forgotten—"

"But you've obviously forgotten who you're married to. Because I won't allow you to place yourself in jeopardy, Felicia. Even if you hate me…"

He's so scared, she thought even as he kept talking. And she understood the feeling. She'd be terrified if she thought too much about all the people who wanted him dead, the Quorum least of all. And she certainly didn't want to die. She wanted to enjoy the life she'd finally managed to attain—with him, the children, and the rest of the vampire clan. The last month had been a dream come true for her. She'd never been happier. Until she'd started to feel unhappy, of course. Confined. Restricted.

Protected, yes, but also smothered. And she knew that in order to safeguard the love she and Knox had always felt for each other, she had to force him to let her breathe, even if it meant she wouldn't be quite as safe as she was now.

"…you insist on leaving, tell me where you want to go. I can teleport you almost anywhere in the world. Somewhere you haven't been. I know you must be getting bored, but—"

She sighed. "This isn't about being bored and you can't accompany me everywhere I go. We can rejoin the team together, but—"

"Fuck the team," he growled.

His bald statement simply made her smile. She knew this male inside and out, and she knew how much the Para-Ops team and every one of its members—even the were, Dex Hunt—had come to mean to him.

"Honestly, I'm not sure you could handle that," she said lightly. She cupped Knox's face in her hands and rose on tiptoe to give him a light kiss. Despite the scowl on his face, his lips immediately returned the gesture. When she backed away, she sighed regretfully at the sheer terror on Knox's face.

She'd known all she would get was resistance. But she'd paved the way and she was going to continue doing so. Right now, she was going to wipe that expression of fear off her husband's face and replace it with pleasure.

CHAPTER THIRTEEN

PALADINE ABBEY
AUVERGNE REGION, FRANCE

Jes lay in bed listening to the sound of rain patter against the window. The tinny beats beckoned to her, urging her to stand, but she didn't move. She hadn't been able to move for days.

The sheets that had always felt luxurious against her skin were a heavy weight. She hadn't changed the bed linens, hadn't been able to get out of bed at all. She'd been too afraid of what might happen.

She curled her knees tighter to her chest, as if that action would protect the tiny life inside her. She didn't look pregnant, of course. Not yet. A vampire pregnancy lasted only a month, and the fetus didn't grow large enough to show until almost two weeks. Her baby was just a week old. But even though no one else could see it, her baby was there, inside her, a part of her.

Even now, it struggled to hang on. Her baby—Dex Hunt's baby—was dying, and there was nothing she could do. She couldn't help wondering if she was being punished. Again.

She shouldn't have been able to get pregnant. The doctors had told her that after the last miscarriage. When she'd found out her night with Dex had led to a miracle, she'd convinced herself things would be different this time. That unlike the others, this baby would flourish with the strength and vitality he'd inherited from his father. After all, if Dex possessed the gift of immortality, wouldn't he naturally have passed along his health and well-being to his child? But it wasn't as if he could actually control that type of thing even if he'd known one of the condoms he'd worn wouldn't block a life determined to be created.

No, Dex Hunt hadn't known he was blessing her with something so precious. Just like he hadn't known she'd taken his blood in order to save the werewolf he wanted to kill.

Due to Jes's weakness, Jes had barely managed to visit Bodin since her return. When she had, the old werewolf had looked horribly gaunt. His hair and beard, once a dark, lustrous black, had turned a shocking white in her absence. He could barely get out of bed now, but still he'd noticed Jes's own weakness and called her on it.

"You need to rest. Go now," he'd commanded.

And Jes had retreated to her bedroom and had been there ever since. Not even the lure of Dex's blood and the experiments she'd planned to perform on it were enough to raise her. As a result, Amanda had once again taken over caring for Jes's patients, including Amanda's own grandfather, and to Jes's surprise, the female was far more nurturing and skilled than she'd ever expected her to be.

Amanda had even shown a modicum of tenderness and affection when she'd come to visit Jes. She and the rest of Jes's makeshift family had rallied around her, but it didn't matter. None of them knew Jes was pregnant. Even if they did, none of them could stop Jes's body from doing what it had always done—losing a baby she so desperately wanted to keep.

Someone knocked on the door. She said nothing, barely stopped herself from hiding beneath the sheets, but Giselle, her feline housekeeper and friend, came bustling in anyway. "I've brought you your favorite breakfast. Morning buns and fresh fruit." She set the tray down on the table next to the bed.

Jes closed her eyes as a wave of nausea rolled through her. "Per—perhaps later, Giselle."

"Cy's downstairs. He wants to see you."

Cyrus Mead was Jes's adoptive Draci brother, one of the males she was closest to, but she didn't want to see him. She didn't want to see anyone. "Please tell him I'm not feeling up to company."

"I've been telling him that for days, but he says he doesn't care anymore. He's worried, Jes. We all are."

"I know, but—" She froze as awareness swept through her. She felt the knowledge in the sudden flutter of movement inside her. More vigorous than ever. Jess sucked in air as an irrevocable yet impossible certainty flooded her. She sat up.

Dex was here. In France. She didn't know how she knew it, but she did. And so did her baby.

Joy and hope infused her, and not just her own.

Somehow her baby had connected with his father, almost as if Dex's proximity had infused its small body with strength.

Energy zipped through her veins, compelling her to move. She reached out and grabbed Giselle's arm. "Giselle, please tell Cy I need to see him. Now."

CHAPTER FOURTEEN

PARIS, FRANCE

Trosseau, the shape-shifter Dex was supposed to meet in the French market, had said he'd be identifiable by his red hair and matching glasses. Of course, he'd be in disguise, taking the form of some human or Otherborn instead of traveling in his true state—smooth translucent skin, large dark eyes with no whites to them, no hair, and a flat nose. He wasn't simply trying to avoid the same staring or even abuse he might encounter in the United States, but because in Europe, Otherborn were still in hiding, hoping to avoid detection given what had happened to their kind when the United States had attempted to integrate them into their population. As it was, even Dex got looks as he traveled from the airport to the heart of Paris. Looks that suggested that people knew his stocky build, hazel eyes, and tawny hair made him part were. Granted, his neatly trimmed soul patch was particularly favored by weres, but still …

Many of those who gave him a second look took care to move out of his way. Any other time, he'd have called them on it. Picked a fight. But he wasn't here for that. He was here for the team and that meant he had to put his own tendencies aside and do the job. Besides, ever since he'd landed in Paris, his beast had been getting more and more restless. His mind more distracted. His senses were filled with the scent of Jesmina. His fingers tickled with the memory of how soft and wet she'd been. His ears echoed with the cries of her passion, each climax seeming to take her by surprise.

He hadn't understood it then and he didn't now. He'd explained away her fear, but not her surprise. She wasn't innocent. She'd told him herself she'd had many lovers. Yet that hesitance he'd sensed when he'd first kissed her had reared its head throughout the night, and no matter how much he tried telling himself it was due to were prejudice, he just couldn't seem to let it go.

Fuck, this was bad. He was distracted. Even if all he was supposed to do was gather intel, he couldn't let his guard down. Enemies could be anywhere. He shouldn't let a piece of vamp ass make any difference, but it did, which was why he wanted to meet the shape-shifter, get the info he needed, and get the hell back to the States.

Of course, also in the back of his mind was the fact Lucy had to be suffering. Before he'd left, he'd tried to talk her into letting him give her sexual release, but she'd completely frozen him out. She'd emphatically told him she wasn't sleeping with him again. And while part of him had been relieved, he'd pushed things the way he always did.

"Yeah?" he'd taunted. "So you've found another male to give you what you need?"

The normally unflappable Lucy had actually sneered at him. "I don't need any male, Dex. I dealt with the heat for a helluva long time before you came along, and I can do it again. Thank you, but your services are no longer needed."

His services.

Dex's mouth tipped up at the memory of Lucy's words.

If Lucy no longer needed *his services*, then that meant he was free to find his pleasure elsewhere. But despite the number of beautiful females all over France, the only beautiful female he was interested in was a vampire who'd vanished into thin air without even bothering to say goodbye. She'd probably been so disgusted with herself for sleeping with a lowly were that she'd run away in horror.

Whatever. He didn't need her. She'd just be a distraction, and if he was going to do his job and deal with his grandfather, Dex needed as few distractions as possible.

He prowled the market, impatiently scanning for the shape-shifter. Since it was past five in the afternoon, many of the merchants were packing up. Almost all of them looked up as he passed. His scowl made them avert their gaze pretty fast, which was why he was surprised when one female merchant stared at him.

To his even greater shock, she motioned him over.

Cocking a brow and unable to resist the sense of intrigue she emitted, Dex strode up to her. He stopped a few steps away, saying nothing. That's when he noticed she had artfully painted on brows. He studied her shiny blond hair, perfectly coiffed, not a strand out of place.

"You're wearing a wig."

Statement, not question, but still she nodded.

"You're a mage?" As a general rule, mages were bald, with no eyebrows or eyelashes.

She looked around, eyes wide, as if she couldn't believe he'd uttered the words out loud. "You're American?"

"What gave me away?"

"You're friends with a mage?"

There was that word again. Friend. Yeah, okay. Why deny it? It was true. "She's a friend, yes."

"A lover?"

"In a way," he said.

"Ah, a mystery. I sensed it about you right away. You are not what you appear. Not what you think yourself to be."

He laughed at that. "I know exactly what I am. I'm a half-breed werebeast on a mission."

"What kind of mission?"

He shook his head, started to walk away, then stopped. He turned back to her. Studied the flasks, herbs, and textiles she had on display. "Do you cater to your kind? More than humans do, I mean?"

"I suppose it depends on what you're looking for."

"The mage I know…she's not an herbalist. These potions. Is there something that will help felines with the heat?"

"If I had that cure, I'd be far richer than I am. Far more popular, as well."

"What about birth control? Something for—for males?"

She frowned. "Afraid of reproducing a feline?"

"Not at all." He stared at her. Let his message come through: Back off.

Only she didn't quite do it. "Ah, afraid of reproducing yourself. I'm surprised. Weres are generally so…proud."

"Do you have anything or not?"

"I don't."

Not surprised, he nodded, then caught a flash of red out of the corner of his eye. He turned. Bingo. Red hair. Red glasses. He caught Trosseau's gaze, but the shape-shifter kept moving.

Dex followed the shape-shifter into an alley straddled by shops, staying several feet behind. The longer they traveled, the more deserted the street became. The more penned in he felt. On either side of him, windowless, towering walls provided little maneuverability.

Dex didn't like it.

He stopped, and as he did, it was as if the shape-shifter immediately sensed it, because he stopped, as well.

The shape-shifter turned to look at Dex. "Problem?"

"My only problem is that I'm here instead of Stateside. Where are we going?"

"Somewhere we can be alone. To talk."

"We are alone. Let's talk here."

"Your friend told me you wanted information about shape-shifters killing shape-shifters." Trosseau jiggled his leg and took a quick glance around. "My informant, the one I'm protecting, the one who has personal knowledge of the bridging, is in hiding. I'm sworn to protect him."

"Bridging? What the hell is that?"

"Not here. I must ensure my informant is kept safe."

"Yeah, so you said. Safe from whom? Other shape-shifters, right? Just how do you plan to do that? By isolating him completely? What's to stop a shape-shifter coming for him in your form? How do you know I'm not a shape-shifter myself?"

"Our kind is easy to spot when you know what to look for. Besides, he's in a place where shape-shifters cannot take another's form. On consecrated ground. "

Well, that was something new. "No shit?"

"No shit. So that answers your question, why there and not here."

He supposed so. "So we're going to a church?"

"We're going to a major church. The second highest point in the city. The Basilica of the Sacred Heart of Paris." Without another word, the shape-shifter turned and began walking again.

Within minutes Dex saw it, glowing in the twilight like a beacon. A long path of stairs, edged on either side by a green lawn, led to the majestic building. Made of white travertine, with several domes and arched details, it was a massive structure, its elaborate architecture gentled by its uniform color, interrupted only by the pale green of two massive bronze figures on horseback. The shape-shifter turned and caught him looking at them.

"They are our national saints, Joan of Arc and King Saint Louis IX."

"Uh huh." As they walked around the building, Dex's eye caught another flash of green. Wings. "And that?"

"The Archangel Michael, defeating the serpent. You can see it there, curled around his legs. A symbol for the devil."

It looked more like a crocodile than a serpent. But when Dex said nothing, the shape-shifter stopped. "Do you believe in the devil, Mr. Hunt?"

Dex immediately thought of his grandfather. The man who'd abandoned him. Hated him. "I believe in evil. Evil that dwells in everyone and everything. Evil that's harbored in little old women. Fathers. Even small children. But just as there can be false Gods, there are false devils, as well. Scapegoats. Your kind knows that just as much as my kind."

"Your kind?"

"Half-breeds. Werebeasts. You can't tell me you don't—" Movement. A shadow. Dex narrowed his eyes. "What the—"

At Dex's sudden exclamation, the shape-shifter whirled in a panic, its gaze flying to the statue of the Archangel. "What do you see?"

Dex shook his head. "It's just—I thought I saw the serpent move."

The shape-shifter's eyes widened. "We must go. Hurry. Around this way. We must go to the great bell, the Savoyarde." He rushed up yet another steep expanse of steps leading to ceiling high bronze doors with foliage designs. When he reached the doors, he turned back to Dex. "Come on."

Dex followed him. When he stepped into the dim interior, he sucked in a breath. The entire ceiling was covered with paint in vibrant blues, golds, and white. The figure of Jesus, arms outstretched, beckoned to him, the glow of his halo virtually hypnotic so that Dex initially didn't spot the triad of shape-shifters that stood solemnly in front of the altar.

"*Merde*," Trosseau whispered when he saw them.

Dex grunted. "I guess that means you weren't expecting them. Who are they?"

"*Diregeants*. Regional leaders. Powerful ones."

Automatically, Dex spread his legs. Balanced his body. Prepared for attack. "Are they dangerous?"

"Not the way you mean. They're probably more interested in shutting me up than harming you."

"And your informant?"

Trosseau looked at Dex and shrugged. "Gone, I'm sure."

"Why don't you confirm that while I have a little talk with your friends here?"

"But—"

Dex narrowed his eyes and Trosseau nodded jerkily. "Yes. I'll do that. But be careful. They hold great influence among my kind. Harming one of them will only make your job more difficult. I'll meet you out front." With a final glance at the trio in front of them, Trosseau backed out of the building.

Dex strode forward, noting that the shifters wore matching white robes resembling the habits of monks only of much finer material. Given the altar in the background, their dress made him think of animal sacrifices and pagan rituals. A shiver streaked up his spine. "My name is Dex Hunt. I work for the FBI."

The shape-shifter in the center inclined his head so he resembled a royal speaking to a peasant. The scent of roses drifted around them, intense and sickly sweet, a stark contrast to their blank expressions. "We know who you are, Mr. Hunt. We know why you're here, as well. We do not need assistance from outsiders."

"No assistance has been offered. Yet. But I'll admit you've got my government curious. Fratricide tends to do that."

"Curious or not, your trip here will achieve nothing."

"Huh. So you just plan on killing each other until you settle whatever disagreement you're having among yourselves?"

All three shape-shifters smirked, their expressions morphing so swiftly and simultaneously it was eerie. The middle one continued to speak for them. "A laughable question coming from one whose nation was recently at war."

"One whose nation is trying its damndest to promote peace," Dex corrected.

"With little success."

"I suppose that's subject to debate."

"We are no more interested in debate than we are in your help," the same shape-shifter said.

Tilting his head, Dex studied them, certain he saw genuine regret reflected in their eyes. So they wanted help? What was stopping them from asking for it? "You're scared shitless," Dex accused, not missing the way each of them looked away. "What's this 'bridging' about?"

The middle shape-shifter, obviously the leader of the trio, shook his head. "Trosseau has said too much as it is. Go back home, Mr. Hunt."

"And what of Trosseau's informant? The one who wanted to talk to me? Is he under your custody and control now?"

"You and your countrymen have done little for our kind in the United States. We have learned to rely on ourselves for protection. We will continue to do so. Please remind Trosseau of that when you join him outside."

"And yet you've dodged my question. Where is Trosseau's informant?"

They said nothing, simply stared at him without blinking. Dex growled in frustration. "Look, if you tell me what's going on, I might be able to help."

The middle shape-shifter sucked in a breath while the other two cast their gazes downward. "At what price? As you said, we're killing our own kind.

That doesn't happen unless something momentous is at stake. Unless we have no other choice. Right now, we have no choice. And we will trust no one, let alone a half-breed were."

Ahh, there it was. The slur Dex had been waiting for. Funny how it still managed to rattle his cage. Instinctively, he clenched his fists and teeth. Yet the desperation radiating from the shape-shifters made it easier for Dex to keep his cool. It was obvious he wasn't going to get anything from them now, but he was right. They were desperate, and that was something he could work with. He had time. And he had Trosseau.

"I'm staying in Paris. I won't be hard to find when you change your minds."

He half turned, but the shape-shifter's voice stopped him. "Staying in Paris might not be a good idea, Mr. Hunt. If I were you, I'd return to the States as soon as possible."

"Is that a threat?" Dex grinned and stepped forward. "Because if it is, I'm not opposed to answering it."

None of them so much as flinched. "It's no threat," the middle one said. "It's merely a suggestion. That which plagues us has spread to the U.S. Perhaps instead of relying on an informant overseas, you should go to your own kind for information. *Obserwować Demonie Krawcy*."

"What the hell does that mean?"

Again, only the middle shape-shifter answered. "Go, Mr. Hunt. Trosseau waits."

CHAPTER FIFTEEN

MANHATTAN, NEW YORK

Zeph Prime had always lived in his big brother's shadow.

Many, including Zeph's father, Dante Prime, had recognized that fact and sought to turn Zeph against Knox. Knox, after all, was a dharmire, one whose human father had been accused of betraying the vampire race. Even so, Knox was the Vampire Queen's firstborn and heir to her throne. Zeph, a full vampire but the product of a mere mating pair between the Queen and his father, was relegated to second best. As such, it should have been easy for Zeph to hate his half brother.

But all Zeph had ever felt for Knox was admiration.

Knox looked after his family and his clan because it was his duty, but also because he loved them. Right now, Zeph couldn't help wondering if Knox's duty or love would enable him to do what Zeph was about to do.

Given that Zeph could barely stand to do it himself, he wasn't so sure.

"Bite me. Do it," the human female underneath him ordered as her nails raked across his back. Zeph gathered her wrists in one hand and slammed them above her head. Though his gaze never strayed from hers, he was ever aware of her bodyguards standing in the shadows with vamp stun guns trained on him. But he didn't let their presence inhibit him. Without an express command from their mistress, they wouldn't intervene, not even if Zeph got rough with her. By now they knew the rougher the sex was, the more she liked it.

"Don't give me orders," he snapped. "Not in bed."

Vanessa Morrison, the First Lady of the United States, struggled vainly against his grip, her mouth twisting into an ugly sneer. "I'll command you whenever I want, wherever I want. Don't forget you work for me."

"I work for the Quorum, not for you," Zeph reminded her. "And I'll do that only while it serves my purposes. This," he said as he thrust deeper into her, causing her back to bow and a moan of excitement to pour from her, "isn't part of my job description, and I'm not even sure why I'm doing it."

"You're doing it because you know how powerful I am and you crave that power. You crave the power that your brother has. Isn't that why you're here? Isn't it the reason for everything you do?"

It was almost funny how one-dimensional people thought he was. If Knox only knew how much impact he had on Zeph's life, he'd laugh his ass off. Well, he'd have laughed at any other time. Right now Knox was too pissed at Zeph for working with Mahone without his knowledge, even though Zeph was just trying to bring Quorum down. But Zeph wasn't going to apologize for doing his part to help the world. He might not be a member of an elite Para-Ops team, but he did have his usefulness.

Unfortunately, right now that usefulness entailed fucking the First Lady because she also happened to be a powerful and elite member of the Quorum, a group of humans bent on Otherborn eradication.

When this mission was over, he'd have to practically parboil himself to get the stink of her off him. Even now, with her grinding her hips and licking his ear, his erection began to deflate.

Damn it, focus, Zeph.

Focus.

Focus on someone you *would* want under you.

And he did.

He imagined *her*.

Knox's wife.

Felicia. Red hair. Blue eyes. Porcelain skin.

He'd wanted her for forever, but Felicia had always been in love with Knox, even when Knox had been married to someone else. If there was anything Zeph resented his brother for, it was having Felicia's love, but that didn't taint his feelings for his brother. Rather, because he loved his brother so much, he felt guilty for fantasizing about Knox's wife, though doing so enabled him to stay hard and fuck the human beneath him.

Disgusted with her and himself, Zeph reared up and bit her neck. Immediately, he blocked the bitter taste of her pure blood from his mind and instead focused on remembering how wonderful Felicia had tasted the one time she'd let him—the time when both of them had faced circumstances that required her to offer herself to him or they'd die.

It didn't matter that he hadn't tasted her since.

It didn't matter that he now received pure human blood from the Quorum in exchange for his alleged loyalty to their cause.

Felicia's essence was inside him. At least he would always have that.

But because he couldn't have more, could never have more, he'd agreed to help Mahone. He'd agreed to leave his home. His family. He'd agreed to it, even knowing that Knox would be angry at Zeph endangering himself.

He could deal with Knox's anger at Zeph acting as an undercover agent, especially because Zeph had kept it a secret from him. What he couldn't deal with was betraying Knox or the possibility that Knox would hate him and disavow him forever because Zeph was in love with Knox's wife.

After Zeph had wrung two climaxes from Vanessa and had managed to come himself, he ripped himself away from her and got dressed. Vanessa continued to lounge in the bed, completely comfortable with her nudity.

She had reason to be. She was beautiful, with a lithe, strong body. It was too bad she was pure evil.

"So as much fun as this little *siesta* has been," Zeph said, "I'm anxious to get back to work. Have you and the other Quorum members decided what your next move is to be?" They'd already gone after the vampires and the felines. Zeph didn't know if they'd be crazy enough to go after the mages or shape-shifters, but he suspected that had to happen eventually if the Quorum was to achieve its goal of Otherborn separatism.

"You know I don't discuss business in the bedroom, Zeph. Certainly not with hired thugs."

He was on her in a second, his fingers wrapped around her throat, his fangs flashing in warning. "Careful, or this hired thug won't be giving you any more help or information, let alone more screaming orgasms, and from the way you soak them in, you definitely need them."

She glared at him. "Arrogant bastard. But then you're a vampire. Enough said."

Zeph laughed and shook his head before releasing her neck and moving to his feet. "Amazing that you dislike Otherborn so much given it takes one to satisfy you when your husband clearly can't."

She rose from the bed, her finger pointing at him in her own warning. "Watch yourself, vamp. My husband is the President of the United States. He's a little busy running the country."

"Too busy to fuck well? Then he's got his priorities wrong. Now, I'll ask one more time. Does the Quorum have a job for me, or not?"

She jerked on a silk purple robe and belted it before answering. "Not…yet. We're assessing our options. Believe it or not, Zeph, you don't have us completely fooled. Isaac might trust you, but I'm not convinced you're not playing us. I'm willing to give you the benefit of the doubt for now, but we'll call you when we have need of you. Until then, you're free to stay here while I return to Washington D.C."

"Here" meaning the expensively furnished penthouse condo in one of the ritziest neighborhoods in Manhattan. Everything about it screamed class and affluence, things that were normally very important to a vamp like him. Given its owner, he'd rather stick knives in his eyes and burn in the sun.

"Thanks, but I'll be seeking my amusement elsewhere. Don't wait too long to contact me. I grow bored really fast. You might just find I've picked up new allies in the meantime."

CHAPTER SIXTEEN

PARIS, FRANCE

"What kind of weird-ass woo-woo shit have you gotten me into, Mahone?" Dex mumbled to himself, shaking his head as he exited the church. He looked around for Trosseau but saw no sign of him. Figured. The guy and his informant were probably miles away by now. Maybe Trosseau hadn't been surprised by the presence of the other shape-shifters, after all. And how coincidental was it that those very same shape-shifters had urged Dex to seek out his own "kind" when he already had plans to do so? Granted, his plans were for a nefarious purpose, but what the hell did "*Obserwować Demonie Krawcy*" mean? He didn't even know what language that was.

He started down the exterior stairs but then spotted Trosseau's red hair about twenty feet away. "Hey, Trosseau," Dex called out.

The shape-shifter ran toward him. Fast. When he got close, Dex noticed his eyes gleaming with some kind of unholy light. What the hell? The guy looked stoned out of his mind. As if he'd been possessed by something not just deadly, but purely evil.

Just as the shape-shifter was about to grab him, Dex twirled, evading his grasp at the same time he brought up his legs in a scissor kick that caught the shape-shifter in the face, knocking his red glasses askew. Instead of staggering back the way he should have, however, the shape-shifter barely flinched. Swiftly, Dex reached for his knife just as Trosseau grabbed his arm and head butted him in the face.

Pain blinded Dex for several precious seconds, allowing Trosseau to get his hands around Dex's throat. Trosseau squeezed, and the power behind his grip was greater than any creature Dex had encountered, including superhuman vamps. Gasping for breath, he stared into Trosseau's eyes. "Tro—sseau," he choked out.

The shape-shifter's eyes flickered and cleared, as if he had momentarily regained sanity and awareness. His fingers loosened. "Hunt?"

Dex closed his fingers around the hilt of his blade. "Yes. I'm Dex-fucking-Hunt. Now let me—"

Shit. The shape-shifter's expression had morphed again. His eyes brightened with blood lust and his fingers tightened once more. Dex managed to pull out his knife and was about to plunge it into Trosseau's gut when—

"Argh." Trosseau's body jerked.

Almost simultaneously, something pricked Dex's sternum, as if it had passed through Trosseau's body and barely missed penetrating his.

Wincing, Trosseau let go of Dex and grabbed at his chest.

Dex hadn't heard anything, couldn't see anything resembling a weapon having struck Trosseau, but blood sprayed out of the shape-shifter's chest and all over him. As Trosseau went limp, Dex cursed, shoved his knife back into its sheath, grabbed Trosseau by his shirt, and whirled in an attempt to get them under cover. If he could get behind one of the stone columns at the church entrance...

Within seconds, something hit him in the shoulder, something with the familiar feel of steel sinking into skin. Only when he lifted his hand, nothing protruded from his flesh. Blood coated his hand, a dark, translucent stain. Dex kept moving until he bypassed the columns. He shoved the shape-shifter through the front doors of the church and then pulled them shut. Diving to his left, he wrenched off his jacket, sweeping it around him like a matador's cape. He cursed as the fabric jumped in several places.

He somersaulted, then took cover behind one of the building's front columns. He removed his knife from its sheath again, but swore again. This wasn't close arm-to-arm combat, but a sneak attack by someone or something that could be hiding several yards away. But who was it? One of the three shape-shifters from inside? Damn. He needed to get to Trosseau. Find out what the hell had happened to make Trosseau freak out on Dex. Find out where Trosseau's informant was hiding and what Trosseau had meant about "bridging." But he wasn't just going to run inside and leave the bastards to think he was running from them. No chance in hell.

He scanned the perimeter, and still seeing nothing, he lifted his jacket and felt carefully within its folds. Several small sharp objects clung to the fabric. He pulled out what looked like small throwing stars, smaller than any he'd ever seen. But they weren't made of metal. Rather, they resembled some kind of natural material. Almost like the stone façade of the church. Smooth yet rough. Like the details on the crocodile wrapped around the Archangel's legs. Fossils? Scales? What the—

"Dex Hunt!"

The shout came from down the steps, a deep but timorous voice that had Dex's brows climbing. Was there anyone in Paris who didn't know who the hell he was?

"I just saved your ass from that shape-shifter. The least you can do is come out. I won't harm you."

"What? You run out of your little throwing stars?" he yelled back.

"Look for yourself."

Cautiously, Dex peeked around the column. A man stood at the bottom of the steps. The dude was wearing nothing but a kilt.

"Unless you think I'll shoot them out from my dick, I assure you, you're safe."

"You're going to have to do better than that."

"Okay. How about this—Jesmina sent me."

Shock upon hearing her name made him jerk. Jesmina? Seriously? How the hell would she even know he was here? Instantly, he wondered if she'd had anything to do with the shape-shifters' refusal to talk to him. Or with whatever the hell had possessed Trosseau. The last time he'd seen her, he'd been attacked by Rurik. Granted, that had been in a dream, but he definitely wasn't dreaming now. "Jesmina, huh? Does she want you to bring me to her with a heartbeat or without one?"

"I assure you, she most definitely wants you to have a beating heart."

At the other guy's words, Dex came out from his cover, his blade in hand, ready to throw it should the male make one wrong move. The dude was obviously trained in weaponry. He was also tall, bulky, a weapon in and of himself. He appeared human...Dex inhaled deeply but couldn't read his scent.

"We must tend to your wound. The poison in the darts will spread and disable you—I'm surprised it hasn't done so already."

"Exactly what you had in mind, I imagine." But despite his caustic words, he could feel himself weakening and struggled not to sway on his feet.

"They weren't meant for you. You got in my way."

"The shape-shifter..." He'd gone crazy. Like he'd been possessed. Yes, there'd been that moment of sanity, but he'd been ready to kill Dex. And he'd had the abnormal strength to do it, too. "Did you know him?"

"Never seen him before, but he certainly looked pissed. You're welcome, by the way."

Dex glared at him, and the male sighed.

"Look, the shape-shifter is dead. I hit him four times. The poison has spread throughout his system. You can confirm it for yourself, if you like. Only quickly, if you don't want to die."

Moving slowly, Dex went to the doors through which he'd shoved the shape-shifter and peeked inside. Sure enough, the shape-shifter was dead. He hadn't died pretty either.

The poison had turned his skin a light puce color. His eyes and every vein on his body were bulging.

Dex really didn't want to end up looking like that. A quick visual search outside confirmed there was no sign of the other shape-shifters. Warily, he turned back to the other male. At some point, the guy had donned a white linen shirt, boots, and backpack, but he'd kept the kilt. "What, were you cold?"

The guy shrugged. "A kilt's easy to get in and out of when I need to move, but I keep extra clothes with me just in case."

Since the guy was clearly waiting for Dex to ask "in case what?" he didn't. Instead, he confirmed, "So you're going to take me to Jesmina, huh?"

"That's right."

"How did you—how did *she*—know I was here?"

"She is the one who sent me for you, Mr. Hunt. As to her contacts or means of information, I would only be guessing."

"And I should trust you why?"

The male sighed impatiently. "Look, I don't want to hurt you. Whoever you are, you managed to make Jesmina happy. At least for a short time, which for her is still priceless."

Dex gritted his teeth. "Who are you to her? Besides her retriever?"

He didn't look insulted by the jab, merely amused. "I'm everything and nothing."

"A riddle. Great. And what am I?"

"You, Dex Hunt, are about to find out that we have much in common. We're both dualities for her."

"What duality am I?"

"You are her life and her death."

"You gonna explain that?"

"I rather think I'll leave that up to her."

CHAPTER SEVENTEEN

PALADINE ABBEY
AUVERGNE REGION, FRANCE

Bringing Dex to Jesmina meant traveling several hours by car and then train. Apparently, it also meant bringing him to an estate fit for royalty. Jes's residence put Knox's well-appointed mansion in the Vamp Dome to complete and utter shame, which was saying quite a lot. No wonder she'd called him "were" with such disdain—forget his mixed-race heritage; he was a virtual peasant compared to the kind of people she must associate with.

She lived in a freaking castle. It was dark out, but the place was awash with light from hundreds of outdoor lamps. He could clearly make out a sprawling green lawn. Fancily trimmed hedges. A vast garden with an enormous iron gazebo and mounds upon mounds of blooming flowers and tall, elegant trees.

Dex and the male who'd finally introduced himself as Cy were just approaching the front entryway when he heard faint shouts somewhere to the east of them.

Cy cocked his head and frowned. "This way," he snapped.

He led Dex to the side of the monstrous estate and to a tall set of wooden double doors through which the voices and shouts were getting louder.

"What the hell's going on?" Dex asked.

"Just a regular day in the life of Jes. I told you, she wants to see you right away. I'm simply following orders." He smirked, as if he found the idea of taking orders from Jes humorous, and Dex understood why. In their short journey to Jes's home, Dex had learned enough about Cyrus Mead to know he didn't take orders from anyone, not unless he had his own reasons.

So what were his reasons for following Jes's orders? What could Cy possibly gain from bringing Dex to her?

As Cy reached out to open the wooden doors, Dex girded himself for his first glimpse of her. He reminded himself that while she might be an immortal and a loaded one at that, he'd seen her naked. He'd seen her perfect body, but he'd also seen her imperfections. She'd been self-conscious when he'd bared her right arm and caught sight of the thick scars that covered it, but her vulnerability had only made her seem more accessible to him. Which in turn had made her even more desirable.

But it didn't matter how much Dex had prepared himself to see her again. Because Dex's first glimpse of Jesmina Martin shocked the hell out of him.

When Cy swept open the big wooden doors, the brightly lit room immediately reminded Dex of a hospital and he saw Jes covered in blood. Thankfully, it wasn't her own, but the five seconds it took his brain to process that made his heart gallop in horror. Leave it to a vampire to look classy even with her hands halfway inside someone's chest.

What also shocked him was the fact she looked nothing like the vibrant vampire he'd met in the United States. She'd dyed her silver hair dark, but it wasn't just that. She looked drained. Weak. Of course, they weren't in the United States anymore. Here in Europe, vampires didn't get to live openly, which meant she probably spent most of her time indoors, hiding who she was and what she needed to survive. In addition, although Europe contained far more immaculates, those humans with pure blood who hadn't taken the anti-vamp vaccine distributed by the United States during the War, it must still be hard to drum up humans willing to give their blood to vampires and at the same time keep their existence a secret. So maybe that was why she looked weaker. Still, Dex couldn't help wondering why she hadn't just stayed in the United States.

She was in some kind of operating room that had been devised out of the basement of the ancient stone building. Like Jes's hotel room in L.A., the room was simple, modern, and clean, but instead of a bed it featured a large surgical table and a host of gleaming surgical tools. Jes glanced up when Dex and Cy walked into the room, but she didn't acknowledge him in any way. She struggled to keep her patient still while another female ran around gathering supplies.

"Cy, help me," Jes shouted.

Cy was already halfway to her, giving her the aid of his greater weight and muscle to restrain the individual on the table. As Dex stepped closer, he could see the patient was a shape-shifter. Sucking sounds emanated from the open wound in its chest and blood frothed against Jes's surgical gloves. The shape-shifter's features, normally uniform and white, were tinged blue.

"What happened?"

"He's been shot. I've found the entry and exit wounds." Swiftly, she tore open a plastic wrapper of field dressing. "Listen to me," she said to the shape-shifter. "Breathe out and hold your breath. I need the air to be out of your chest before I seal this wound. Do you understand?"

The shape-shifter didn't answer; hell, Dex didn't even know if he was conscious.

Jes watched his chest, then flattened the dressing over the wound right after he exhaled and before his chest rose again. The sucking sounds ceased. She nodded to the woman who was assisting her, a werewolf who kept glancing at Dex with a curious expression and... He immediately bristled at the hint of disdain he saw. It was so common, something he almost always saw when he encountered a full-blooded were, but it still bugged him every single time.

"I have to close the wound." Jes glanced at Dex. "I'm sorry, but I'm going to be a while. Cy, can you take Dex inside?"

"Isn't there someone else who can do this? You look ready to collapse," Dex asked. He looked at Cy, who shrugged.

"I'm not medically trained. Are you?"

Dex knew enough that he could have triaged the chest wound in preparation for a surgeon to take over, but that was about it.

"I'm fine. I'll be inside soon," Jesmina insisted. "Go."

Her words were curt and dismissive. Dex frowned at the air of indifference and command she was emanating, but she'd already turned away. He followed Cy outside. His last glimpse was of her swiping at her forehead with her arm and leaving a swath of blood across her face.

He turned to Cy. "Why don't you tell me what the hell's going on? Why am I here?"

Cy stared stonily at him. "Sorry. No can do. But tell you what. If you can read, you might be able to figure out some of it yourself. You can read, can't you?"

Dex answered the man's sneer with his own. "How about you read this?" he growled just before he punched Cy in the face.

***

Rurik had lost track of time and space. He didn't know what day it was or what state he was in, or even if he was in the United States anymore. He suspected he wasn't, given the various languages he'd heard being spoken around him, but his consciousness faded in and out and his body throbbed in protest every time it was invaded by the dark creature manipulating it.

If he could, he'd have gladly killed Dex Hunt. He wished he'd accomplished the task long ago. That way, the Dark One would have no reason to be going after Dex now and no reason to use Rurik to try and get what it wanted.

That was the only thing Rurik knew for sure any more. What the Dark One wanted from Dex. It wanted his body. Not just because any body would do. If all the Dark One wanted was a body, he'd be satisfied with Rurik's. But the Dark One wouldn't be satisfied until he'd found a way to invade Dex's *immortal* body.

When he'd first heard them talking about Dex as an immortal, Rurik had laughed, but his laughter had choked off really fast, not just because it had angered the Dark One, but because Rurik had finally put two and two together.

He'd told that bitch of a vampire that Dex's health had seemed unnatural. That answer had been in response to her specific questions, which he now realized had to have been prompted by the same information the Dark One had.

Wasn't it just like Dex Hunt to cause Rurik grief even years after he'd left the Ferals?

Damn bastard.

For a moment, Rurik's anger pushed a surge of adrenaline through his veins and he felt hope. That is, he felt hope until he heard the Dark One laugh eerily inside his head.

It was feeding off Rurik's hate for Dex, as well as his own anger, Rurik realized.

In feeding, it was growing more powerful. Its possession of Rurik's body expanded and intensified, creeping into the smallest corners of Rurik's mind until his vision began to black out and he couldn't recall who he was anymore.

"Dex," he managed to gasp out before he lost consciousness completely. He no longer thought of Dex as the enemy, but as a male who'd once ridden and fought alongside him. "Dex," he muttered. "Beware…the…Demon Tailors."

CHAPTER EIGHTEEN

After several minutes of giving Dex back as good as he got, Cy eventually pulled away and dabbed at his bloodied lip. "Fuck. Now look what you've done," he groused. "Jes is going to have my hide." He dragged himself to his feet, walked away, then glanced back at Dex over his shoulder. "Come on."

Side aching from where Cy had repeatedly punched him, Dex narrowed his eyes but obligingly followed the other man into the bowels of Jes's castle. Cy led him past one lavishly appointed room after another before pausing outside another set of solid double doors. "You can wait for her here. If you pay attention, you might even learn a few things."

With that parting shot, Cy disappeared.

Dex opened the doors and stepped into what was clearly Jes's personal library. Floor to ceiling shelves were filled to bursting with books. A massive trestle table in the center of the room had been strategically placed in front of a large fireplace. Feminine touches—a vase of flowers here, an ornate letter opener there—told him this was likely Jes's haven. A gilded clock indicated it was half past midnight. Several papers on the desk bore chicken scrawl writing that, if it was indeed hers, amused the hell out of him. It was ugly as sin, completely contrary to how the handwriting of an elegant vampire like Jesmina's should look. He bet it annoyed the shit out of her, and why didn't she have a computer somewhere—

Ah, there it was. A laptop peeking out from a pile of paper and medical journals. Dex frowned as he spotted several picture frames displayed on a table next to the desk. Smack dab in the front was a picture of a smiling Jes with her arms around a broadly grinning Cyrus Mead. It didn't matter that Jes's smile looked slightly sad. All he could wonder was whether this was what Cy had wanted him to see.

Had Cy brought Dex here so Dex would know Jes belonged to another man?

He wiggled his jaw where Cy had gotten in a particularly good punch.

Right now, he was really wishing he hadn't taken it easy on the guy. He should have pulled his knife and sliced the bastard open.

Dex reached out to slam down the framed picture of Jes with Cyrus, but before he could his gaze caught on a thick book spine just to the right of it. "Jes's Otherborn Research" it read, along with a date seventy years earlier. The print was blocky and childlike.

He pulled the book out, lowered himself into an armchair in front of the fireplace, and began reading. It looked like a journal a child might keep, but the handwritten notes—in the same chicken scrawl as the papers on Jes's desk—used fancy language and seemed to describe not only the biology of random Otherborn, but various medical conditions he'd never heard of.

Minutes ticked by and Dex became more and more engrossed in what he was reading. When he was done, he selected another book. He was flipping through a third when Jes walked into the library.

She'd washed up and was dressed in a simple long-sleeved sweater and slacks, her hair tidily swept back into a low ponytail. His eyes narrowed when Cy followed her into the room and affectionately tugged on her hair.

Dex stood, trying to resist the impulse to pull her away from the other male. He couldn't believe how strongly connected he felt to her. It was almost as if something supernatural was at work. He'd always had a thing for vampires, and he'd had an exceptionally strong reaction to this one, but now he wanted to run to her, sweep her up in his arms, and race away.

His skin prickled with possessiveness as she turned and gave Cy a hug. It was to be expected, he told himself. The last time he'd seen Jes, they'd just had hours of mind-blowing sex. It was no wonder his first inclination was to rip the other man apart limb from limb, something Cy probably knew given the look of amusement he shot at Dex.

"How's your patient?" Cy asked Jesmina while still staring at Dex.

"I think he's going to be okay."

"Who the hell shot him?" Dex snapped out. Damn if he was going to let her ignore him any longer. After all, she had brought him here, not the other way around.

She turned to face Dex. "I—I don't know. And I don't need to know."

"Why's that?"

"It's part of what I promise my patients. I treat without discrimination. I don't interrogate. For example, I'm tempted to ask you and Cy how you both managed to sustain fresh bruises to your faces since I saw you last, but you'll notice I'm not asking you that."

Cy winced but Dex managed not to do so. Barely.

He strode closer to Jes, satisfied when she took a step back and started breathing faster.

"If you don't question your patients before treating them," he queried, "then how do you know you're not helping a bad guy?"

She shrugged. "Good. Bad. It's a matter of opinion, isn't it? From my perspective, all life is precious."

"Seems like a dangerous rule to live by." Recalling the stuff he'd read while he'd been waiting, he couldn't resist asking, "Is there really such a thing as a centaur?"

"Yes."

"And saber tooth vampires?"

She nodded. "Believe me, if you were a vampire with that particular condition, you wouldn't need to ask."

Huh. He'd have to ask Knox about it, if only to give the dharmire a bad time. "Why didn't you tell me you were a doctor?"

"Well, for one thing, you never asked."

"True. We didn't really talk much at all, did we?"

Her mouth firmed and she looked at Cy, who got the message.

"Why don't I leave the two of you alone?" Cy said, even though he didn't look happy about doing it. "I know you have a lot of catching up to do. Just know that Mr. Hunt isn't in top form, Jes. We had some trouble and I hit him with some of my throwing stars. Quite by accident. I already gave him the proper inoculation and he's fine, but he's likely to be weak."

"Don't count on it," Dex shot back. "I feel fine."

Cy raised a brow. "Still, you used considerable energy while I was...giving you a tour of the place. Don't do anything overly vigorous while I'm gone."

Jes flushed at Cy's words.

Cy chuckled before gently rubbing her cheek with a knuckle.

Okay, enough was enough. Dex growled, the sound an obvious warning. In case Cy missed it, however, Dex ordered, "Get your hands off her."

Cy flipped him a look. "Who's going to make me?"

"You'll find out in about two seconds. And this time, I won't bother playing nice."

"Nice, huh? Interesting," Cy muttered, but he dropped his hand. "Like I said, I'll give you two time to talk."

He left.

Dex and Jesmina stared at one another for several tense moments before she spoke. "I'm sorry you got hurt. Let me see..."

Dex heard her words. He saw her lips moving as she formed them. But they were a distant thing in his mind. He found himself walking toward her without any intent to do so. Saw her eyes widen just before he swept her up in his arms and took her mouth with his.

She tasted as sweet as he remembered. Even sweeter. She'd welcomed him before, but not as she did now. Now, she clung to him, pulling him into her body with an obvious desperation that told Dex she'd thought of him too. His hands swept into her hair, but he didn't like the dark strands, missing the silver that sparkled and shimmered like jewels. He lightly ran his arms over her, her breasts, her hips, her thighs.

She gasped and it took him a moment to realize she was pushing him away.

"Wait. Stop, Dex. I—I didn't bring you here for this."

He blinked and took a step back, breathing hard, fists clenching.

"I—I need a minute. Please. Let me sit down."

Taking her arm, he guided her to the same armchair he'd used earlier.

Shakily, she sat down.

He pushed several strands of hair out of her face. "What's wrong? Are you sick?"

"Yes, I am. And I need to feed. I need pure blood from an immaculate. I've arranged for someone to come to me."

"Fast food delivery? At this late hour?"

She gave a ghost of smile. "Something like that. He was supposed to be here a while ago, before you showed up, but he was delayed."

"He?" She was going to drink from another male. While Dex was here. And he couldn't help the jealousy and possessiveness that once again swirled through him. This time, considering the guy was nowhere in sight and was going to be her meal and not her lover, the emotions bothered him. A lot. He had no true connection to this woman. No rights. Why was he acting as if he did?

"Yes. He's one of the few immaculates nearby that I trust."

"How long—"

"I've used him a few times only. But he's young. His blood is very potent."

I'll bet it is. "Why am I here, Jes? And how did you know I was in France?"

She hesitated and bit her lip. "Listen, Dex, I—"

A young Adonis, blond and tall and muscular, walked into the room. Dex growled at the interruption, but mostly it was with renewed jealousy. Of course this was the immaculate she was going to feed from. Only the best for Jes. The guy was so good looking he even put Caleb O'Flare to shame.

"I'm so sorry I'm late, Jessie." He held out a hand to Dex. "I'm Raul Merced."

Dex glared at the guy until his hand fell.

Jes stood. "We'll talk when I get back, Dex. I'll return in a moment."

"No."

Equally startled, Jes and Raul stared at him.

"Excuse me?" she asked faintly.

"You don't need to drink from him. You can drink from me."

Her eyes rounded with shock, her pupils expanding so they shone like the moon, wiping out nearly every trace of her dark irises. She blinked, but she couldn't disguise the glitter of her desire. Desire for him. It took her several tries before she could speak. "For nourishment, vampires need pure blood. Blood from humans or animals. Can't be anyone with Otherborn heritage, not when I'm weak and hungry, or else it'll make me sicker than I am now. You've dated many vampires. You've got to know that."

How the hell did she know he'd dated many vampires?

And why was that the part of her statement he'd focused on?

Fuck.

He swiped his hands over his face. He knew she needed human blood. It had been stupid for him to suggest otherwise. But the idea of her feeding from this man—Raul, he thought nastily—made him want to howl in rage. "You'll drink from his wrist?"

Raul, Dex noted, looked thoroughly amused. Lucky for him he kept his eyes downcast.

Not Jes. She raised her chin, her eyes flashing. "What business is it of yours?"

"I'm here, aren't I? You asked Cy to bring me here. And the only reason I can think of is because you want to continue what we started in the States. Or am I wrong?"

She glanced at Raul while once again blushing an endearing shade of pink. He hadn't noticed that before, but she tended to blush a lot.

"Right now I want to get my strength back."

"Then tell me you're going to drink from his wrist. Because that's the only way I'm going to let it happen."

They stared at each other, with her looking as shocked as he felt, but he meant every word he'd said.

He didn't know what was driving him to make the demands he was making. All he knew was he wasn't backing down until she gave him the answer he wanted.

Finally, she nodded.

Reluctantly, he released her.

She left the room with Raul, leaving Dex to stare out the library window.

A vampire feeding was a private thing, and he'd have to be given certain privileges before he was allowed to watch it. That was the only reason that he hadn't insisted she drink from Raul in front of him. It would have suggested an intimacy that he couldn't afford to foster, not given how damn obsessed with her he already was.

Several minutes later, he heard the library door open.

He turned.

Jesmina stood in the doorway.

She looked healthier already. Her skin looked pinker. Her cheeks slightly fuller. Her eyes sparkled in a way they hadn't before. Better but still not fully recovered. Maybe it just took awhile for the full effects of the feeding to settle in.

"He—he's gone."

Dex walked up to her and rubbed her cheek with his knuckles, deliberately caressing her where Cy had touched her, as if he could wipe away the other man's touch. "Did he taste good?"

She bit her lip, as if she knew it was dangerous to answer.

He rubbed his thumb over her lip until she loosened the plump flesh. "Did he?" he demanded.

"Yes," she breathed.

He stared at her consideringly. "I want you to taste me. I want to eradicate the taste of him from your lips."

Her eyes flared. Then, although she hesitated, she leaned up to kiss him.

He pulled back and shook his head. "I wasn't talking about my lips."

Jes's shocked gaze dropped, causing his muscles to tighten with anticipation. He loved shocking her and making her blush. It was quickly becoming one of his favorite things.

But not his favorite, of course.

He clearly remembered the feel of her sweet mouth wrapped around him. She'd made him feel like a fucking god, one being pleasured and worshipped by a goddess.

He wanted to feel that way again. Right here. Right now. But first...

"But first you need to tell me, Jes. How did you know I was in France, and why did you bring me here?"

***

Jes heard Dex's question but didn't immediately answer him.

She couldn't.

Joy at seeing him competed with the knowledge that she felt better than she had in days. More alive. Healthy. Powerful. And the same was true for the life inside her.

And it wasn't because of Raul. Not completely.

She'd barely given herself time to take what she needed from Raul because she'd been so anxious to get back to Dex. Seeing him in her own private sanctuary was surreal and combined with the shock of pregnancy, part of her still wondered if she was dreaming. But if she was dreaming, they'd already be naked and some part of him would already be in some part of her. Right now, she wasn't particular about what parts went where, only that it happen. She took a step closer, but her lust-induced haze must have been evident to him because Dex shook his head and took a step back.

"Not yet. How'd you know I was in France, Jes? Have you had someone watching me?"

He looked extremely pissed off at the thought. If he only knew everything she'd done, he'd be rabid with anger. The knowledge tempered the joy and the lust she was feeling.

What was she going to do? How was she going to explain the powerful connection they now had, the important connection he had to the baby growing inside her, when she didn't even understand it herself? If she told him basic facts, that she was pregnant and he was the father, what was to stop him from freaking out and leaving them?

What if he thought she'd lied about being able to conceive? What if he thought she'd deliberately gotten pregnant to trap him? Granted, it would be hard for him to blame her given the fact he'd used protection, but what if—

Dex lightly grasped her arms and gently shook her. "Damn it, Jes. What's going on? Answer me. Were you having me followed?"

"No," she said. Or at least, that's what she meant to say. Her mouth opened and closed but she didn't hear any words escape her lips.

He glared down at her, his eyelids heavy, his lips flat, his nostrils flaring.

He looked so angry, she thought once again, but she didn't care.

She didn't care!

Right now, none of it mattered. Her quest to prolong life. The gift he might possess. The duty she owed Bodin and Dex's contrary intent to kill him. All that mattered was Dex.

He was here. When she'd thought she'd never see him again. He was touching her. He'd given her what she'd always longed for, a baby. One more chance to love and be loved by a child of her very own flesh.

And she was acutely aware of what else Dex had given her.

What he could give her again.

Pleasure.

Sheer ecstasy.

The ability to momentarily forget everything else and focus purely on her own carnal needs.

She licked her lips, remembering how he'd tasted. How much she'd wanted to bite him. How, even when she'd been gulping down Raul's blood, she'd imagined the sweet nectar flowing from Dex and—

He growled. "Jesus, you're incredible. You want me, don't you? You want me so fucking bad you can't even answer my question. Can't wait."

He pulled her against his chest and slammed his mouth down on hers. His tongue thrust between her lips, penetrating her so thoroughly that she whimpered with relief. As soon as she made the sound, he tore himself away from her and sucked in several breaths.

He looked as shell-shocked as she felt.

"What the hell is going on?" he muttered, but he didn't wait for her to answer. He swept her up into his arms, marched to the chaise lounge on the other side of the room, and spread her out like she was a five-course gourmet meal and he was absolutely starving for her.

CHAPTER NINETEEN

Dex covered Jes's body with his and stared into her dark midnight eyes. Electricity crackled between them, causing warmth to infuse his skin. That warmth grew sizzling hot wherever their bodies touched. She whimpered and the sweet feminine sounds soon became a steady chorus, ratcheting up his desire until he felt dangerously poised on the edge of sanity.

Closing his eyes, Dex took a deep breath. It was amazing, this connection he had with her. Proximity was enough to make his head spin with desire but actual contact? As it had in the States, touching Jes resulted in a feeling of intense relief that immediately skyrocketed into a desperate, mind-blowing need. He'd never needed anything like he seemed to need her. Not sex or food or companionship. Hell, not even revenge.

His eyes popped open and he furiously tossed his head as if he could shake that errant thought out of his mind. Her cool smooth palms stroked his back and thoughts of revenge were swept away. Lust surged through him, concentrating in his groin until he couldn't help but thrust his hips, notching his thick aching flesh into the cradle of her hot center. The way she strained to get even closer to him took his breath away.

Yes, he thought. Need me. Need. Me.

He framed her face in his hands and took her mouth with his. Groaned as their tongues butted and battled for dominance. He held himself back as long as he could before wresting it from her. His tongue was aggressive in a way his body wanted to be but couldn't manage, given the clothes they were still wearing. He penetrated her mouth with a thoroughness designed to both satisfy and entice. At the same time, he pushed himself slightly up on his knees and began tearing at her clothes, hungrily taking in each patch of pale creamy skin as it was exposed.

This time when she whimpered, he thought he heard fear in the sound. He froze and raised his gaze to hers. She looked drugged, her pupils so dilated now her eyes were almost completely silver, with only a thin black ring of her irises showing. He saw his own reflection in the shimmering silver globes and shock jolted him. He looked more animal than human with his brows furrowed, his skin pulled tight over his cheekbones, his lips pressed back from his teeth to reveal his canines in all their glory.

Shit. No wonder she'd sounded scared.

Trembling, he released her. "I'm sorry. Fuck, I didn't mean to go at you so rough. I know you're not feeling well." He tried to move off her, but she wrapped her legs around his waist, locking him in place.

"No. *S'il te plait.* Don't go. I want you. Just—can you slow down? Touch me a little…softer?"

Softer? He was so hard he could hammer nails with his dick and she wanted…soft? But as he looked down at her, noted her flushed skin and the vibrant light in her eyes, he wanted to give her anything and everything she wanted. She looked even stronger than she had after drinking from Raul, and that made him feel possessive all over again. Possessive and satisfied.

She was a vampire but he was feeding her with nothing but his kisses and touch.

Outside, wind buffeted the lead paned windows. He took another deep breath and shuddered. It was touch and go for a second, but he managed to push back the need demanding he get her naked and get himself inside her. Gently, he cupped her breasts, stroking the soft, dainty globes as if he was cherishing them. She bit her bottom lip and he groaned, wanting to suck the pink plump flesh for all he was worth. Hell, he wanted to eat her up. Gulp her down until the gnawing hunger he felt was appeased. Instead, he swiped his thumbs over the hard, needy points of her nipples, drawing a whimper from her that no longer held a trace of fear.

"I can give you soft," he said, as much to reassure himself as her. "With my hands. My lips. My tongue. But…" He reached down and eased one of her hands to his crotch, where his dick jumped and quivered in protest at what wasn't happening. "Not with this." Easy boy, he thought grimly, groaning when her fingers stroked him, exploring his length through his pants as if she was blind and committed to memorizing every detail.

"I don't want soft here," she breathed. "Never here."

He gave a bark of laughter. "That's good. Because I can't control something like that. Damn it, even though I know I shouldn't be, I'm glad you sent for me. I look at you and I'm hard."

She smiled, pleased by his statement, and released him to relax back against the chaise. She extended her arms over her head. "Then look at me, Dex. Look at every single inch of me until you're so hard you can't think of anything or anyone else."

I'm already there, he thought, but didn't say it. His hands returned to her clothing, this time unbuttoning and slipping and tugging rather than tearing.

Even though he clenched his teeth so hard they should have cracked, he kept his touch gentle.

When she was completely naked, he knelt back on his haunches and took her in. Abruptly, he scrambled off her until he stood at her feet.

She lifted herself up on her elbows. "No! Where are you—"

"Shhh," he soothed. "I want to touch every inch of you, from your toes to the top of your head." He gave her a devilish grin. "Think you can handle that?"

Her eyes narrowed as she absorbed his challenge. Even so, she shook her head. "*Je ne sais pas.* I don't know."

The honesty of her response had him scrambling on top of her again, bracing his weight on his hands and knees so he didn't touch her but merely hovered over her, teasing both of them with his closeness. He brushed the lightest of butterfly kisses against each of her cheeks before sipping at her lips, lifting away when her tongue tried to tangle with his. "I think you can, Jes. I think you can handle anything I can give you."

He gave her another brief, close-mouthed kiss before moving off her. Once again, he stood at her feet. Bracing a knee on the chaise, he lifted the foot closest to him and kissed her big toe. He did the same to the next adorable digit, and then the next. Then he returned and nibbled each of the toes he'd kissed. Then returned again and licked them.

When he sucked the first toe into his mouth, her leg jerked. He wrapped his fingers around her ankle to hold her in place. Suddenly, moving slow and touching softly didn't seem to be as difficult as it once had.

He'd never savored a female during sex, he realized. Not like this. He'd loved receiving and giving pleasure, of course, but he'd always dived right in, wanting it intense and hard, going for broke with everything he was worth. Even with Lucy, when he'd held back it had never been to relish the touch, sound and taste of her, but simply not to hurt or scare her.

Now, even as he took care not to hurt or scare Jes, it became less about giving her what she needed and more about experiencing what he'd never had before. This wasn't just about sex and physical pleasure or about using his knowledge to press where he needed for as long as he needed to get his partner to climax. Instead, it was about exploring every inch of something warm and beautiful and precious until he knew it even better than his own body. Just for the sheer joy it brought him.

Joy. Contentment. Belonging. They weren't words he'd ever thought of in conjunction with himself, but every time he was with Jes, they somehow managed to sneak into his subconscious. Unease poked at him, but he shoved it away, unwilling to stop what he was doing.

He kissed and nibbled and licked his way up her smoothly toned calves until he reached her thighs. He tugged them further apart and stared at the feminine pink flesh glistening with the proof of her desire. As he watched, even more moisture pooled out of her, the cream dripping down her thighs and calling to him like a siren's song.

Soft, he thought again. Who knew soft could be so damn intoxicating?

He curled his fingers into the cushions on either side of her thighs, grounding himself while he leaned in close, his face hovering just an inch over her soft curls; they were her natural color, a beautiful shade of silver that made him think of spun silk rather than a metal capable of killing his kind. He breathed in deep and heard her moan of mortification. She writhed and tangled her fingers in his hair, trying to push his face closer to her core. He resisted, shaking his head and growling until she released him. Her arms fell away and her hands clenched into fists.

"Remember," he said. "You asked for slow and soft. And that's exactly how I'm going to give it to you." He extended his tongue and lapped up the dribbles of juice that covered her thighs. Then slowly, softly, he laved his tongue through her wet cleft. Her hips jerked and arched upward, burying his face in her musky heat.

He groaned and rubbed his face against her, covering himself with her arousal.

"I can't!" she said, her head thrashing against the cushion that even now he was struggling not to rip to shreds. "*Mon dieu*, I can't stand it. Please."

"No," he said. "I'm only halfway there. I want to suck your nipples. Don't you want that, too?"

She sobbed as he pushed a thick finger into her honeyed depths then circled her clit with his thumb. Again, he kept his touch gentle, not enough to give her the release she craved. "Don't you?" he crooned.

"Yes, please. Now!"

He moved to obey, then caught sight of the scarred flesh on her arm. He remembered how she'd flinched away from his touch the last time they were together. "In a minute," he said. "First…"

He lifted her arm and started at her fingertips, lavishing them with the same attention that he'd given her toes. Then he smoothed his tongue over the scars trailing up her arm. Once again, she tried to pull away, but he wouldn't let her.

"You're beautiful," he said, half-aware that his voice sounded slurred. As if he was getting drunk on the taste of her. Instead of bothering him, the thought made him crave her more. If he was drunk, he didn't have to think about the past or his revenge or even his duty to talk to the shape-shifters, despite their resistance. He could lose himself in this moment. Lose himself in her.

"Dex, please," she wailed. "*S'il te plait.* I'm going to come and I want you inside me when I do."

His gaze jerked to her face. Her breath was hitching, and sure enough she looked like she was about to come. Like she'd been pushed to the edge by him licking her fingers and arm. He swallowed loudly and suddenly couldn't resist any longer. He shifted, pressed the head of his cock against her, then froze.

Fuck! He wasn't wearing a condom. He hung his head and groaned.

"*Quel est mauvais?* What's wrong?" She arched up, rubbing him with her folds, as if determined to get him inside her.

Goddess, he wanted to be inside her!

"I don't have protection."

"Oh." She went rigid for a second, then relaxed. "You can't make me pregnant by coming in me now, Dex. I swear it."

She'd said the same thing to him in L.A. Then, he hadn't taken any chances. Now, for some crazy reason, he was tempted to.

To hell with it. Since he knew she couldn't lie, he gave in to temptation. Flexing his hips, he pushed into her, and although his thrust might not have been soft, at least it was slow and steady.

Her tight flesh resisted him, but for the first time, he felt the slick heat of a woman's core on his bare flesh. Her muscles contracted and pulsed around his dick as if they didn't know whether to keep him out or invite him in. He didn't give her a choice. He pushed in, tunneling into her, penetrating her until he was locked deep, unable to go any further. Then he bent down and sucked one of her ruby nipples into this mouth.

She screamed and started coming. He released her nipple with a loud pop and stared at her as her face contorted with her release. The tight clasp of her body embraced his dick like she'd never let it go, and he began thrusting, prolonging her pleasure while racing toward his.

Forget soft. Even slow wasn't an option anymore.

He didn't know how long he thrust or how many climaxes he gave her. Eventually, her release passed and she lay limply beneath him, her sated gaze locked with his. Her breasts jiggled and the wet sounds of their slapping flesh echoed around them. Their combined scent invaded his pores and settled into his skin and hair until he knew he'd never be able to escape her. His arms trembled until he feared he wouldn't be able to hold himself up. But he didn't stop or slow down. Instead, he lowered himself fully on top of her, pressed their bodies so tightly together that nothing could come between them, wrapped his arms around her, and thrust inside her until the chaise shook and wobbled.

He buried his face in her neck and realized that, once again, she hadn't bitten him. But when she'd been lying passively beneath him, dazed with her release, he thought he'd seen—

He shoved himself up to look at her, his dick swelling even more at the sight of her unsheathed fangs. "Oh yeah," he muttered, even as he lowered his face and curled his tongue around first one fang, then the other.

Her body jerked and her arms flew around him, suddenly no longer passive but demanding more. But she held back, turning her face away. "Dex," she gasped. "Stop."

"You can drink my blood now without getting sick, can't you?"

She tucked her bottom lip behind those gorgeous fangs, saying nothing.

He stopped thrusting his hips and instead swiveled them so his pubic bone ground against her clit. "Can't you?"

"*Mon dieu*," she mewled. Her eyes fixated on his neck.

"Do it, Jes. Take my blood."

"No. No, I can't."

"Jes, look at me."

Her gaze flickered to his.

"Make me come, Jes. Please. I need it. Bite me."

Her control shattered. He realized it one second before her fangs pierced his skin, flinging him into a pleasure that annihilated him, incinerating him as if he was a fireball and she was the sun. His balls tightened and he shouted as he exploded.

He shot streams of come into her body, his body jerking with each burst as a long, drawn-out moan was pulled from him. She milked his cock, hugging him there just as tightly as she did with the arms she'd wrapped around his body, as if no part of her ever wanted to let him go.

CHAPTER TWENTY

Lying in Dex's arms, Jess could no longer deny the truth.

Having sex with him in L.A. had created a very real, biological connection between them.

Having sex with him just now had only cemented it and confirmed what she'd suspected.

Her wellbeing, her very future, now depended on him. Somehow, Dex being here—Dex being inside her again—had not only made her stronger, but his presence was doing the same for her baby.

Drinking Raul's blood hadn't helped the way she'd expected.

The purest human blood no longer nourished her.

But Dex's proximity and his possession of her did.

She didn't know why, but she knew without a doubt that the key to keeping their child healthy was to keep its father close.

Reaching out, she caressed his cheek, sucking in a breath when his eyes immediately opened. He stared at her, his expression blank, the hazel of his irises nearly matching his hair. Even lying down, he vibrated with power and energy, and she immediately leaned toward him, wanting to absorb all that vitality inside her.

"Were you lying to me when you said you couldn't get pregnant?"

She couldn't say she was surprised by the question or the sudden rigidity in his body as reason returned to him. "No," she said, almost wincing at the relief that flooded his expression before he wiped his expression clean again. If he only knew she couldn't get pregnant because she was *already* pregnant.

"We need to talk." He swung his feet to the ground, stood, and gathered their clothes. He tossed her clothes to her then started getting dressed, watching her as she used her panties to wipe away the sticky come he'd left on her. Averting her gaze, she shoved her panties into her pants pocket and slipped on the pants.

"What brought you to France?" she asked him. He was completely dressed now and still watching her as she struggled to get back into her shirt.

He cocked a brow. "How do you know I didn't come to see you?"

Finally, she managed to get the damn shirt on and sat back down on the chaise. "Other than the fact that I had to send Cy to fetch you? I don't think you were sightseeing. You're here on a mission, aren't you?"

"I am. I was very much engrossed in my mission when Cy interrupted me. How familiar are you with shape-shifters?"

She frowned. His question eerily echoed the question Mahone had asked her when she'd first talked to him on the phone. She told Dex the same thing she'd told Mahone. "Not very. They're a hard race to track down, the most obvious reason being their ability to hide in plain sight. Why?"

"I'm investigating what seems to be a high number of shape-shifter murders. These murders have been committed by other shape-shifters."

Jes blinked in surprise. "That's unusual. They're usually closely knit."

"Exactly. So what would cause a close-knit race to turn against its own?"

Why was he was asking her? Because he really valued her opinion? Pleasure, this time wholly unrelated to her physical response to him, shimmered through her again. She scrambled for a response that would make sense. "What if individual shape-shifters were doing something immoral? Or dangerous to their own kind? People can justify almost anything if it's under the guise of protecting themselves or others from a physical or even spiritual threat."

"That makes a lot of sense. But what is it that shape-shifters could be doing to warrant retaliation by their own kind, and why would they reject outside help so much they'd kill anyone who offered?"

At what had to be a confused look on her face, he explained, "Before Cy found me, I ran into a triad of shape-shifters. My contact called them *diregeants*. They stonewalled me. Implied I should get back to the States, and fast. Right after that, my own contact tried to kill me. Coincidence? I don't think so."

He spoke so matter-of-factly, as if unconcerned by the fact someone had tried to kill him, but Jes's heart nearly stopped at the news.

"I need to go. Tell Mahone what happened and figure out—"

Now her heart did stop. She shot to her feet. "No! You can't leave!" Her voice rang out, loud and desperate.

Dex stared at her and she blushed.

What was she doing, shouting at him like that?

"I mean—I know a lot about shape-shifters. Nothing about the murders, per se, but I have a friend who is an Otherborn Ambassador. He tries to promote peace between Otherborn races. If you're looking to meet with the shape-shifter leaders, he might be able to help."

Dex looked suspicious and well he should considering she was thinking of Bodin. Of course, she had no intention of telling Dex that, but that didn't mean she couldn't ask Bodin for the information or for help.

"Is this person someone you trust?" Dex asked.

"Yes. I've known him a long time. He's trustworthy. But he's sick right now. I'm not sure he's in a state of mind to help."

"He's sick." Dex's eyes rounded. "Shit. Are you talking about the shape-shifter you were treating when I arrived?"

"No. But besides, what are the chances he knows anything? I mean, I don't even know who he is."

"Did he say who shot him?"

"I told you, I didn't ask."

"Then his assailant could very well have been another shape-shifter, right?"

"Maybe," she said slowly. "But that's a pretty big conclusion you're drawing."

"I want to talk to him."

Whoa. He'd switched gears so fast her mind was spinning. She hadn't even had a chance to tell him she was pregnant and he was already moving on to his mission. It was great he was no longer talking about leaving, but she knew he'd get back to the topic soon.

Right now, he wanted to talk to her patient. With his mind on his mission, now was not the time to talk about the baby.

Automatically, she shook her head. "Wait. No. *T'es fou?*"

When he cocked a brow, she said, "It means, *Are you crazy?* He's recovering from a critical wound. He needs rest."

"How much rest are you talking about?"

"Days, at least."

Dex ran his hands through his hair in obvious frustration. "Damn it. In days, there could be several more killings. I'll leave. Come back—"

"No!" She fought to keep the desperation out of her voice.

Dex put his hands on his hips. "You don't seem keen on me leaving anytime soon. And that brings us right back to my initial questions, doesn't it? This time, I want you to answer me, Jes. How'd you know I was in France, and why did you bring me here?"

"If I tell you how I knew you were here, you're not going to believe me!" she cried.

"Try me."

"Fine." The stress of the past few days—hell, the stress of a lifetime spent desperately clinging to love only to lose it over and over again—suddenly became too much for her. In her mind, Dex was pulling away and ready to walk out the door. All she knew was that she couldn't let him leave her. Not like everyone else in her life had. Not this time.

"I'm pregnant," she said.

***

Dex didn't react for several seconds. When he did, it was only to turn pale. Finally, he repeated, "You're pregnant."

Since she knew it wasn't a question, just an echo of the shock she'd given him, Jes didn't reply.

He blinked several times. "You just said you couldn't get pregnant."

Again, she said nothing and his expression darkened. "Because you *are* pregnant? And I'm to assume by the fact that you're telling me this that, what, the baby's—"

"—yours," she confirmed.

"Bullshit," he gritted out.

"*C'est vrai.* It's true."

He laughed. Out loud.

Then grew completely quiet again.

They stared at each other, as if each was daring the other to speak first.

"You want to tell me how the fuck that's even possible?" Dex asked softly.

"You were there. All four times. I think you know."

He shook his head. Began pacing the room while raking his hands through his hair. "You told me in L.A. you couldn't get pregnant. Even if you were lying—"

"I—truly thought I couldn't get pregnant. I'd been told by my doctors that I couldn't."

He kept talking despite her interruption. "I wore condoms—"

"Which aren't foolproof," she retorted.

He stopped pacing and pointed his finger accusingly at her. "It's been just over a week since we were together."

She crossed her arms protectively over her belly. "Vampires have a different gestation period than humans. It's short, and a successful fertilization presents itself almost immediately. I'll give birth within a month, but I'll begin to show within days."

He grasped his temples. "This is crazy. This is—" He looked frantically around him, as if searching for an answer he wasn't going to find. "So this is why you brought me here? Because you thought—what? I had a right to know? That I'd propose, and we'd be one big happy family?"

He was yelling now. She'd known he would react this way. She strove to keep her own voice calm, but inside, she was crying. "One out of two isn't bad," she said softly.

"What's that mean? That you *don't* want me to propose? Good! But if you don't want me to be part of some farce of a family, then why? Why am I here?"

"For one reason and one reason only. Because I need you."

"You need me," he sneered. "Yeah, you sure needed me an hour ago. What, did you think fucking me would make me more receptive to your little bombshell?"

"Listen to me," she said quietly. "The sex we just had wasn't about anything but me wanting you. I should have had more self control but—"

"Damn straight you should have!"

She kept talking over him. "I should have had more self control, but the fact remains I'm pregnant with your child."

He grew deathly quiet at her flat statement, until all she could hear was his labored breath. Until she could see the realization in his eyes.

He was beginning to believe what she was telling him.

She licked her lips before continuing. "The reason I knew you were in France is because our baby sensed it. We felt it. Together. And you can't leave. Not to go back to the United States. Not to talk to shape-shifters. Not for any reason. Because if you do, our baby will die."

***

Dex seriously felt like his brain was about to explode.

If he didn't know better, he'd think he was dreaming again.

No, not dreaming. Having the worst fucking nightmare of his life. And that was counting his years in the orphanage and the dream where Rurik had him cornered naked and helpless in a damn bathroom.

"You're crazy, lady," he managed to choke out. "And even if you're not, what do you expect me to say to that? You expect me to be shackled to you so you can—you can—"

"Keep your baby alive."

"It's not my baby. You tricked me. Lied to me."

"I didn't lie. I told you, I believed—"

"I know a vamp can lie," he said desperately, remembering how Knox's brother, Zeph, a full vampire, had lied. He'd heard that from Knox himself. "It's possible." But while that might be true, it didn't really matter if in the end all Jesmina had lied about was her ability to conceive. The question was, was she lying about being pregnant?

"I'm not denying that. There are things that can be done to enable a vampire to lie. They're not necessarily pretty, but if someone is determined enough, they can make it happen. I haven't developed the ability. I really thought I couldn't conceive."

"And you expect me to believe you why?"

"I. Am. Pregnant. With your child. I'm asking you to stay with me. To give my baby a chance to survive."

"Stay with you? Here? For a month? I have a fucking job to do!" He was shouting so loudly, he expected her to flinch back. She didn't.

Incredibly, her expression turned haughty and she actually sniffed.

Sniffed!

"And there's no one else who can do it?" she practically jeered. "You, Dex Hunt, are the only one who can successfully get the FBI the information it needs?"

"I need to get out of here. I need to think." He strode to the library doors, then froze. She'd said she needed him to stay with her or the baby might die. He didn't want to believe there was a baby, or that the baby's life depended on him, but what if? What if she was telling the truth? He couldn't take that chance. Not when he was still reeling from the shock of her revelation. He turned back to her. "How close do I have to stay to do what you"—he waved his hand in an all-encompassing gesture—"I mean, to keep the baby safe?"

"I don't know. You just being in France has already helped. The baby was dying. But then I felt—felt your presence. Felt the baby rally. But I didn't truly feel stronger until you arrived and after we—"

He averted his gaze. Stared at a point just over her right shoulder and gritted his teeth. "If I stay on the grounds, will that be okay?"

"I think so. I don't think you have to stay that close to me to—to help us."

"Good," he bit out. He whirled, grabbed the door handles, and flung the heavy oak slabs wide open. "Because being next to you is the last thing I want."

Behind him, she gasped, as if his words had caused her intense pain, but he didn't look back.

He couldn't.

He was too afraid of what else he might say, what he might *do*.

Practically staggering, he rushed through the castle halls, retraced the path Cy had taken from the entrance to the library, then pushed open the front doors with something like desperation. When he stepped outside, he sucked in the crisp evening air as if he was starving for it. Dots flashed in front of his eyes and he automatically bent over, head down, palms braced against his thighs.

The same litany kept repeating over and over in his mind.

Can't be. Can't be. Can't be.

He'd vowed never to have kids.

Kids were soft. Fragile. Easily hurt.

Life was hard.

He was hard.

He'd never wanted to be the source of pain for any child and he knew, with him for a father, a child was bound to suffer. If not physically, then because of Dex's careless way with words. And if not by that, then by neglect. Or if a miracle happened and Dex somehow managed to be a decent father, his child would still suffer the stigma of being part dog. A mongrel. One with a half-breed father whose own family had abandoned him…Sent him away to live with a bunch of other unwanted werebeast children who were sometimes abused, sometimes starved, and sometimes even worse.

Dex's heart constricted, as if someone had reached inside him and mercilessly squeezed it, and he grasped at his chest. His left knee gave out and crumbled, hitting the ground. The world around him swirled, faster and faster, like he was on a merry-go-round from hell. The dots grew bigger, blacker. He heard the pounding sound of running feet and wondered if the devil himself was chasing him.

***

From somewhere outside, the sound muffled by distance, came a man's scream. Jes bolted to her feet, straining to hear. To her horror, it wasn't an isolated sound, but kept on coming. Her shock morphed into panic. Dex. Dex was in trouble. She barreled after him, her breath nearly choking her when she realized he wasn't screaming, but shouting. She could barely make out what he was saying, but the words sounded like: "can't be." He was yelling over and over again, but it was his tone, not his words, that sliced into her. He didn't just sound angry, he sounded overwrought. In pain.

Because of her.

When she finally made it outside, he was illuminated by her house lights. He was half-kneeling, one leg bent, one knee and one hand on the ground, and the other hand grasping at his chest as if he was having a heart attack. Fear made her stumble. "Dex! Oh Goddess, no!" she shouted.

The ground shook behind her an instant before Cy barreled past, getting to Dex before she could.

"Shit! What the hell's wrong with him?" Cy shouted.

She shook her head. "I don't know. We talked. He was angry. But not crazed. Not like this. Maybe he's having a heart attack." She stepped closer.

"Stand back, Jes!" Cy gripped Dex's arm and called his name.

***

Dex heard shouts.

Jesmina's faint voice in the distance.

Strong fingers gripped his arm. "Hunt! What are you feeling?"

That sounded like Cy, the male who'd brought him to Jesmina. But why would Cy care how he was feeling?

Didn't make any sense.

Cy wanted Jes, didn't he?

Did he want Dex's baby, too?

From out of nowhere, that thought became Dex's sole focus.

Danger.

Jesmina. His baby. His.

No one was going to take what was his away from him.

No one.

Kill. Kill the man who was trying to take what was his.

The pain in his chest intensified at the same time a heady power surged through him.

With an inhuman roar, he straightened, grabbed Cy by the arms, and even though the other man was several inches taller, Dex lifted him into the air, then body slammed him to the ground. Before Cy could recover, Dex grabbed his throat and squeezed, not satisfied until Cy began to gasp and wheeze for air.

Kill him.

Do it now.

***

With a feral scream that made Jes's skin crawl, Dex exploded into movement until he had pinned Cy to the ground, his fingers wrapped around his throat.

"No!" Jesmina leaped forward and latched on to Dex, clawing at the arm he was using to strangle Cy. "Stop. Dex!" But despite her pleas and her attempts to loosen his grip, Dex didn't relent. He didn't even look at her. His twisted features appeared demonic. As if he was crazed. On drugs. Completely focused on killing Cy.

"Mine. Kill," he spat out.

"Jes—" Cy's voice was thready.

A quick glance confirmed he was running out of air. Though he was trying to extract himself from Dex's grip, he seemed to be holding back. With shame, Jes realized it was because of her. Cy knew Jes cared about Dex. Because of her feelings for the were, Cy was reluctant to hurt him. But if he didn't do something fast, Dex would kill him. "Cy, shift. Use your power. Make Dex let go of you."

Cy's watering eyes widened for a split second before he gasped, "Get back."

Swiftly, Jes obeyed, stumbling backward as her gaze skipped between the two men. This was all her fault. Dex had been driven mad by the news she'd given him and now he was hurting Cy. Killing him. They—

It took mere seconds for Cy to shift. One moment he looked like his humanoid self, a tall handsome man struggling to breathe, and in the next, his body went rigid and seemed to turn to stone. His hair and flesh fossilized, turning egg-shell white just before it began to glow, as if being heated from within. Wisps of smoke wafted around him as his body heat rocketed to a sizzling seven hundred degrees Celsius before bursting into flames.

Upon Cy's ignition, Dex screamed and automatically let go of the dragon-shifter.

In slow motion, Dex careened backward, his palms blistered and smoldering, his arms windmilling, before he hit the ground with a resounding thud.

Keeping an eye on the mass of fire that had swallowed Cy, knowing it would take a few moments for the flames to dissipate, Jes rushed to Dex. She bit her lip, whimpering when she saw that parts of his clothing had burned away, leaving scalded, bubbling skin behind.

"Giselle!" she screamed, hoping her friend was nearby. "I need my triage kit. Hurry!"

Quickly, she stripped back Dex's clothes and assessed the damage to his body while still keeping an eye on the flames behind her. Even now they were dwindling. "Cy!" she called.

The flames flickered and then went out completely, leaving what looked like a huddled human form, charred black. As she watched, Cy's black outer exterior cracked and crumbled until it fell away completely, peppering to the ground and exposing Cy's stone-encased body again. In seconds, that exterior also gave way, this time dissolving without leaving any trace of itself, until Cy was once again flesh, blood, and bones. Nude, but alive. Jes moaned with relief when Cy moved, then came to crouch beside her.

"Are you okay?" she sobbed. Her gaze swept over Cy for signs of injury, but there were none, enabling her to accept his curt nod.

"How's the were?"

Swiftly, Jes returned her attention to Dex. Physically, he was going to be fine. He'd sustained third degree burns in several areas, primarily his hands, but he was lucky his injuries weren't worse. He was unconscious. Her body shook from shock and distress, but gently, she ran her hands over his skull, searching for bumps or bleeding. He had a small lump on his left side, but it didn't appear serious. "He blacked out. I don't know if it's because of the fire or when he hit his head. I don't know. But he's okay." Turning to Cy, she grasped his arm with one frantic hand, desperate to make him understand. To forgive her. "I'm so sorry, Cy. It's my fault. He went crazy when I told him."

Cy broke her grip, grabbed her arms and gently shook her, abruptly stopping her words. "It's okay, Jes. I'm fine. Tend to him."

Giselle ran up and sank down next to them with Jes's bag of emergency medical supplies. Jes took a deep breath and dove into the duffel. She pulled out antiseptic and bandages, her movements crisp and efficient. Suddenly, she was calm. In control. All emotion pushed aside so that she could tend to the patient who needed her. But as she did so, she was ever aware of Cy's eyes on her and the echo of her own words.

He went crazy when I told him.

And that's exactly what had seemed to happen. Dex had seemed to be caught in the grip of insanity as he'd choked Cy.

Would he still be that way when he woke up?

CHAPTER TWENTY-ONE

Dex woke disoriented and feeling like he'd been dragged behind a car for several blocks.

Make that dragged behind a car for miles across mountainous, rocky terrain, then dumped down a steep ravine covered in shards of broken glass and left to the mercy of a dozen hunger-crazed vultures.

On top of that, his mouth felt dry, his head fuzzy.

Where the hell was he?

After several failed attempts, he finally managed to open his eyes. He blinked until the world stopped spinning and came into focus.

He was surrounded by white. White walls. White sheets. Sunshine spilled into the room from a window where heavy drapes were pulled to the side. He heard the beeping of a monitor beside him and figured he was in some kind of hospital. But the last hospital he'd been in had been in L.A. to talk to the wounded shape-shifter. He was supposed to be in France now.

Colors exploded through his mind. Red hair—Trosseau. White robes—the trio of shape-shifters. Grey on green—a castle on a lush expanse of land.

A rainbow of ivory and pink, silvers and blacks—Jesmina.

France. Jesmina.

Jes.

Pregnant.

Oh shit.

He bolted to a sitting position, wincing when his head violently protested. Instinctively he raised he hands to press against his temples, frowning when he saw they were covered with bandages. Why? Had he cut them?

No, he realized. Not cut. Burned. In some kind of explosion that had sent him flying off the man he'd been fighting. The man he'd been choking and trying his damndest to kill.

Jes's friend, Cy.

But why? Sure, they'd gotten in a few punches before Jes had shown up, but they hadn't actually been trying to kill each other.

"Cy—" He croaked out, not really expecting him to answer. Only he did.

"Yeah, man. I'm here."

Dex caught a flash of movement out of the corner of his eye and jerked his head to the right. Sure enough, Cy sat next to Dex's bed, his hands folded against his chest and his body deceptively sprawled back in a straight back chair, despite the tension emanating from his tightened shoulders and the scowl on his face.

Cy looked pissed but otherwise normal. Not like a creature that could transform itself into a fireball. But he had. At least, that's what Dex remembered.

"What—what happened?" he asked, then winced. What was wrong with his voice? He sounded like his throat had been scraped raw.

Cy straightened and leaned forward. "Funny, I was going to ask you the same thing."

Dex shook his head to indicate he didn't understand. He'd been talking to Jesmina in her library and things had gotten pretty hot pretty fast. Although he'd been troubled by not knowing why she'd sent for him, he'd also been relieved to see her again. To be inside her again. Only those feelings of relief hadn't lasted long before the tides had turned, and things had gone to hell in an instant. Why?

He strained to remember. It was on the tip of his tongue. He'd remembered it a second ago, but it was gone again. She'd been telling him something. But what? He scanned the room. He and Cy were alone.

"Where's Jes?"

Cy's mouth flattened into a thin line. "She's finally catching up on some sleep. She was up most of the morning worrying about you. Worrying about the baby and what's going to happen next."

"The what?"

"The baby," Cy repeated, his face going eerily blank.

Baby.

Clarity and memory combined to ruthlessly drop kick Dex in the head.

In a flash, he remembered everything again. Him and Jes having sex. How right it had felt. Then her telling him she was pregnant. That he had to stay with her through her pregnancy or the baby would die. He'd responded with denials and recriminations before freaking out completely and running outside into the night. There, he'd suddenly been overcome by a sharp stabbing pain in his chest. Automatically, he raised his hand and rubbed at the spot that still throbbed.

"I lost it," he muttered.

"Yeah, you could put it that way." Cy shoved to his feet and stepped closer until he towered over Dex. "Can't say I completely blame you, given the shock you'd just had. But frankly, you losing it isn't what has me worried."

At the other man's threatening posture, Dex's muscles automatically tensed. He braced himself to take a blow or to deliver one. "What do you mean?" he asked. At the same, he deliberately rested one hand against the small table to the right of his bed and gripped the edge; if he had to, he'd use the table as a weapon and bash Cy's head in.

Cy's gaze followed the small movement. He frowned, then took a step back and held up his hands, silently indicating he wasn't a threat. Dex relaxed, but only marginally.

"What I mean is that you lost it for a while there, but then you were gone. And whatever was in your place instead wasn't lost—it was exactly where it wanted to be. Inside you and wanting you to kill. A *diabol*."

CHAPTER TWENTY-TWO

Dex glanced at the small clock by his bed. Seven p.m. Roughly eighteen hours had passed since Dex had tried to kill Cy, and Jes still hadn't been by to see him.

Go figure.

Instead, Jes's assistant, the full-blooded werewolf who'd looked at him with such disdain the day he'd arrived—had that been just yesterday?—occasionally stopped by to check on him. She did her job, taking his vitals and changing his dressings, but she barely looked at him and only spoke when she needed to, which was pretty much not at all.

If he'd been physically capable of it, he would have gotten out of bed immediately after talking to Cy several hours ago. Unfortunately, any time he'd tried to stand, his limbs had crumpled like straws under an elephant's feet. He'd finally decided to take it easy for a while rather than risk falling flat on his face and not being able to get up again without someone's help.

But despite the werewolf's final instructions to take the pills she'd left him and get some sleep, Dex couldn't take it anymore. He'd go mad if he stayed in bed any longer.

Assuming, of course, he already hadn't.

Damn Cy for dropping his bomb and leaving to let Dex stew about it, which the other male had no doubt done deliberately. At first, when Cy had implied Dex had been possessed by some kind of dark spirit, Dex had laughed his ass off. But then he'd remembered the look on Trosseau's face just before the shape-shifter had done his best to kill him and his laughter had quickly faded.

With Dex stunned into silence, Cy had turned on his heel and walked out. Dex had been too busy weighing the possibilities, including the status of his own mental health, to even think about stopping him. What was so ludicrous about a person being possessed by a demon? He'd thought the same thing himself—that Trosseau had been possessed, his actions completely outside his own control except for that one flash of clarity when he'd seemed to recognize Dex and had said his name.

Was that what had happened to Dex? Had someone or something been controlling him? Because why else would he have tried to kill Cy when the male hadn't even been the one to deliver the news that Jes was pregnant?

Right. Can't forget that little fact, Dex. Jes had told him she was pregnant with his child and he'd sure as hell responded well to that, hadn't he?

Not.

He'd practically run from the room. But that time was over.

He was going to have to find Jes, get the truth out of her, and then get the hell back to the States. Only he hadn't yet done what he was supposed to do in

France. He needed to check in with Mahone, tell him about his meeting with the shape-shifters, and figure out what to do next.

Call Mahone first. Then see Jes. But he'd already checked and there wasn't a phone in the room.

Dex shoved back the bed linens and swung his legs off the side of the bed. He was feeling almost normal and surprisingly, his burns weren't as bad as he'd thought. They'd appeared badly burned, but with each hour, they'd improved until they were slightly chapped. As always, Dex's body had healed quickly. Now, he just hoped he had enough strength to get out of the damn bed. He was just about to put it to the test when Cy walked into the room unannounced.

"Ah, I'm just in time, I see."

Dex glared at the other male. Cy was beginning to annoy him even more than the pretty boy psychic on his team, O'Flare. "In time for what?"

"In time to watch you make a break for it. Or maybe I'm wrong? Perhaps you've gotten over your shock at being a daddy and are about to pledge your eternal love and devotion to your baby-mama?"

At Cy's taunts, Dex's composure, already shaky at best, fled completely. His fear and anger upon learning about Jesmina's so-called pregnancy came barreling back at him. He gripped the mattress hard when what he wanted to do was shout in denial. Only, he'd already done that several times before. He wasn't going to amuse Cy by doing it yet again.

So Cy apparently believed that Jes was pregnant with Dex's child. Did Cy also know Jes wanted Dex to stick around so the baby actually lived long enough to be born? She'd said the baby would be born in less than a month, and for a second he tried to imagine it—him at Jes's side for all that time, slowly adjusting to the idea of becoming a father.

Predictably, his thoughts gave way to a whole new set of denials. It didn't matter what Cy thought. Jes was lying. Or she'd made a mistake about him being the father. At the very least, she was wrong about the affect of his proximity on her pregnancy—

"Nope, I guess not," Cy drawled, stopping Dex's runaway thoughts. "You just don't have the look of a proud papa. Too bad for Jes."

Dex ground his teeth together before asking, "So you knew she was pregnant when you brought me here? Did you also know she wants me to stay close in order to prevent losing the child? Because it doesn't matter. I'm not staying."

"I suspected she was pregnant. I didn't realize she's been banking on your presence to keep the baby healthy. And as for you not staying?" Cy shrugged. "I didn't expect you would."

His utter lack of concern threw Dex off. He'd been expecting Cy to plead Jes's case. To start talking about how much a child needed a father figure. The fact Cy didn't simply further annoyed Dex for some reason. "So then what happens?" he challenged. "To her? To the baby?"

"If she's right about needing you around, she loses the baby, just like the others. It will hurt her, but she'll survive. No matter how much she doesn't want to."

They stared at each other for several tense seconds. "What others?" Dex finally asked.

"The other babies she's miscarried," Cy said softly. "And in case you're wondering, there's been a lot of them because she had no qualms about trying artificial insemination." Suddenly, his voice turned tight and guttural. "Who knows, you might get lucky after all, and Jes will lose this one, too. Problem solved, right?"

"Get the fuck out of here," Dex snapped, though he wasn't quite sure what had set him off. Unless it was hearing that Jes had miscarried. A lot. But since he thought she was liar and a manipulative bitch, why should he care?

Instead of complying, Cy shook his head. "No. You need to hear this. Jes has tried to have a baby for years. She can conceive just fine, she just can't carry a baby to term. It's actually not that unusual for vampires. Most give up after the first two or three losses. Not her. But it didn't matter. No matter what race the father was, whether she used artificial means or not, she could never keep the pregnancy. She always lost the child within the first week. This one's held on longer than most."

Dex felt another surge of discomfort, irritation, pain. Whatever it was, it swirled through him like a slow winding tornado picking up speed. He wanted to punch Cy in the face, if only to stop him from talking. Dex couldn't deny it—he barely knew Jes and he was angry as hell with her, but a part of him suddenly ached for her, too. Not wanting to examine why, he sneered, "Did she try to have a baby with you, too?"

The question seemed to rankle Cy like nothing else up to now had. "I'm only sixteen years old and Jes views me as a dear little brother. But we aren't connected by blood, and when you leave, I'll have an even better chance of reminding her of that."

The male's statement of intent rubbed Dex raw, but he was too busy reacting to Cy's stated age to immediately respond. "Sixteen? You're bullshitting me." Cy looked like a fully matured, well-experienced male who was at least thirty. Then again, Dex looked about the same age but was over eighty.

"No," Cy said simply. "I'm not."

"In what world are you sixteen years old?"

"In the Draci world."

"Draci?"

"I'm a dragon-shifter."

A dragon. In a strange way, it made sense. "You burned me. After you shifted. But you didn't look like any images of dragons I've ever seen." No, Dex recalled, Cy had looked like himself, only he'd transformed into a marble statue just before he'd exploded in flames.

"That's because I can shift into three forms. You saw form number one."

A dragon-shifter with multiple forms. Of course. Why not? Dex was a were. He served on a team with a ghost, a psychic, a vampire, and a feline mage. Why shouldn't dragons be a represented Otherborn, too?

Dex shook his head and raked his hands through his hair, thankful that at least his head had stopped throbbing even if his mind was still spinning. His gaze dropped briefly to Cy's kilt. It was different from the one he'd worn yesterday, but it was still a kilt. "So I guess that's why you need to get in and out of clothes so easily. Because you're naked after you shift?" Before Cy could answer, Dex said, "Let me guess. In another form, you have a tail and can breathe fire?"

"Pretty much. You got a problem with that?"

Dex actually laughed. "Problem? No. You forget I have a tail when I shift, too."

"Ah, that's right. I'd like to see that someday."

"I bet you would." He bared his teeth in a facsimile of a smile.

Cy narrowed his eyes. "Meaning?"

"Meaning, when I shift, it hurts like hell, and I assume you'd enjoy seeing that."

"Damn straight. But luckily shifting doesn't hurt me. Which I suppose is a tradeoff of sorts. For you, it hurts when you shift, but you get to live hundreds of years. Me..."

"You?" Dex prompted. "It doesn't hurt when you shift, so you..."

"Let's just say my time on earth is more limited than yours. Which is why I don't fuck around when it comes to going after what makes me happy."

"Let me guess again. Jes makes you happy?"

"Yes. But to be fair, an average life span of thirty years is also one of the reasons she's not interested in me, so you can take your own pleasure in that."

Draci only lived an average of thirty years. Cy didn't seem all that broken up about it. Dex supposed to him, a life lived was a life lived, no matter how short. Didn't butterflies live between a few weeks and a few months? Yet Dex had never felt particularly sorry for the beautiful creatures. And speaking of beautiful creatures... "If you want Jes for yourself," he asked, "why bring me here in the first place? Why not just get rid of your competition?"

The right side of Cy's mouth tipped up in a hint of a smile. "One of my poisonous throwing stars should have been more than enough to do the job."

"So how come I'm not dead?"

"I don't know. But maybe one day I'll get the chance to find out."

Yeah, and if it was up to him, one day would come sooner than later. So fine. He couldn't put if off any longer.

Slowly, steadily, Dex pushed himself to standing, thankful that someone had dressed him in a loose pair of sweats rather than one of those ridiculous hospital gowns that would have left his ass exposed. Still, he wasn't quite steady on his feet, which Cy would plainly be able to see, but no way was he going to sit and let Cy tower over him while they talked. "So why are you here, Cy? You planning on trying to kill me again?"

The other male's silence was telling.

Dex took a step toward him.

But Cy sighed and rolled his eyes. "No, I'm not here to kill you. Now sit down before you fall down." He dropped himself into the same chair he'd occupied earlier and then looked at Dex.

Dex waited several beats before sitting back down himself.

Cy leaned forward while clasping his hands between his knees. "Look, I'm not going to lie. I didn't want to bring you back here, but I didn't shoot you deliberately; it really was an accident. That said, I was perfectly willing to take advantage of a little bad aim, only you didn't cooperate. Maybe it has something to do with why Jes thinks you can save the baby. Either way, I'm not going to kill you in cold blood, especially now that Jes needs you. The only reason I'm here now is because she asked me to see you."

"And you always do as Jes asks?"

Again, Cy's mouth tipped into that one-sided smile. "Always."

Cy's smile hinted at an intimacy with Jes that made Dex want to choke him again. Easy, he thought. First Raul, now Cy. He had to stop thinking of Jes as his. She wasn't his. The baby wasn't his. This monstrosity of a castle wasn't his. And he wasn't staying. "So does Jes think you can keep me here?"

"Not at all. She made it quite clear you're free to leave whenever you want. But she did say you were probably bored and she asked me to entertain you."

Cy gave an exaggerated wince, but Dex didn't smile. So he was free to leave whenever he wanted, huh? While Dex was glad he wasn't going to have to battle his way out of Jes's castle when he was feeling as weak as a newborn colt, he wasn't exactly pleased with what Cy had said, either. "I don't need a damn babysitter," Dex groused.

"No. But I've thought a lot about it, and you deserve to know about Jes. And if you're willing to listen, I'm willing to talk."

The guy was just full of surprises, wasn't he? "Why would you want to help me understand her? You've already admitted you'd like nothing more than to get me out of the picture."

"I want you to understand her because I care about Jes and I'd rather know that when you hurt her—and you will hurt her—that you'll be doing it deliberately, with full knowledge of all the facts, rather than hurting her inadvertently because you're bumbling around in the dark and don't know any better. Also, I have no doubt you're going to leave, whether it's before the baby's born or after. But in the meantime, Jes is pregnant. She's vulnerable and fragile. If she's going to keep this baby, I want to give her every shot she has. And if that means trying to reason with you or even having to play nice, then I'll do it."

Damn dragon was making it really difficult for Dex to stay pissed off at him. He appeared to be a good guy. A good friend to Jes, even if he did want to be more.

And the thing was, Cy had already made Dex understand Jes better. Now that he'd had the shit kicked out of him and had spent hours lying in a damn bed, Dex was finding it easier to think of Jes, even a pregnant Jes, without getting quite so angry. First, just knowing that she'd suffered because of her desire to have children made him less prone to view her as a cold-hearted calculating bitch. Second, if she really was pregnant, that meant she'd told him the truth despite knowing he wouldn't like it. In Dex's book, honesty was a major factor in her favor.

"Tell me, Hunt. You close to your family?"

Cy's abrupt question made Dex instantly suspicious, but his response was as natural as the rising sun. "I don't have family."

Cy smiled, which made Dex's hackles rise even more.

"What's funny about that?"

"Nothing, except it proves just how much you and Jes have in common. Jes is an orphan, too."

Dex gestured around him. "Yeah, well, it hasn't seemed to impact her too badly."

Cy's expression swiftly became serious. "That's where you're wrong. Jes's life hasn't been easy. She lost her parents when she was young and my people adopted her. Can you imagine how that must have been for her? To lose her parents, then adjust to a new family only to have to stand by and watch them die, one by one, over and over again? Because every few years, that's what happens to Jes. She loses someone she loves, and even if she did believe in an afterlife, which I'm not sure she does, she can't even comfort herself with notions of post-death reunions. Not when she's immortal. That's why having a baby is so important to her. She's desperate to love someone who won't leave her."

Dex got what Cy was telling him. And if Dex was the key to keeping Jes's baby alive, could he really jeopardize her chance at motherhood, let alone be the cause of extinguishing a budding life? But neither could he put his life on hold and just chain himself to her side. Even if it was just for a few weeks, that time was enough to make a difference. To his team. His plans for his grandfather. Wasn't it? "She can never be sure of a love that won't leave her," Dex pointed out. "Even immortals can die given the right circumstances. Death comes for all of us at some point."

"Yeah, but usually other people's odds aren't quite as bad as hers." Cy stood and clapped his hands. "Okay, so I've said my piece. Mostly. I just have one more thing to say."

Dex arched a brow.

"I told you Jes wants someone who's not going to leave her. That's not me, but it's not you either, Hunt. Maybe someday she'll find someone who can give her that, but until then, all she has is this baby. If you care for her at all, you'll give her the chance to have it."

"I'm not going to rip the baby out of her."

"No, but you've already upset her more than you can imagine. That can't be good for the baby and it can't be good for her. So don't wait. Either decide you can support her or leave now."

"You'd like that and believe me, I'd be happy, in this one case, to help you out. But I really don't understand you. You act like you care about her, but aren't you jealous? Of her? Hell, of me? We live so much longer than you."

Instead of blowing Dex's question off or making some flippant response, Cy seemed to give it careful consideration. When he answered, he spoke slowly. Thoughtfully. "I'm not sure if you'll believe this or not, but here's the thing. In the grand scheme of things, my life on this earth will be relatively short. I know that. But I also know my time is precious. And I will be happy, no matter what it takes. You and Jes? You're two of the saddest people I know. I wouldn't trade places with you even if I could."

***

After talking to Cy, Dex took several moments to inventory what he was feeling. Yes, he was still pissed at Jes, or more specifically at the idea of her being pregnant, but he was also beginning to come to terms with it and accept it wasn't her fault. Condom or not, he'd stuck his dick in her several times. He'd even done it again yesterday despite knowing full well he wasn't wearing protection. But regardless, if she was pregnant with his child, he had to take his share of responsibility for that. It didn't mean he was any happier about having a child with her, but she'd only asked him to stay until the baby was born; she'd made it clear she didn't want them to be one big happy family.

He should be jumping for joy, right?

Because that meant she could have the baby and it wouldn't affect him directly. Not if she was the one who kept it and cared for it. But hell, he didn't even know her well enough to trust in her ability to be a good mother.

It didn't matter that he didn't want the baby—if Jes gave birth to his child, Dex needed to know the child would be well taken care of. No child deserved to suffer, not even his.

Fortunately, there was no reason to think Jes would hurt their child. In fact, if Cy could be believed, she'd likely cherish the kid within an inch of its life. So he wasn't going to add yet another worry to the heaping pile he was accumulating.

Right now, he was going to call Mahone and let him know about his meeting with the shape-shifters.

Although it took longer than he'd have liked, Dex finally managed to get dressed and retrieved his things from the bedside cabinet. He punched Mahone's number into his cell phone, cursing when he didn't get a signal.

Impossible. She had to have cell service here.

Moving slowly but ever more steadily, Dex stepped out of his room and into a hall with several closed doors. He opened one and found another recovery room, the bed made up but empty. Door number two yielded the same results. The next door he opened led him outside and he immediately recognized the outer doors to Jes's surgical room nearby.

The sun had set but the grounds were once again lit up with bright lights. There were several structures on the perimeter of the property, including a small shed a few hundred feet away, likely a woodshed given the split logs piled next to it. He heard voices in the distance and followed them. When he turned the corner of the castle, however, he froze.

A kid who looked to be about seven years old was making a rather pathetic attempt at what he could only assume were cartwheels. The kid—he couldn't tell if it was a boy or girl given the baggy jeans, sweatshirt, and knit cap—wasn't very graceful but was certainly persistent. As Dex watched, the kid bounced and kicked on all fours like a drunken toad at least ten times before giving up.

When the kid picked up a stick and began using it like a fencing sword, Dex assumed it was a boy. Unbidden, he remembered himself as a child, wielding a wooden sword and running up a hill. Shortly after that, moments before his grandfather had sent him away, he'd hugged his mother for the last time.

A familiar anger boiled within his veins and along with it, a pinch of pain ached in his chest. He was rubbing the renewed ache when the boy looked up and saw him.

"Hi," the kid said.

Dex frowned. Considered walking away without responding. But ultimately he nodded in greeting. "Hey."

"Wanna play sword fighting?"

"No." Dex's negative response was instinctive, but because his memories were still raw, it came out harsher than he'd intended. He waited for the kid to pout or cry, but he didn't. Like Cy had done earlier, the kid merely shrugged.

"Okay."

He threw the stick down and started doing those pathetic cartwheels again.

Dex walked past him and was about a hundred feet away before he stopped and looked back. He winced when the kid bobbled and landed heavily on his side. Again, Dex waited for the kid to cry. Again, he didn't. With a determined look on his face, he started hopping around again.

"Oh come on," Dex snapped out in exasperation. "Surely you can do better than that."

The kid stopped and pushed his bangs out of his face. "Huh?"

"Have you actually seen someone do a cartwheel before?"

"Sure. I see Jes do them all the time. I do them just like her."

Dex arched a brow. If that was true, than Jes wasn't very coordinated, but he knew for a fact that she was quite limber...at least when it came to sex.

"You show me," the kid demanded.

"What?" Dex scowled. "No. I just came out here to make a phone call." He dug his cell phone out of his pocket and held it up as if the kid was a juror and the phone was a piece of evidence.

"Please?" the kid said.

"Don't try looking all sad and pathetic. It won't work with me."

The kid shrugged, said, "Okay," then went back to his drunken hopping.

Dex grunted. Watched. Grunted again. Damn it. What kid gave in that easily? It made him think the kid must be used to disappointment. That in turn made him think of Cy and what Cy had said about life being too short not to be happy. At least, he'd said something like that, hadn't he?

"Okay, fine," he said, as if the kid had been pleading with him for five minutes straight. "I'll do a cartwheel. But I'm only going to do it once, okay? So pay attention."

The kid stepped back and watched expectantly.

Still holding the phone in his hand, Dex did a smooth cartwheel. Even with his burns and the time he'd spent in bed, the movements were graceful and strong. "See how I kept my legs straight and up in the air? That's what you need to do."

The kid jumped up and down. "Okay, okay." Then he did the same bad version of a cartwheel he'd already been doing. Looking pleased with himself, he said, "Like that?"

Dex was about to say no, but just managed to stop himself in time. "That was okay. Just keep practicing."

"Okay. Thanks. Can I try it one more time?"

"Sure."

The kid's tongue stuck out of his mouth as he concentrated. He raised both his palms and this time, when his palms slapped the ground, his legs were a lot straighter than they'd been before.

Dex nodded. "Good. Keep practicing and you'll have it down in no time."

"Thanks, mister." The kid pushed at his bangs again and inadvertently shoved the knit cap off his head.

Light brown hair came tumbling down across his face.

Uh, make that her face.

He was a *she*.

Never a good mistake to make, Dex thought. At least he hadn't called her a boy to her face.

"What's your name?" he asked, not even sure why he had.

"Ella," she said. "What's yours?"

From somewhere behind the castle, a voice called. Ella turned toward it. But rather than leaving, she looked back at him expectantly, obviously waiting for him to answer her question.

"Dex," he said.

She nodded. "Bye, Dex. I gotta go. See you later." She waved and ran off.

Dex watched as her little legs carried her away. When he realized he was staring after her, he picked up the stick that she'd been using as a sword. He stared at it for a long time as well, before flinging it to the ground. When he looked up, Ella had been joined by a woman. The woman crouched down in front of Ella and they talked for several seconds before Ella ran off again.

The woman straightened and walked closer to Dex.

It was Jes.

***

Jes froze when she saw Dex Hunt standing in front of her.

As both Cy and Amanda had indicated, he seemed composed. Nothing like the crazed were he'd been when she'd last seen him conscious.

But what was he doing out of bed? Her initial instinct was to scold him and shoo him back to his room, but she stopped herself just in time. Mothering him would be the last thing that Dex would want. So instead of walking toward him, she stood where she was, some distance away, wondering if he would simply turn and walk away from her without saying a word.

To her surprise, he approached her, stopping only when he was about ten feet away. "I'm not going to hurt you," he said.

She startled. "I didn't think you were."

"Why not? From what I hear, I tried to kill Cy in front of you. Shouldn't that make you at least a little nervous?"

She cleared her throat. She'd already talked to Cy about what had happened. Cy seemed to think Dex had been possessed by some kind of dark power, but she figured Dex had probably been in shock after the news she'd delivered. "You were upset. Cy startled you when he grabbed you. People do things they wouldn't normally do when they're upset and surprised." She certainly knew that was true. Look at all the things she did out of desperation. And they were things, at least she hoped it was the case, that didn't really reflect who she was inside. "Besides," she said, twisting her mouth, "It's not like you can actually kill me or anything."

He frowned. "I know better. Vampires can die."

"Yes, but no matter how much you hate me, I'm not going to just stand here and let you rip out my heart and burn it, so I think we're okay."

"Oh yeah. That's right. You're a super-strong badass immortal vampire, right? Lucky you." He seemed to be watching her closely as he said it.

She smiled tightly, her face feeling so stiff she was surprised it didn't crack. "Yes. Lucky me." Suddenly feeling cold, she stuck her hands in her jacket pockets and hunched her shoulders. "Your hands are okay?"

He held them up for her inspection. His palms were still pink, but the blisters and raw burns were gone, having healed far faster than they should have. Further proof of how incredible this were was. Yet she'd made up her mind. She couldn't force him to stay, not even to protect her child. "So…was there something you needed before you go?"

"Go?" he asked, obviously surprised. "But I thought—" He narrowed his eyes. "So now that I almost killed your boyfriend, you don't want me to stay. You no longer care whether your baby lives or dies. Is that it? Or was it all just bullshit after all?"

Her first response was fury. How dare he imply she didn't want her baby to live? When that's what she wanted most right now. Yet, she was also confused. What was he talking about? What boyfriend? Unless he meant—

"Cy is not my boyfriend. He's my adoptive brother."

Dex grunted, but said nothing else.

"And as for wanting you to go, I don't. Want you to, I mean. I asked you to stay. I told you why. But I'm not going to keep you here against your will, Dex. And you made it more than clear yesterday that you don't want to stay. I just want to say again, I didn't trick you into getting me pregnant. I really didn't think it was possible, with or without the condoms."

He was silent as he seemed to contemplate what she'd said. She held her breath, hoping he wouldn't sneer or snarl or accuse her of lying again. Goddess knew she'd deceived him, yes, even lied to him in a way, but not about their baby. Never about something like that.

When he nodded, she breathed a sigh of relief.

"Okay. I believe you."

"Thank you."

"Don't thank me, Jes. If you're going to have the baby, you can't expect anything from me. I'm not parent material. I don't want to be. I have a life in the States and things I need to do. Thing I've been needing to take care of for a long time."

Things like killing his grandfather? Since she only knew it because she'd read his mind in L.A., she didn't say it out loud. Nor would she mention that his grandfather was a patient in the very castle he was standing next to, and not in the States as she knew he probably thought. "Okay," she said cautiously.

He held up his cell phone. "I need to call Mahone, my boss. Tell him what's been happening and check in. Only I haven't been able to get a strong enough signal."

"I don't have a phone line. I—uh, generally don't need it, since I can teleport and talk to people directly. Plus, since others live here, it's easier to use individual cell phones. The best hot spot is actually in the gazebo over there." She pointed.

He frowned and looked like he wanted to ask her something. Instead, he said, "We'll talk afterward."

She nodded. "Okay." And despite herself, despite how horribly he'd reacted yesterday, she couldn't help but feel a spark of hope that maybe, just maybe, Dex Hunt would give her what she and her baby so desperately needed—himself.

***

Thirty minutes later, Dex pressed the disconnect button of his cell phone and cursed.

Damn Mahone, Dex thought. Leave it to that son of a bitch to send him to France without giving him all the facts. Like the fact that several of the murders he was investigating had been linked to dark magic and rituals to raise the dead. Like the fact all the shape-shifters who'd confessed to killing their own in self-defense had said they'd acted in order to protect themselves and others from evil spirits trying to come back to earth. Of course, no one had really emphasized that part of the confessions in their reports because the responding officers had thought the shape-shifters were spouting some made-up bullshit but still...

Dex didn't think it was bullshit.

He knew what he'd seen. And he knew what he'd felt. And most of all, he knew what Cy had told him.

That he hadn't looked like himself when he'd gone after the dragon-shifter.

Just like Trosseau hadn't looked like himself when he'd gone after Dex.

So what did it all mean? That there was some kind of dark spirit floating around and following him, trying to find a comfortable body to inhabit so it didn't have to return to hell?

Even if that was the case, Dex didn't know what to do with that information any more than he knew what to do with the news of Jes's pregnancy.

Fuck.

Jes's pregnancy. She'd asked him to stay. He knew he couldn't. Not for three weeks. But he needed to regroup and...he needed to call Lucy and tell her he was probably going to be gone longer than he thought.

"Lucy," he said when she answered her cell.

"Dex. Is everything okay?"

Hell, no, he wanted to say. Instead, he said, "Yes. But I haven't had any luck with the shape-shifters here yet. I'm hoping that'll change. I've—uh, managed to track down Jesmina Martin, the vampire we met in L.A."

"Yeah, I remember who she is," Lucy drawled.

Dex winced. Of course she did. He shoved a hand in his hair as he paced. "Turns out she lives in France and she has some leads for me to pursue. But it might take me a few days. I wanted to make sure you're okay. That you're not...suffering."

"You need to stop worrying about me, Dex. I'm fine. I've arranged to talk to the same shape-shifter who tried to take me from that club, but he was transferred to another facility just before you left. He has a new attorney who's slowing things down."

He frowned. "I told you I already talked to him. He gave me some names to explore, but said he didn't know anything about the shape-shifter murders."

"I know. But he likes felines. He might be willing to tell me something he wasn't willing to tell you. How's Jes, by the way?"

Not missing her teasing tone, he muttered, "She's...okay."

"Are you sure nothing's wrong? You sound weird."

Maybe I sound like an expectant father, he thought. A shell-shocked one. "I just called to let you know where I was and that you can still call me if you need me. But cell service is pretty spotty here. If you can't get through, leave a message and I'll call you back. Also, I wanted to fill you in on some things. There's some weird shit going on, Lucy. Black magic type stuff—"

"What?" Static crackled on the line. "Wh...say...ear...ex..."

"Damn it. Lucy?"

"Losing...say..."

"Lucy, can you hear me?"

When she didn't answer, he cursed, hung up, then texted her, his fingers fumbling with the tiny keyboard on his phone.

Call Mahone. I gave him info u need 2 know. Shape-shifters calling forth dark spirits. Be careful.

About a minute later, his phone finally bleeped as she texted him back.

Got it. Take care. Have fun. :)

Dex snorted. He'd worried Lucy couldn't manage the heat without him. Leave it to her to still be playing matchmaker between him and Jes. Hell, if only she knew about the baby...

Someone behind him cleared her throat.

Dex whirled around.

It was Jes.

"Hi," she said. She notched her chin at the tray she carried. It was stacked with several plates and bottles. "I figured you'd be hungry, and you said you wanted to talk after your call. Or I can leave you alone if you want?" In addition to her words, her expression evidenced her uncertainty of her welcome. As he gazed at her, Dex didn't dwell on the way they'd fought yesterday, but on how good it had felt to hold her. To be held by her.

He cleared his throat and pocketed his phone. "No. I am hungry. Thanks."

She stepped into the gazebo and they sat across from one another at the small table and chair set. She pointed to the food on the tray. "It's nothing fancy. Lettuce and toasted bread with grilled goat's cheese and apples in caramel."

"Looks good."

They ate in polite silence. Made painfully superficial small talk. They were being so civilized, in fact, it was burning his ass. Desperate to make some kind of significant subject change, he asked, "So who's Ella?"

Her face softened in obvious affection for the girl. "Ella lives here. She's an orphan. I have about six orphans who live on site."

"You've adopted six kids?" Had she done that after all the miscarriages? And were they the only individuals who lived on the grounds with her, or had she been talking about Cy earlier? Just as he had then, Dex bit back the question.

"No. I'm more of a house mistress. They don't really need a mother."

Dex frowned. "Don't need a mother? How old is Ella? Seven? Eight?"

"She's seven. But she's a dragon-shifter, like Cy."

When he just continued to look at her blankly, she frowned. "Cy said he'd explained to you about their life span."

"An average of thirty years. Yeah, he told me. So?"

"So although a seven-year-old human child would need to live with a parent, Draci often live independently by the time they turn five. But since Ella came to me when she was three, well, I told her she could stay here as long as she wants. She and the other children have chosen to do so."

"She looks to be her age, but Cy looks a lot older than sixteen."

"In a couple of years, Ella will start aging more rapidly. Right now, it's mostly emotional and internal maturation that's accelerated."

He nodded. Then shook his head while blowing out his breath. "Weird."

She laughed. "I know it must seem that way, but I've lived with the Draci for almost a century. I've grown used to them."

Cy had said she'd come to live with the Draci after her parents died. Dex wondered how it had happened.

"So you called your boss," she said. "Mahone, right? What now?"

According to Mahone, he was supposed to get his ass back to the church in Paris, track down the trio of shape-shifters, and make them talk. But he hadn't told Mahone about being summoned by Jes or about her pregnancy, and although he'd told Mahone that he thought Trosseau had been possessed, he hadn't told him the same thing about himself. "I don't know," he told Jes. "You said you need me to stay, but that I don't have to stay too close. Why don't you tell me what that means?"

"Honestly, I don't know. I'm kind of playing it by ear right now."

"So this connection we have, the one that makes the baby stronger, it's not typical for vampires and their…" He stopped, not sure what to say. Child's father? Lover? He didn't feel comfortable saying either one.

"No. Not at all. I've never heard of it before. Certainly never experienced this. But I have no doubt it's real." She pressed her hand against her stomach. Was it his imagination, or did her waistline look slightly thicker?

"You said your pregnancy will last a month. So the baby will be born in a little more than two weeks?"

"Yes. Maybe even sooner."

He saw the flash of hope in her eyes and shook his head. "I can't stay that long, Jes. I have work to do." He also had his revenge to think about. And despite her assurances, Dex needed to consider Lucy. He'd promised to be there for her during her heat. Every day he was away meant she suffered. Although she'd wanted to terminate their arrangement before he'd left, she'd likely change her mind when the heat got bad. He didn't want to leave her hanging, even if spending an extended amount of time with Jes could be…nice.

Jes bit her lip, clearly struggling with the desire to persuade him to stay and the need to let him do what was right for himself. "Can you stay a week? Ten days? You don't have to stay here, on the grounds. The baby started getting better as soon as you were in France. I know you have your mission to consider. In fact, I asked Cy if he'd take you to the village come daylight."

He couldn't stay ten days. Not even one week. But her comment about Cy and the village distracted him from saying so. "What village? Why?"

"You said your main objective is to get intel on these shape-shifter murders, right? But that the *diregeants* had stonewalled you?"

"Yes."

"Maybe someone in the nearby village knows something that can help you."

"Why would they? Who lives in this village?"

"Mostly dragon-shifters, but there are a few Otherborn, as well. No humans, so we can all live relatively in the open."

He reached out and touched her hair. She seemed to hold her breath until he drew back him arm. "Why the dye job, then?"

"I'm a doctor. Never know when I'll be called to help someone. Slipping sunglasses on to cover my eyes is one thing, but with the hair, it's just easier this way."

"Hmm," he said. "Are there shape-shifters in the village?"

"Not that I know of. The Otherborn are mainly Giselle's family. Felines. And a couple of mages."

Mages, huh? That could be useful. Now that he was dealing with shape-shifters killing shape-shifters, and dealing with some kind of dark force, too, maybe a mage would know something useful. But was it worth risking the baby's health on the chance he could get some information that may or may not be helpful? "What if going to the village is too far? What if it's dangerous for me to leave and you end up losing the baby?"

Clearly upset by what he was saying, Jes looked away. "I've given that a lot of thought. But you staying here could very well endanger the baby, too."

He stiffened. "You said you weren't afraid of me."

She covered his hand with her own. The light touch hit him harder than a heavyweight knockout punch. He felt it everywhere. Inside him.

She hissed and pulled her hand away, as if she too had felt the contact intensely enough to scare her. She shook her head. "I'm not afraid of you. But Cy thinks something possessed you, something he called a *diabol*. I'm not sure if it's true, but it could be. You weren't yourself when you attacked him. If something made you act that way, it could do so again. If you go into the village, a mage might be able to give you a protection spell."

He smiled at how eerily her thoughts echoed his own, but he still hesitated. Funny, just yesterday he'd completely rejected the idea of having a child. Now he was having to weigh his every move against the risk of harming one.

"What if you start to weaken in my absence?"

"I'll call you."

"Your cell service sucks."

"True, but the village isn't that far away. Plus, I've been to the village, which means if I need you, I can teleport there in seconds."

"I don't know. Yesterday you were begging me to stay close. Now you're sending me away? You can try to persuade me to stay put. Why aren't you?"

She smiled sadly. "I tried that already. It didn't work out so well, remember? Besides, I honestly don't think I'd be endangering my child. If I did, I wouldn't be suggesting this. I know nothing is foolproof or guaranteed. I know it's a small risk. Given my history, it's a risk whether you stay or not."

Dex nodded. "Okay. We'll try it your way for now."

"Good," Jes said. She rose. "I'm sorry, but I need to get some wood to replenish the fireplaces. I'll—I'll see you later?"

"Uh, yeah." Dex stood, as well. He remembered the woodshed he'd seen earlier and knew carrying wood to the castle over such a distance wouldn't be easy for Jes. She looked healthier than before but she was pregnant. Yes, he knew she was a vampire who was probably stronger than he was, but he still wasn't going to let her haul wood by herself. "I'll help you," he said.

"You don't have to do that!" Jes said. "You're still recovering and—"

She bit her lip as he glared at her, arms crossed over his chest. "Okay, I'm sorry. What I mean is, thank you. I'd appreciate that."

He smiled and she laughed and he was filled with shock at how much he was enjoying her company when neither one of them was even naked. Silently, she led the way to the woodshed, occasionally sneaking glances at him. At one point, he felt her gaze on him and turned. When their gazes locked, she flushed, and he knew immediately she was remembering the two of them together, bodies straining toward climax.

Quickly, she looked away. "Uh, here we are," she said needlessly.

The woodshed was bigger than it had looked to be in the distance. A stump and ax were to his right, but there was plenty of split wood to collect already. Dex looked around for some kind of basket.

"There are rucksacks inside. Let me just—" As she spoke, she pulled open the shed door and flipped on the light switch.

Since he was looking at her, he noticed the way her eyes rounded and her cheeks lost the color they'd only recently regained.

"*Mon dieu!*" she gasped.

He stepped behind her and looked inside. "What's wrong? Is there—oh fuck," Dex breathed. He put a hand on Jes's shoulder and said, "Go get Cy."

"But—but maybe I can help."

"He's dead." Turning her to face him, he repeated, "Go get Cy, Jes. Now."

She nodded and stumbled back, then began to run while calling Cy's name.

He watched until she made it inside, then he turned back, his gaze landing on the body of the dead werebeast inside.

It was Rurik Pitts.

CHAPTER TWENTY-THREE

Thirty minutes later, Dex paced in Jes's library. He and Cy had carried Rurik Pitts's body into Jes's surgery room, leaving him there so Jes could later conduct an autopsy. When Jes handed him a glass of scotch, he noticed how calm she appeared. He, on the other hand, was more rattled than he cared to admit. Even Cy looked a little shaken up. Aside from her initial shock at the woodshed, Jes seemed the most composed. Why? Because she was a doctor and dealt with life and death every day?

"Come morning, you and Cy should still go to the village," Jes said. "I'll do the autopsy while you're gone."

What? Was she serious? "I should stay here," Dex insisted. "Rurik Pitts was a member of a U.S. biker gang, the Ferals. I rode with them for a while and they're not a nice bunch of guys. He was obviously murdered and left in that woodshed for me to find."

The question was why. Part of him had always known that someday Rurik would come after Dex to avenge his brother's death, but why now? Why in France? Did Dex's weird dream in L.A. have anything to do with this?

He plowed a hand through his hair. How had Rurik ended up dead? It didn't make sense, which meant he wasn't leaving Jes alone even to investigate the nearby village with Cy. What if Rurik's murderer was hanging around just waiting to claim another victim?

Only problem was, Jes was looking at him with a combination of exasperation and flinty determination, clearly not liking what he was implying: that she needed him to protect her.

"Let's be logical about this," Jes said. "First, you don't know the werebeast was murdered. Maybe he came to see you and died of natural causes before he could. We won't know for sure until I complete the autopsy."

"He died of natural causes while waiting in your woodshed? Even if that's true, he was sneaking around and he likely wasn't alone. That means someone else is sneaking around, too, and is still a potential threat."

"But if this hypothetical companion came with Rurik, and Rurik came to see you, it's likely his companion came to see you, too. Whether it was to talk nice or not, you're probably the target. Am I right?"

She was right, but Dex really didn't want to admit it. Compromising, he grunted.

Next to Jes, an impatient Cy rolled his eyes.

"Okay, then don't you think leaving the castle grounds for a while actually makes sense? Chances are the guilty culprits will follow you, leaving the rest of us safer than we are now. Plus, someone in the village might have seen Rurik. I guarantee you, strangers would be noticed, especially someone as rough-looking as him."

Dex frowned in frustration. A quick glance at Cy proved he wouldn't be getting any help from him. "Everything you say makes sense, but—"

"But you're worried about me." Jes covered his hand with hers, but quickly withdrew it when a sizzle of awareness flashed between them. She flushed. "And that's very sweet, Dex, but I'm not an ordinary female. I'm a vampire. I've lived in this isolated part of the world for almost one hundred years, protecting myself and others from all kinds of intruders, including weres. I don't need you here. Not for this," she said quickly when he opened his mouth to contradict her.

He closed his mouth with a snap.

She stood and nodded, as if things had been decided.

"I don't want to be blamed for interfering with your mission. Go. Talk to the villagers. As we discussed, I'll find you if I need you. Barring that, I'll see you when you return. Right now, I have an autopsy to perform."

After nodding to Cy, she turned on her heel and left. Dex stared after her in amazement. He felt like he'd been twisted and turned and generally worked over by a pro.

Cy burst into laughter. "Man, if you could see the look on your face." Shaking his head, he rose. "Might as well give in gracefully. One way or another, you and I are going to that village or Jes will make you miserable. By the way you both reacted when she touched you, I'm betting you'd rather go now and reap the rewards of having pleased her later."

***

Dex wasn't sure what he was expecting of Cy's village, but this wasn't it.

He supposed that since Jes's home was a castle, he wouldn't have been surprised to find a village of cramped dingy huts and a bunch of morose dragon-shifters bemoaning their short life spans. Instead, Montpeyroux Village was both modern and quaint, bustling with life despite the fact it only had about 189 residents. If he didn't know better, he'd swear the village was inhabited by regular old humans. No wraiths, vamps, or weres in sight.

As Cy led him down the main thoroughfare, they passed outdoor cafes where a few couples sat outside. Several people walked the street with them, some pushing prams or carrying nappies or picnic bags. There were several restaurants, including a pub that caught Dex's attention—damn, he could use a beer right about now—as well as several businesses. The Draci were obviously a creative, artistic bunch. On one street alone he passed sculptors, wood crafters, leather crafters, ironmongers, painters and a poet reading his work in front of a bookstore.

Across the way from them, there was a small water fountain where several children played. To Dex's surprise, the sight of children playing and the sound of their laughter didn't have their usual effect on him. Whenever he'd seen kids playing in the past, he'd inevitably remembered the suffering he'd witnessed at the were orphanage and during the War. And he'd always renewed his vow never to bring another child into the world. Now, with Jes pregnant, it was too late for that. Still, the thought came without regret or anger. He seemed more inclined to remember Ella, the cartwheeling girl. Even more amazing was the fact he wanted to smile at the memory.

Cy stopped outside a *creperie*.

"You like ice cream?" Cy asked.

Was the guy joking? "Not particularly."

Cy shrugged, went inside and ordered a double-scoop of Rocky Road and vanilla.

Dex watched the entire transaction, then fell back in step beside him. Cy was one surprise after another. He was huge, looked like a linebacker, yet had no problem ordering and licking a double scoop ice cream while they walked.

Cy finished off the cone, tossed the wrapper in a garbage can, then grinned before turning to Dex, catching him staring at him. "I'm freaking you out, aren't I?"

Dex coughed. "A little."

"I told you." Cy gave one of his common shrugs. "I have to enjoy my life while I can. If I feel like having an ice cream cone—and unlike you I have quite a fondness for ice cream—I'm not going to stop myself from having one because someone else is gonna see it as unmanly, you know? Isn't there anything that you've wanted, that you knew would make you happy, and you just took it, damn the consequences?"

"Yeah. That didn't work out too well." He was thinking of Jes and their unplanned pregnancy. And he had the feeling Cy knew it. Especially when he said, "Show's not over yet. Who knows what will happen."

As they continued to walk, the dragon-shifter greeted those they passed. Those same people looked at Dex with fascination, but no one seemed to be scared or disdainful of him. Which Dex found interesting.

"You get many weres around here?"

"At one time, quite a few. At various times they've been enemies. Allies. Peacefully indifferent. Right now, we're at the peacefully indifferent stage. We have been for a long time. We're hoping that's not going to change."

"Why would it?"

"The were leader who controls the packs around here promotes peace and everyone knows the punishment he'll impose if they countermand him. Unfortunately, he's dying. Those set to take over aren't quite as open minded."

"And what will you do once this were leader is dead and the others don't cooperate?"

Cy shrugged, but this time his expression was hard. "Whatever we have to do. Same as you would."

Dex was about to ask him the were leader's name when Cy stopped. "We're here."

"Here" was a little shop complete with wind chimes and a banner that advertised palm readings. "You're kidding, right?"

Cy opened the door and motioned Dex inside.

A mage came out from the back room. He recognized her immediately. It was the blonde from the farmer's market in Paris.

Her eyes widened when she spotted him, then she smiled. "Hello, were. You still looking for something to help your lover ease the heat?" she asked. A second later, her gaze dipped to his chest then back up to his face. Was it his imagination, or had her smile dimmed slightly?

Before he could respond to her question, Cy grabbed him by his shirt and hauled him to him. "What is she talking about?"

Dex shoved him away. "What the hell business is it of yours?"

"You know why it's my business. How do you two know each other?"

"We met at the farmer's market before I ended up at that church where I met you."

"And this lover in heat?"

"She's a lover. End of story."

"You've been with her since meeting Jes?"

"Does that surprise you? Did Jes imply we'd made promises to each other? Because we haven't. I hardly know her. I wasn't looking for a relationship or family. I'm still not." But even to him, his protest sounded a little weak. Why? It was true. Wasn't it?

"Yeah, well, like I said before, it's your loss." With a final look of disgust, Cy turned back to the mage. "Dex needs to ask you some questions. He's a friend of Jes's, so you can trust him. For now."

The mage looked at Dex, her expression serious, all trace of sweetness and light gone. "What do you need to know?"

"What do you know about shape-shifters and dark spirits?"

"*Diabol*s? Why?" Again, her gaze darted to his chest before returning to his face.

Automatically, Dex rubbed at the tender area just over his heart. Was it his imagination, or had she honed right in on it? "Because shape-shifters are killing shape-shifters and I'm trying to help stop it."

This time, she looked down at her suddenly wringing hands before she seemed to consciously relax them. "And what if you can't?" she asked softly.

"Excuse me?"

"I said, what if you can't?"

"Why wouldn't I be able to?"

"There are some things so powerful, they can't be stopped. Not by mere mortals. Maybe not even by immortals."

"Yeah, well I don't buy that," Dex reassured her.

"I suppose that's good. Maybe it'll help you."

"Help me what?"

"Help you fight the *diabol* that's after you."

***

So far so good, Jes thought.

She didn't seem to be suffering any negative effects because Dex was off the castle grounds, and neither did the baby. Its life force was a comforting presence inside her. Though it didn't move, its energy intensified whenever Dex was in the room. In case it was worried, she rubbed her stomach and said, "Don't worry, little one. Your father will be back soon. Stay with me, okay?"

It was nice to feel hope again. At first, she'd been so worried about losing the baby then about Dex's reaction to the news that she'd barely allowed herself to imagine what her life would be like once the baby was here. It was partly a defense mechanism; experience had taught her that the more she envisioned that kind of life, the more devastated she'd be when it didn't happen. Right now, she needed to be smart, stay healthy, and keep her focus.

Finding Rurik Pitts's body in the woodshed had certainly thrown her equilibrium off. At first she'd thought the werebeast had come after her, either to kill her or to extort more money. A host of questions had swiftly followed: Did he know Dex was here? Had he come to warn Dex about her? Had he brought anyone else who knew about her? And, of course, who had killed Pitts, and why?

Thankfully, she'd managed to keep her composure and Dex had taken care of the rest, immediately assuming that Rurik had traveled to France because of *him*. Even as relief had overcome her, she'd been tempted to tell Dex the truth—not just about Pitts, but about everything.

The legend. His grandfather. The blood she'd taken.

Aside from freaking out about the baby and trying to choke Cy to death, Dex was proving to be enjoyable company. Revealing bits and pieces about himself through his actions and so far confirming why she'd liked him from the very beginning. Then there was the fact he'd been so tender when they'd made love in the library…

She wanted to get to know *that* Dex Hunt better.

And telling him the truth would ensure that never happened.

So she hadn't told him the truth.

Hadn't told him anything.

Even though part of her wondered if Pitts's death had anything to do with Dex's crazed behavior and possible possession by a dark spirit.

Instead, she'd convinced him to go to the village with Cy. She'd obviously meant it when she'd said she didn't want to interfere with his job. She wanted him to help keep their baby alive, but his job put a lot of pieces in motion, and ignoring any one of them could prove disastrous.

At least her autopsy of Rurik Pitts had been fruitful. The werebeast had died of a heart attack. His presence in France was still a mystery, but he'd died from natural causes, which made it less likely something dangerous was lurking on the castle grounds.

Since Dex and Cy were still gone, she decided to take advantage of Dex's absence to continue working in her lab. She collected the vials of Dex's precious blood and ran several more tests. The results were similar to the others. Except for his vampire ancestry, Dex's blood showed no signs of extraordinary power. Unfortunately, that meant she had to move to the experimental phase of her research sooner than later.

Her first plan was to see if Dex's blood had any healing or life-prolonging properties even though her initial tests hadn't shown it. Using laboratory mice infected with a debilitating virus, she injected them with Dex's blood. She took another set of mice and slathered the blood on them topically. Then she slipped a couple of vials of blood into her lab coat pocket and headed off to see Bodin. She wouldn't inject him with the blood yet, but if the mice didn't suffer any ill effects, and if Bodin's health continued to decline, she might not have any other choice.

On the way to Bodin's room, she wrestled with whether she should tell him about Dex. She'd been going back and forth on the subject since Dex had arrived. Would it be wise to alert Bodin to Dex's presence, even if Bodin had acted in Dex's best interests when he'd sent him away?

Her steps slowed for a moment. She supposed part of her didn't believe that. When it came down to it, Bodin hadn't necessarily acted in Dex's best interests. He'd acted to keep Dex alive, which wasn't the same thing at all. Still, his actions were understandable. Those of a man left with few choices, all of them difficult ones.

Still undecided about what to do, she knocked on Bodin's door. He was in an isolated room meant to house quarantined patients. It was on the other side of the castle from Dex's room, and one had to get through several locked doors to get to it; only she and Amanda had the keys.

"Come in."

At Bodin's soft call, she stepped inside. When she saw the werewolf leader, she strove to keep her expression blank. Now he had deep wrinkles tracking his face to go with his white hair.

Yet when Bodin looked up and saw her, his eyes lit up with the same intelligence and vibrancy that they'd always held. He reached out his hand. "Jes," he said softly.

Even his voice is different, she thought. It used to boom with authority, and now it was barely more than a whisper. She took his hand and kissed it. Held it for several seconds against her cheek, yearning for the strength he'd once possessed and that she'd so infrequently been able to lean on.

"You look good," he murmured. "You've been resting."

"I have. Yes," she replied.

"Good. That's good. Amanda came to see me earlier. She said you had another patient. A werebeast. Do I know him?"

Would he know him? She sighed, unwilling to lie, given Bodin's direct question. On some level, she was certain that's why Amanda had mentioned Dex to him in the first place. "Actually, I think you do know him. But I need to talk to you about something first. Something important."

"All right."

She sat in the chair next to the bed. "As you know, I've been furthering my research on extending life. I had a lead in L.A. and—and I've brought something back with me." She held up the vial of Dex's blood.

Bodin's brows furrowed even as he smiled. "What's that?"

"It's blood. It's blood that I think is very powerful. The blood of a werewolf. And a vampire."

Bodin's quizzical expression slowly disappeared. "Vampire? And werewolf?"

Jes simply continued to look at him, saying nothing.

If possible, Bodin paled to almost the exact same color as his hair.

"No. No, Jes. No."

"Shhh. It's okay," she said. "I heard about the legend from the Draci. The day you brought me here, I saw how you reacted when Lacrosse asked you about it. I knew that—"

"Damn it, girl. What have you done?" he shouted. With more strength than she'd expected him to have, he grabbed her arm. She automatically tried to pull away, but he yanked her closer.

"What have you done?" he asked.

She scrambled for something to say. All that came to mind was, "I met Dex. *Il est ici.* He's here."

Bodin blinked. Slowly, his fingers loosened and he fell back against his pillows.

"Dex? The Boy is here?"

"Yes."

"You're sure it's him?"

She nodded. "Yes." Her eyes filled with tears, not because he'd grabbed her but because she could see the sheer love and relief that flashed across his face, as well as the way he blinked away moisture in his eyes.

"He's alive," he clarified. "You've met him? What's he like?"

She laughed. "He's handsome. Stubborn. Strong. He works for the FBI, on a team comprised of humans and Otherborn. He doesn't lead the Para-Ops team, but he's a commanding presence on it. Essential to its success. To peace in the States."

Bodin nodded. "A warrior. I always knew that's what he was. So you know that he's the one? The one to fulfill the legend?"

"Yes," she said gently. "At least, I believe he is. I put things together. Lacrosse's question. Your response. And Rita, the Draci seer—"

"The mysterious one who wore that damn cloak all the time," Bodin bit out.

Jes nodded. "She helped me, too. I asked around, but very discreetly. Most of all, I know you. I knew you wouldn't ostracize your grandson simply because he's a half-breed. Or if you did, it was so you could protect him."

"Foolish girl. How can you know that?"

"Because that's what you did with me. You saved me. And you knew I couldn't live with your pack and remain safe. So you brought me here."

"You've always thought too good of me, Jes." He picked up her hand and squeezed it.

Jes frowned. His fingers were cold. Too cold. She said, "And you've always given me reason to."

"So you're trying to confirm whether the legend is true. By testing his blood?"

"My initial tests were inconclusive, showing only his heritage but not whether he has an immortal gift. I'm running tests on actual subjects now. Using his blood. But do you know another way? Do you know how Dex would be able to gift another immortality?"

Bodin shook his head and for a second looked immensely sad. "Does he know what he is?"

Disappointment weighed heavily on her shoulders. Since the legend didn't specify the exact nature of the immortal gift, she hadn't really expected Bodin to have the answer, but she'd hoped. "No. He doesn't know. And he doesn't know what I suspect."

"I don't understand. Then why is he here?"

"He came to France for a mission. Something about shape-shifters killing shape-shifters. But he hasn't gotten much information from the shape-shifter leaders."

Bodin scowled. "Shape-shifters are nothing but trouble. Let them kill each other."

Jes's eyes widened in shock and he obviously noticed. His gaze flickered with regret. "I told you, you've always thought too good of me."

Not willing to believe that, she said, "You—you promote peace between Otherborn."

"Shape-shifters are different," he answered. "Dark. With the ability to consort with darkness."

Darkness? As in a demon that might possess a werebeast so he tries to kill someone he just met? "What darkness—" she began, but Bodin cut her off.

"No more talk of shape-shifters," he commanded. "Why else is Dex here. With you? In this castle?"

This time, she hesitated several beats, not wanting to drop the subject of dark shape-shifters but also for another reason she couldn't quite comprehend…But Bodin was as much a father to her as any she'd had. Part of her couldn't resist sharing her joy with him. "I'm pregnant. I'm carrying your great-grandson."

Bodin didn't even look surprised. Had he guessed?

He only nodded. He sank deeper into the bed and pulled the sheets up around him, as if he was ready to fall asleep. He even closed his eyes. "You need to send Dex away. Trouble will follow him. The legend isn't true. But if you believed in it enough to find him, others will, too."

"You don't understand, Bodin. I can't let him leave. I need him here. My baby needs him. If not in the castle, then at least in France. We're connected somehow, and it's through Dex's strength that my baby keeps his own."

Bodin's eyes flickered opened and this time his expression was devoid of all emotion. "Does he know I'm here?"

"I haven't told him yet."

"Don't tell him. If he finds out, he'll leave. He hates me. Likely wants to kill me. Whether or not he'd actually try, we can't know for sure, but I do know this—he will leave you."

CHAPTER TWENTY-FOUR

Dex didn't even bother protesting the mage's words. She believed a dark spirit was targeting him and he wasn't taking any chances. Better that she turn out to be wrong than he make the mistake of not listening to her when she was right.

The mage led them to a room at the back of her shop and waved at them to sit at a small table. When they were all settled, Dex urged, "Tell me about this *diabol*."

"They are everywhere. Always. The dead who haven't been allowed entry into the Otherworld, but have been banished to hell for their cruelty and misdeeds. Their hell is to walk beside the living, unseen and unheard. Forever reminded of the life they squandered. They have an energy. An aura. I can sense traces of the aura on you." She reached out and lightly touched his chest. "In you."

Dex swallowed loudly and shifted away from the mage's touch. "If they're everywhere, how can you tell the spirit's been inside me?"

"They are everywhere, but also nowhere. Normally they don't have the power to interact with the living. When they acquire that power, their aura changes. Becomes brighter instead of its normally subdued gray."

"And shape-shifters? What's their role in all this?"

"It's rumored that certain shape-shifters can create a bridge that connects a *diabol* to the world of the living."

"And in doing so, shape-shifters can facilitate individuals being possessed by *diabol*s?"

"Yes. Once the bridge to the living is made, a *diabol* can thereafter possess an individual that's weak enough."

Cy coughed, earning a glower from Dex. Dex turned back to the mage. "What do you mean, weak? I'm not weak, and the shape-shifter who attacked me wasn't weak, either."

"Not weak in the physical sense. But people have natural barriers that protect them from darkness. Those barriers falter when the person is experiencing intense negative emotion."

"Like?"

"Anger. Guilt. Jealousy."

"You wouldn't have any experience with those emotions, would you, Hunt?" Cy taunted.

But Dex didn't even look at him this time. He'd felt all those things since meeting Jes, and he'd been beyond distressed after she'd told him she was pregnant. It would have been the perfect opportunity for some dark spirit just waiting to get the jump on him.

"So possession is random?" he asked, trying to understand. "A *diabol* waits to find a weakness and then exploits it?"

The mage shook her head. "No. It's extremely rare for *diabol*s to connect with the living world. When they do, they usually have an agenda. A particular person they attach to. For some reason, this *diabol* has attached to you. You have something it wants. Or you can lead it to what it wants."

"The way Trosseau led it to me."

"It appears so."

"Why me? Why not him?" Dex notched his chin at Cy. "He was there, too."

"That I do not know." The mage stood, almost as if she wanted to end their conversation. Dex remained planted in the rustic wood chair. He did, however, rub his hands together, conscious of the sudden chill in the air that existed despite the temperate weather outside.

"But why would the *diabol* try to kill me? If he wanted to possess me, why have Trosseau attack me?"

"Perhaps it only looked like he meant to kill you when what the *diabol* really wanted was to weaken you so you'd let it inside you. Then it could control you, if only for a short time."

"What do you mean?"

Beside him, Cy shifted and leaned forward, his expression one of rapt attention.

"In creating a bridge," the mage explained, "a shape-shifter enables the *diabol* to take on the disguise of another. The shape-shifter gives it form. Dresses it, if you will. That's why shape-shifters who've pledged themselves to *diabol*s are sometimes referred to as Demon Tailors. They help demons access the living through the physical world as well as through dreams."

Dex felt his brows shoot up. Seeing this, the mage's eyes widened.

"You already know this?" she asked him.

"I had a weird dream before coming to France. A dream in which an old friend visited me and tried to kill me. But after I arrived in France, after I was possessed—assuming that's what happened, of course—we found him nearby. Dead."

The mage actually backed several steps away. "*Protéger cette âme des esprits sombres.*"

Dex stood. "What does that mean?"

When she just shook her head, Cy said, "It means 'protect this soul from dark spirits.' A protection prayer."

"Will that ward off possession?"

Cy shrugged and Dex pinned the mage with his gaze.

She raised a shaky hand to her temple, then took a deep, calming breath. "If I did a full protection spell, it could. But the spell is only as strong as my power, and there are ways for a *diabol* to circumvent it. Especially if it seeks to possess a dreamer. That kind of possession is rarer than the other and is far more dangerous."

She took her seat again and motioned for Dex to do the same. When he did, she asked, "Tell me, did this old friend appear in dreams while you were here in France? Before you were possessed?"

"No. But that's because I never had a chance to actually sleep, not in France, at least not before I was possessed. I never had a chance to dream. After I was possessed, I lost consciousness but—"

"It could have come to you then. Either you don't remember or your friend was already dead, in which case the *diabol* could not use him as a guise."

"Why is it more dangerous for a *diabol* to possess a dreamer?"

"In real life, a *diabol* can only possess someone for a limited time. During that time, the body it possesses will be infused with the power of dark magic. Likely this will be evident through the host's supernatural strength. But in a dream, the *diabol* must approach the dreamer in the guise of someone familiar. Not necessarily someone he trusts, but someone he believes would be in his dream. So if a *diabol* entered my dream disguised as you, that would be expected, familiar, since we've met. Do you understand?"

"So far. Go on."

"In my dream, you could only do what I expected you to do. Your strength would only be evident to the degree I expected it."

"So if I knew the strength of this person firsthand, it would be delineated as such. In the dream, I mean."

"Yes. Because the *diabol* and its guise are joined, with the spirit knowing what the guise knows and acting the way the guise would act, it fools your mind into letting it in."

So Dex's subconscious had presumably forced this *diabol* to disguise himself as Rurik in order to enter Dex's dream. "But after I woke from my dream, certain things occurred that copied the dream, while others didn't. Identical conversations. Thoughts. Something like deja vu."

"That was an indication that the guise or the *diabol* had been watching you for some time. Following you. Following your friends. It knew what was going to happen before it actually became clear to you."

"But why invade through dreams at all? What does the *diabol* gain?"

"Life. If a *diabol* disguised as a familiar succeeds in killing the dreamer in his dream, it's said he has the power to take over the dreamer's body. Permanently."

Permanently. The word echoed around him until urgency poked at Dex like a cattle prod. Fear caused him to break into a sweat. He suddenly remembered Jes's patient, the shape-shifter who had been shot. She'd said he would be recovering for days, which meant he was likely still at the castle. If that was the case, that shape-shifter would have been close enough to bridge the dark spirit that had possessed Dex.

"The shape-shifter at the castle," Dex gritted out.

Cy's eyes widened.

"I need to get back to the castle. Fast," Dex told Cy. "I'm going to shift and run." He turned back to the mage. "Can you come with us? I need you to put a protective spell in place. Can you protect a castle? A group of individuals?"

"I can try."

"You think Jes is in danger?" Cy asked.

"If Trosseau led the *diabol* to me, how do I know I didn't lead it to Jes, or to one of the other people at the castle?"

"That doesn't make any sense."

"No, but it doesn't make sense that a dark spirit wants something from me, either."

"That's not true. You work for the FBI. If a *diabol* possessed your body, it would be able to access people and places that could impact a whole helluva lot of people."

Shit. Cy was right. But that didn't mean Jes wasn't in trouble, did it? He couldn't be certain. He stood. "I'm shifting." He didn't waste any time finding someplace private to do it.

His skin tightened until it felt agonizingly too small. His bones and organs expanded, rippling inside him, forcing his skin to stretch as tawny fur began to sprout from his follicles. The rippling was in his face, too, threatening to push his eyeballs out of their sockets. His teeth sharpened and elongated, and he clenched them together to stifle his moans. Finally, bones broke and blood stained his fur as his form shrank. The pain smothered him until he wasn't even sure who he was anymore.

Then it was over.

He was wolf.

He raised his muzzle to look at Cy, who was staring at him in horror.

"I guess I don't enjoy seeing you in pain as much as I would have thought," the male said faintly.

Dex bolted out of the mage's shop and down the main street of the village.

As he ran, he tried telling himself that Jes was fine. There was no reason to think she was in danger. It was just all the talk of dark demons and devil spirits trying to take over people through their dreams that had him edgy.

But he wasn't taking any chances, either.

Earlier, he'd enjoyed dining with her almost as much as he'd enjoyed having sex with her. Nor had he imagined the tremendous respect he'd felt for her when she'd urged him to go to the village, either. She'd wanted to give Dex what he needed, even though she wanted to protect her baby—*their* baby.

For the first time, thinking of himself as a father didn't seem so wrong.

He made it to Jes's castle in record time. Quickly, he shifted, the transition from wolf to human form slightly less painful but enough to leave him sweaty and breathing hard. Running to where he'd left his things, he pulled on some clothes, then went looking for Jes.

He called out for her, but heard no answer.

He raced around Jes's home, searching, growing tense with the sight of each empty room. She wasn't in the living area, library or the surgery space. Maybe she was in one of the recovery rooms with a patient? Maybe even with the shape-shifter?

What if the shape-shifter had been shot because one of his brethren had found him trying to raise a dark spirit? Or trying to create a bridge for one? What if he was doing it again? Here? Now?

Dex's heart almost stopped. "Jes! Where are you?"

"Why are you yelling?"

Dex whirled around.

It was the female who'd been assisting Jes the day Dex had arrived. He strode up to the werewolf, stopping right in front of her.

She sniffed, then stepped back. "You shifted," she accused.

He frowned. She could smell that on him? "Where's Jes?'

"What's wrong?"

"Damn it, just tell me where she is."

"She's in the nursery."

"Where is that?"

"On the third floor, but—wait!"

He headed for the stairs, but she grabbed his arm, clinging to him despite his efforts to shake her off.

"You can't go in there. She's delivering a baby."

"Let go, damn it. I need to talk to her. To make sure she's okay."

"I just saw her. She's fine. You'll have to wait."

For some reason he needed to confirm she was okay himself. "No."

"Yes," a male voice suddenly boomed out. "Dex, calm down. It's all right."

Dex turned to see Cy standing with the mage. Fuck, had he been arguing with the werewolf long enough for Cy and the mage to walk back from the village?

As if Cy had read Dex's mind, the dragon-shifter shook his head. "You're not the only creature that can shift for speed. And I've got wings."

"She says Jes is in the nursery," Dex said.

"Then she's fine. You can't go in there now, Dex. She'll be busy."

What the hell was wrong with them? "I've seen babies being born before," he pointed out. "It's not like the sight of blood will make me faint."

"You haven't seen anything like this before." Cy turned to the werewolf, who nodded her head. Cy turned back to Dex, a pained expression on his face. "It's a Draci birth."

"And?" Dex asked impatiently.

"It's just different. Let's get the mage started on the protective spell. By then, Jes will probably be done."

Damn it. He didn't want to do that, but he'd also come to trust Cy to a degree. Cy knew Jes and her way of life in a way that Dex couldn't. As much as that bothered him, he had to accept Cy's place in Jes's world.

"What's your name?" he asked the werewolf.

She practically sneered at him and there was something familiar about her expression, something that made Dex frown. He shook off the feeling, trying to stay focused on Jes. He stared at the werewolf until she answered.

"Amanda."

"You were operating on a shape-shifter when I first arrived, Amanda. Is he still here?"

Amanda hesitated, then said, "He left against our advice. Seemed in a big hurry, too."

Although her news seemed to confirm his fears, Dex hoped the shape-shifter had gone for good and wouldn't return. But he'd still have to warn Jes. "Go in and check on her," he ordered Amanda. "Then come out and report to me or I'm going in there myself."

Amanda glared at him.

But she did as he said.

***

In minutes, the mage had gathered all her supplies—crystals, a feather, and some lit incense. She strolled through the castle, quietly chanting. Dex and Cy followed a short distance behind her.

"Tell me about Draci births," Dex ordered Cy. "What's so different that I couldn't be there to talk to Jes?"

"A Draci birth is a somber occasion. Jes would never have let you stay as it would have been the height of disrespect for the delivering mother."

"Why isn't it a happy occasion?"

"It's both happy and sad," Cy conceded.

"The duality thing again?"

Cy nodded. "Exactly."

"Tell me what you mean."

"Right now, Jes probably isn't just dealing with birth, but with death, too. Welcoming the new arrival but also preparing to bury the mother."

"Wait, you know her? Is the mother particularly ill or is this pregnancy just risky?"

"Any Draci pregnancy is risky. Fatal, even. Draci are very similar to vampires in that giving life weakens them. For vampires, miscarriages are frequent. For Draci, maternal deaths during childbirth are most often the result. It keeps my race's numbers down."

Shit. "And Jes doesn't mind having to be there?"

"It's part of us, just as she is. Jes was there for my birth and my mother's death. I imagine she'll be there for my death, too."

So Cy had lost his mother. And unlike Dex, he hadn't even had those first few years of life with her to remember her by. "Thirty years. You said that was a Draci's average life span."

"Barring the unexpected illness. Or for females, the mixed blessing of giving birth."

"So Jes is doctor, midwife, and mortician?" Did the suffering never stop for her? Just how strong was she expected to be for the sake of others?

"Jes is everything to the Draci. We rely on her as a stabilizing force in our community. We probably rely on her too much, I know. But she encourages it, too."

"And what of her own race? Does she ever see them?"

"Jes has never associated with other vampires. She lost her parents early on and my people adopted her. She's pledged her allegiance to us. She treats Otherborn who show up here, but the rest of her time she spends trying to help her own."

"Her own, meaning the Draci?"

"Yes. You might say that being a doctor in the Draci community is a twenty-four/seven job."

"And what about what you told me when we first met? How am I Jes's life and death?"

Cy's expression became mulish. "That's something you're going to have to figure out on your own."

"And that's a bullshit answer. Am I just supposed to accept that? Hope neither of us ends up dying just like Jes is hoping the female giving birth doesn't die?"

Cy shrugged. This time, the gesture of acceptance seemed infinitely sad.

"Just so I'm clear on this...bearing children is a virtual death sentence for your females? How does your race manage to reproduce at all?"

"Draci females enter a lottery. The loser—or the winner, depending on who you're talking to—is chosen to produce. That female is revered in our community in the same way saints are in the human world."

"That's barbaric," Dex breathed out.

"It's a necessity if we want our race to survive. We're on the endangered species list as it is."

"Maybe that's where you belong. Maybe that's what nature intended."

"I've told Jes the same thing."

"And I've told you," Jes's voice suddenly reached them. "I don't believe that. And I won't stop trying to find a way to undo it."

Dex turned, ready to question what she meant by "undo it," but he was distracted by the sight of the infant she cradled in her arms.

"The mother?" Cy asked.

Jes shook her head. Cy bent his head and looked at the floor.

Dex couldn't manage the gesture of respect. The baby's smell was sweet and milky, and its eyes had opened and attached to him like a heat-seeking missile. It looked robust and healthy. Jes, however, did not. She looked pale. Tired. No wonder. She'd been up all last night and this morning.

She swayed slightly and he cursed. Grabbing her arm, he nonetheless hesitated to take the baby from her. Good thing she seemed to have a good grip on it. "Damn it. You're weak. Because you're tired or because I was gone? You didn't call."

"I'm a little weaker, but the baby's fine. Both of them are. I'm feeling better already." She pulled away and forced a smile. "Remember. I can't lie."

He reluctantly released her. "We've brought someone back with us. A mage who will put a protection spell on the castle. Cy knows her."

"If Cy trusts her, then so do I."

The statement didn't bother him as it once might have. If she drew any comfort from her relationship with Cy, Dex was glad. It told him just how much he was starting to care for Jes.

She caught him looking at the infant. "Do you want to hold her?"

He stared at the little girl in Jes's arms. He was tempted to say yes. But then he remembered the other babies he'd held. Young ones at the were orphanage. Babies who'd been hurt and abused. Babies that Dex hadn't been able to help.

Automatically, he took a step back. "Why would I want to do that?" he asked.

Jes's smile dimmed and she nodded. She took several steps back. "Just let me get the baby settled and I'll meet you and the mage in the library."

CHAPTER TWENTY-FIVE

Before meeting Jes in the library, Dex did a sweep of the castle just to make sure the shape-shifter wasn't lurking around. Cy agreed to check the main living quarters while Dex checked the lower area where the recovery rooms were located.

Dex probably should have asked Jes for permission first, but he hadn't wanted to put her in a position to say no. Or rather, he hadn't wanted to put *himself* in a position to be told *no*. She'd feel obliged to consider her ethical duties as a doctor—not to mention her privacy—and what was in her patients' best interests, but he had to consider the bigger picture—the safety of the castle's inhabitants as well as any global threat from the *diabol*s and the shape-shifters that were invoking them. In Dex's mind, the wounded shape-shifter was a potential threat simply because of what he was.

Dex winced.

Whoa. Had he actually thought that?

Talk about racial profiling, he chided himself. For a werebeast who'd suffered discrimination from the entire world, most of all from his full-blooded werewolf ancestors, he'd thought himself immune to racial bigotry. He didn't like where his thoughts had taken him.

Still, he didn't backtrack. It wasn't that he was prejudiced against shape-shifters in general, he assured himself. It was simply better to investigate now, and if he had to, apologize to the shape-shifter or Jes—or both—later.

Yet Dex didn't kid himself. There was another reason he hadn't asked Jes's permission to search the grounds for the shape-shifter. He'd had to get the hell away from her as soon as he could. Not her, exactly, but the sight of her holding that tiny, newborn baby.

The Draci baby was cute, sure, but it was the picture they'd made together that had knocked him for a loop. He'd taken one look at that baby and Jes, the vampire he was drawn to both because of her outward appearance and inner strength, and immediately imagined her cradling *his* child. Then he'd taken that image and run with it.

Soon, it would be his child she held in her arms. His child nursing at her breast.

His child being rocked to sleep while she sang to him.

His child that went to sleep only after she kissed him goodnight.

And with all those thoughts came another inescapable one—he was going to miss all of it. Going to miss seeing all the ways Jes and his baby bonded after he returned to the States. If he went through with his original plan, that is...

If?

If he went through with his original plan, meaning his plan to get revenge on his grandfather?

Since when had there been any doubt that was what he would do?

Since he'd met Jes, he realized. Even before he'd learned she was pregnant, he'd found himself doing things that did nothing to further his goal for revenge, and he hadn't cared. He'd gone to her hotel room knowing they'd fuck, but also knowing it wasn't just about fucking her. Afterward, instead of leaving, he'd stayed the night, holding her in his arms, enjoying it too much to pull himself away. And he'd even considered seeking her out in France. Couldn't deny that part of him had jumped at Mahone's request to question shape-shifters here simply because it would bring him closer to her...

So what now?

Could his original plan and his new desires be morphed into something new, a compromise that allowed him to have his revenge, work on the team, and also have a life with Jes and his child?

The logistics might prove difficult, especially given the fact they lived on different continents, but he wasn't one to turn away from a challenge.

He searched, finding no trace of the shape-shifter. Eventually, he came to the room where he'd recovered. Finding it empty, he checked the two rooms next to it and confirmed they, too, were still empty. He walked past the door that led outside to that patch of grass where Ella had been doing her cartwheels. There was one other door down the hall from it. He knocked then opened it. Empty.

He quickened his steps. At the end of the hallway, he came to a T. The path to the left led to a large door marked "No Entry." Sure enough, when he tried it, it was locked. He frowned and checked the hallway to the right. This time, he walked quite a bit before seeing another doorway. Next to it squatted a small figure, hands covering her face.

It was Ella. She appeared to be shaking while she struggled to hold back tears.

Shit. Not again.

Maybe he could turn around before she saw him.

Swiftly and soundlessly, he turned on his heel and walked a few steps. She didn't call out to him, but she suddenly sobbed, the sound aching and lost. It froze him in his tracks.

He swiped a hand over his face. Hell, he wasn't going to be able to leave with the child crying like that. Something serious could be wrong with her.

Backtracking until he towered over her, he crossed his arms over his chest. She seemed unaware of his presence. He sighed. "What's wrong?"

Ella's head jerked up and she stared at him wide-eyed before glancing away, scrubbing furiously at her face. "Nothing."

He harrumphed and sank down until he was sitting on the floor next to her with his back braced against the wall.

He didn't push her. Didn't say anything at all. He just stared at the wall across from them and twiddled his thumbs. He suddenly wished one of his Para-Ops team members was here—when it came to comforting anyone, let alone a kid, even Knox or Caleb would make more sense. Knox had kids and Caleb was a healer. Hell, the only team member who might not be a better choice than him was Wraith.

Ella glanced at him several times before wrapping her arms around her knees. Her sweater sleeves, long enough to dangle past her wrists, brushed the floor.

"I need to have tests done," she finally said, "but they hurt. I know I shouldn't be such a baby about it, but—"

Dex spoke swiftly, though a lump had formed in his throat. Ella was sick? "Fearing pain doesn't make you a baby."

"Really?"

"Nope." He paused, not sure he wanted to know, but feeling compelled to ask anyway. "These are medical tests?"

She nodded.

"And Jes says they're necessary?"

"She's explained why it's important to test my blood."

"Then you need to listen to her. She's a doctor. She's just trying to help." In fact, Dex felt better already knowing that Ella was under Jes's care. If there was anything to be done to help her, Jes wouldn't give up until she'd explored all the options.

"I know." Ella blew out a long breath, her face scrunching up as if thinking things through. "And I want to help. I want to help everyone. But I wish I didn't have to." Her eyes welled with tears but she rapidly blinked them away, obviously not wanting to cry in front of him again. "It just—it hurts."

He looked away in order to give her the privacy she needed to compose herself. Or maybe he did it so she wouldn't see his expression as memories assailed him.

It hurts, Dex. It hurts.

The voice from his past filtered through his mind and he clenched his teeth and fists in response.

The little werebeast who'd often spoken those words to him had been named Elliott. He'd been chubby when he'd first came to the were orphanage, but his frame had soon grown thin and frail. Elliott would always go to sleep in his own bed the way he was supposed to, but sometimes he'd sneak into the older boys' wing and try to crawl into bed with one of them. He'd gotten slapped down a time or two before he'd approached Dex. To this day, Dex still didn't know why, but he'd let the kid crawl into bed with him. Eventually, the boy became comfortable enough that he'd talk rather than just sleep. He'd tell Dex the horrors he'd encountered that day and more times than not, before he fell asleep, he'd tell Dex how he hurt.

Dex had never known what to say to the boy to comfort him. He'd wanted to be strong. To help. To kill the ones who hurt them. But he'd only been nine. And he'd been scared, barely managing to handle what was happening to him. So instead, he'd done nothing. Said nothing. Yet night after night, Elliott had climbed into bed with Dex and talked to him.

Until the day came that Elliott couldn't do anything anymore.

"Here's the thing," Dex said, still averting his gaze. "Sometimes, when things you don't like are happening to you, it helps to think of something else. Another place."

"You mean like pretending I'm at my favorite spot? Someplace nice?"

"Sure." Although in Dex's case, he'd mostly imagined himself somewhere horrible, a place even worse than the orphanage. He'd told himself that what he was enduring was only preparation for the greater suffering that might await him. Basic training. And in a way, he'd been right. It was because of his childhood that he'd been tough enough to survive during the War. But none of that would be helpful to this young dragon-shifter right now. "What's your favorite place?" he asked.

"The river. I love the water. I feel so peaceful when I'm near it."

Involuntarily, Dex mentally shuddered. Weres generally hated water because it was the only thing that prevented them from shifting into their immortal wolf form. Still, he tried to sound encouraging. "Okay, then when you're having your blood drawn, think of the river. That's not being a coward, that's taking control. You stay the same. You just change your circumstances."

"But the change isn't real," she argued.

"It's real in your mind. Why is that so different? What happens to you is just stuff. It's not you and it doesn't define you. You do the best you can, that's all. You can't let outside stuff affect the way you think about yourself."

She didn't look like she believed him. He had to admit, he was having a hard time selling what he was saying. Almost everyone ended up hating themselves because of the crappy stuff life threw at them. Lucy hated herself because of her heat. Before recent events, Wraith had hated herself for being the undead, unable to be touched without feeling pain. And Dex?

He resisted answering the question, but as he stared at Ella, he saw more than a scared young Draci—he saw Elliott. For him, for her, he forced himself to be honest.

Dex hated himself for what had happened to him and the other boys at the orphanage. He hated the stuff he hadn't been able to stop.

But most of all, he hated the stuff he hadn't even tried to stop.

That's why he'd craved revenge against his grandfather for so long, Dex realized. Dex had disposed of the actual perpetrators. He'd even killed Ramon, Rurik's brother, after Dex learned about Ramon's involvement with the orphanage. After that, he'd needed someone else to blame besides himself.

But maybe he'd begun to forgive himself more than he'd ever realized. Maybe that's why he hadn't been able to resist the temptation Jes represented.

Because somewhere along the way, he'd lost the need to hide from his own shame, and at the same time, he'd lost his thirst for revenge.

If all he'd really wanted was to kill his grandfather, Dex hadn't needed to strike an immunity deal with Mahone. Hell, he knew he was capable of killing the werewolf leader and disappearing so the authorities never caught him. But by striking the deal with Mahone, he'd justified his place on the Para-Ops team. What he couldn't have known was how much he'd like it. He'd experienced something he'd never felt, even when things had been good with the Ferals.

For the first time in his life, he'd belonged.

Just like he belonged with Jes. Just like he belonged right now, sitting with Ella in this hallway, helping her face something unpleasant because it was the right thing for her. Did he really want to lose his newfound place in the world for revenge?

No, he didn't.

Love. He'd never thought it was something he could have.

Did Jes love him—could she love him—or was that just wishful thinking? They hadn't known each other long at all, yet when they were together, the world just felt right.

She seemed to enjoy his company. Was certainly drawn to him physically. Whether she called it love or not, or whether he called it something else, it didn't matter. She was his. The child in her belly was his. And if accepting that meant he had to live in this castle and give up his plans for revenge against his grandfather, so be it.

Abruptly, he became aware that someone was tugging on his sleeve. He looked down, surprised to see Ella. For a second, he'd forgotten she was there.

"I asked if it works for you. Imagining you're someplace else," she clarified.

"It works," he said, his voice gruff with emotion. How could he have known that meeting this girl was what he needed to see himself and the world so clearly?

She sniffed and nodded. She raised her chin and pushed her sleeves up as if readying for battle. "Okay, I'll be brave."

She pulled herself to her feet and walked toward the nearby door. As she did, Dex caught sight of the skin on her arms. Inch-wide splotches of pink and angry red dotted the otherwise smooth surface.

The splotches resembled burns. Or the scars that covered Jes's arm. He looked harder. They looked more like strips of healing skin, as if the top layer had been ripped away in several places. Deliberately and methodically.

She'd said Jes tested her blood, but the wounds on her arms didn't look like something a disease would leave behind. They looked man-made.

"Ella, what illness do you have? Why does Jes need to take samples of your blood?"

Ella turned her head toward him just as she reached for the door handle. "Oh I'm not sick."

"What do you mean you're not sick?" He surged to his feet and held out his hand, indicating he wanted to look at her arms. "What are those marks I see?"

She frowned, glanced down, then gasped as if just realizing she'd shown him something she wasn't supposed to. She quickly pulled her sleeves in place.

"Answer me. What are those marks on your arms?"

"Nothing!" She paled to a sickly white. "I just fell down and hurt myself. When I was doing the cartwheels."

A bad feeling formed in the pit of his chest. It wasn't like that intense pain he'd felt when a *diabol* might have possessed him. This monster was different.

It hurts, Dex. It hurts.

"It's okay, Dex. It doesn't hurt, honest."

"Let me see your arms, Ella." His tone brooked no disobedience. Although Ella initially hesitated, she finally stepped closer and held out her arms. Dex tugged up her sleeves and examined the marks. The patches ran from her wrists to her elbows, the wounds shiny and still healing.

"These are skin graphs. Why? If you're not sick, why would—"

"Please don't tell Jes," Ella pleaded, on the verge of crying again. "Don't tell her you saw. She's just trying to help us."

He struggled to get past his confusion. "Us?"

"The Draci. She wants to help us live longer and I want that, too. I don't care how much it hurts. I'll do what you say and Jes will keep doing her experiments and she'll find a way to make us live longer. That's all that matters."

"She's experimenting on you?" Dex breathed out, his head starting to pound.

Dex, it hurts so much.

Denial pushed into his brain and outward. He grabbed his head and groaned. No, no. Not Jes. She made him feel good. She helped others.

Didn't she?

He swept Ella up in his arms and ran.

CHAPTER TWENTY-SIX

WASHINGTON, D.C.
FBI HEADQUARTERS

Lucy burst into Mahone's office with his secretary close on her heels.
"Ms. Talbot, you can't—"
"You bastard," she gritted out, barely restraining herself from shouting at him. "You—you stinking piece of shit!"
"I'm so sorry, sir. I tried to stop her but she—"
"It's all right, Kara," Mahone said. He didn't even bother rising from behind his desk. Instead, he leaned back and pressed his fingertips like a steeple against his chest. "Please close the door behind you."
He simply stared at her, without remorse, without guilt, as Kara shut the door.
"So what can I do for you, Lucy?"
His calm demeanor catapulted her into the stratosphere.
Before she knew what she was doing, she used her power of telekinesis to lift Mahone out of his chair and slam him hard against the window behind him. A spiderweb of fractures appeared in the glass. Mahone's eyes were so round with shock she almost laughed, but her disappointment and anger wouldn't allow it.
"You obviously don't know me very well, Mahone. By nature, I'm a pacifist, but if you needed someone willing to overlook your machinations against the Para-Ops team members, you should never have recruited me. Because if there's one thing I am, it's loyal. Let me get close to someone and I will protect him with my life. Even if I have to protect him from you."
"Does that go double for a male you're fucking?" Mahone said softly.
Lucy sucked in a breath. She didn't move. She didn't need to. The power of her thoughts sent Mahone hurtling into the right wall of his office. He grunted as picture frames broke and crashed to the floor.
"Mahone!"
Someone, presumably Kara, started to open the office door, but Lucy divided her powers in order to keep it shut. "I gave you the benefit of the doubt with Caleb. You didn't know any of us in the beginning, not really, so getting him to test Wraith was halfway understandable. But you went too far this time. Dex and I are the only active members on the team and he flew to France

despite knowing the poor reception he'd receive as a were. But he didn't know the half of it, did he, Mahone?"

"The were knows better than to let down his guard completely, Lucy. Especially when it comes to me. And if he forgot that, he needed a reminder."

As shouts and thuds continued to be heard from outside, Lucy propelled Mahone across the office into the left wall. This time, when he hit, he yelled, "Damn it, Lucy. Let me the fuck down now! That's an order!"

"An order? You think I'm going to take orders from you? You led Dex in front of a firing squad while he was completely blind. I can't help wondering how long it would have been until you'd have done the same to me."

"I had no choice, damn it. If you let me down, I can explain."

Lucy let him hang there. She couldn't imagine how he would explain his actions, but what she'd said was true. She was loyal. And a part of her, despite what she'd recently learned, still hoped her loyalty toward Mahone hadn't been misplaced.

Still, she didn't bother easing him down gently. She abruptly withdrew her power so Mahone fell heavily to the ground. He grunted but immediately sprang to his feet to glare at her, breathing hard.

"Tell them to go away," she ordered.

Mahone clenched his jaw, then called, "Kara. I'm okay. Call off security and back off. Now."

"Are you sure, Mahone? How do I know—"

"Now, Kara. Please."

Maybe it was the fact he said please, but something convinced Kara to call off Mahone's guards and leave them alone. Soon, the sounds of multiple footsteps faded and Mahone's office grew quiet. He straightened his tie and jacket, then once again took his seat behind his desk. He waved for her sit down.

Narrowing her eyes, she stepped closer but remained standing.

She caught sight of several photographs and papers on Mahone's desk before he shoved them back in their file folders. She swore she'd seen a picture of a dragon—

"What do you know? And *how* do you know?" Mahone gritted out.

"I've been doing what you asked of me, looking into shape-shifters murdering shape-shifters in the United States while Dex did the same in France. After Dex called, after you filled me in on the possible connection with dark magic, I went looking for the one shape-shifter I knew had a fondness for felines. So much so that he was willing to perform involuntary sterilizations on them in order to 'help' them."

"The shape-shifter the others caught trying to take you from that L.A. club," he guessed.

"Right. And apparently the same shape-shifter you paid a visit to before Dex left for France. The same one you had transferred to a low-security facility and hooked up with high-powered counsel. The same one who happened to witness your accidentally-on-purpose verbal slip about Dex being some kind of carrier for immortality, with the power to transfer it to others."

"Are you saying you didn't know anything about that?"

Her eyes widened. "Of course I didn't. And I'm betting Dex didn't know it, either. Is it true?"

Mahone shrugged. "I don't know. My source seems to believe it is. But whether it's true or not didn't really matter, did it?"

She laughed bitterly. "No. What mattered was setting Dex up as bait so that shape-shifters wanting to help dark spirits take over the world would have something special to offer them. What better way than offering them a host that can turn a whole bunch of other hosts into immortals?"

"And you think what, Lucy?" Mahone asked as he suddenly shot to his feet. He rounded the desk, stopping several feet from her. "That I set Dex up as bait because I hate him? Because I want him dead?"

Lucy remained stubbornly quiet. She knew that hadn't been Mahone's intentions, but she couldn't condone what he'd done.

"Of course I didn't," he said. "It was my safety plan in case Dex couldn't get any of the shape-shifters to talk to him. And that's exactly what happened. Properly motivated, the shape-shifters will go to Dex. I have enough faith in Dex's ability to take care of himself and fend off any attacks."

"How convenient for you," Lucy said.

With a disgusted shake of his head, Mahone snatched up objects that had fallen to the floor when she'd smashed him into the wall. He stacked frames together and tossed shards of glass in the waste bin. Finally, he stood and stared at her with his hands on his hips.

"Why didn't you just tell Dex?" she asked, then frowned. "Or did you? Am I wrong about that?"

"No. You're not wrong. I didn't give him any warning."

"Why?"

"Because that would have led him in a certain direction and it might have been the wrong one. It was better that he investigate without preconceived ideas. Plus, Dex doesn't know anything about this so-called gift, Lucy. And I don't even know if it's true. If I'd told him, he would have been distracted, wondering why his grandfather hadn't told him or if it was the reason his grandfather sent him away. Which, by the way, I think it is. I didn't have anyone else I could rely on. I needed you here. Him there. I couldn't afford to lose either one of you! Plus—"

He bit off what he was about to say.

"Plus what?" Lucy prodded.

Mahone shook his head.

"Tell me, Mahone!" Lucy shrieked.

She must have looked ready to hurl Mahone into the window again because he started talking.

"I didn't tell him because I knew he'd ask me how I'd found out and wouldn't have stopped until I'd told him. Again, Dex would have been out of his mind, wanting revenge. He'd have gone to France all right, but not to talk to the shape-shifters. He'd have been too busy hunting down the vampire who'd not only fucked him, but fucked him over."

Lucy drew back in shock. "Jesmina? She came to you with some story about Dex? When?"

"Before he left. Before he slept with her."

"He—he actually slept with her?"

"Unless they were playing poker all night. Does that bother you, Lucy?"

She shook her head in confusion. "What? That she slept with Dex knowing she'd betrayed him?"

"No. That she slept with him at all."

"Dex is free to have sex with anyone he wants."

"Even when he's supposed to be having sex with you? No one told me, by the way. I figured it out on my own. He's very protective of you."

"He cares about me. Maybe too much, which he'd be horrified to hear. But I regretted accepting Dex's offer to help me with my heat almost immediately. So no, it doesn't bother me to know he slept with the vampire. It gives me hope he's finally found someone that can mean something to him. At least, she might have meant something to him if she hadn't screwed him in another way altogether. I need to talk to him—"

"And tell him what? That I set him up?"

"Why shouldn't he know? If you're right, shape-shifters and dark spirits are gunning for him because they think he's some kind of legend and—"

"Dex already knows he's in danger. He knows to be wary of shape-shifters even as he seeks them out. What will telling him any of this serve? Other than pissing him off and risking that he'll abandon the two things that, as far as I can tell, mean the most to him—his place on the team and Jesmina."

"So you're doing him a favor?"

"No. I need Dex's head in the game, not on his own shit, but if Dex's personal life benefits, too, then all the better. He's happy, which makes him a team player, one who owed me in a way."

"You're incredible, Mahone. But I'm his friend. I can't let him get further involved with Jes without telling him she played him."

"But you came to me before talking to Dex about the legend. Why? Because you trust me. Because part of you knew I'd kept that from him for a good reason."

He was right, Lucy thought. She didn't like it, but he was right.

"And you trusted Jes, too, didn't you, Lucy? Trusted her enough to think that she could have been special to Dex. You know what? I think the same thing. Jes might not have been completely honest with Dex, but she's a good person. One who might be able to give Dex everything he's ever wanted. You gonna be the person that takes that away from him?"

"Damn you. You'll never play fair, will you?" But Mahone's words were having their desired effect. Lucy was actually considering not telling Dex what she'd learned. After all, he knew about the most important things now—the connection between the shape-shifters and dark spirits, and the threat they posed to him. Given that, the rumor about his alleged gift and Jes's knowledge of it didn't seem significant. On the other hand, what if Mahone was right? What if Jes really could mean something to Dex? Lucy had believed the same thing from the beginning. Did she want to ruin any hope Jes had of winning Dex's heart?

"So now what?" Mahone asked.

She sighed. "Now you need to stop what you set in motion. We need to give the rebel shape-shifters what they want. Before it's too late."

CHAPTER TWENTY-SEVEN

Jes and the mage were waiting in the library for Dex to arrive when he suddenly burst in. She stood and smiled at him. Despite his resistance to holding the newborn Draci baby, she'd seen the way he'd looked at them. With fear, yes, but also wistfulness. "Dex—"

"You damn bitch," he snarled, coming at her so fast he was on her in seconds. He grabbed Jes's arm and drove her backward until her back bumped up against the wall. He didn't hurt her. Hadn't shoved her hard enough to hurt her. But he was trembling and she could feel the effort he was making not to unleash his anger on her.

Her eyes darted to the mage. Had he been possessed by the *diabol* again? Why was he looking at her like that? Like she disgusted him? Like he hated her again?

"You're running fucking experiments here, aren't you? To find a way to prolong Draci life?"

She stared at him, too stunned to respond. Had he found out why she'd sought him out? Did he know she'd taken his blood? How? But did it really matter? Shame swept through her. Shame and fear. Fear not just for her child, but for herself. She wanted her baby beyond imagining, but she couldn't deny what she'd been fantasizing about, either. She wanted Dex, too. She wanted both of them.

"Answer me!" he shouted.

"Dex, perhaps you need to—"

He turned to the blond mage. "I'm not talking to you and I haven't been possessed by anything other than my own fury. This is between her and me, got it?"

The mage's gaze darted to Jes, then back to him. "Then let her go and I'll let you talk to her. But she's pregnant, and I'm not going to let you manhandle her in front of me. If I have to, I'll use the same power that enables me to keep demons away to send you straight to hell."

A slight exaggeration, Jes was sure, since she'd never heard of a mage that powerful. Still, Dex turned back to Jes. Studied her. Instinctively, she knew he saw the shame that she'd felt just now, but he clenched his jaw and breathed in furious breaths before slowly releasing her.

Both Jes and the mage let out sighs of relief.

"Say it. I'm right, aren't I? About the experiments."

"It's been my life work," she admitted. "To find a way to prolong life. Not just for the Draci, but for all mortal races."

"Is that supposed to make a difference? That's even worse!"

"Why?"

"Because you're using Ella, a little Draci girl, and you're willing to hurt her so you can find a cure for people she doesn't even know."

Ella? "What are you talking about, Dex? What did Ella tell you?" A strange hope filled her. Maybe this was just some kind of misunderstanding. Maybe the hate in his eyes would disappear as soon as he realized that.

"She told me she didn't want to have her blood drawn because it hurts. But that you said she needed to, so she was willing to do it!"

Okay, so he had his facts straight. Hope vanished and guilt once again replaced it. She'd known drawing blood from Ella would hurt the girl a little, of course, even if the pain was minimal, but she'd given her the option of helping because she'd seen it as the girl's right. Jes had never thought the blood tests were something that haunted her. Unable to stand the disgust contorting Dex's face, she tried to explain. For some reason, even though the opinion of others hadn't swayed her before, it seemed imperative she convince Dex she wasn't a person to revile. "I've explained to her it was important, but I've never pressured her. I've never forced her. I've merely given her the facts and the choice."

"She's seven! She shouldn't be making a choice like that."

"Dex, I've explained that even at seven, Ella is emancipated in the eyes of the Draci. I have to treat her that way, as well." She frowned. "Besides, the procedure is slightly uncomfortable, yes, but if it gets too bad, I stop."

"Until you start up again, you mean."

This time, his sneer of disgust didn't hurt her so much as anger her. He had no idea the type of pressure she was under. That with every hour that passed, her failure to find a cure for the Draci, or for the werewolf slowly wasting away in this very abbey, haunted her. Instinctively, she took a step forward, thrusting her face closer to his.

"You think I want to cause her pain? That I want to cause anyone pain? I don't, but sometimes doctors have to cause pain to heal, Dex."

He pointed toward the doorway. "She's not sick. She doesn't need to be healed."

"I'm trying to prolong the lifespan of an entire race. I can't do that by myself," she cried.

"So you do it by using children. Children who can't refuse. And to think I was talking her into cooperating until I realized it was unnecessary."

"That's a matter of opinion and it hasn't been hers."

"You disgust me," he said.

Somehow, the words hurt her more than the expression on his face had. She felt her mind close in on itself, erecting walls to block him out, telling herself he simply didn't understand the importance of the work she did. "I'm sorry you feel that way, but you can't possibly understand their situation. Or the situation of most mortals. Your natural life span is six to eight times longer than the Draci. Does that seem fair to you? If I can help prolong their lives at very little cost to anyone else, why shouldn't I?"

"Little cost?" He shook his head in disbelief. "What about the Draci? Have you even bothered to ask what they want? Because as far as I can tell, most of them seem quite content. You're all fired up to extend their lives so they'll be more like you, so you won't have to be alone, but is that even what they want?"

"Of course it's what they want! You think you know them? *Je les vois tous le temps.* I see them every day. How they mourn for each other. How they long for the time to do things they'll never be able to. Be more. Go more. Do more. Don't tell me you know them, because you don't."

He gripped her chin, his fingers still gentle although his eyes flared with fury. "Oh but I do know you, Jes. I know that you're so obsessed with yourself that you can't accept others can live fulfilling lives even if they're not like you. You're so selfish, you don't care about peeling the skin off of a young girl as long as it advances your agenda. You dish out pain and poor kids like Ella just have to take it."

She jerked her chin out of his grasp. "*Qu'est que t'en parle?* What do you mean I peel the skin off a young girl?"

"I saw the graft scars on Ella's arm, Jes. She admitted they were for the experiments and begged me not to tell you!"

Again, although there was no hope this time, confusion barreled down on her. "Wait. Ella showed you these scars? She told you they were for experiments?"

"Why are you bothering to act surprised? Yes, she did. They were—"

She grabbed his arm. "Where is she?"

"What?" He looked down at her hand as if he wanted to fling it off her. Instinctively she released him. "Where is she, Dex?"

"You think I'm going to tell you? She's waiting someplace safe while I—"

She laughed harshly. "While you what? Accuse me of torturing a child for my own selfish whims? I've never asked Ella to undergo skin grafts. I've never performed them on her!"

He stared at her, eyes narrowing suspiciously. "What are you saying? That she was lying?"

"If you saw the scars, no. But did she specifically tell you I was doing the treatments?"

He pursed his lips, considering what she'd asked. Slowly, he shook his head. "No. She said you drew her blood. And when I saw her scars, she begged me not to tell you. I assumed—"

Yeah, he assumed I was a monster, she thought. Because obviously that's what he believed of her. He probably still believed she'd tricked him into getting her pregnant.

He pressed his lips together. "So if you didn't perform skin grafts on Ella, who did?"

A name immediately came to mind, but she had to be careful. She wasn't going to repeat Dex's mistake by accusing anyone of something so horrific without more evidence. "*Je ne sais pas exactement.* There's really only one logical explanation but—"

"Amanda, right? She's medically trained."

She swallowed loudly. To avoid answering him, she turned toward the mage only to find she'd managed to sneak out without either of them noticing. She turned back to Dex. "I need to talk to Ella. I need to see her right now. So please, take me to her."

"I can't. You'd have to go outside. In the sun."

"If she's still on the grounds, it doesn't matter. Tell me."

His expression was unreadable as he stared at her. His jaw ticked. Then he said, "I took her home."

***

An hour later, Dex stood to the side and watched as Jes argued with Amanda, who they'd found working in the laboratory.

"As a Draci, Ella's skin can transform itself to stone and back again. It's a form of regeneration—*stone doesn't age*—and you might be able to replicate the process. I knew you wouldn't ask her because of the pain the test would cause, but having Draci blood isn't enough," Amanda insisted, her tone pleading. "The pain was minimal. If you're going to find the key to prolonging life, if you're going to help my—"

"You went too far, Amanda. I trusted you to treat my patients in my absence, and you betrayed that trust. I want you to pack up your things and leave. Today."

"You know I can't do that. Not without—"

"He can't be moved. If you want, you can stay at an inn in the village and visit, but only when I'm present. Otherwise, I'll tell him what you did myself. I'll bring him Ella and show him."

Amanda turned her head and glared at Dex. "This is because of him. He's turning you against us. Distracting you from your duty."

"No one can distract me from my duty, Amanda. Not even you."

Amanda looked like she wanted to say more, but Jes cut her off. "Go. Now. If you say anything else, I'll retract your access to the castle altogether. I don't want to do that."

After a tense moment, Amanda stalked past Dex and out of the room. Good riddance, he thought.

Jes closed her eyes, leaned against a tall counter-high lab table, then held a hand to her temple as if it ached.

To avoid the sun, she'd led him through a maze of underground tunnels to reach Ella's cottage. There, the girl told Jes how Amanda had come to her while Jes was in the States. Amanda had insisted they do the skin grafting on their own. She'd told Ella that even though Jes believed the grafting was necessary, she was too weak to ask Ella herself, and that Amanda and Ella needed to be strong enough to do the right thing for her.

As he'd listened to Ella's tearful explanation, Dex knew she'd been telling the truth. And that meant Jes had known nothing about the skin grafting.

He felt like shit for how he'd treated her. Even so, he told himself to be realistic. She'd admitted she was testing Ella's blood to further her life-prolonging experiments. Maybe she hadn't authorized the skin grafts Amanda had performed, but would she hesitate to do them if she really thought it would help her cause?

The question nagged at him, but he couldn't bring himself to ask Jes. Not now. She looked tired. Drained. And that's exactly how he felt, too. Just an hour earlier, he'd been ready to give up his revenge against his grandfather. To open himself up to a fantasy—one in which he devoted his life to Jes and their baby. Maybe that had been foolish, but he mourned the loss of his dream. And he regretted being the cause of the pain Jes was now suffering.

"I'm sorry," he said.

Her head jerked up and she looked confused, as if she'd really forgotten he was there. "Why? You came to Ella's defense because you thought I was hurting her. I'm glad you did."

"I should have listened to her more carefully. I should have known you wouldn't hurt her that way."

Her mouth twisted. "But you couldn't have known that, Dex. How could you, when I don't even know it myself?" she asked tiredly.

When he didn't answer, she raised a brow. "Shocked?"

He still didn't answer. He didn't know what to say. He'd been thinking it himself. Only he knew she wasn't that selfish. She'd been willing to let him go despite the fact his absence might endanger the baby.

"I don't agree with what Amanda did," she continued. "I certainly don't condone it. But I also don't believe the skin grafting was necessary to accomplish what we want. If I did, if I truly thought skin grafting was the key to finding the secret to immortality, would I hesitate to explore that theory because it would cause Ella pain? *Je ne sais pas*."

"*I* know." he said quietly. Despite his previous doubt, he spoke without hesitation. He stepped closer, until there was barely any space between them.

She shook her head and raised her fist, then repeatedly hit him in the chest, although the force she exerted was negligible. "How can you say that?"

He wrapped his fingers gently around her wrist, holding her hand against him when she would have pulled away. "Because you couldn't even ask me to stay with you for three weeks to save the baby once you knew it wasn't what I wanted. And you arranged for Cy to take me to the village even when you knew it might weaken you. You think of what you need and what those you love need, Jes, but you always temper that by considering what you're asking of others. I just lost sight of that for a while. I'm sorry." He cupped her chin with his other hand and tilted her face up. "I'm so sorry."

She frowned, obviously struggling to accept what he was saying. When she finally nodded, he drew her into his arms. He rested his cheek on the top of her head and breathed in deeply.

He rocked her for several minutes, until she closed her eyes and seemed to fall asleep. But he knew she hadn't and something was still bothering him.

Something triggered by the similarity between Ella's graft wounds and the scars on Jes's arm. "Can I ask you something?" he asked.

Her eyes fluttered open and she leaned back. "Of course."

He lifted her arm, pushed back her sleeve, and lightly brushed his fingertips against the thick-ridged scars crisscrossing her skin. Again, she tried to pull away. Again, he wouldn't let her. "What happened?"

***

Jes winced at Dex's question. "I know it's ugly." She also knew she couldn't tell him the truth. Lord, given the way he'd reacted to Ella's wounds—

"No," he said. "It's not ugly. Nothing about you could ever be ugly."

Her chest felt too tight. She wished that were true, but Dex had seen the ugliness inside her. He'd made a mistake by believing she'd performed skin grafts on Ella, but that didn't mean he was completely wrong about her. She was willing to do bad things for her cause.

She'd lied to him. She'd taken his blood without asking.

In some way, her scars were the outward manifestation of the ugliness inside her.

He continued to caress her scars and eventually, amazingly, she stopped fighting him altogether. The air seemed to thicken and wrap around them, making her mind feel fuzzy and her blood roll through her veins like honey oozing through a straw. Her heart pulsed and, between her thighs, desire throbbed in an echoing beat.

"How did you come to be with the Draci?" he asked softly, either forgetting his earlier question or deciding not to push her. His fingers trailed up her arm and across her shoulder until he cupped the side of her head. His thumb stroked her cheek. His touch felt so good that she didn't stiffen at his probing, personal question. "I mean, I know they adopted you, but did your family know them? Is that why you were sent here?"

She nuzzled his hand before his questions registered. When they did, she gasped and pulled away. She immediately mourned the loss of his touch, but they were walking on treacherous ground. She didn't want to lie to him, not any more than she already had, but she couldn't just blurt out that his grandfather had been the one to save her and bring her to the Draci.

She tried to give him an answer that, while not completely truthful, wasn't a lie either. "You know it's very dangerous for Draci women to have kids."

Dex nodded and reached out to touch her again, rubbing her arm in small circles. Then he bent down and lightly kissed her throat.

The affectionate gesture, committed so casually, startled her. Something about him seemed different. Now that he no longer believed she'd hurt Ella, he was acting as if he liked her. Maybe even—She trembled and tried to keep her mind clear.

"After I lost my parents, I—I was brought here because the Draci queen wanted a child but the king didn't want to risk her life. My benefactor knew that giving me to her would finalize a peace treaty that had just been instituted between his race and hers. So I became her daughter. And she loved me like her own. I loved her and we were happy for ten years until she died. Then I was sent to live with a new family, and then a new one, each one welcoming me as their own. I've never lacked for love."

"Why do you sound surprised? Of course they loved you. Who wouldn't?"

She suddenly couldn't breathe. He looked as shell-shocked as she felt. As if he'd just realized what he'd implied—that even *he* couldn't resist loving her either. But despite having almost thought it herself, that Dex could love her was crazy. Wishful thinking resulting from the gentle way he was touching her. Still, she was so shaken by the idea of Dex loving her, too intent on denying the possibility, that she spoke without her normal caution.

"Part of them loved me because I served a need for them. Do you really think I'm the first to try to find the secret of prolonging life?"

With horror, she realized what she'd said almost immediately.

Dex didn't miss a thing. "What's that supposed to mean?" he growled.

She shook her head and backed several steps away. "I shouldn't have said anything. It doesn't matter—"

For every backward step she took, he moved forward, tracking her with a predator's glint in his eye. "The hell it doesn't. Are you saying the Draci used you while trying to find a way to prolong life? Did they experiment on you? Is that what your scars are from?"

Fool, she berated herself. But it was too late to shake him off the scent. Instead, she said, "The clan's seer, an old Draci named Rita, she was certain I was the key to prolonging Draci life. She convinced the others to do tests. But I wasn't forced. They gave me the option, too."

Dex paled, as if she'd told him something too horrible to imagine. But it hadn't been like that.

"How old were you?"

"I was eight."

"And not a Draci eight, but a vampire eight, which means you were considered a child. Too young to make that kind of choice."

She smiled sadly. "I was eight, but I was quite mature. Probably more mature than even Ella. *C'est bien*, Dex. I just meant I served an important role for the Draci, but it doesn't mean they loved me any less. In some ways, I think they loved me even more because they envied what I had. The long life they'd never have. They cherished me."

His gaze flickered to her arm. "Jesus, they cut you. Repeatedly. And you let them?"

She sighed. "They did what they thought was needed and what I agreed to. It hurt but I was always glad to give what I could for them. I still am. The Draci are my family. I love them and I will always fight to help them. Please, I don't want to talk about it anymore. It's part of who I am, but it's not my present. Not my future."

He didn't look ready to let the matter drop but he seemed to calm. "And I called you selfish? Damn, you're so selfless it scares me. But despite what an ass I've been, despite thinking the worst about you concerning Ella, I want you to know this, Jes. I know you're going to make a wonderful mother to our baby."

He lowered his hand and cupped her belly. There was no mistaking it now; her belly had thickened with her pregnancy. Given the way his brows lifted, she could tell he'd noticed the change.

"The baby's growing much faster than normal." She covered his hand with hers and, despite everything, let herself feel hope again. "You're not angry about the baby anymore?"

"I'm in awe of the baby's mother. How can I be angry? I'm going to stay with you, Jes. I—I want to be part of the baby's life. And your life, too. I don't know what that'll look like, but I'd like to explore it with you. If you want the same thing. Do you?"

She could hardly believe what he was saying. At first she thought this must be some kind of trick. But as she looked at him she saw his sincerity, as well as the hint of fear that edged it. Fear that she would reject him.

How could he think she'd reject him? He'd given her everything. He'd given her even more by wanting to share it with her. She pulled him into her embrace.

Whispered, "Yes."

And kissed him.

***

There was something sacred about the way Dex returned Jes's kiss. Nothing about it resembled the way he'd kissed his other lovers. It was also nothing like the way he'd previously kissed her. He noticed the difference immediately. He was more tentative, less focused on the clamoring demands of his body and more concerned with the foreign emotions that were swirling through him. And what was more astonishing was that he wasn't even bothering to deny or fend off those emotions.

Not anymore.

He loved her, he finally admitted to himself.

In the private recesses of his mind, he could say it. He loved this female.

That's why this kiss was so different. He'd never kissed a female he was in love with before. Never been so scared.

What terrified him most wasn't what he was feeling, but that Jes would guess. She already influenced him, more than he'd ever thought possible. He could imagine the power she'd wield if she actually knew how much he wanted to be inside her, but also how much he longed for her to be inside him. Her fangs, her body, her heart. He wanted to absorb all there was of her so he could keep her safe and carry her with him always. For an eternity.

With a sigh, she wrapped her arms around his neck. He reveled in her embrace and locked his hands together at the small of her back. Her breasts pushed against the hard planes of his chest, her nipples drilling into him, prodding him into action.

He swept her up in arms, breaking their kiss despite the way her mouth chased his. "I want a bed this time. Your bed. Where is it?"

"On the top floor."

She directed him to her room, apparently not caring that someone might see them. When he reached her bedroom door and walked through it, he was eerily reminded of how a groom traditionally carried his bride over the threshold. The gesture gained even more significance given he'd never actually been in a woman's bedroom before. All the others—including Lucy and even Jes in L.A—he'd always fucked in hotels rooms. It felt strange being granted access to Jes's intimate space but only after he'd been given the same access to her body. Strange but good.

The shadowed room was decorated in cream and rose and sage. It was more feminine than he'd expected it to be, with romantic iron candelabras bolted to the stone wall, the burned-down candles telling him she liked the ambience they provided. Wall-to-wall bookshelves were filled with the same kinds of bound books he'd seen in the library. Another chaise had been strategically placed in front of a large fireplace, but he ignored it for the bed.

It was a queen, smaller than he would have liked. Plush pillows were propped against the iron scroll headboard, virtually covering the top half. Holding her to him with one arm, he shoved at the pillows, sending them tumbling off the other side of the bed. Only when the linens were clear did he lower her to the mattress.

She gazed at him with a serious expression, her brow furrowed.

"What is it?" he asked, praying she hadn't changed her mind about wanting him. Now, here in her bed, or later, in her life.

"I—" She shook her head. "Nothing. It's just... You were so angry with me. And now you're being so gentle."

"Yeah," he sighed as he smoothed her hair away from her face. "I'm a bundle of contradictions. I don't know what the hell I'm doing here. I'm just— I'm just glad I'm here."

"Me, too, Dex. Me, too."

She opened her arms wide, beckoning him to her, and with a groan he lowered himself until his body covered hers. Pressed against her, he couldn't help noticing once again that she'd gained weight in her middle. Earlier in the lab, when he'd flattened his palm against her and felt the outward manifestation of her pregnancy, an electric current had zipped up his arm, connecting the three of them—him, Jes, and their baby. For the first time, he'd felt the evidence of his child within her, and along with it, an inescapable awareness of its growing vitality.

The irrefutable evidence of the baby's existence had shocked him enough to eradicate all hesitation and doubt. He'd flirted with the idea of giving up his quest for revenge for Jes and the baby, but as he'd cradled the life in Jes's belly, he'd committed himself to it. He'd never felt more sure about anything and that had given him the strength to voice what he wanted. He'd allowed himself to be vulnerable because the chance of getting what he wanted—in this case, Jes and the baby—had seemed well worth the risk of rejection.

Electricity once again coursed through his body and he wondered if she felt the same thing, for she trembled, as well. She hugged his hips with her thighs and lifted her hands to frame his face. Her gaze wandered over him, as if she was searching for an answer to some unknown question. When she smiled, he breathed a sigh of relief, overcome with the knowledge that whatever she'd been looking for, she'd found.

"*S'il te plait*. Kiss me," she urged.

She didn't have to ask twice. He pressed his mouth against hers and his control slipped. His dick throbbed, urging him to celebrate their newfound connection in the most primal way possible. But he was suddenly afraid of making the wrong move. Of breaking the fragile almost holy bond that had seemed to form between them.

Uncertain in bed for the first time in his life, he broke away from her and rolled until she was on top of him, her eyes rounded, her fingers digging into his shoulders. He planted his feet on the mattress and raised his knees, then gently pressed on her shoulders until she leaned back. He'd never let a lover top him before, so this would be another first, and his anticipation was enough to make him dizzy.

She recovered fast. With a saucy smile, she moved her hips, rubbing her bottom against his painfully aching shaft until he wanted to howl in frustration. But he had invited this. Needed it. And now he'd let her play all she wanted.

As she undressed him, her hands shook with need. She kissed every patch of skin she revealed, pausing a particularly long time to suck at his flat brown nipples. He buried his hands in her hair and held her head close. Then, without even knowing he was doing it, he pushed her head downward, directing her to his dick. As he peered down at her, he could see she was smiling and that her hands were steadier as she unsnapped and unzipped his pants.

She licked her lips as if her mouth was watering for him. She tugged him out of his pants and enveloped the tip of his dick in her mouth. He groaned and fell back as she sucked hungrily. As if she couldn't get enough of him. Her hands joined her lips, firmly clasping the base of his shaft even as her mouth took him deeper. She kept going until her lips met her own fingers and then she slowly pulled back. She did it again and again, sucking harder, moving faster until the sounds of her sucking combined with the tight clasp of her mouth and shoved him over the edge.

Greedily, without hesitation, she swallowed his seed. When she finally raised her head and licked her lips, he cupped her beneath her arms and dragged her up his body. Not bothering with the rest of her clothes, he shoved down her pants and underwear, and plunged two fingers inside her. She screamed with pleasure as her muscles clenched and fluttered around him. He withdrew his fingers, stirring them around her cleft, then parted her flesh and positioned her over him.

As a were, he had greater sexual stamina than most, but even he was amazed at how hard he still was. He ached for her. He couldn't imagine a time when he wouldn't.

"Take me," Dex growled. "Take all—" She impaled herself on him, taking every rock-hard inch. Before he could catch his breath, she lifted herself up then slammed down on him again. She flew into motion, riding him for all she was worth.

"Oh Goddess," Dex gasped, grasping her hips but determinedly not guiding her. It was exactly what she was in his mind. A goddess. He wanted all of her. He wanted to know that every move she made was hers alone, spurred on by her sheer desire for him.

Her hands lifted to cup her own breasts and she tweaked her nipples, harder than he would have expected. She mewled and flung her head back. "Dex, it feels so good. Soooo….goooood."

"Oh yeah," he growled as she began shaking with her release. She ground against him, keeping him lodged deep as he reared up to kiss her. He swallowed her moans as she came. When she collapsed on top of him, he rolled until she was once more beneath him.

His dick, as heavy as a metal pipe, couldn't hold still. It slid out of her and then back inside again, the movements as smooth as pistons. He butted against a special spot inside her that made her gasp, and in seconds she once again hovered on the edge of orgasm.

"Yes. Come again, Jes. Come with me." His gaze held hers so she couldn't look away. As her hips rolled, searching for the pleasure that only he could give her, he slipped his hand between them and pressed against her clit. She went bow-tight, then exploded.

"Yes," she sobbed. "Dex, *Jes t'aime*. I love you so much."

He jerked and squeezed his eyes shut as her words set off his release.

Jes, he thought. His body shook and shuddered. She was the only female to ever take his seed inside her body, and that knowledge kept him pouring into her, one stream of come following the other until he was sure she'd suck him dry. She was pinned beneath him, his cock shoved up inside her, his heavy weight making it impossible for her to escape even if she'd wanted to, but he was the one who felt helpless. Powerless.

And at the same time, he felt more powerful than he ever had.

CHAPTER TWENTY-EIGHT

Jes struggled to breathe in enough air. She was on the verge of tears, overwhelmed not only by the pleasure Dex had drawn from her, but also by the emotions. For some reason, when she was in his arms, she was able to forget her research and her experiments. Forget he was a legend who could gift another with immortality. Her heart and soul didn't think of Dex that way. She saw him only as an honorable male who could be a wonderful father and partner if he'd only let go of the horrors of his past.

Sweeping her hands over his muscular back, Jes decided it was time to tell him about his grandfather. Dex deserved to know Bodin wasn't the monster Dex thought him to be. After all, Dex had been wrong about her and Ella's skin grafts; because of that, maybe it would be easier for him to accept he'd been wrong about his grandfather, too. She couldn't endanger Bodin by alerting Dex to his presence on the grounds, but she could at least try to pave the way for peace between them. "Dex," she said. "Do you remember when I told you someone brought me to the Draci? After my parents were killed?"

"Hmmm," he said, even as he lifted his head to kiss her. He groaned as he rolled to his side, then propped himself on one elbow and drew lazy circles on her belly with his fingertips. Instinctively, her stomach muscles clenched, her desire renewed far faster than she would have thought possible.

She inhaled, trying to memorize his scent. His touch. "Dex—"

"Has it been hard for you? Adjusting to life here?"

"Not really," she murmured. "I was so young when I came to live with them. It wasn't long before I barely remembered living with other vampires."

His fingers moved to her arm, first the unmarred one, then the other. His fingertips traced her scars the way they often did and she knew his frown wasn't because the scars were ugly, but because they evidenced the pain she'd gone through getting them. "Your parents were killed?" he asked. "As in murdered?"

"Yes," she answered, even as she tried to block the rash of awful images his question brought to her mind. Images of her mother and father, staked down beside her, trying to comfort her as the sun rose.

"Don't look," her father yelled.

"Close your eyes, Jessie love, and it'll soon be over. Please, close your eyes" her mother begged.

And as she always did, Jessie listened to her parents. Because she was so young, because she hadn't acquired vamp powers or weaknesses, she wouldn't burn in the sun, but her parents would. She couldn't bear to see it. She closed her eyes but they flew open when something landed with a thud beside her. A werewolf, like the others. He tore off her restraints. She immediately tried lunging toward her parents, but the werewolf picked her up and ran.

"No!" she screamed. "Mama. Daddy!"

Sunlight painted the ground and moved inexorably closer to where her parents lay. They stared at her, matching smiles of relief on their otherwise terrified faces just before the light hit them. Simultaneously, they flinched.

The werewolf carried her under a sheltering tree and covered her body with his. By twisting her head to the side, she could still see her parents' writhing bodies. She fought to get away from him, but within seconds her parents burst into flames.

Jes closed her eyes and turned away, sobbing.

The werewolf said he was sorry her parents had been killed. That he'd protect her until the sun went down. For hours, she'd been too traumatized to tell him the sun couldn't hurt her because she hadn't reached puberty.

"Don't look at them," he urged when she would have done so. "Remember how they were. Remember how they loved you."

And that's exactly what she'd been trying to do ever since. Trying to remember her parents and how much they loved her, and trying to make them proud.

Bodin was the only reason she'd survived that day. If he hadn't arrived, the werewolves who'd left them to burn would have seen she was still alive and killed her themselves. She owed him her life and her loyalty. But would the fact Bodin had saved her be enough for Dex to overcome a lifetime of hatred? Could he ever forgive his grandfather for what Bodin had done to him?

"So we're both orphans," Dex said quietly. "Did Ella's mother die in childbirth?"

"Yes." Ella's mother, Helen, had been Jes's friend. Almost like a sister.

"What about her father?"

Jes smiled sadly. "He died when she was three. That's when she came to live with me."

"When did she move into her own quarters?"

"When she was five. That still bothers you, doesn't it? That she had to fend for herself so soon?"

"It's just hard to wrap my mind around. She looks too small and fragile to be emancipated."

"She'll begin to age faster over the next few years. But I know the concept of Draci family is a weird one for most people to accept."

"I've never had any kind of family so I really shouldn't talk about what's normal or not."

"No family at all?" she asked, even though she knew better.

"No. I—I was abandoned by my maternal grandfather."

It was such a small thing, but the way he'd opened up to her made her feel so much closer to him. She shifted, raising a hand to stroke his cheek.

"What about your *maman*?"

He flinched, but caught her hand when she would have withdrawn it. He pressed it against his skin. "She killed herself before I was twelve. Because of Bodin, my grandfather. One of the instructors at the were orphanage took great joy in telling me. After my grandfather sent me away seventy-five years ago, she stayed with her pack, but losing me was her death sentence. He hated me for being a half-breed, but she loved me. I only have snatches of memory but I remember her gentleness most of all. Her voice. She used to sing to me."

"And your father?"

"I never knew him. Not even his name."

So much pain, Jes thought. In some ways, Dex blamed himself for his mother's death, just like she blamed herself for not being able to save her parents. He didn't even know his father had been vampire. What a sad pair they made. "Have you ever tried getting in touch with your grandfather?"

"Not yet. But I will. Soon. That's one of the reasons I was reluctant to stay until the baby was born."

He spoke in the past tense. As he'd indicated earlier, he now wanted to stay with her. But her happiness dimmed when she realized he still intended to kill Bodin. She dropped her hand.

"You must hate him," she whispered.

"I've never hated anyone more."

"Because he sent you away?"

"That. And because of my mother. Because he's such a power-mongering bigot that he cared about nothing but keeping his werewolf line pure."

"But what if—what if your grandfather didn't send you away because he hated that you were a half-breed? What if he did it to protect you?"

Dex laughed bitterly. "Well, there's no chance of that, so…"

"There is a chance, Dex." She took a bracing breath, pulled away, and sat up. "In fact, that's what I believe happened."

He stiffened and slowly sat up, as well. "What the hell are you talking about? How do you know anything about it?"

"Because—because I met your grandfather. Bodin. A long time ago. And he always struck me as being an honorable, kind individual."

"You met my—" He shook his head. "Bodin denounced me. Sent me off to a were orphanage to be—to be on my own. He never visited. Never wrote. He didn't give a shit about me."

"But that doesn't mean he didn't care. Maybe he felt it was better for you if he stayed away."

"Better for me? To be beaten? Starved? Abused? Because that's what happened to the boys at that orphanage. And no one did a damn thing to stop it, least of all him."

"Oh Dex, *je suis si désolé*." She kissed his shoulder and then the other, smoothing her hands over them when they trembled. "But maybe your grandfather didn't know."

"He knew."

"I—I don't think he did."

"Like you would know." He laughed. Shook his head. Once again moved away from her. "What the hell's going on, Jes? Just how did you meet my grandfather?"

"I met him before I came here, Dex."

"How?"

"He's the werewolf who brought me to the Draci."

CHAPTER TWENTY-NINE

VAMPIRE DOME
PORTLAND, OREGON

"I need you to contact Zeph." Mahone kept his voice insistent despite his uncertainty and frustration. "All my attempts to do so have failed." What Mahone didn't say was that his frustration wasn't solely the result of Zeph Prime dodging him.

Oh no. With each passing hour, Mahone found himself more and more frustrated with the bitch who seemed to take pleasure in his misery. After Lucy's little visit, he and the Goddess Essenia had had the mother of all showdowns. He was still surprised he'd managed to survive. He hadn't meant to be so disrespectful, but how the hell did she expect him to respond to her constant, "I know all and see all but I'm compelled not to tell you" bullshit? How could something powerful enough to create life or end it have her hands tied when it came to telling him how to find Zeph Prime or being able to send some sorry-ass demons back to hell?

"I don't know where my brother is," Knox responded.

"Don't bullshit me, Knox." Mahone barely refrained from pulling his hair out. He paced Knox's study, not missing the way Lucy's and Felicia's gazes flitted between him and Knox. "I believe you when you say you don't know, otherwise you couldn't have said it, but I know you—you would have arranged for a way to get in touch with Zeph, no matter how pissed off you were that he was working with me. I'm telling you, you need to send out the bat signal. We need him to act as our representative with the Quorum."

"Our representative?" Knox sneered. "You mean our negotiator. But I'm not negotiating with the organization that placed a hit on my wife. And I thought the U.S. government didn't negotiate with terrorists either."

"As a general rule, we don't. And that's certainly the President's stance. Me? I'm feeling a little more open-minded considering we're talking world invasion by evil spirits who are looking for a way to permanently escape hell."

When Knox remained silent, Mahone snapped, "Damn it, do you think I want to go groveling to the Quorum? I don't. But the intel Lucy got from the shape-shifter makes sense. I didn't tell him anything about the link between shape-shifter deaths and black magic. Rebel shape-shifters, both domestic and abroad, have unified. They plan on harnessing their collective power to create a bridge—a fucking huge one—between the living and the death. We're not talking about raising a few evil spirits here and there, although that would be bad enough; we're talking about letting loose the entire population of hell. The only way I can think of stopping it is to contact the First Lady, a known Quorum member, and hope she'll convince the President to give the shape-shifters what they want—some damn respect."

"Your plan has one major flaw," Knox said stubbornly. "There's no reason to believe she'd help us. She's more likely to use what we tell her to further her anti-Otherborn agenda."

"Not in this case," Lucy interrupted, and Mahone was thankful for her assistance.

While he was still pissed at her for tossing him around like a rag doll, the mage was exactly what she'd said she was—loyal, to the team and to society at large.

"The shape-shifters aren't discriminating against Otherborn," Lucy continued. "They're out to avenge themselves against everyone who has persecuted them, humans most of all. That's why the shape-shifter told me what he did. He thinks there's still a chance to stop them, which tells me the shape-shifters actually want to be stopped. They're acting out of desperation, because they feel they have no other choice. But it's the U.S. shape-shifters who sought the help of those in Europe. And they only did so after the President vetoed their application for funds to increase public awareness and tolerance for shape-shifters."

"So they wanted to run a 'hug a shape-shifter campaign' or the equivalent? How do you even know your source was telling the truth about that being the shape-shifters' motive?"

"Because I've confirmed it!" Mahone bit out.

Knox glared at him. "With whom?"

With a Goddess who has apocalyptic plans of her own, Mahone thought, regardless of the fact that Essenia had no dominion over hell or the dark demons there. At least, that's what she'd told him. He couldn't exactly contradict her, could he? "I can't tell you my source, Knox, so don't even ask, but believe me when I say I would not be asking this of you, of any of us, unless I felt there was absolutely no other choice. Let me talk to Zeph. Let him communicate our plea to the First Lady. All we're asking for is a temporary cease-fire. If she can persuade the President to authorize a federal grant, it will be a show of good faith and might stop the shape-shifters from going forward with their plan. We can't stop them all, Knox. Some of them, maybe, but not all."

Knox turned to look at Felicia, who stood across the room, her gaze troubled. She nodded.

"Fine," Knox said. "I'll contact Zeph. But if he thinks approaching the First Lady is too risky, I won't put him in danger. He's already left the safety of the Vampire Dome because of you and the Quorum. I won't let him risk his life any further. If I have to, I'll go to the President himself."

"The President's a good man, Knox, but he won't move, not without more evidence than this. Not unless he's influenced by someone more important to him than me. He loves his wife. He trusts her and he listens to her. If we're going to stop hell from invading the world, like it or not, we need her."

***

Dex pulled away from Jes so fast it scared her.

"You told me someone gave you to the Draci to seal a peace treaty between his race and theirs."

"That's true. It was a treaty between the Draci and the European wolf packs."

"Bodin rules U.S. werewolves. He has no dominion over those overseas."

"That's not true. He merged his pack with those in Europe. They follow him, for the most part. There are always exceptions, of course, but the European packs are hopeful that as werewolf rights expand in the U.S., Bodin will make sure the same happens here."

"You're actually telling me that Bodin of Hammersham is the werewolf who brought you here?"

"Don't you see? It's why I don't believe he intentionally hurt you, Dex. I believe he made mistakes, but his actions were intended to protect you. He's not evil."

"And yet as soon as I show up here, so does Rurik Pitts, a werebeast with damn good reason to want to see me dead. Do you really think that's coincidence?"

What he was implying couldn't be true, Jes thought. Bodin hadn't even known Dex was here until earlier today. But what if she was wrong? Bodin had said Jes thought too well of him, something he'd seemed to confirm when he'd talked so disdainfully of shape-shifters. What if Bodin had known about Dex and summoned Pitts to deal with him? Yet Pitts was dead and nothing made sense. "I—I don't know why Pitts was here," she exclaimed. "Since I know Bodin, maybe Pitts was here because of me, not you. I should have thought of that earlier."

Dex slowly shook his head. "How long have you known Bodin was my grandfather? Did you know this in L.A?"

She swallowed hard. Even though he looked surprised and angry, he wasn't reacting the way she'd feared. He wasn't railing at her or threatening to leave. For that she was grateful. "Yes."

"Did you seek me out in hopes of reconciling us?"

She hesitated, aware that this could be the bomb that set him off. "I hoped that would happen."

"Was fucking me part of that plan?"

"No! I swear it, Dex. That had nothing to do with accomplishing what I wanted. I was drawn to you. I slept with you because I couldn't resist my attraction to you."

"Damn it, I want to believe you."

"Then do. Please." She took his hands in hers. "I know about your gold charm but I could have gotten it away from you. Then I could've simply used persuasion on you. Hell, I could've *made you* forgive your grandfather. But I didn't. I wouldn't. Please believe me."

It took a few seconds before his fingers curled around hers. When they did, she wanted to weep with relief.

"If my grandfather helped you," he said slowly, "he didn't do it out of compassion or kindness. He had his own agenda, which was to use you as a bartering tool with the Draci."

"That's not true. He thought of it later, because he knew he couldn't bring me to live with his pack."

"And why couldn't he do that, Jes? He's the pack ruler. He couldn't do it because it went against his rules. His beliefs. He hates all races but his own. Thinks of himself as a superior power. It's why he sent me away and it's the same reason he rejected you. That's why he brought you here."

"But Dex, that can't be. Over the years, he's done much to promote peace with Otherborn. Not just with the Draci but—

He released her hands and turned his back on her. "Damn it, don't keep defending him to me. He's a bigot and a murderer and I'll never forget what he did to me or my mother. He's got you fooled and everyone else, too. If the only reason you're with me is to convince me to forgive him then—"

She wrapped her arms around him from behind, not letting go even when he tried to pull away. "No! Dex, that's not it at all. I promise. I love you. I want you. I want to raise this baby with you. I'm sorry. I won't talk about him anymore. It was only because he helped me and I wanted to tell you and—"

Slowly, he relaxed, turned, and put his arms around her. "Shhh," he soothed. "Calm down. It's okay."

When she stopped shaking, he raised her face to look at him. "Did you mean that? That you love me and want to raise the baby with me?"

"Yes. I want that more than anything."

"That's what I want, too. But you won't sway me on this. I understand why you'd be grateful to him. But I don't want you to ever mention that bastard's name again. Certainly not to defend him. I mean it, Jes."

"Okay, Dex," she said, but she knew her expression remained worried. Sad.

He kissed her lips. She could tell he regretted talking to her so harshly. She knew he wanted to give her what she wanted. What she needed. But he couldn't. He'd never think of Bodin of Hammersham with anything but utter hatred.

"At least my grandfather did one damn thing in his life that was good. He saved you," he whispered before kissing her and sweeping her up into his arms again.

She curled into him. She may not have told him everything, but hopefully she'd told him enough. She couldn't lose him. Not now. Not ever.

CHAPTER THIRTY

Vanessa Morrison stared at Zeph as if he was insane. He hadn't thought it was possible for the beautiful woman to look as ugly as her insides, but he'd been wrong. She looked positively hideous.

"You've been in contact with your brother and you expect me to believe this isn't a trap? You forget, I'm intimately acquainted with the procedure that enables vampires to lie."

No shit, Zeph thought. The Quorum had been the one to apply that little "procedure" to him and he still had nightmares about it sometimes. Vampire biology was designed to prevent them from lying and reversing such age-old instincts had taken a whole lot of blood, sweat, and tears, all on his part. As soon as she saw the expression on Zeph's face, she instinctively cringed. She'd probably be doing more than cringing if it weren't for the vamp stun guns her bodyguards constantly had locked on him, whether they were talking or fucking. Just once he'd love to see her cowering in terror, knowledge of her imminent death in her eyes. "Knox came to me, not the other way around," he said softly. "I'm merely delivering a message. One I think you should listen to if you want humanity to survive the coming Armageddon."

"Again, why should I believe anything you let alone your brother says?"

It was the same thing he'd asked Knox when his brother had arranged for them to meet at their preplanned spot. Knox had delivered Mahone's message clearly but with obvious reluctance. He knew Knox's hesitation was about not wanting to endanger Zeph just as much as it was about not wanting to go to the enemy for help. The fact that Knox had done what Mahone asked despite his misgivings told Zeph how critical the situation was.

"I don't expect you to believe Knox," he said. "I didn't simply take my brother's word on this, either. I talked to my own contacts. And I'm encouraging you to talk to yours. I'm sure I'm not the only Otherborn you've managed to turn against his own kind. If you have shape-shifters on your payroll or otherwise under your thumb, talk to them. Have them confirm what Knox has said. If they don't, we'll know Knox has uncovered the means to vampire falsity himself. Otherwise, I'd advise you to take his request seriously."

She still looked suspicious. "That assumes I'd trust a shape-shifter any more than I'd trust you. Which I don't."

"Fine. Then deal with the consequences." Despite the urgency driving him, Zeph pretended to examine his nails in a "you can die for all I care" way. If it was just her, of course, that would be true, but how could they risk a demon takeover of the world? "I'm not too keen on seeing what a world run by hell demons will look like, but I am immortal." He raised his gaze and pierced her with a look. He wished he could simply persuade her, but she was never without the gold that blocked vampire powers. In any event, Mahone had been quite clear about giving Vanessa the leeway she needed to hang herself. "I have no doubt I will live to see it."

He turned and walked out of the room. He was already to the front door, vamp stunners trained on him the whole way, when she stopped him.

"Wait," she said. "What has your brother offered in exchange for my help in this matter?"

"Nothing. He believes you'll help because you want humanity to survive."

"Then your brother isn't as smart as he's rumored to be."

Zeph rolled his eyes. "Believe me, he's smarter. I'm the only chance you've had of defeating him, and now...well, let's just say I'm willing to suffer Otherborn integration into human society a little while longer if it means keeping demons out of the mix."

"Stop," she commanded.

"Look," he said in an irritated voice. "I delivered the message. If you're not going to do what Knox has asked, then I'd just as soon get the hell out of here and enjoy what time I have left in the world as I know it."

"I'll do what you've suggested."

He couldn't help it. He whirled around in surprise.

She smiled tightly. "I'll get in touch with my contacts. And if I have reason to believe what your brother has told you, I'll consider helping. But only under one condition."

"I told you. Knox isn't going to negotiate with you. Not about this."

"Maybe not. But perhaps you will."

"I'm already on your payroll, Vanessa. You don't have to bribe me." And please don't let her be talking about sex because he wasn't sure he could stomach sleeping with her right now, even to seal this deal. Hearing Knox's voice had reminded him of all he'd lost in recent months. His torture had been twice as intense because he'd wanted to ask about Felicia. He hadn't, of course. His longing for his brother's wife was so bad he was sure Knox would have heard it in his voice.

"Just the same, I want to make my offer," the First Lady insisted. "You support the Quorum's goal to divide humans from Otherborn, but you harbor love for your family and clan. You want them to survive. I believe you'd be willing to give me something special to help them."

"What do you want?"

"I want you to turn me into a vampire."

CHAPTER THIRTY-ONE

Several days had passed since Jes had told Dex about her connection with his grandfather. Since then, she hadn't said another word about Bodin, and even though Dex had been tempted to question her about it—how well she knew his grandfather, how long she'd stayed with him before he brought her to the Draci, if his grandfather had ever mentioned Dex or his mother—he managed not to do so. Their closeness was still new and fragile, their future uncertain. He didn't want to cause more strife between them. As each day passed without them discussing the elephant in the room, he found it easier and easier to put it out of his mind.

Her belly was round now. At two-and-a-half weeks, the baby was moving. "It's amazing," Jes had breathed at one point. "It's growing so fast. I don't think it will take the full month." She'd hugged Dex tight. "It might decide to be born this week!"

She'd laughed, the sound trembling with joy, and Dex had felt the same joy course through him. One week and he'd be a father? It was so fast, but he'd fallen in love with Jes in virtually the same amount of time.

Dex's cell phone rang but he ignored it, just the way he'd been ignoring it for the past few days. He didn't want to talk to Mahone. He didn't want to talk to any of the Para-Ops team, even Lucy. Instead, he wanted to hold reality at bay for just a little longer. He knew it was a dereliction of his duties. That he'd sworn to protect and serve the citizens of the U.S., Otherborn and human alike. But he was so damn tired of acting solely out of duty. If things were critical enough, Knox could damn well teleport to France and find him. Until then, he'd concentrated on binding Jes to him more and more. He lavished her with love and affection in a way he'd never allowed himself before, and he lavished that attention on their baby as well.

"Where is the baby going to sleep?" he asked as they lay in bed together, their bodies still warm from their recent lovemaking. He plumped her breast in his hand. As always, he was fascinated by the resilient, smooth flesh but now he was even more fascinated by the way it and its companion had swelled in size. Like her ever-expanding abdomen, the pregnancy was making itself more apparent with almost every hour that passed. He placed a gentle kiss on both her nipples, then covered her stomach with his hand.

He often tried picturing the babe, but despite the knowledge that the baby would inherit Jes's vampire traits, he'd never actually seen a newborn vampire. Would it have silver hair? Would its eyes be black or that hazy blue that human babies often had before their true eye color emerged? A part of him had even begun to contemplate names, and he wondered what Jes would think of the name Elliott...

"It'll sleep with us. Here. In a bassinette."

She stroked his hair and he closed his eyes to savor her touch. Now that he'd let her in, Dex had been the happy recipient of Jes's affectionate nature. She loved touching him almost as much as she loved being touched by him, he realized, grinning to himself.

"I've set up a meeting between you and the shape-shifters," Jes said.

Involuntarily, he stiffened and sat up.

"I've asked Cy to accompany you, and he's agreed," she continued and began to fiddle with her own hair. The dark dye had faded enough that hints of her natural silver color peeked through. She'd commented that she needed to dye it again, but he'd begged her to wait just a little longer.

Begged her, he realized.

Her words and his realization combined to leave him with a feeling of unease. Who was he? Had he transformed into his true self or merely a shell of who he'd once been?

Wincing, he rubbed at the sudden pinch in his chest, and even that was enough to alarm him. He'd run miles with an open wound and felt far more pain every time he shifted. Yet now he was rubbing at the smallest of twinges?

He abruptly stood, stalked to his clothes, and jerked them on.

"Dex? Did you hear what I said about Cy?"

He glanced at her. She was sitting up now, still naked, her knees bent and her arms wrapped around them. He could see the ample sides of her breasts and the tease of pink flesh peeking out here and there. He was tempted to climb back into bed with her before he remembered her question.

"I heard what you said," Dex mumbled. "And of course Cy agreed to go with me. Cy will do any damn thing you ask him to." Not that Dex had seen much of the dragon-shifter lately. Why was that? Did Cy simply want to avoid seeing Dex and Jesmina together? Avoid seeing Jes as she plumped up, ripening right along with the baby inside her?

"Dex, let's not make this about Cy and me."

"Why not? After all, you sent him for me. You seem to know each other pretty well. Very well," he amended. He knew he sounded like an ass, but it still bothered him that Cy knew more about Jes than he did. He was slowly getting to know more about her, but he had to face the ugly truth—over the past few days, he hadn't just refrained from asking her about Bodin, he'd avoided asking her much of anything at all.

He knew her favorite color was pink, that she adored gelato, and that even though she couldn't derive nutrition from his blood, sinking her fangs into his inner thigh was enough to make her orgasm right along with him. But they didn't discuss deeper, more treacherous things. Like how far she was willing to go to find the secret to prolonging life. Like whether she'd ask their child to undergo the same kind of blood tests she'd asked of Ella—

Stop, he commanded himself. Don't go there. Like Jes told you, Ella's considered an adult among the Draci. Jes wouldn't ask that of an ordinary child, certainly not her own...

Would she?

His niggling doubt was enough to make him to glower at her. "Nothing to say about Cy?"

She threw back the sheet and pulled on her clothes. He wanted to weep at the sight of all that pale flesh being covered up. But her "He's like a brother to me," comment made him snort at her naiveté.

"Believe me, the feelings he has for you are far from brotherly."

Something flickered across her face. Something that made him curse and pounce on it. "You knew? Yet you let him wander around, giving him free rein?"

"Don't be absurd, Dex. Cy's expressed interest before but that doesn't mean I'm going to banish him from my life. Especially because we both know why he'd be prone to have a crush on me. He knows loving a Draci can have certain consequences, so why not turn his attention to a vampire female who he believed to be sterile?"

He supposed that made sense. But there was something about the way she'd looked just now, something that told him Cy hadn't been the only one to suffer from a crush. "So you were never tempted to make your relationship with him into something more intimate?"

"I didn't say that." She put her hands on her hips. "But if I was briefly tempted, I didn't act on it. I could have, of course. I wasn't in a relationship at the time."

"You damn well are now," he roared, causing her to stare at him in amazement.

"I know that, Dex. Believe me, it's a little hard to ignore given the baby growing inside me." Her expression softened as she approached. When she stood before him, she lifted both hands to frame his face as she often did. "And I've never been happier," she said softly. "You have no reason to be jealous. I haven't had sex with anyone—haven't even thought about having sex with anyone—since the day I met you."

The relief he felt was instantaneous. Because of her confession, however, he couldn't help thinking that, unlike her, he'd had sex with another female after he'd met her, and he'd *thought* about having sex with Lucy again even after he'd had Jes. Granted, Lucy had declined but— Jes must have seen uneasiness in his expression because she dropped her hands and narrowed her eyes.

"Let me ask you this, Dex. After we had sex in L.A., have you wanted to have sex with any other female?"

He stared dumbly at her, like a damn animal caught in a hunter's crosshairs. Dimly, he wondered if his mouth was opening and closing like a caught trout struggling to breathe.

"Still helping Lucy out?" she asked lightly, even though he saw the hurt she was feeling.

He lifted his hand but she flinched away from him, so he let it drop to his side.

He had two choices—let the guilt swallow him or defend himself. Apparently some of his survival instincts had managed to stick around because he said, "I didn't sleep with Lucy after we were together. I mean, I offered but she said no and—"

Jes paled and clutched at her stomach, as if she suddenly felt nauseas. Goddess help me, he thought, but he knew that wasn't going to happen. Like always, Dex needed to get himself out of this mess.

"What I mean is, she's decided to deal with the heat on her own. I thought you knew about Lucy and the bargain we'd struck. It's not like—"

"What?" she sneered, obviously ready to throw down the gauntlet. "It's not like you enjoyed it? Come on, you really expect me to believe that? Lucy's beautiful!"

He could hardly deny that so he did the smartest thing he could think of— nothing. Until, despite himself, he smiled. He couldn't help it. He didn't enjoy hurting her, but he'd been the one acting like a jealous ass; to know she wasn't immune to the same irrational feelings heartened him. It made him feel more confident about the feelings they had for one another.

"You think this is funny?" she hissed in disbelief.

"What? Of course not." Dex wiped the smile off his face, but obviously not fast enough for her. "Look, Lucy really likes you," he began, trying to appease her.

"And I really like Lucy," she emphasized. "I know she only turned to you out of desperation, nothing more."

"So what's the problem then?"

"Nothing." She stomped her foot.

"Then come here and give me a hug," he challenged. Looking at her all flushed and squinty-eyed, with her newly plump breasts quivering and her belly sticking out made him hot and hard. Was this their first fight? Because he'd never had make-up sex before. From what he'd heard, it could be damn good...

She smiled sweetly at him. "Sorry, but I've got a date with some shampoo and a carton of ice cream." She whirled around, stomped into the bathroom, and slammed the door. He heard the lock being thrown into place. "Hurry up and find Cy or you're going to be late for that meeting," she called.

It took Dex a moment before he could react. All he managed to say was a soft, "Shit." But when he left, he left with another smile on his face.

***

PARIS, FRANCE

Several hours later, Dex was back at the Basilica of the Sacred Heart of Paris. This time, there were pockets of tourists outside, but he and Cy followed Jes's instructions until they found a secret door near the bronze statue of Michael and the serpent. They traveled down a dark corridor until they came to a small room lit with primitive torches on the wall. Waiting for them were the three *diregeants* he'd spoken to just before Trosseau had gone apeshit and attacked him. He wasn't inclined to believe the trio didn't know anything about that.

"Well, would you look at this," Dex drawled. "If it isn't the shape-shifter equivalent of Larry, Moe, and Curly."

Next to him, Cy elbowed him in the side.

"What?" Dex asked innocently.

"We're not surprised to hear you being so cavalier, Mr. Hunt," the shape-shifter spokesperson, still positioned between the other two, said. "A shame, really, given that Trosseau sacrificed his life as a result of trying to help you."

"Trosseau tried to kill me," Dex responded. "At least, someone made damn sure it looked like that. I'm thinking it was a *diabol*. But you wouldn't know anything about that, would you?"

"It could very well have been a *diabol*. We never denied knowledge of the trouble brewing. Only that we needed help from outsiders."

"And you've changed your mind about wanting help from this outsider because...?"

The shape-shifters smiled eerily in that synchronized way they had.

Next to him, Cy winced. "This is damn freaky," he whispered.

Dex grunted. "Stick around. I think it's going to get freakier."

"Despite our warnings that you leave, you didn't. You've been asking questions about shape-shifter murders. You even contacted a mage in the Montpeyroux Village and asked her to perform a protective spell for you. Why?"

Dex managed to hide his surprise at their mentioning the mage. "Apparently, you already know. Why don't you tell me?"

"You've been targeted by a *diabol*. And you're afraid it will harm those close to you."

"That's right," he said. "I want to prevent that. I want to prevent the loss of further life in general. Despite what you think of me, I don't enjoy needless killing or suffering."

The center shape-shifter inclined his head. "So your liaison has said. We just weren't sure whether to believe it."

He assumed they were talking about Jes. Then again, she'd denied having any connections to the shape-shifters. How had she set up this meeting then? She'd mentioned an Otherborn Ambassador before. Could she have meant Bodin?

Dex felt his eyes widen. "Who convinced you to meet with me?" he asked.

Please don't let it have been him, Dex thought. Not the same werewolf who'd saved Jes, making her believe he was some kind of supporter of Otherborn rights. But despite Dex's horror, he knew it was a very real possibility. If Jes's goal was to help him, she would do whatever she thought was necessary, even if it meant relying on someone he hated. As much as he didn't want to admit it, he couldn't really blame her. A part of him admired her ruthlessness.

"Answer me," he prodded the shape-shifters.

"It doesn't matter, Mr. Hunt. We've had our eye on you. Now that we've run out of time, we have no other choice but to accept the help you've offered."

"What do you mean, you've run out of time?"

"We've suffered a revolution of sorts. Many shape-shifters are tired of trying to make progress the civilized way. They're fed up with being treated as parasites undeserving of even the government's most basic protection."

"How can they be fed up when European shape-shifters haven't even exposed their existence to the government?"

"U.S. shape-shifters have asked for help from shape-shifters world-wide. They are no longer willing to rely on peaceful negotiation and some are willing to take their chances by joining forces with another oppressed group."

"Oppressed group? Tell me you're not referring to *diabols* as an underrepresented minority."

"The *diabols* you speak of are demons, cast into hell, persecuted for their past mistakes. They long for a second chance at life, and that's exactly what our rebel shape-shifters want as well. In a few days, the solstice gates will open and for one hour conditions will be such that shape-shifters all over the world can work together to create a bridge. One large enough to carry every *diabol* in hell into the living world."

As he listened, Dex shivered, not so much because of the shape-shifter's words but because of the expression on his face. They'd already given up, he realized. They held no hope that they'd be able to stop the mass bridging they were talking about. Or that Dex and the U.S. government would either.

"If a few shape-shifters can work together to create the bridge, why can't the rest of you work together to destroy it?"

"We've tried on a smaller scale, but not every shape-shifter knows how the bridge is made. It's taught to us by the evil ones. Obviously, unless we open ourselves to communication with them, a dangerous prospect indeed, we can't know how to counter what they've started. Not effectively enough to change things."

"But if we can stop it…if this solstice gate closes…"

"Then the threat of mass bridging is significantly reduced. Shape-shifters can, of course, continue to bridge *diabol*s in small numbers, but those are intermittent situations we're more equipped to handle. As we have been."

"Of course. So how can I stop the bridging? Or even better, how can I close this solstice gate?"

"*Obserwować Demonie Krawcy*. It means 'watch the demon tailors.' The phrase is part of your heritage as a were. At least, it would have been if you'd been raised by your pack as was right."

Dex didn't bother asking how the shape-shifter knew he hadn't been raised by his pack. "That phrase. It's the same thing you said before, at the church. And the mage I spoke to, she called shape-shifters working in league with *diabol*s 'demon tailors.' How do weres watch them?"

"No one outside the pack knows. It has something to do with protecting the sanctity of the solstice gates. With being able to travel through them."

"That's not a whole lot of help," Dex snapped.

"Which is why we told you to seek out your own in the States."

"My werewolf grandfather. You were talking about him?"

"A were with knowledge of your pack's inherent power. That is all that matters."

"Great. I'll just find a werewolf, ask him, and I'm sure he'll spill all his secrets to me."

"Now you know why we hold little hope of stopping these sad events, Mr. Hunt. But we thank you for meeting with us."

He'd been dismissed. And he supposed there was really no reason for him to stay. He had the information he needed. He just didn't know what the hell to do with it. "Thank you," he said gruffly, and he could tell he'd surprised the shape-shifters. "For finally trusting outsiders. I don't know what difference I can make, but I'll do everything I can to help."

Turning, he bumped into Cy, who was looking at him with a flat, unreadable expression.

"Mr. Hunt."

The voice that spoke was one he'd never heard before. He turned back to the shape-shifters, surprised when it was the one on the right, and not the center, that addressed him.

"You're different than you were when you first got here," Righty said.

Dex was too shocked by the seemingly innocuous comment to respond at first.

Cy slapped a hand on Dex's shoulder. "Dex here's now expecting a baby, and you know how that affects a male. He's over the moon with happiness."

Dex glowered at the dragon-shifter even as he knocked Cy's hand off him. "Shut up, Cy," he said, not liking the taunting tone the dragon-shifter had used.

He also didn't like the way Righty reacted to Cy's words.

Eyes wide, Righty asked "A child? You? But aren't you staying in Paladine Abbey? With the pretty vampire doctor?"

An expression of unease washed over Cy's face as he realized how much he'd revealed. Dex barely managed not to hit him.

"The vampire is helping my cause," he said, "but we're not lovers. She doesn't mean anything to me. The female I've impregnated is back in the States."

"That's good," the center shape-shifter said. "Because vampires have a natural resistance to possession by *diabols* and other spirits. That's not true when the vampire is pregnant or otherwise weakened."

"I'll remember that," Dex said, pretending the shape-shifter's words hadn't scared the shit out of him. But Dex knew Righty hadn't been fooled.

CHAPTER THIRTY-TWO

After Dex left, Jes was appalled by her childish reaction to the news he'd almost slept with Lucy again. Oh she knew her reaction was understandable given how close she and Dex had become. What female wouldn't be pissed to learn the male she loved had thought about screwing another female after her, even if it had been for a practical, medically-related reason?

Had things really changed? If Lucy asked to sleep with him tomorrow, would he do it? Because if he would even considerate it, they were going to have a serious discussion. Right now, however, all she wanted was to see him. To discuss his meeting with the shape-shifters. To repair any damage that had been committed as a result of her jealousy.

But at the same time, her thoughts were weighed down with a more imminent and pressing concern. Bodin.

Days ago, he'd rallied. In a moment of lucidity, he'd asked about Dex again. About his work with the Para-Ops team. Jes had told Bodin about Dex's current mission. The fact that *diabols* were somehow involved. Upon hearing that, Bodin had arranged Dex's meeting with the *diregeants*.

Now that the meeting was taking place, however, Bodin had slipped into unconsciousness and Jes didn't know if he'd come out of it. She and Amanda sat beside him, each fearing his next shuddering gasp for air might be his last.

Amanda sobbed. Jes placed a hand on the grieving werewolf's shoulder. Since Jes had kicked her out of the castle, Bodin's granddaughter had visited her grandfather everyday, always in Jes's presence, but during those times, the two females hadn't spoken.

Amanda turned to Jes. "He's going to die soon, isn't he?"

"I—I don't know, Amanda. I'm sorry. I've tried everything I can think of, including injecting him with Dex's blood and my own. Nothing has helped."

"But you collected your blood under normal circumstances, right?"

"I don't understand."

"You haven't tried collecting your blood when your body is in duress. You have the power of regeneration, Jes."

Although it had never occurred to her before, it should have. She knew immediately what Amanda was asking but said nothing.

"I know you think I'm horrible," Amanda pressed on. "For what I did to Ella. For what I'm asking of you. But I'd do the same thing. In fact, I will. I won't ask you to do what I'm not willing to do, as well."

"No," Jes began. Amanda's desperation was causing the werewolf to grasp at straws. Even so, she remembered all the times she'd allowed herself to be experimented on when she was younger. Instinctively, she smoothed her fingers over her scarred arm. She wasn't willing to let herself be used like that again. Was she?

"You haven't done everything you can, Jes. You know you haven't. Weres can't be killed in their wolf form."

"We've taken your blood in that form. There was nothing—"

"You haven't taken the blood while I've been in wolf form *and* regenerating. Perhaps there's a special property that comes out at that time. Something you can't isolate otherwise."

Jes steeled herself. She knew what Amanda was going to say next. And she knew that eventually she was going to go along with it.

"I want you to wound me and collect samples as I'm regenerating," Amanda said. "And I want to do the same to you."

***

"Find Jes," Dex told Cy as soon as they returned to the castle grounds. A quick glance confirmed the sun was moments from setting. "Bring her here to me."

"Where are you going?"

"I haven't been able to get a damn signal to call my friends at the FBI. I need to go to the gazebo where the reception is best. We've got another agent investigating the shape-shifter murders in the U.S., but my boss can send more men to the weres. They can ask the weres about the solstice gates."

Cy looked like he wanted to argue with Dex, but he didn't. "I'll be right back." He ran in the direction of the castle.

When he reached the gazebo, Dex had to dial Mahone's number several times before the call went through.

"Where the hell have you been?" Mahone snarled.

"Out of touch," was all Dex said. "I need you to do something."

"I'm a little busy right now trying to—"

"Listen to me, Mahone. There's a group of shape-shifters who are pissed by the way the U.S. government has treated them. They plan on helping a bunch of hell demons invade the living world. We only have a few days to try and stop them."

"How do you know this?"

"I finally got some high level shape-shifters to talk to me. You need to send men to interrogate the werewolves. Even my grandfather," he added, surprising himself. "Tell them they're being asked to do their duty. They need to block demons from traveling through the solstice gates."

"Solstice gates? What the hell does that mean?"

"Just do it, Mahone," Dex snapped.

"Fine. But you should know, Lucy discovered most of this days ago. Just not the part about the weres and the solstice gates. We've been working on a solution but it's still touch and go. It involves having to rely on Vanessa Morrison."

"The First Lady? The woman who is part of the Quorum? Are you crazy?"

"We didn't have any choice," Mahone said. "You've been off radar and we went with the intel we had. I'll send a team to the weres but in the meantime we'll keep the other plan in motion."

"Fine. I need to go."

"Dex. Wait!"

He brought the phone back up to ear. "What is it? I need to find Jes."

"Look, who set up this meeting with the shape-shifters?"

"Jes. Why?"

"Does she know about this so-called were power to walk the solstice gates?"

"I don't think so. She wasn't there."

"Talk to her, Dex. I have a feeling she might know something about it. Something about you."

About me? What the hell did that mean? "Mahone, what are you—" But the line was dead again. He didn't know if Mahone had hung up or if they'd just lost their signal again, but it didn't matter. Where was Cy? What was taking so long?

He waited two more minutes before he went looking for them. When he rounded the corner of the castle, he saw Cy at the front entry. He was leaning against the exterior wall, looking like he'd just been sick.

"What are you doing? Did you see, Jes?"

Cy raised his head and blinked at Dex. "Yes. But she's in the middle of a procedure right now."

"In the surgery room? Who's she working on?"

Cy shook his head. He looked like he was in shock. Unsure of what to do.

Dex grabbed him and shook him hard. "Answer me. Is Jes okay? Cy, tell me—fuck!"

Grimacing, Dex let go of Cy. His head was throbbing and from out of nowhere he heard a whimper of pain. It sounded like it came from Jes.

"Did you hear that?" he asked Cy. "Did you hear her?"

"What? No." Cy looked baffled.

Dex heard her whimper again and whirled. This time, she had seemed closer. "I can hear her." I can *feel* her, he realized. He was hearing Jes moaning in his head somehow. She was in pain but she was stifling the sound, trying not to be heard. He hissed and grabbed at his own arm when it inexplicably began to throb. What the hell?

"It's okay," Cy was saying. "You must be connected with her through the baby somehow. She's in pain because they don't want to use anesthesia or pain meds. They're afraid it'll compromise the results of the procedure, but she'll be okay."

"What are you saying?" Dex demanded.

"Dex—"

"What's going on? Why is she in pain? Never mind, I'll go to her myself." He whirled around and headed for the surgery room he'd seen when he'd arrived.

"It's not that one," Cy choked out. "She's in a secondary surgery room."

"Where is it?"

Cy shook his head.

Dex almost couldn't contain his panic. For Jes's sake, he did. "Is she hurting herself? Allowing herself to be hurt for some kind of experiment?" He could tell by the guilty expression on Cy's face that he'd guessed right. "Don't do this, Cy! I thought you cared about her."

"Damn it, I do. That's why I understand her. I know what's driving her. And she's done it before. She was fine then and she'll be fine now."

"This is different," Dex urged, his desperation rising with every second and each stifled moan he heard. On some level, he knew she wasn't in agonizing pain. It was manageable, but the thought of her in any pain at all was too much for him to stand. "Anything they're doing to her they're doing to the baby, as well. Have you thought of that?"

"Jes wouldn't do anything to jeopardize the baby." But Cy looked unsure.

"Not intentionally. But remember how you didn't want me to upset her? This is upsetting her, whether she knows it or not. Now tell me where she is." He clasped Cy on the shoulder and stared into his eyes. "I'm begging you, Cy. Let me help her."

Cy nodded as if coming to a difficult decision. "This way." He led Dex downstairs until he came across the same door that Dex had, the one locked and expressly denying them entry. The door was enormous and likely reinforced, but Cy didn't bother fiddling with the lock. He turned to Dex. "It'll take me a while to recover. Keep going." As soon as Dex stepped away from him, Cy shifted, turning himself into marble before bursting into flame. The fireball he threw incinerated the door.

Dex didn't hesitate to run through it. When he realized his clothes were on fire, he simply slapped out the flames and kept running, letting his instincts as well as the increasing volume of Jes's moans guide him.

When he came to the doors marked *Surgery*, he barreled through them.

Jes was strapped down to a table, a piece of leather in her mouth. She was biting down on it to stop from screaming while Amanda cut her arm.

He growled and lunged for the werewolf. "You bitch!"

Amanda dropped the scalpel and scrambled away, crashing into a tray of surgical tools. "She agreed to do it! She did the same thing to me. It's painful, but she regenerates. It's not like she's going to die!"

"Get out of here before I kill you," he gasped out, meaning every word.

After glancing at Jes, Amanda ran from the room.

Breathing like a locomotive, Dex turned to Jes. And he could tell she wanted to run, too.

***

Thankfully, Jes didn't fight Dex when he gathered her into his arms and carried her to her bedroom. She knew better than to agitate him given the anger that was thrumming through his veins. As soon as they were inside and he'd placed her on her feet, she'd wobbled briefly, excused herself, went into her bathroom, and shut the door.

They hadn't said one word to each other.

Dex wasn't sure if and when he'd be capable of speech.

He was too afraid that the minute he or she started talking, he would finally lose it and say something he would regret.

When she turned on the shower, Dex took a deep breath and closed his eyes, trying to calm down. He knew she was hiding, but he'd give her a few minutes to herself. He figured he'd need that long just to get his anger under control.

He was about to sit on the bed when he saw traces of blood smearing his clothes. It wasn't a lot. She hadn't been bleeding enough for her blood to soak through. But it was enough. Too much. He stripped off his shirt, balled it up, and threw it across the room, his anger returning full force.

How dare she allow herself to be hurt? How dare she lay there and let Amanda slice her open? It didn't matter that the wounds couldn't hurt the baby. That the cuts had only been on her arm, the one unmarred by scars. The cuts had been deep, some almost to the bone…

He agonized over her injuries for several minutes.

When she finally opened the door, steam billowed out of the bathroom. She stepped out wearing a shell pink robe.

Lying on the bed, his hands tucked behind his head, Dex refused to look at her.

She padded over and sat beside him.

Neither one of them spoke until . . .

"My wounds have already healed, Dex," she said gently. "Unlike the ones I sustained as a child, these wounds won't even leave scars. See for yourself."

"I don't want to see," he snapped as his gaze honed in on hers. "I can't forget the sight of Amanda cutting you while you laid there and let her do it!"

"I know it looks bad, that it's hard to understand, but we needed to try it. Our bodies have healing properties. We never thought to take our blood as we were regenerating. If I can harness that power to help others—"

He pushed himself to a sitting position and took her by the shoulders. Although he wanted to shake some sense into her, he kept his touch gentle. "Damn it, you have to stop! Your life isn't all about helping others live longer. You have your own life to live, too, and you need to do it!"

"I have an eternity for that, Dex."

"And just when will your eternity start, Jes? You're already almost one hundred years old and believe it or not, you can be killed. Knox's first wife was a full vampire and she was murdered; when he found her, she had a gaping hole in her chest, one that all the experiments in the world couldn't heal. Even now, with our baby inside you, you can't let yourself be happy. Why?"

"That's not true. This baby means so much to me. I have him. And now I have…" She looked away. Despite their talk of a future, he realized, she didn't feel she could say it out loud. But he did.

"You have me. Me, Jes. You said you love me. Well, you know what? I love you, too. I want to know I can fulfill you. Not every part of you, but a part big enough and deep enough that you can let go of your damn guilt and be happy!"

"What?" she asked, the question simple and designed to deceive. She'd probably wanted to say: "I don't feel guilty." But she didn't, because she couldn't, because that would have been a lie.

"You feel guilty that you survived and your parents didn't. You feel guilty because you're immortal and the Draci aren't. Hell, you probably even feel guilty that you got pregnant, despite the fact you didn't think you could and we used condoms. Goddess knows that if that's true, then I contributed to your guilt. For that I'll always be sorry. But I don't blame you anymore, Jes. And you have to stop blaming yourself. For all of it."

She pulled away from him, walked across the room, and turned her back on him. But he didn't give up. He came up to her. Close enough that she'd feel him even though they weren't actually touching. "Why are you the only immortal here?"

She whirled around. "Excuse me?"

"Why haven't you brought in other vampires to help you? Surely there are some who'd be willing to do what you do. Some that are medically trained, in fact. Why do you do things all on your own?"

"This village is virtually unheard of. We want to keep it that way. It's how we're able to maintain some level of peace. Besides, I don't know any vampires. Not anymore."

"It wouldn't be too hard to find them. I can talk to my friend Knox. He has connections."

"No," she said coolly.

"No?" he repeated. "Just like that?"

"That's right. I don't want vampires—I mean, I'm fine with things the way they are."

"I bet you are. It puts you in a pretty important position, don't you think? Everyone around you either ill or dying. Almost like you're some kind of Goddess. That would change if all of a sudden you brought in another immortal."

"All that would change is that the Draci will have exposed their weaknesses to more people, more people who can turn against them, more people they can't trust. Or are you telling me that you trust others? Even this Knox you're talking about?"

"There are not many I trust," he conceded. "But I have good reason for that. What's your reason? Just who staked you and your parents out to die?" He reached over and lightly caressed her scars. This time she managed not to flinch. "Was it vampires? Is that why you don't want to bring your own kind here?"

"No. *Ce n'était pas des vampires*. It was werewolves."

"What?" It was the last thing he'd been expecting her to say.

"That's right. It's ironic, don't you think? A were killed my parents. My mother and my father. But a were also saved me, and then another gave me a baby. Maybe it's some kind of cosmic fair play."

"If werewolves killed your parents, why would Bodin have intervened? They must have been acting under his orders."

"They were. At least, initially. They were searching for a vampire among my villagers, but they couldn't find him. They didn't believe us when we said we didn't know where he was. Or even who he was. Bodin told them to find the vampire so he could talk to him, but he never authorized violence. Bodin's men went crazy. They overpowered several of us. We weren't used to fighting. We were a peaceful clan. They took us and staked us, not realizing I was too young to have vampire powers or vampire weaknesses, either. And then Bodin arrived and he saved me. Then he punished his men. Each and every one of them. So it's not vampires I hate. I don't hate anyone, Dex. Not even weres. I hate the ones who did what they did. But I don't hate the whole race."

"Then you're better than me. Better than most people. I don't think I could be that evolved. In fact, I know I can't. Did Bodin ever find the vampire he was looking for?"

***

At Dex's question, Jes said, "I don't—" but her claim of ignorance stopped mid sentence.

Because something had suddenly occurred to her. Something alarming.

It was so obvious, but she, who prided herself on gathering information and wielding her scientific mind like a finely honed scalpel, hadn't even thought of it.

The day Bodin had saved her, his weres had been searching for a vampire. That had also been around the same time Bodin had sent Dex away. Could it be that Bodin had been looking for Dex's vampire father? And if so, why? To talk to him? Or to kill him?

A shiver of doubt swept through her. Was it possible that Dex was right about his grandfather after all?

"Jes, if you don't hate any particular race, why won't you bring other immortals here?"

Her answer was an easy one given what she'd just been thinking. "Because while I don't hate," she answered slowly. "I also don't trust. Like you, I've lived long enough to know that everyone is motivated by their own selfishness, and that includes me. You asked if I want to be a goddess? Yes. I do. I wish I had the power to create and manage life. Because I think I'd do a much fairer job than those currently in power."

He obviously had no response for that. How could he? Life was filled with unfairness. Dex had to know that better than most.

It was just too bad creationism, and if it existed, individual cosmic power, weren't ruled by democratic vote. Or maybe, given what a bad job the world's current democracies were doing, it wouldn't even matter.

"I'm sorry, Jes," Dex said. "I know you're doing what you think is right. But you can't continue to hurt yourself in a desperate attempt to alter nature."

She smiled. Appreciated that even now he was trying to protect her. Convince her that what she was doing was wrong. But she didn't believe him. She probably never would. "Dex, the night I met you, you were with your Para-Ops team. How long have you been together?"

"What does that have to do with anything?"

"Please. Just answer my question."

He did, albeit impatiently. "A few months."

"I saw for myself how well you work together. Do you consider the Para-Ops team your family?"

"No."

She smiled sadly at his swift response. "Let me guess. You think of them as better than your family, don't you? So let me ask you this, and answer honestly, please. Would you die to protect one of them?"

He didn't want to answer. He didn't. Not for several tense, prolonged seconds. Then, with great reluctance, he admitted, "Yes."

She nodded at the confirmation of what she'd already known. "Then why can't you understand that I'd do the same for the Draci? Because they are my family. If I can help them, even if it means suffering a little pain, then so be it. I'm an adult. I can make that decision. And I'm sorry, but I won't stop trying. Ever."

CHAPTER THIRTY-THREE

A few hours later, Jes finally fell asleep. She was obviously exhausted, the trials of the past few weeks as well as her pregnancy causing her internal clock to shift. It was another hour before Dex accepted he wasn't going to rest as easily. Silently, he left her room and walked into the garden, heading for the iron gazebo where they'd had their first meal together. He was almost to the structure when shadows moved.

Cy said, "So you're still here, huh? I thought if anything would make you run, it would be that."

Dex stepped closer and saw the dragon-shifter. He was in his favorite sitting position, sprawled out and limbs splayed, swigging back something clear from a bottle.

"I'm not running," Dex confirmed, bracing himself against the gazebo's opening. "Today only proved how much Jes needs me here."

Cy nodded and pointed the neck of the bottle at him. "Because I can't take care of her the way you think you can?"

The dragon-shifter was clearly inebriated. Slurring his words. His manner more aggressive than usual. Dex sighed. "You're too close to the subject, Cy. Too willing to give her what she thinks she needs."

"You think I let her hurt herself because it might end up saving me?" He shook his head. "No. I let her do what she needs to in order to have any semblance of happiness."

"Maybe she needed her quest in order to be happy at some point, but not anymore. She has me and the baby now."

Cy laughed. "Oh wow. That's a good one. So when I wasn't looking, you decided to pledge your love and devotion to her after all?"

Dex straightened. "That's right. I know you aren't happy with that, but if you want to continue being part of Jes's life, you have to accept it."

"You mean: if I want to be part of her life for the next fourteen years of the life that I have left, right? And even then, only if I'm lucky."

For the first time since Dex had met Cy, the guy looked morose. Completely without hope. If Dex hadn't been so messed up himself, unsure of how to handle Jes and her obsession with prolonging life, he might have even felt sorry for the other male. "I didn't say that, Cy."

"You didn't have to." Cy shot to his feet, weaving slightly before catching himself. "Damn it, it's not fucking fair. She just met you but you're going to get everything. Her. The baby. Hundreds of years with them."

When he put it like that, it did sound pretty damn unfair. Exactly the reason Jes wanted to prolong the Draci lifespan in the first place. But everyone had their baggage. He understood wanting to change things for the better, but how far did that extend? Far enough that someone like Jes gave up her own chance for happiness in order to give it to others? He wasn't going to let that happen, and he sure as shit wasn't giving up his chance for happiness with her. "You said you were happy, Cy. If that's true, you've had fourteen years of the happiness I've just discovered is possible."

Cy threw the bottle against the side of the gazebo, shattering it into a hundred pieces. "This isn't as easy as buying a fucking ice cream cone," Cy snarled.

"I know that."

"No," Cy said. "You don't." The dragon-shifter stumbled toward him while Dex held his ground.

The closer Cy got, the more sure Dex became that the one bottle had simply been the first of many. Cy reached out and thumped Dex on the chest with the flat of his palm. "You don't know anything, Dex Hunt. You certainly don't know Jes." He slapped Dex in the chest again. "Not what drives her. Not if you actually believe that you and the baby will make her so happy that she'll stop being obsessed with her research."

This time, when Cy moved to slap him, Dex shoved back. Hard. Cy toppled backward, landing on his ass. To keep him down, Dex pushed his foot against Cy's chest. "Whatever I don't know about her, I'll learn. I know it won't be easy and I'm not expecting a miracle overnight. But we're going to have the time to figure it out together."

Cy struggled beneath Dex's foot before surrendering. With that, Dex released him and stepped back. Cy immediately clambered his way to his feet.

"Only until you leave her," Cy spat. "Remember, I told you that. I know you'll leave her."

"I'm not leaving her."

"You're wrong. What if she continues to experiment on herself? What if it goes beyond cutting and she wants to explore regeneration by having someone cut off one of her limbs? You going to stay with her then?"

"I'd never let that happen. I'll protect her, and I'll help her find other ways to get what she needs. If what she needs is to find a way to lengthen life, then fine, I'll do everything I can to help her. But she'll damn well learn to balance things and look out for herself, too."

"What if she asks you to do something?"

"What? She can have anything she needs from me. Hell, she can have my blood before I'll let her shed any more of her own."

"Too late for that," Cy taunted.

"What are you—"

"You have no idea what Jes would demand of you. What if she wanted your loyalty?

"She has it."

"What if she wants you to pledge your loyalty to someone else? Someone you hate? What if she wanted you to *save* someone you hated?"

"Stop fucking around, Cy. If you have something to say, then just say it."

"Fine. Bodin of Hammersham."

"Nice try. But I already know he's the one who brought Jes here."

Cy's eyes rounded with shock but Dex felt no pity for him.

"She told you that, huh? Well, did she tell you he's here? Because he is. He's been here the entire time."

***

Something woke Jes and she automatically reached for Dex. She frowned when she found the space beside her empty. Where had he gone? And was he still angry with her?

She closed her eyes, wishing things between them weren't so complicated. Hating the fear and uncertainty she'd seen in his eyes when he'd discovered what she and Amanda had been doing. But Dex had hated his grandfather his whole life. Had probably plotted to kill him for most of that time. He didn't understand the urgency she and Amanda had felt as they'd stared down at Bodin and—

She abruptly sat up.

Bodin. She'd intended to check in on him immediately after she and Amanda had concluded with their research, but once Dex had arrived, she'd forgotten. Then she'd fallen asleep.

She leaped out of bed, and finding herself still in her robe, didn't even bother to dress. She grabbed her keys, the ones that would enable her to get to Bodin, and rushed out of her room.

When she arrived, Bodin was either still unconscious or asleep, but he'd kicked all his covers off. Occasionally, he muttered to himself and writhed restlessly on the bed, as if he had something important to do. Something urgent. Only someone or something was keeping him from it.

She picked up the covers and tucked them carefully around him.

"Camille, my darling girl. Dex—" he whispered.

It wasn't the first time he'd called to them in his sleep.

"Shhh," Jes soothed and placed her hand on his forehead. Despite all the antibiotics they'd been giving him, he was burning up. It wasn't the heat of infection, but the heat of his ancestors calling him home after a long life lived. No matter how they'd fought it, she knew it was Bodin's time.

Grief overrode her feelings of failure.

The worst thing about seeing him approach his end was that he was doing so with regrets. He was clearly haunted by the things he'd done in his past. And she knew most of his demons came from guilt over Dex.

She raised his weathered hands to her lips and kissed them.

She didn't completely discount what Dex had claimed. That Bodin had merely seen her as a pawn to use with the Draci. She also still harbored questions about whether the vampire Bodin's men had been searching for on the day he'd rescued her had been Dex's father. But she had only to be near Bodin to feel the goodness in him. That, at least, was true. If Dex saw his grandfather, would it help him see that goodness, too?

She hadn't told Dex that Bodin was here because she'd feared what he would do. But now there was nothing Dex could do that nature hadn't already taken care of. He deserved to see Bodin before his grandfather passed. "I'll bring him to you," Jes whispered "I'll bring Dex."

"No need. I'm already here."

She jumped and whirled.

Dex. His hate-filled gaze was latched onto Bodin. And when he turned his gaze on her, that hatred didn't diminish.

"I didn't believe Cy. Not until I saw him with my own eyes. How long has he been here?"

Dex hadn't bothered talking quietly, yet Bodin seemed unaware of their presence. That told her he wasn't asleep but still unconscious. "He's been here several months," she said. "He knew his time was coming and—and he sought my help."

Dex nodded. "You'd be the one to see, I suppose. Given the little display I just saw, you love him, just not enough to sacrifice your own life, right? Otherwise, you'd have turned him into a vampire."

"If it was that easy," she said, her voice shaking, "I'd have turned a whole bunch of others into vampires. But you're right, considering I'd have been risking my life, I didn't make the offer to anyone. Anyone but Bodin, that is. But he refused and I already told you, I don't make people do things against their will."

"No. You just make sure they don't have the knowledge to protest. You trick them, so you can justify your actions and tell yourself they were committed without force. So long as you get what you're after, that's all that matters. That's why you didn't tell me you knew my grandfather or that he was here. Because you knew you wouldn't get what you were after. Me. Isn't that right?"

When she didn't answer, he moved aggressively forward. "Isn't it, Jes? Answer me."

"Yes, you're right," she whispered.

His aggression slipped away and was replaced by genuine confusion. "Why? Why did my grandfather send you after me?"

"He didn't send me, Dex. I was the one who wanted something from you. I wanted to test your blood. I—I took several vials from you while I was in L.A. After we made love—I mean, after we had sex." She would always remember it as making love. That's what it had been every time they'd been together. But she knew Dex no longer viewed it that way.

"My blood? Why? You already had Amanda, a full-blooded werewolf. Any healing properties my blood carries are diminished compared to hers."

"That would be true if you were an ordinary werebeast. But you're not."

"I'm not, huh?"

"No, Dex. I'm afraid not. You're a half-breed, but you're not half were and half human. You're half were and half vampire."

He barked with disbelieving laughter. "For a scientist, you haven't done your research. Dharmires, no matter what type of race mixes with vampire blood, always present as vampires."

"You're an anomaly. One that's been foretold for centuries."

"Bullshit."

"It's not. It's called the Legend of Wolves. Legend has it that a half-werewolf, half-vampire who presents as a were will have the ability to gift immortality. Because Bodin knew you were half vampire but presented as a were, he believed you were the one to fulfill the legend. He sent you away, Dex, because it was the only thing he could think of to protect you."

"You can't know that."

"I can. You can. I see it in your eyes."

"All you see in my eyes is disgust. For him and for you. I knew you'd do anything to help your cause. Why not add whoring to the list?"

It hurt more than she'd thought it would. It hurt so bad she wasn't sure if she could survive the pain.

His gaze returned to Bodin. The hate was still there, but so was a flash of longing. A longing that he extinguished as easily as he could choke the life out of the weak, aged were. His gaze slid back to hers. "It's just too damn bad," he said, "that we conceived a child from your lies. Now another child has to suffer, stuck with freaks like us for parents. One more life my grandfather has had his hand in ruining. But this time, he had your help."

CHAPTER THIRTY-FOUR

After Dex left his grandfather's room, Jes saw very little of him. He remained on the grounds, and despite the vast depression Jes had slipped into, their baby continued to thrive. Occasionally she'd venture from her bedroom and she'd catch a glimpse of him, but he'd immediately disappear.

Days passed. Bodin was on the verge of death. Soon, she began keeping vigil by his bedside, trading shifts with Amanda, often sleeping in the chair next to his bed. When Jes wasn't caring for him or comforting Amanda, she forced herself to sleep and eat for the baby's sake.

She was doing just that, sitting in the kitchen and forcing herself to drink bottled blood and choke down soup, when Dex appeared in front of her. She dropped her spoon and stood, swaying slightly. He looked both bad and good. Bad because he looked tired. Troubled. But good because he was him, and she wanted nothing more than to draw him in her arms and beg his forgiveness.

"Congratulations," he said, his tone as cold and unforgiving as ever. "I didn't realize I could think less of you, but I just talked to Lucy. She told me you talked to Mahone before leaving the States. And that you told him about this legend of yours. Even managed to get some money out of him for your trouble. For your research, right?"

She sank back into her chair. "That's right," she said softly, though she sounded nothing like herself. Did that faint, scratchy, defeated voice actually belong to her? "You might as well know I spoke to Rurik Pitts, too. Before I returned to France. I paid him for information about you, so he probably traveled here for me."

His expression darkened before he composed himself again. "It doesn't matter. Not anymore. There's something going down. I'm returning to the States."

"What?" she asked in disbelief. He was leaving her? "Today?"

He averted his gaze. "I leave tonight. Lucy and I are going to meet with shape-shifters in the States and try one last time to negotiate with them."

Since Dex had never told her what he and Cy had learned from the shape-shifters, she wasn't certain what that meant. All she knew was that she didn't want him to leave. "Why—why can't Lucy handle it herself?"

He scowled. "Because Lucy's been doing everything herself while I've been wasting my time here with you. I need to get back and do my job. You said the baby's been growing. That it's almost ready to be born. It should be fine. Unless there's something I don't know. If so, just tell me."

He couldn't even look at her, she thought. She disgusted him and he wanted no part of her. But of course that was true. She'd done nothing but lie and deceive him since the moment they'd met. No matter what her intentions had been, she'd acted with dishonor and he'd never forgive her for that.

Still, she felt compelled to ask him one last question. "So you're not going to be here for the birth? You—you don't care about the baby?"

He turned toward the door. Over his shoulder, he said, "I'll check in when I can. If the baby's born before then…" He shrugged, dismissing the birth and her, and at the same time giving her the answer to her question.

***

That evening, Dex held his phone to his ear as he stood outside Jes's castle. For once, his cell reception was crystal clear. Good, because he wasn't standing in that damn gazebo ever again.

"I'm not expecting much from this meeting," Mahone said, "but it's all we've got. We haven't been able to get anything from the weres. Bodin's MIA, and they refuse to say anything until they hear from him."

"What about the First Lady?" Dex asked, his voice flat. He wasn't going to discuss Bodin with Mahone. Not yet.

"No word. But the President has called a press conference. It's scheduled for tomorrow evening. Seven p.m."

"My flight will just have arrived."

"And we'll know, one way or another, if going to the Quorum was a lost cause or not."

"Right," Dex said. "I'll check in when I get Stateside."

"Dex..."

"Yeah?"

"I'm sorry about Jes. I don't think she meant any harm, which is why I didn't say anything."

Dex heard a noise behind him. He sensed Jes. Smelled her. For a second, he closed his eyes, wishing with all his heart things could've been different for both of them. But they couldn't. She'd lied to him. One time too many. He no longer trusted her.

"It doesn't matter," he forced himself to say to Mahone. "Jes means nothing to me, Mahone. Less than nothing." He hung up. Stood there. Expected her to scamper away. But she didn't. Instead, she spoke.

"Dex. Please don't leave."

Her plea stunned him. He knew how proud she was. Knew she'd heard what he'd said to Mahone. How could she think she could sway him? Why did she want to even try?

Slowly, he turned.

At some point, the dark dye had completely faded and he hadn't even realized it. Standing under the entryway lights, she looked like the same vamp he'd first met in L.A. Well, except for the fact she looked decidedly pregnant. But her lush curves only made her more attractive. Too bad all she'd wanted from him was what she thought he could give others—immortality.

"It's no use. I don't fulfill any crazy-assed legend. Even if I do, I don't know how to gift immortality. I can't help you."

"I don't care about that," she cried, walking closer to him. "I mean, I did. That's why I deceived you. And I'm so sorry for that, Dex. But I've changed. I understand what's important now, and that I've been denying myself a real life because I didn't think I deserve it."

"And now you do?"

"I don't know if I deserve it," she conceded, "but I know I want it. I want you. Not for my experiments, but because you make me happy. I love you and I know you can love me. Love our child."

"It's too late."

Her expression crumpled and tears fell from her eyes. It was the first time he'd ever seen her cry, he realized. And the first time since he'd been a child that he felt the sting of moisture in his own eyes.

"I'm sorry, Dex! I'm so sorry. *S'il te plait me pardone-moi.* Please forgive me. Please stay with me."

"I said no," he snapped, too tempted by his own need to forgive her. But he couldn't give in. He'd been a fool to think Jes was different. To think that he could be different with her.

His harsh tone seemed to jolt her. "Is it because of Lucy? You don't need me anymore because you'll be fucking her?"

"Stop it, Jes. You know that's not true. Even if it were, so what? Lucy has never lied to me. When she was using me, I knew exactly what was going on. That's the difference between you and her."

"But she doesn't love you, Dex. Not the way I do."

"Goddess save me from your kind of love, Jesmina. If this is love, I hope I never love again."

Her stricken expression was the last thing he saw before she finally gave up. She whirled and ran from him.

And although Dex took a step toward her…

Although he wanted to chase after her and tell her he'd changed his mind…

He didn't.

He swiped at his face and any trace of tears that might have lingered in his eyes. After taking a deep breath, he forced himself to recall Mahone's last words. He'd said the weres wouldn't talk until they'd heard from Bodin.

Fine.

Dex would just have to make sure that happened.

Without hesitation, he retraced the path to Bodin's room. Although he'd half-expected Jes to have moved him, she hadn't. He was still in bed. Pale. Old. Helpless.

Harmless.

But he hadn't always been that way, Dex reminded himself.

He stepped farther into the room, determined to shake the old were to consciousness, but he froze when he saw Amanda. She sat in the chair next to him, looking like she hadn't slept in weeks. She stood when she saw Dex.

"Come in," she whispered, shocking the hell out of him.

Not waiting to see whether he complied, she bent down, kissed Bodin's cheek, and spoke in his ear. Then she straightened and walked past Dex. Before she walked out, she paused to look at him. "I know why you hate him," she said, her voice barely audible. "I hate him for the same reason."

"Really?" he drawled in patent disbelief, telling himself not to be swayed by the sadness in her eyes. "Tell me about it," he said, even though he just wanted her to go.

"You hate him because he sent you away and your mother never recovered from it. She fought her depression, even married and had other children, but she never got over losing you. She ended her life rather than face her loss."

Okay, so she did know why he hated him. But what did that have to do with her?

"You still don't get it, do you, brother?" She laid a hand on Dex's arm and squeezed softly. "Can't you see who I am?"

"No," he choked out, jerking his arm from her touch. She was full were. She looked nothing like him. But something reached way back into his memory... If he allowed himself to remember the beautiful visage of his mother, rocking him to sleep and singing him a lullaby... He pictured a face startling similar to Amanda's.

"I never condoned what he did. Nor did our mother. We loved him, but we hated him. And we grieved for you, Dex. We all did. Bodin most of all."

While he was still in shock, she slipped out of the room.

Silence surrounded him, broken only by Bodin's slow, weak breathing.

As if he was in a trance, Dex walked to his grandfather.

He stared down at the werewolf he'd hated for so long, and he tried to feel pity for him.

Forgiveness. Compassion. Something. But he couldn't.

"I hope you rot in hell," he said, before whirling around and going after Amanda.

Bodin wasn't able to tell him anything about the solstice gates.

But maybe Dex's sister could.

CHAPTER THIRTY-FIVE

As soon as Dex's plane landed in the States, Lucy met him at the airport. She hugged him hard. When Lucy had told him about Jes contacting Mahone, Dex had filled Lucy in on the Legend of Wolves and the reasons Jes had sought Mahone out. Lucy hadn't said much then, and she didn't now, either. She simply asked, "Are you okay?"

She was his favorite Para-Ops team member for a reason, he thought tiredly and nodded his head. "I will be. What's going on with the press conference?"

"It's about to start. Let's find a television and check it out."

They found a bar and pissed off a few football fans by changing the channel on the big screen TV, but the bar pretty much cleared after Dex's colorful response. Lucy smiled and shook her head. "I'm glad to see you're the same old were."

"What did you expect? That less than two weeks in France would make me a better man?"

Despite his attempt at humor, his joke fell flat. Lucy looked away and Dex swore she was trying not to cry.

Fuck. "Lucy—"

But he was interrupted by the sounds of the Presidential Address commencing. Grim-faced, he and Lucy watched as the President was introduced.

He spoke on various topics, domestic and international. Just when it appeared he was winding down, he said, "Recently, I vetoed the award of federal funds that Congress set aside for a shape-shifter awareness campaign. My thinking was the money would be better served to hire more border agents. I've given it more thought. I've weighed the importance of strengthening the relationships between our citizens versus protecting our nation's resources. As we're still recovering from war, it's often easier to look outside ourselves and see enemies when what we must do is look within. I don't know how much you know about shape-shifters, but in truth, I probably don't know much more. That can't continue. Many fear shape-shifters because they are a mystery. Today I'm challenging us all to learn more about them. In order to let go of our bloody past and embrace a brighter tomorrow, I am authorizing the funds for a shape-shifter awareness campaign."

The journalists in the room exploded into action, peppering the President with questions.

Lucy turned to Dex, her gaze mirroring his own disbelief.

"We did it. The First Lady did it. She convinced the President to change his mind."

"I don't believe it," Dex said. "She must have some ulterior motive."

"Of course she does," Lucy said, slapping Dex's arm. "But for one second, can we simply enjoy this small victory? We need to confirm the shape-shifters are actually going to abandon their plans now. And we're still going to have to attend the meeting and propose a long-term plan in order to avoid something like this happening again. But right this minute—"

She grinned and for a second, Dex's mood, weighed down by his grief over Jes, lightened slightly. "Yeah," he said. "Only I'm not relying on the shape-shifters just telling us they've changed their minds. We have to assume a great number of them will still try to bridge demons through the solstice gates. We need to stop them. We might not be able to stop them forever, but if we can ensure they don't do anything now, when emotions are still high, we might buy the President the time he needs to prove he's serious about working with them."

"But how can we stop them?"

"I spoke to a werewolf in France, one who believes I can help close the solstice gate in the United States while she tries to close the one in Europe."

"Is this about the legend Jes told Mahone about?"

"Not necessarily. Apparently, werewolves have been charged with this duty for centuries. They fight the demons in human form; it's the only form they can take once they enter a solstice gate."

"Then they—*you*—can be killed."

"But if I am part of the legend, maybe I can prevent one of them, a significant one, from being killed."

"Small problem. You don't know how to access your gift to give it to anyone. Do you?"

"No. Jes tested my blood but came up with nothing."

"Who's this were you're working with? You trust her?"

"I have no reason to trust her, yet I do. At least with this. She's my half sister, a werewolf sworn to protecting the solstice gates. She says her destiny and the destiny of all weres is to prevent demons from crossing into earth. She was in France with my grandfather. Before I left, she gave me this." Dex reached into his backpack, then pulled out an envelope with a worn piece of paper inside. He showed it to Lucy. "According to Amanda, it's the only known recording of the Legend of Wolves."

They scanned the print together.

Protect the wolf whose ancestry none can see.
Protect the one who can gift immortality.
Cast him out before you let him be found.
He'll drive hell's demons back underground.

His…will give eternal life to a… ther
But only if he's gifted his…

Obserwować Demonie Krawcy.

"The last line means 'Watch The Demon Tailors.'" Dex explained. "Amanda said the solstice gate in the U.S. is near Death Valley, near Bodin's compound. That the pack is gathered there, prepared to drive demons away until the gate closes again."

"Dex, you can't know for sure you're this prophesized were! Besides, even if you are, you don't know how to gift immortality to anyone. Plus, how are you going to choose the right were? How do you know he won't abuse the privilege? And according to the legend, you need to have gifted *something* to *someone* before you can give someone eternal life anyway. This is all crazy!"

She had valid points. It *was* all crazy. But something was driving Dex. A feeling that, whether he was part of the legend or not, he had to be part of this battle. "Look, to gift immortality, I'd probably need to be in my immortal wolf form. If that's the case, how can I gift a piece of myself? Blood, semen, body, or bite, right?"

"I—I guess. I mean, that part sounds logical, at least."

"Jes didn't find anything in my blood that showed signs of an immortal gift, but she confirmed I'm half-vampire and half-were. If I *am* the were spoken of in the legend, the most logical way for me to gift anyone anything would be through my bite."

"Haven't you ever bitten another were while you were in wolf form?"

"Several times. And I killed them afterwards, so my bite obviously hadn't turned them immortal. But maybe that's because the solstice gate wasn't open.

And I wasn't near one at the time. Plus, if I'm supposed to have gifted someone something else, look at everything I've given in the last few months. Even to you," he tried joking. "Maybe that'll be the key."

"You're reaching, Dex. This is all speculation! That piece of paper is so faded and ambiguous, we can't know a damn thing for sure."

"You're right, but I have to try, Lucy. And I'm going to."

Lucy bit her lip in indecision. Then she held out her hand. "Give me the paper," she said. "Let me try a spell to make the faded words more clear."

Instinctively, Dex held the paper away from her. "Have you done that before?"

"No, but you haven't gifted anyone with immortality before either, have you?"

With a snort, Dex handed her the paper.

Gingerly, she held it between her fingers, closed her eyes, and started chanting. Bar patrons had already been shooting furtive glances at them, but now they stared. Since the paper in Lucy's hands had started to glow, Dex didn't blame them.

Dex peered over Lucy's shoulder. "Shit! It's working." The faded print wasn't reemerging, but the paper itself was glowing so the surface revealed a faint imprint from where the ink had been. Dex silently read the words.

*His **bite** will give eternal life to **another***
*But only if he's already gifted his **heart** to **a lover**.*

A quick glance confirmed Lucy's eyes were still closed. What a cluster fuck, he thought. He'd given Jes his heart. Granted, she'd taken it and sliced it open, but it didn't matter. She might be the key to accessing his gift, after all. "It worked," he said quietly. "You can stop."

Lucy eyes abruptly opened and the paper stopped glowing, returning to its original form. She scanned it with an impatient frown. "What did it say?"

"I was right. I need to bite another were."

"But what about the condition? What did you need to already have given?"

Dex shook his head and glanced away. He didn't want to think about Jes again. Didn't want to think about those fleeting days where he'd basked in her attention and love. It had all been a lie. *She'd* been a lie. "It doesn't matter. I've already done it."

"But—"

"Drop it, Lucy. We need to go. Amanda has already contacted a volunteer. He'll be waiting for me at the gate. Even if I don't gift him anything useful, I'll be there to guard the gate myself."

Lucy stared at him with uncertainty, then nodded. "I'll go with you—"

"No. The gates are werewolf domain. They won't let a non-were close. But come to California with me. We'll postpone the meeting with the shapeshifters and check into a hotel. I'll report back as soon as I can."

"I don't know, Dex. What's this really about? Why not go to the meeting and see if Mahone's plan worked?"

Agitated, Dex ran his fingers through his hair. He tried to explain the mix of urgency, restlessness, and purpose he was feeling. "I just—I need to fight, Lucy. I'm a were. I've rejected my heritage all my life, but if this is what I was born to do, if I really am meant to fulfill some kind of legend, I need to know. And I need to act. Can you understand that?"

She searched his gaze for several seconds before nodding. "Yes," she whispered. "So when do we leave for California?"

Dex pulled two tickets out of his backpack. "Right now."

***

ALABAMA HILLS, CALIFORNIA
JUST OUTSIDE LONE PINE & DEATH VALLEY

Dex stared unflinchingly at approximately thirty werewolves standing in front of him. They stared back with expressions ranging from suspicion to disdain and from hope to envy. Amanda had told him they wouldn't use guns because of the tight quarters and the danger of friendly fire. Nonetheless, the werewolves were armed to the hilt, dressed in leather and gripping axes, maces, or clubs. At the moment, their guns were holstered and knives sheathed, but they looked like they had itchy fingers. If Dex was wrong about being able to trust Amanda, he was shit out of luck. He wouldn't go down without fighting, but he was definitely going to go down in an extremely painful way.

His gaze flickered beyond the werewolves, to the hills that stood like silent sentinels guarding the gateway to the snow-capped majesty of Mount Whitney. All around him, the prevalent colors of nature were grey and brown, complimenting the black hair and dark skin of the full-blooded werewolves. Although the colors should have reminded him of barrenness and death, they didn't. Energy pulsed off the sharp granite edges of the Sierras, filling Dex with determination. At this moment, he truly felt he was facing his destiny head on. If that resulted in his death, so be it.

A flicker of doubt invaded his mind along with an image of Jes cradling a baby. *His* baby. If he died, he'd never see her again. Never see his child.

But as he'd told Lucy, he knew this was the right thing to do.

"So what's it going to be," he called out. "Was I wrong to trust Amanda? Do you want my help or not?" He deliberately glanced at his watch. "Because according to my sources, the solstice gate is going to open in just over an hour.

A broad bulky male holding a wicked-looking scythe, stepped forward and kept coming. The guy towered over Dex by several inches and probably outweighed him by fifty pounds. Dex didn't back away and respect softened the other male's features. His gaze flickered to Dex's hunting knife, sheathed at his waist. "I'm Hal. You came with a pretty small weapon, were."

"Big or small, it'll get the job done, just like I will."

"That's what Amanda says. Bodin, too."

Dex frowned but refused to utter one word about his grandfather.

Hal continued. "Your grandfather has a message for you. One I'll deliver *after*—if you're still alive, that is. Agreed?"

"Fine," Dex gritted out. "Now tell me, who am I going to bite?"

"You're not biting anyone."

"What? Amanda said she'd arranged for someone to—"

"It was Bodin's order. He said the gift of immortality couldn't be given lightly, not even to one of his own, unless you were sure it was meant to happen. Are you?"

Hell no, Dex thought. He didn't even know if defeating hell's demons was conditioned on him gifting immortality in the first place. That's what they'd all assumed, but it wasn't like the legend spelled it out. Plus what his grandfather had said made sense. Years ago, Bodin's own weres had tried to kill Jes and her parents, forcing Bodin to intervene. What if one of those weres had been immortal? How ironic that he had the very thing Jes had spent her whole life searching for, but when it came to dispensing it, he was as cautious as his grandfather. "Damn it, I'm not sure of anything except that I need to be here. That I need to fight."

Hal shrugged in a movement that reminded Dex of Cy. "Then fight. Fight next to us the way you always should have. Not as a legend, but as a were."

Dex glanced at his watch again. "We're wasting time."

When Dex looked up, Hal had already turned back to the others. "Brothers, we fight. Let us keep all the demon spawn where they belong. On the other side of the gate!"

Roars and cheers came from the crowd. The werewolves no longer looked at Dex. They turned and marched toward the mountains behind them.

Over his shoulder, Hal glanced at Dex. There was a question in his gaze. Dex answered by following him.

Within an hour, they entered a canyon that dead-ended into a group of boulders and a small cave that looked like a pig's snout.

"That's it," Hal said. "The solstice gate is inside that cave. In order to get out, the demons must take their original form," Hal explained, "The only difference is their red eyes and razor-sharp claws. With the return of their human form comes weakness. Mortality. If we kill it here, it goes back to hell and must wait months before it can be bridged again."

"And if it passes through the gate?" Dex had asked.

"It loses form until it finds a host. Through life or through dreams."

Hal's words were consistent with what the blond mage from Jes's village had told him. The werewolf held out his hand. "Good luck."

Dex hesitated only briefly before shaking the werewolf's hand. "Thanks. You, too."

The next twenty-four hours passed in a blur, one dominated by werewolf blood and pain and desperation. The werewolves were greatly outnumbered but somehow they were managing to hold off the masses of dark spirits who'd taken human form and came at them one after another.

Screams and the clash of steel echoed all around him. Werewolf blood painted the floor of the caves—apparently, demons didn't bleed even when in their human form. Hours passed before Dex caught sight of Hal again, caught in a corner fighting a demon. Using his scythe, Hal severed a demon's head from its body. Instantly, the demon's remains vanished, leaving no trace of itself.

A demon came at Dex, swiping at him with his claws. Dex ducked and elbowed the thing in the neck. When it staggered back, Dex jammed it in the gut with his knife. It howled before disappearing.

Another demon stepped in front of him. Dex slapped both hands against the demon's face, then followed up with an elbow strike before snapping the demon's neck.

Next, two demons came at him, one on either side, and Dex leaped in the air, striking out at one with his knife while kicking the other in the chest. The one he'd cut collapsed, but the other regained its feet faster than Dex expected. It barreled into Dex and took him down to the ground. Dex dropped his knife and grunted when his head struck a rock, but he managed to stay conscious as he grappled with his attacker.

In the distance, Dex saw a demon rip the arms off one werewolf, then another.

There were too many demons.

The werewolves were tiring.

Even Hal was being driven back. Several demons pushed him closer and closer to the entrance of the cave. Dex screamed when the demon he was grappling with sliced his shoulder. At the sound, the demon grinned, certain of its victory.

No fucking way.

Bringing his knees to his chest, Dex pushed out with his feet and sent the demon flying. Immediately, it charged him again, scrambling on all fours like a spider. Dex rolled to his knife and just managed to grip the handle. Twisting onto his back, he held the blade up just in time to impale the demon as it threw itself on top of it.

Scrambling to his feet, Dex glanced around. About half of the werewolves were dead. Even so, despite their exhaustion, they pressed on. Hal had managed to stop his backward approach to the cavern entrance and was cutting down one demon after another.

Dex's werewolf blood pulsed through his veins and filled him with a sense of pride. Finally, he was one with his pack. With a battle cry, Dex jumped back into the fray.

***

Later, when Dex finally walked into Lucy's cramped motel room in Lone Pine, he was covered in blood—his own and that of his fellow weres—but he couldn't stop grinning. He'd killed before. Battled with others for a higher cause. But fighting with the werewolves in the midst of those bleak mountains had fed something in him. It had healed him in a way even his work on the Para-Ops team hadn't. "We did it," he told Lucy. "We held them off until the gate closed. A few got past us—I spoke to Amanda and the same thing happened in Europe—but the *diabols* won't be a global threat for at least another year. The few *diabols* that escaped will be hunted down by the shape-shifters as they have been for the past few years and months."

"That's wonderful, Dex." Not caring about the blood or grime, Lucy threw her arms around him. He'd hugged her before, but this time, despite the rush of his recent battle and victory, thoughts and images of Jes bombarded him. Abruptly, he pulled away. "Don't—please don't," he growled.

After the battle, Hal had relayed his grandfather's message to him. "Don't repeat my mistake. Don't throw away what's yours because of fear." But Dex hadn't walked away from Jes out of fear. She'd pushed him away with her lies and deceit. Hadn't she?

"Dex?" Lucy whispered.

A pit of desperation formed inside him, spreading and threatening to swallow him whole. How was he ever going to fill it?

The feelings magnified while he was in the shower. By the time he was dressed and standing in front of Lucy again, he wasn't sure he could survive his grief. Had he fought hell's demons and won only to undergo a mental collapse as a result of losing Jes?

No.

He couldn't give Jes that power over him. He wouldn't.

He gripped Lucy's arms. "Would you do something for me, Lucy?"

"What?"

"Would you have sex with me? Right now? If I told you I needed to wipe my mind clean, that I needed a distraction, that I'd be using you just like I let you use me, would you sleep with me? No love. No feelings. No nothing."

"Yes," she said simply. "I would. But I don't want to. And I know you don't want to, either, Dex."

"Maybe it's exactly what I need," he began, but the ring of his cell phone interrupted him. He hadn't taken it with him, so it rang from his backpack. Lucy pulled away from him, retrieved it, and handed it to him. He checked the screen, frowning when he didn't recognize the number.

"Dex Hunt," he said when he activated the call.

"Dex, this is Cy. Thank God I finally reached you. I swear, we're going to install a fucking satellite phone in the castle. I've been trying to reach you for hours."

"I've been a little busy, Cy. You wouldn't have been able to—forget it. What's wrong?"

"It's Jes. She's gone into labor early. The baby's coming, but it's not going smoothly. She's struggling, Dex, and she's calling for you. I'm sorry, but—"

The phone went dead. Dex cursed and redialed Cy's number, but he couldn't get a connection no matter how many times he tried.

"Dex."

He barely heard Lucy's voice, but he felt her hand on his arm. It was enough to jolt him out of his paralysis. He'd thought today was about victory, but it might be about failure instead. The worst failure imaginable. "Help me, Lucy," he said. "Please help me."

CHAPTER THIRTY-SIX

"We need Knox," Lucy insisted. "He used to live in France. He can meet us someplace close, then teleport you to Jes."

"He won't do that," Dex said. "He'll worry about Felicia. Teleporting me will drain him of his powers so he won't be at full strength, which means he'll be less able to protect her. He won't want to take that chance."

"You can't assume that. Knox cares about us. About you. You need to ask him for help."

Dex knew that's exactly what he needed to do. He just didn't want to. He hated asking for help from others because he was always certain he'd never get it. That he didn't deserve it. After all, Elliott had come to Dex for help in the orphanage, and Dex hadn't done a thing. Yet what choice did he have now? Despite Jes's warnings that leaving could hurt the baby, that's exactly what he'd done. Now the baby was coming early and both of them were in danger. Jes needed him and all he could remember was the last time she'd come to him, begging for his forgiveness. Instead of giving it to her, he'd lashed out instead. And the sad thing was, he wasn't sure he'd act any differently even if given a second chance.

He knew Jes wasn't a bad person, but she did bad things to feed her obsession, and someone like that could not be trusted. But that didn't mean he'd abandon her or their child when they needed him.

He turned to Lucy. "I need you to come with me."

She flinched in surprise. "What? Why?"

"Your powers might be useful. You can enchant her so she'll feel less pain. Or maybe you can move the baby out of her..."

"Dex, I've never tried that. I don't even know if it's possible."

"I don't care. I need you there with me, Lucy. Knox can teleport both of us. One at a time. Just like he did on that mission in Korea. Please."

She nodded. "Fine. If Knox agrees to teleport us both, I'll go. But if he can only teleport one of us..."

"Then I'll go by myself."

It was a testament to Knox and his honor that he didn't even hesitate when Dex explained the situation. "Meet me at the main entrance to Death Valley National Park. I'll be there in about an hour."

Dex was so stunned and grateful he could barely choke out, "Thank you, Knox."

"You're welcome, Dex. We'll get you there. What you do next is up to you."

After Knox hung up, Knox's parting salvo didn't leave Dex's mind from that moment on. In less than an hour, his friend teleported both him and Lucy thousands of miles to a location familiar to him, one just miles from Jes's castle. "I'm sorry I can't get you any closer, but since I've never been there..."

"I understand. This is good." A quick glance at Lucy confirmed she was still catching her breath after the painful teleportation. Dex held out his hand to Knox.

Knox clasped it. "Good luck," he said

Dex turned away, but something made him look back. Knox was staring at him with an intense though unreadable expression.

"What is it?" Dex asked.

"You'll remember your promise, won't you?"

His promise? The one Knox had extracted from him at the hospital? "Of course, Knox. You'll never have to worry about Felicia while I'm around. I told you that."

"Thank you. I hope you know I'd do the same for you."

Dex swallowed hard. "You just did. But why are you—"

"Go on," Knox said. "Go to her. She needs you. I know you'll be a good father, Dex. I believe in you."

O-kay. Now Dex was more confused than ever. It was great that Knox had faith in him, but why did the vampire sound like he was saying goodbye? Before he could question him, Knox vanished.

Dex turned to Lucy, who appeared equally confused. But they'd have to figure out Knox later. "I'm going to shift. I'll get there faster."

Lucy nodded. "I'll be there as soon as I can. Go, Dex."

And he went. He didn't even feel the pain as he shifted. He couldn't feel anything but fear. While he'd gotten to France in record time, it might not have been fast enough to save them. Jes or the baby.

When he arrived at Paladine, the grounds looked exactly as they had when he left. He shifted back into human form, then checked the surgery room that had access to the outside. It was empty, but he grabbed some surgical scrubs and threw them on.

He ran inside. "Cy!" he yelled. "Jes! It's Dex. Where are you?"

He headed to the second surgery room, the one where Amanda had been cutting Jes.

But it was empty, as well.

He hadn't seen anyone. Hadn't heard anyone. Where the hell were they?

He whirled and almost ran into Cy.

The dragon-shifter looked exhausted, with dark grooves under his eyes. He shook his head. "You're too late," he said.

Dex snarled and lunged at him, grabbing his shirt and shaking him. "No! Damn you, don't say that! Don't tell me they're dead."

"Dex! Stop it." Cy shouted. "I didn't say they're dead. You missed the birth, that's all. They're okay. It was touch and go there for awhile, but they're both okay. You have a son. Congratulations."

Dex couldn't tell if Cy was being sarcastic. He didn't care. "Jes is okay?"

"She's exhausted. Asleep. She tore and lost a lot of blood, so Amanda gave her a sedative. I need to get some sleep. I'm going to crash in one of the recovery rooms. I've been up for almost forty-eight hours. I'm so out of it, I'm not even going to ask how you got here so fast."

"Shut up and tell me where she is, Cy."

"She's in her bedroom. With the baby. Giselle's been checking in on them."

"Can I—can I see her?"

Cy laughed but there was no humor in the sound. "It's your kid, Dex. And Jes? She belongs to you, too. The question is whether you'll finally accept that, or if you're going to prove me right and leave her again."

"Isn't that what you want?" Dex growled.

"All I want is for Jes to be happy. And to hope that maybe I can be happy again, too. I'm not sure either will ever happen. You hurt her, Dex. Bad. I knew you would." He walked away, muttering, "I knew you would."

"Cy," he called out one more time. "What of Bodin?"

Cy shrugged. Shook his head. Then was gone.

So his grandfather was dead. Why wasn't he happy at the news? He'd wanted his grandfather dead most of his life, but now it didn't even matter.

Dex made his way to Jes's room, trying not to feel like a prisoner being led to his execution.

He remembered lying in bed with Jes, thinking about baby names and wondering what their baby would look like. If it would have silver hair. Even now he wondered if it would be as pale as Jes or more toasty like Knox.

As he climbed the stairs and paused outside her bedroom door, he second-guessed whether he should go to them. After all, Cy had said they were okay. The dragon-shifter was watching over them, as was Giselle. Why should Dex bother seeing them if he was just going to leave again?

But there was no way he was leaving without seeing his son. He pushed open the door and gasped.

Jes lay in her queen bed, looking small and lost under the sheets. He walked toward her. She was beyond pale now, with dark shadows under her eyes and sunken cheekbones, evidence of the arduous trial she'd just undergone. As he peered down at her, he couldn't help but remember the precious few times they'd bantered and touched and even laughed together. Was that really going to be gone from his life forever? Was she?

Knox's words echoed in his brain. *What you do next is up to you...I know you'll be a good father, Dex. I believe in you.*

Knox believed in him and Knox was the most honorable man Dex knew. He was, Dex admitted to himself, a true friend.

Taking courage from his friend's words, Dex turned toward the small bassinet he'd glimpsed when he'd walked into the room. When he peered inside, his blood froze.

The baby was awake, staring up at him with eyes that weren't black like his mother's, but a golden, tawny brown. Just like Dex's.

His son was part vampire and part were. He should look like a vampire. But like Dex, he was an anomaly.

The kind of anomaly that could prove a legend true.

In that second, there was no doubt in Dex's mind of what he had to do.

All he could think of was protecting his son.

***

When Lucy finally arrived at Paladine Abbey, she was breathing hard but patting herself on the back. Who knew she could run so fast for so long? Why, she'd bet Dex hadn't beaten her by more than twenty minutes, she mused. She eyed the massiveness of Jes's castle as she started to climb up the entryway steps.

The front door swung open and suddenly Dex was there, a wild look in his eyes as he cradled a small cloth bundle to his chest. He was kind of holding it like a football, but if she wasn't mistaken—

"Dex?" she asked slowly. "Where are you going with the baby?"

His gaze jerked to hers and she caught her breath at the terror reflected in their depths. "He's a were, Lucy. He looks just like me."

Oh shit. What was wrong with him? "Poor kid," she tried to joke. "But Jes found you attractive. I'm sure he's not that bad off."

"No." He shook his head fiercely as he stared down at his son. "You don't understand. He's like me. He's part of the legend. The one Jes told Mahone about. The child of a vampire and a were that doesn't look like a vampire. Which means he's just like me. Why does he have to be just like me?"

His question sounded so tortured that Lucy almost cried out. "Dex, stop it. Why shouldn't he be just like you? You're wonderful. Brave. Strong. A good friend."

"I'm a coward," he shouted. "A fucking joke. A whipped dog."

"No! That's what others have called you, Dex, but it's not true."

"It is," he said. "It is. I didn't help him. Elliott. When he came to me at the orphanage, I didn't help him and because of me he got hurt. He died."

"Oh Dex." Lucy felt lost. She didn't know what to say. She knew he'd suffered abuse. It had been so obvious. But she'd had no idea that he blamed himself for the abuse another had suffered. No wonder he'd been so protective of her. She was the most youthful looking of the Para-Ops team. The most innocent. He'd have seen her as his second chance to help the child he hadn't been able to save. "Dex, you've helped so many people. You. Me. The Para-

Ops team. We're all doing good. We're making the world a better place for your baby. You and Jes will be wonderful parents."

He scowled at her when she mentioned the baby, pulling the bundle closer to his chest. "No. She can't have the baby. She'll use it for her experiments. I won't have him suffer like that. Not even for her."

"Okay," Lucy said, moving toward him. He wasn't himself. He was distraught and wouldn't listen to reason right now. She just needed to get the baby from him.

To her surprise, he held the baby out to her. "You take him."

"Uh, what?" But the next thing she knew, she was cradling the baby, gazing into the cherubic face of an adorable werebeast baby that had Dex's eyes and Jes's nose and mouth. "Dex, he's beautiful. But what do you want me to do with him?"

"Take him. Meet me at the airport. We'll leave together."

"Dex, no! Are you crazy? Where's Jes?"

"They gave her a sedative. She's asleep upstairs."

"Are you kidding me?" she yelled, jiggling the baby when he startled and began to fuss. "Dex, you can't take him. She'll never forgive you."

"It doesn't matter. He'll be safe. That's all that matters."

"Dex—"

"Lucy." He spoke firmly, his gaze suddenly clear. He seemed cognizant now, completely aware of what he was doing and why. "Trust me. I have to do this. Are you going to side with Jes or me?"

She didn't even hesitate. "You. You know that, Dex. But this is wrong."

"I'll meet you at the airport."

"But where are you going?"

"Once you're far enough away and can get a ride to the airport, call me. At that point, I'll tell Cy, Jes's brother, what I've done. You'll be too far away for them to stop you, but they'll know the baby is safe. I—I owe them that much."

"I hope you know what you're doing, Dex."

Dex placed his hand on the baby's forehead, the first sign of affection he'd shown his son since she'd arrived. "I'm doing what I have to do, Lucy. I promise."

***

Dex waited in the iron gazebo. About an hour after Lucy left, she called him on his cell phone and told him she'd caught a train and was on the way to the airport. They'd be there in a little over three hours.

After thanking her and disconnecting the call, Dex went inside to find Cy. He was headed toward the recovery rooms when he heard a scream coming from upstairs.

He winced. It was Jes.

There was another scream. A low agonized howl of pain. And then another.

Shouts. Unintelligible for the most part except for two distinct words.

My baby. My baby.

He couldn't do it. No matter what she'd done, he couldn't let her wonder what had happened to her baby. She wouldn't understand that Dex had taken him to protect him. But he'd explain and—

He caught movement out of the corner of his eye and whirled.

"You bastard," Cy roared, coming at him with fists swinging. "What have you done?"

"Cy, wait!" Dex yelled

But the dragon-shifter was incensed and punched Dex in the face so hard Dex wondered if he'd shifted into marble first. He hadn't done it the first time they'd fought, but this time—Dex hit the ground and skidded several feet before crashing into a wall. He blinked and regained his feet in time to see Cy running in the direction of Jes's screams.

Dex followed on his heels.

"I'll kill you!" Cy yelled over his shoulder.

"I had to take the baby away. He looks like a were. She would have hurt him. Experimented on him."

Cy careened to a stop, whirled, and punched Dex in the face again. At least he tried to. Dex dodged and blocked the punch with his arm. They strained against one another, Cy's face inches from Dex's. "You idiot. Jes would die for that baby. She'd die for you. Hell, she'd fucking die for me. And you really think she'd do anything to hurt a child? Let alone hers?" Cy shoved Dex away. "You don't fucking deserve her."

He whirled, leaving Dex to stand there, stunned, too paralyzed to move as words rained down on him.

Cy's words.

Jes would die for that baby. She'd die for you. Hell, she'd fucking die for me.

Jes's words.

If it was that easy...I'd have turned a whole bunch of others into vampires. But you're right, considering I'd have been risking my life, I didn't make the offer to anyone. Anyone but Bodin, that is. But he refused and I already told you, I don't make people do things against their will.

Even Mahone's words.

I'm sorry about Jes. I don't think she meant any harm, which is why I didn't say anything.

As soon as the words faded, he was bombarded by other memories.

Lucy trying to play matchmaker between them. Ella trusting Jes to take care of her. Bodin going to Jes when he knew the end was near.

The signs had been everywhere and he'd chosen to ignore them.

Jes loved. She was loved. Everyone who met her, no matter the circumstances, respected her and believed in her innate goodness.

Dex had been the only one to ever doubt that.

Of course Jes wouldn't hurt their baby.

She'd done a lot of things that could be classified as mistakes, all with good intentions, but she'd never intentionally hurt another living thing. All she'd done was try to heal and help others. And what had Dex done in return?

Taken the one thing she wanted most in the entire world. A love that would never leave her.

Her baby.

Suddenly, he was moving again. But when he heard the next high-pitched scream, he knew it was over.

* * *

When Dex made it to the foyer, Cy was kneeling at the bottom of the stairs next to Jes's crumpled body. The look on Cy's face was pure horror.

"No!" Dex shouted, fear pulsing through him. He ran to them, wincing when he saw a trickle of blood on Jes's temple.

Cy looked at Dex, his eyes shimmering with tears.

"What happened?" Dex demanded.

"I—I don't know," Cy said shakily. "One minute she was standing at the top of the stairs, screaming. I shouted for her to calm down. That the baby was all right. But she wouldn't listen. When I reached her, she—" Cy closed his eyes as if trying to block out some kind of horror.

"What, damn it? What did she do?"

Cy's eyes popped back open. "She—she looked at me as if she didn't know who I was. She said she was going to kill me. And she—she tried to rip my throat out. Literally. She came at me with her fangs. I'd never even seen them before! I struggled with her, tried to restrain her, but she was so fucking strong. She pulled me down the stairs with her and now—now she won't wake up."

The sound of a baby crying interrupted them. Their heads snapped up.

Lucy stood in the doorway holding the baby. Her gaze moved from Dex to Jes. "I couldn't do it. I lied, Dex. I never went to the airport. I thought you'd be gone by now and I could give the baby back to Jes. I'm sorry."

"It's okay, Lucy," Dex said, trying to keep everyone, including himself, calm. "She's hurt. We need to help her. Jes is hurt."

"I can see its aura," Lucy said. "It's inside her."

"What is, Lucy?" Dex asked, even though he knew.

She raised her terrified gaze to his. "A dark spirit has possessed her."

CHAPTER THIRTY-SEVEN

It was funny how Jes could see and hear what was happening even though she shouldn't have been able to. After all, her eyes and ears no longer belonged to her anymore, but to the power that had claimed possession of her body and even now was trying to overtake her mind.

For a moment, she ceased her frantic struggles.

She'd been struggling, she realized. Fighting.

Why?

She couldn't even remember.

She remembered pain as her baby had tried to slip from her body.

Pain as she'd held her baby and felt only the loss of his father.

Pain when she'd awoken and found her baby missing. Taken from her.

Pain when her chest had caught on fire.

Pain when she'd seen Cy and realized he'd been the one responsible.

Pain upon pain upon pain.

She was a doctor, wasn't she? Why couldn't she stop the pain?

But she had, she realized. She'd stopped the pain.

She was dead. She could see her body lying on the floor. Dex was there. So was Cy. Even Lucy. And Lucy—

Whatever was left of Jes's spirit cried out at the sight of Lucy holding her baby. Why did she have him? Had Dex given him to her? But no, Lucy handed her baby to Cy and told Cy to watch him. "Watch him for Jes," Lucy whispered.

She calmed and turned her attention back to Dex. His face was contorted in anguish. He looked so sad, as if he couldn't bear the thought that she was dead. For a moment, Jes ached to comfort him, but of course she couldn't. She wasn't even here anymore.

"The other mage," he said to Lucy. "She said a *diabol* could only possess a living person temporarily. That it's only in dreams that a possession can become permanent."

"But she's unconscious," Lucy countered. "How do we know she's not dreaming right now?"

Huh, Jes thought. That made sense. She'd always known Lucy was a smart one.

The baby started to fuss in Cy's arms and Jes frowned. Why was he holding her baby? She wanted to comfort her baby. Sing to him. Take care of him with Dex's help. Only Dex didn't want them. He'd taken the baby away from her…

"Jes. What are you doing? You should be in bed."

Giselle materialized. Giselle had helped deliver the baby, but she hadn't been here a moment ago. Where had she come from?

"I'm here to help you," Giselle said.

That sounded right. Giselle was always helping Jes. Giselle had been there for Jes when Dex hadn't been. Instinctively, Jes moved toward her.

"She's letting go! I can feel it," Lucy screamed.

Jes flinched at the sound and turned her head—

"No," Giselle soothed. "Don't listen to any of that. You're tired. You need to rest. As soon as you do, you'll have the baby again. It'll just be the two of you. Forever. Just like you always wanted."

Just like she'd always wanted, Jes thought. Yes. She moved forward, ever closer to Giselle.

But unfortunately, Dex wouldn't stop talking.

"Don't leave me, Jes," he begged. "I'm so sorry for what I did. I just wanted to protect the baby, but I should have known you would never hurt him. Even if the legend is true, you'd never do anything that would endanger him. I should have trusted you. Believed in the power of your love. After all, it had the power to change me. You taught me to love, and that's a fucking miracle right there."

She thought she heard him sobbing, but that couldn't be right. Dex wouldn't cry. Dex wouldn't say any of that to her. Lucy was right. She must be dreaming.

And that meant she could go with Giselle.

***

"Damn it, we're losing her again," Lucy cried.

"No!" Dex framed Jes's pale face in his. "Hang on, Jes." He'd been getting through to her. She'd heard him. He knew she had. "Don't you dare give in! Fight!"

"This dark spirit's powerful," Lucy said. "But if he's in Jes's head, what does it want?"

"It wants to live," Dex said, remembering what the mage in the village had told him. "To take over her body permanently."

"How?"

"By using a guise. The mage in the village told us that when a person is unconscious, a *diabol* could enter her mind the same way it would if the person is sleeping. As a dream. But the *diabol* would have to present itself as someone the dreamer knew and trusted. But who—" Dex's gaze jerked to Cy. "You said Giselle was checking on Jes and the baby, but I haven't seen her."

Cy nodded and handed the baby to Dex. "I'll see if she's in her room."

"No wait," Dex said, thinking. "If she's been possessed and the *diabol* is using her as a guise, that means there's probably a shape-shifter nearby, the same one who created the bridge." Torn, Dex looked down at Jes. "I can't let you go by yourself, but—"

"It's okay, Dex, go. Leave me the baby," Lucy said. "You and Cy find Giselle. It might be the only way to save Jes."

Lucy was right. Dex knew that. But he couldn't bear the thought of leaving Jes this way. Of losing her.

Gently, Lucy took the baby from Dex. "Dex, I'll stay with her. I promise. I'll guard her with my life, just like I know you'd do for me. Trust me."

Lucy meant every word she said. She'd guard the baby and she'd guard Jes or she'd die trying. Gently, he kissed Jes and climbed to his feet. "Don't let her go, Lucy. Keep talking to her. Keep telling her how sorry I am and that I love her."

***

As they ran to Giselle's room, Cy leading the way, Dex gripped his hunting knife. "You have any of those poisonous throwing stars?" he asked Cy. "Because they'd sure come in handy right about now."

Breathing hard, his expression grim, Cy nodded. "Yeah. Give me a second to shift. When I'm ready, bust down the door. I'll be right behind you."

"How will I know you're ready?"

Cy grinned. "Believe me, you'll know." He turned a corner before slowing down and pressed a finger to his lips. "This way," he said softly.

Stealthily, they walked until Cy stopped in front of a door. Cy stood on one side of the door while Dex stood on the other. Cy looked at Dex and mouthed "form number two" then started to shift. Dex recalled Cy saying he could shift into three different forms, only one of which gave him a tail. Within seconds just as it had before, Cy's body marbleized. Instead of bursting into flames, however, it became covered in sharp scales. But then something even more amazing happened.

Cy disappeared. Into thin air. As if he had the power to teleport. Or, Dex realized, to render himself invisible. Fuck. That was a sign if there'd ever been one.

Dex kicked in the door and burst into the room, leaving space for the dragon-shifter to navigate around him. Giselle was lying on the bed, restrained, eyes closed, seemingly fine but for the thing undulating inside her. Next to the bed stood not one shape-shifter, but two.

It wasn't the sight of more than one shape-shifter that caused Dex to freeze.

It was the sight of who was with them: Ella.

One shape-shifter held the little girl in front of his chest, one arm around her waist, her feet dangling off the floor, a knife to her throat. Ella's eyes were wide, her fear apparent despite the way she struggled against her captor's grip.

Dex held out his hands. "Hold on, hold on. Don't do anything rash."

"Put down your knife," the shape-shifter yelled. As soon as he spoke, Dex recognized him. It was "Righty," the *diregeant* shape-shifter who'd only spoken once, and only then to ask Dex if he'd impregnated Jes.

"Now," Righty yelled when Dex didn't immediately comply. He tightened his hold on Ella, making her whimper.

"Okay, it's okay. I'm putting it down." Slowly, Dex bent to lay the knife on the floor. As he did so, he said, "It's okay, Ella. I won't let him hurt you. I promise."

"Be quiet!" Righty yelled.

But as soon as he did, his companion did a stupid thing. Instead of maintaining a position of safety near Ella, it ran. Not toward the outer door through which Dex and Cy had passed, but toward an open doorway to the right, likely the bathroom. If it was configured like Jes's bathroom, it had a large window that accessed the outside.

Righty automatically watched as the fleeing shape-shifter cried out. His body convulsed several times from the impact of Cy's throwing stars before falling to the ground.

Dex didn't hesitate. As soon as Righty turned its head, Dex lunged for his knife, grasped the hilt, and threw it. It whistled through the air and plunged into the shape-shifter's right temple.

Righty howled. Blood sprayed out of his head and he released Ella. Ella immediately sprang forward and ran to Dex.

She launched herself into his arms and he hugged her, saying, "It's okay. You're okay." He held her out in front of him so he could examine her. "Did he hurt you?"

Ella shook her head. "But Giselle," she whispered. "It—it's hurting her."

A spark of energy shook the air just as a naked Cy appeared beside them. He immediately checked to make sure both shape-shifters were dead, nodding to Dex in confirmation. Cy grabbed a sheet and wrapped it around himself.

Dex hurried to Giselle but could only look down at her helplessly.

He didn't know what to do.

Her body was still undulating, which meant the *diabol* was still inside her.

***

Where had Dex gone? He'd been yelling at her, commanding her not to go, but then he'd left. Had he remembered that she'd lied to him? Had he decided he didn't love her after all?

"Come, Jes. Come let me hold you," Giselle said.

Giselle was a great hugger, Jes thought. But then another voice reached her.

"Dex was right, you know." It was Lucy. She sounded like she was crying. "You changed him. You performed a miracle, Jes, and you can perform another miracle. Come back to us. Don't let this thing take you away. Please. Dex loves you. He'll always love you. And he'll always love your son."

Dex. He loved her. He would miss her, she realized, but he'd also have Lucy to take care of him. Him and their baby.

Although it made her sad, the thought also made her happy.

It's okay, Dex, she tried to say, though she didn't know where he'd gone or if he could hear her. It's not your fault. I understand why you did what you did. Considering how I lied to you, what else were you going to think? But don't worry now. Our baby will always have you. I know you'll take care of him. I know you'll love him the way I love him. The way I love you.

"Stop it," Giselle growled. "Stop it and come here, you bitch."

Jes startled. Had Giselle just called her a bitch? Prim and proper Giselle, who never swore? Who wasn't hateful or mean?

In front of her, Giselle's form shimmered until it grew dark. Ominous. Evil.

Ah, now this dream makes sense, Jes thought.

A *diabol* was inside her, trying to lure her to it so it could kill her in her dream and possess her body. And the reason it was freaking out was because the emotions that had allowed it to enter her in the first place—her horror and grief and terror over losing her baby—were fading. She'd begun to do what Bodin had urged her to do. She was letting go of her pain.

It was the last thing Bodin had told her before he'd died. In one last bout of clarity, he'd called for her. When she'd arrived, he'd pulled her close.

"Live, Jes. Do good but be happy. It's the best weapon of all. Demon Tailors help dark spirits called *diabol*s enter a person's dreams. Their power is in negative emotion. Let go of the emotion, the hate, and the fear, and they have no power over you. Tell Dex to let it go before it kills him. Ask him to try and forgive me. And tell him I'm sorry. I wanted to love him. I would have. I did."

I did, Bodin had said before he'd died. Meaning, he'd loved Dex.

Just as Jes loved Dex.

And her love was the best weapon of all.

She stared at the evilness in front of her and smiled. Foolish, she thought. It had been so foolish to think she'd surrender anything to it.

"I forgive you, Dex. *Je t'aime*," she whispered.

She heard the *diabol* scream in fury.

Then she was no more.

***

Jes was so still.

She had been still for almost twenty-four hours. Ever since the *diabol* had been expelled from Giselle's body and Jes's mind. One minute Dex, Cy, and Ella had been watching Giselle's body undulate and then it had stopped. Giselle had groaned and seemed to come back to herself. While Cy and Ella stayed behind, Dex had run back to Jes.

"It's gone," Lucy had said. "Did you—"

Dex had nodded. "Hopefully Giselle will be okay. The shape-shifters that were bridging the *diabol* are dead. Why isn't Jes waking up?"

But Lucy hadn't known why Jes remained unconscious. Or whether she'd come out of it.

After checking her for injuries and determining that, physically at least, she was okay, they brought her into her bedroom, hopeful that the familiar surroundings would soothe her and encourage her to come back to them.

Dex and the baby never left her room. After checking with Knox to make sure it was okay, Dex sent Cy for formula to feed the baby. His son drank it somewhat reluctantly but it was enough to curb his hunger. At one point, Cy came in to report Giselle had woken up. She was shaken and traumatized, but would be fine.

Dex prayed the same would be true for Jes.

As he watched over her, her body occasionally flinched, as if she was still fighting something inside her. Dex told himself that was good. It meant she was fighting her way back to them.

Sitting on the bed beside her, Dex held their son. Gazing into the baby's wide, serious eyes, Dex said, "She's a fighter. Your mother will fight to the death to come back to you. To us."

The baby gurgled as if agreeing. Dex rested his forehead against the baby's tiny chest and listened to the strong, reassuring beat of his heart. He allowed his tears to flow freely. There was no shame in loving Jes as much as he did or in fearing the loss of her. He prayed one day his son would find a mate to love just as much. He also hoped he'd be smart enough to cherish that mate from the very beginning.

But no more regrets, Dex told himself. Jes wouldn't want him carrying on so.

There was only the present now, and if the Goddess granted it, their future. So Dex began talking to Jes.

He told her things he'd never told anyone.

He told her exactly what happened at the were orphanage.

About Elliott. How they'd been beaten and starved and yes, even raped. How years later, he'd hunted down the perpetrators and killed them. How he'd believed that would set him free, but when it hadn't, he turned his focus on the grandfather who'd abandoned him, blaming him for Dex's suffering.

"I even blamed my mother," Dex confessed. "For letting him send me away. I cursed her. I wished her dead. And I got my wish, didn't I? She killed herself."

He paused, but she didn't respond.

"Aren't you going to tell me I'm being stupid? That I shouldn't blame myself for her death? That what I was feeling was natural? Because I really need to hear that from you, Jes."

She remained silent.

It didn't matter.

Hour after hour he told her stories.

About his time with the Ferals.

"You wouldn't have liked them, but there was this one guy who wasn't bad. And we rode to some amazing places. You'd like Yellowstone. I'll take you there someday."

About the Para-Ops team.

"You never got to see Wraith in action since she'd just been shot. But let me tell you, she was a sight to see. She almost blew her top when Felicia lectured her about verbal judo but she wasn't as tough as she pretended. O'Flare saw that right away."

About a bunch of random things.

"Lucy brought the baby back to you, Jes. She knew even when I didn't that you'd never hurt him, and I'll never forgive myself for that. But you never have anything to fear from her. Lucy's my friend and that's all. You're the only female I've loved. The only female I've needed so badly I thought I'd die if I didn't have. After that, I can't go back to being Lucy's fuck buddy. I won't. We'll find someone for her. I was hoping Cy might be a good choice, but then he went and pissed her off. They've been fighting like crazy, and if you know Lucy, you know she doesn't like fighting. So I'd really like you to come back now, Jes. I'm not sure how long I can keep them from killing each other."

Most of all he talked about their baby.

"He's gorgeous, Jes, even if he does look a lot like me. He smiles when he hears my voice. And he smiles when he sees you. See, he's smiling right now. I was wondering if you like the name Elliott? I told you about Elliott, remember? I know it's a little, well, less than masculine, but we can call him Eli. That's got a nice ring to it, don't you think? I'm thinking that—Jes? Did you just move? Jes!"

With his heart slamming against his chest, Dex kissed his son on the cheek and said, "Hang on, buddy. I think your mom might be waking up now. She'll want you close when she does." As he'd frequently done, Dex shifted Jes and positioned the baby so that he was pressed close to her side, propped up by pillows and the cradle of her arm.

The baby cooed and blinked owlishly at him.

"You think you can open your eyes now, Jes? I miss you so much. I love you."

There it was again. That flicker of lashes as she struggled to open her eyes.

Hope swelled within him.

After several tries, she finally opened her eyes. She frowned and he held his breath.

She looked down at the baby.

Looked back at him.

"Dex," she whispered. "Let's call him Eli."

CHAPTER THIRTY-EIGHT

Jes walked down the center of the great hall, her smaller strides keeping pace with Cy's longer ones. She remembered that night so long ago, when she and Bodin had made a similar walk to the Draci leaders who waited for them. To the female Draci waiting to take Jes in. Jes had been so scared. Wondering what the future had in store for her. Wishing the werewolf who'd saved her loved her enough to keep her.

So many things had changed since then.

Today, Dex and Eli were the ones waiting for her. This castle wasn't cold or gloomy. It was her home, filled with memories both good and bad. The room was lit not by torches, but by halogen bulbs, strings of twinkle lights, and hundreds of candles, all of them creating a warm, dreamy glow that complimented the bouquets of lush, fragrant flowers and the fairy-tale simplicity of her ivory gown. Her friends were here. Her family, both old and new, smiling and anxious to witness her union with Dex Hunt, the werebeast who'd once sworn to never have kids, never forgive his grandfather, and never give his heart to anyone, let alone a female.

Jes and her brother came to a halt several feet from Dex. Dex wore a formal tux that perfectly hugged his taut, muscled frame. Its elegance did little to diminish the bad-boy vibe spurred on by his thick tawny hair, neatly trimmed soul patch, sensual mouth, and heated gaze. He was the perfect blend of devoted husband and father, passionate lover, and kick-ass whatever-it-takes-to-get-the-job-done male.

She flushed as she recalled how thoroughly he'd been "working" these past few weeks—specifically, on convincing her that he'd protect, cherish, and love her for all eternity. Though she'd long ceased having any doubt of that, she hadn't called a halt to his ministrations. She wasn't a fool and he kept promising his best work was yet to come.

They grinned at one another.

Dex cradled Eli protectively close to him even as his appreciative gaze swept over Jes's body, causing bolts of desire to course through her. His grin widened, telling her he hadn't missed her response.

Although he still struggled with resentment and anger at times, he was working on forgiving his grandfather. It wasn't easy, but it seemed to be a huge factor in Bodin's favor that his final words had helped Jes fight off the *diabol* that had possessed her. It also helped when Jes and Amanda told Dex about all the good Bodin had accomplished in his life.

Amanda seemed to be making positive changes due to Dex's influence. Still, the situation with the weres posed the biggest concern. With Bodin gone, several factions were vying to replace him, and no one was certain what role Dex would play in things. However, Dex would serve as Mahone's liaison with the werewolves, and the FBI was keeping a close eye on matters. The FBI was also going to continue funding Jes's research, including her research into the Legend of Wolves. But Jes's research would be Top Secret classified and she had Dex to keep her avocation from becoming an obsession again.

Jes still struggled with balancing her personal and professional lives. She'd hired several scientists, some of them vampires, to help her with her research. But questions about life and death still plagued her. Why had she lived when her parents had died? Why was she immortal when the Draci lifespan was so short? Wasn't it cosmically unfair for the world's creatures to have such differing life spans, and why shouldn't she try to even the playing field? Of course, that meant Dex continued to worry about her. In turn, she worried he'd remember how she'd begun their relationship by deceiving him and would change his mind about wanting to be with her.

But for now, for today, none of that mattered.

Today was a celebration of their formal union and Dex's greatest victories. He had a son. Someday, Jes knew he'd forgive Bodin. But her greatest joy was knowing that Dex had given his heart to others and opened himself to love. Love from the Para-Ops team, of course. But most of all, from Jes.

***

As soon as the wedding ceremony was over, Ella ran to Dex and held her arms out for Eli, not caring a fig when the baby's slobber stained her pretty pink flower girl dress. As she jiggled him, Ella scanned the massive hall that had been transformed into someplace magical.

She could tell Cy was feeling a little sad. Mostly, however, he seemed distracted by the pretty feline mage named Lucy. Ella liked Lucy, even if she did tend to glare at Cy a lot. Which Ella didn't really understand since Lucy didn't glare at anyone else.

Ella still needed to learn more about Dex's other teammates. She liked that Knox, the vampire, was so protective of his human wife, Felicia. Felicia was beautiful, with red hair and blue eyes, and she laughed as she talked with the pretty man named Caleb and his girlfriend, Wraith. Despite Wraith's name, she didn't look at all scary. They looked like fun and she'd gather up the courage to talk to them soon. For the most part, Knox looked as happy as the rest of them, but sometimes he stared at Felicia with a desperate, mournful expression. Like he was about to lose her or something. She'd have to cheer him up, but first...

She turned back to Dex. "I want to show Eli that spot outside. Is that okay?" She wasn't asking him permission, not for her anyway, but Eli was his baby, so she figured it was only right.

Dex frowned in that protective way of his and Ella's shoulders sagged. She supposed she'd understand if he said no. Everyone was busy and he'd be worried about the baby and—

"Hey, Mahone," Dex called. "Come here."

As Ella watched, Dex waved over a human male with light brown hair. He wasn't overly large, but he looked strong and healthy, and his gray eyes didn't seem to miss a thing. Slowly, he made his way to Dex. Or rather, he made his way to Jes, who stood at Dex's side.

He held out his hand to the vampire doctor. "Congratulations," he said simply. Jes smiled, took his hand, and to everyone's apparent surprise, leaned in and kissed Mahone on the cheek. Mahone flushed, scowling when Dex laughed.

"Listen, Mahone. Ella here needs to show Eli something outside. Would you be a sport and accompany them?" Despite his casual tone, Dex stared intensely at Mahone, as if communicating something important to him.

Mahone gave a beleaguered sigh that immediately made Ella mad. What was up with the human? He seemed okay, but he kept himself apart from everyone else even when people surrounded him. Maybe he was just shy, she decided. She felt shy sometimes, though she rarely let that stop her from doing what she wanted.

The human male looked down at her. "Let's go, kid."

Kid? Ella scowled but obligingly followed Mahone outside, bouncing Eli as they walked. She reminded herself he'd made a common mistake. Most people viewed her as a kid. Sometimes even Dex still did. They'd figure it out eventually.

Soon, they were outside and standing in the same spot where Ella had first met Dex. "This is it, Eli," she crooned. "It's the perfect spot for running and sword fighting and doing cartwheels. Don't worry if you don't get the hang of cartwheels at first. Even Jes still has trouble with them. But I'm a pro. I'll be able to teach you in no time."

After giving Eli the time to properly appreciate the spot, Ella turned to Mahone. He watched her intently.

A figure appeared behind him and Ella gasped. It was a woman surrounded by light, her long hair floating around her. Ella thought Jes was beautiful. She thought the same about Lucy, Wraith, and Felicia. But this woman...she looked like a queen. She looked like beauty in its most basic form, one that would never fade or tarnish. By her very presence, she made everything around her shine with the same glory.

"Mahone," Ella began, but he'd already turned toward the castle, seemingly unaware of the Goddess standing beside him.

"Let's go, kid." To her surprise, he held out his hand.

Ella took Mahone's hand, curling her fingers around his while at the same time cradling Eli's sturdy body in her other arm. Together they walked back inside. At the last minute, Ella turned back to the Goddess, who appeared to be gazing at Mahone in the same manner Jes often gazed at Dex.

A musical voice whispered in her mind. "Isn't the human handsome?"

Ella smiled and glanced at Mahone.

"Yes," she said, answering the Goddess's question out loud. "He is."

Mahone frowned down at her. "What? He's what?"

"Handsome," Ella clarified.

"Uh, yeah," Mahone said before escorting her to Dex and Jes.

At the doorway, though, he turned back to look at the iron gazebo surrounded by the green grass, a wistful expression on his face. The warm light shone on him, glimmering like it was alive, and a small smile formed on his face. The expression smoothed out the worry lines and tension that normally made him appear aloof. He looked almost relaxed. Not quite happy, but different. Hopeful, maybe.

And Ella felt hopeful, too.

THE END

ABOUT THE AUTHOR

Virna DePaul is a former criminal prosecutor and now National Bestselling Author for Berkley (paranormal romantic suspense), HQN (single title romantic suspense) and HRS (category romantic suspense).

www.virnadepaul.com

Twitter: @virnadepaul

Email: virna@virnadepaul.com

Facebook Fan Page: http://www.facebook.com/booksthatrock

ADDITIONAL TITLES

Paranormal Romantic Suspense:
  Chosen By Blood (A Para-Ops Novel, Book 1, Berkley)
  Chosen By Fate (A Para-Ops Novel, Book 2, Berkley)

Contemporary Romantic Suspense:
  Dangerous To Her (Harlequin Romantic Suspense)
  It Started That Night (HRS, May 2012)
  Shades Of Desire (HQN, SIG Series, Book 1 – June 2012)
  Shades Of Temptation (HQN, SIG Series, Book 2 – September 2012)

Contemporary Romance:
  This Magic Moment (A Dalton Brothers Novel, Book 1)

Novellas:
  A Vampire's Salvation (A Beyond Human Novella)
  Wild For Him

Erotic Novellas (Writing as Ava Meyers):
  Copping To It (Red-Hot Cops Series Novella 1)
  Cop Appeal (Red-Hot Cops Series Novella 2)
  Copping Attitude (Red-Hot Cops Series Novella 3)

Made in the USA
Lexington, KY
16 October 2012